Praise for the works of Lisa Kleypas

"Once more, Kleypas proves why she is the grand dame of the genre."
—*RT BOOKreviews* (starred) on *Devil in Spring*

"A funny and charming story that will delight readers from the first page to the last."
—*Kirkus Reviews* (starred) on *Devil in Spring*

"Quirky, witty, and sexy, this compelling romp is absolute bliss. An addictive tale that readers won't want to put down."
—*Library Journal* (starred) on *Devil in Spring*

"Kleypas is a masterful writer, and her latest offering will be welcomed by fans old and new."
—*Kirkus Reviews* (starred) on *Marrying Winterborne*

"Emotional depth, appealing characters, strong story-lines and sexual tension are what make Kleypas' novels reader favorites . . . but what will truly captivate them is watching the characters grow as love makes them the best they can be."
—*RT BOOKreviews* (starred) on *Marrying Winterborne*

". . . insightful characterization, an abundance of super-charged sexual chemistry, a dash of dry humor, and a to-die-for hero, all of which will have the author's legions of fans giddy with [?] to historical romance."
—*Booklist* (starr[?]

Praise for the works of Lorraine Heath

"Heath's passionate romance exposes the underside of Victorian London society, drawing readers into a dangerous world."

—*Publishers Weekly*
on *The Viscount and the Vixen*

"A winning Victorian romance with a *Pretty Woman* vibe—complete with a hot piano scene."

—*Kirkus Reviews*
on *The Viscount and the Vixen*

"Heath is nothing if not original, unconventional, and a continuing innovative voice in the genre. The pages are brimming over with humor and poignancy, sexual tension, and emotions that run deep."

—*RT BOOKreviews* (top pick)
on *The Viscount and the Vixen*

"Sexy, clever, and emotionally wrenching, this heartfelt story breathes new life into the classic marriage-of-convenience plot and adds another winner to Heath's addictive series."

—*Library Journal* (starred)
on *The Viscount and the Vixen*

"A steamy romance that uses the strict rules of Regency Britain to excellent effect."

—*Kirkus Reviews* on *The Earl Takes All*

Also by Lisa Kleypas

Also by Megan Frampton

LADY BE BAD
MY FAIR DUCHESS
WHY DO DUKES FALL IN LOVE?
ONE-EYED DUKES ARE WILD
NO GROOM AT THE INN (novella)
PUT UP YOUR DUKE
WHEN GOOD EARLS GO BAD (novella)
THE DUKE'S GUIDE TO CORRECT BEHAVIOR

Also by Vivienne Lorret

The Season's Original Series
"The Duke's Christmas Wish"
in ALL I WANT FOR CHRISTMAS IS A DUKE
THE DEBUTANTE IS MINE
THIS EARL IS ON FIRE
WHEN A MARQUESS LOVES A WOMAN

The Rakes of Fallow Hall Series
THE ELUSIVE LORD EVERHART
THE DEVILISH MR. DANVERS
THE MADDENING LORD MONTWOOD

The Wallflower Wedding Series
TEMPTING MR. WEATHERSTONE (novella)
DARING MISS DANVERS
WINNING MISS WAKEFIELD
FINDING MISS MCFARLAND

LISA KLEYPAS

LORRAINE HEATH

MEGAN FRAMPTON

VIVIENNE LORRET

A Christmas to Remember

AN ANTHOLOGY

AVONBOOKS

An Imprint of HarperCollinsPublishers

"I Will" was originally published in 2001 in the anthology *Wish List*, by Leisure Books.

"The Duke's Christmas Wish" was originally published in 2015 in the anthology *All I Want for Christmas Is a Duke*, by Avon Impulse.

First Avon Books mass market printing: October 2017

Print Edition ISBN: 978-0-06-274723-5
Digital Edition ISBN: 978-0-06-274725-9

Cover design by Guido Caroti

Cover images: © Zamurovic Photography / Shutterstock (background); © Africa Studio / Shutterstock (ribbon)

FIRST EDITION

17 18 19 20 21   QGM   10 9 8 7 6 5 4 3 2 1

Contents

I Will

❦

LISA KLEYPAS

Chapter One

It was not easy to ask a favor of a woman who despised him. But Andrew, Lord Drake, had always been beyond shame, and today was no exception. He needed a favor from a morally upright woman, and Miss Caroline Hargreaves was the only decent female he knew. She was proper and straitlaced to a fault . . . and he wasn't the only man to think so, judging by the fact that she was still unmarried at the age of twenty-six.

"Why are you here?" Caroline asked, her voice threaded with quiet hostility. She kept her gaze fastened on the large square frame propped by the settee, a wooden lace stretcher used to reshape curtains and tablecloths after they were washed. The task was a meticulous one, involving sticking a pin through each tiny loop of lace and affixing it to the edge of the frame until the cloth was drawn tight. Although Caroline's face was expressionless, her inner tension was betrayed by the stiffness of her fingers as she fumbled with a paper of pins.

"I need something from you," Andrew said, staring at her intently. It was probably the first time he had ever been completely sober around her, and now that he was free of his habitual alcoholic haze, he had noticed a few things about Miss Caroline Hargreaves that intrigued him.

She was far prettier than he had thought. Despite the little spectacles perched on her nose, and her frumpy manner of

dressing, she possessed a subtle beauty that had escaped him
before. Her figure was not at all spectacular—Caroline was
small and slight, with practically no hips or breasts to speak
of. Andrew preferred big, voluptuous women who were willing to engage in the vigorous bedroom romps he enjoyed.
But Caroline had a lovely face, with velvety brown eyes and
thick black lashes, surmounted by dark brows that arched
with the precision of a hawk's wing. Her hair was a neatly
pinned mass of sable silk, and her complexion was as fine
and clear as a child's. And that mouth . . . why in God's name
had he never noticed her mouth before? Delicate, expressive,
the upper lip small and bow shaped, the lower curved with
generous fullness.

Right now those tempting lips were pulled tight with
displeasure, and her brow was furrowed in a perplexed expression. "I can't conceive of what you could possibly want
from me, Lord Drake," Caroline said crisply. "However, I
can assure you that you won't get it."

Andrew laughed suddenly. He threw a glance at his friend
Cade—Caroline's younger brother—who had brought him
to the parlor of the Hargreaves family home. Having predicted that Caroline would not be willing to help him in any
way, Cade now looked both annoyed and resigned at his sister's stubbornness. "I told you," Cade murmured.

Not willing to give up so easily, Andrew returned his
attention to the woman seated before him. He considered
her thoughtfully, trying to decide what approach to use.
No doubt she was going to make him crawl . . . not that he
blamed her for that in the least.

Caroline had never made a secret of her dislike for him,
and Andrew knew exactly why. For one thing, he was a bad
influence on her younger brother Cade, a pleasant-natured
fellow who was far too easily swayed by the opinions of his
friends. Andrew had invited Cade along on far too many

wild evenings of gambling, drinking, and debauchery, and returned him home in a sorry condition.

As Cade's father was dead, and his mother was a hopeless feather-wit, Caroline was the closest thing to a parent that Cade had. She tried her best to keep her twenty-four-year-old brother on the straight-and-narrow path, wanting him to assume his responsibilities as the man of the family. However, Cade naturally found it more tempting to emulate Andrew's profligate lifestyle, and the two of them had indulged in more than a few dissolute evenings.

The other reason that Caroline despised Andrew was the simple fact that they were complete opposites. She was pure. He was tarnished. She was honest. He tailored the truth to fit his own purposes. She was self-disciplined. He had never restrained himself in any regard. She was calm and serene. He had never known a moment's peace in his life. Andrew envied her, and so he had mocked her mercilessly on the few previous occasions when they had met.

Now Caroline hated him, and he had come to ask for a favor—a favor he desperately needed. Andrew found the situation so amusing that a wry smile cut through the tension on his face.

Abruptly he decided to be blunt. Miss Caroline Hargreaves did not seem to be the kind of woman who would tolerate game playing and prevarication. "I'm here because my father is dying," he said.

The words caused her to accidentally prick her finger, and she jumped slightly. Her gaze lifted from the lace stretcher. "I am sorry," she murmured.

"I'm not."

Andrew saw from the widening of her eyes that she was shocked by his coldness. He did not care. Nothing could make him feign sorrow at the passing of a man who had always been a poor excuse for a father. The earl had never given a damn about him, and Andrew had long ago given up trying to earn the love of a manipulative son of a bitch whose heart was as soft and warm as a block of granite. "The only thing I'm sorry about," Andrew continued calmly, "is that the earl has decided to disinherit me. You and he seem to share similar feelings about my sinful way of living. My father has accused me of being the most self-indulgent and debased creature he has ever encountered." A slight smile crossed his lips. "I can only hope that he is right."

Caroline seemed more than a little perturbed by his statement. "You sound proud of being such a disappointment to him," she said.

"Oh, I am," he assured her easily. "My goal was to become as great a disappointment to him as he has been to me. Not an easy task, you understand, but I proved myself equal to it. It has been the greatest success of my life."

He saw Caroline throw a troubled glance at Cade, who merely shrugged sheepishly and wandered to the window to contemplate the serene spring day outside.

The Hargreaves house was located on the west side of London. It was a pleasant Georgian-style manor house, pink-washed and framed by large beech trees, the kind of home that a solid English family should possess.

"And so," Andrew continued, "in an eleventh-hour effort to inspire me to reform, the earl has cut me out of his will."

"But surely he cannot do so entirely," Caroline said. "The titles, the property in town, and your family's country estate . . . I would have thought they were entailed."

"Yes, they are entailed." Andrew smiled bitterly. "I'll get the titles and the property no matter what the earl does. He can't break the entailment any more than I can. But the money—the entire family fortune—that is not entailed. He can leave it to anyone he wishes. And so I'll likely find myself turning into one of those damned fortune-hunting aristocrats who has to marry some horse-faced heiress with a nice fat dowry."

"How terrible." Suddenly Caroline's eyes were lit with a challenging gleam. "For the heiress, I mean."

"Caro," came Cade's protesting voice.

"That's all right," Andrew said. "Any bride of mine would deserve a great deal of sympathy. I don't treat women well. I've never pretended to."

"What do you mean, you don't treat women well?" Caroline fumbled with a pin and stuck her finger again. "Are you abusive?"

"No." He scowled suddenly. "I would never physically harm a woman."

"You are merely disrespectful to them, then. And no doubt neglectful, and unreliable, and offensive and ungentlemanly." She paused and looked at him expectantly. When Andrew made no comment, she prompted with an edge to her tone, "Well?"

"Well, what?" he countered with a mocking smile. "Were you asking a question? I thought you were making a speech."

They regarded each other with narrowed eyes, and Caroline's pale complexion took on the rosy hue of anger. The atmosphere in the room changed, becoming strangely charged and hot, snapping with tension. Andrew wondered how in the hell a skinny little spinster could affect him like this. He, who had made it a lifetime's habit never to care about anything or anyone, including himself, was suddenly more troubled and aroused than he could ever recall being before. *My God*, he thought, *I must be one perverted bastard to desire Cade Hargreaves's sister.* But he did. His blood was pumping with heat and energy, and his nerves simmered relentlessly as he thought of the various ways he would like to put that delicate, innocent mouth to use.

It was a good thing that Cade was there. Otherwise

Andrew was not certain he could have stopped himself from showing Miss Caroline Hargreaves exactly how depraved he was. In fact, standing up as he was, that fact was soon going to become all too obvious through the thin covering of his fashionably snug fawn-colored trousers. "May I have a seat?" he asked abruptly, gesturing to the chair near the settee she occupied.

Unworldly as she was, Caroline did not seem to notice his burgeoning arousal. "Please do. I can hardly wait to hear the details of this favor you intend to ask, especially in light of the charm and good manners you have displayed so far."

God, she made him want to laugh, even as he wanted to strangle her. "Thank you." He sat and leaned forward casually, bracing his forearms on his knees. "If I want to be reinstated in the earl's will, I have no choice but to indulge him," he said.

"You intend to change your ways?" Caroline asked skeptically. "To reform yourself?"

"Of course not. My cesspool of a life suits me quite well. I'm only going to *pretend* to reform until the old man meets his maker. Then I'll be on my way, with my rightful fortune intact."

"How nice for you." Distaste flickered in her dark eyes.

For some reason Andrew was stung by her reaction—he, who had never given a damn what anyone thought of him. He felt the need to justify himself to her, to explain somehow that he wasn't nearly as contemptible as he seemed. But he kept silent. He would be damned if he would try to explain anything about himself to her.

Her gaze continued to hold his. "What role am I supposed to play in your plans?"

"I need you to pretend an interest in me," he said flatly. "A romantic interest. I'm going to convince my father that I've given up drinking, gambling, and skirt chasing . . . and that I am courting a decent woman with the intention of marrying her."

Caroline shook her head, clearly startled. "You want a sham engagement?"

"It doesn't have to go that far," he replied. "All I am asking is that you allow me to escort you to a few social functions . . . share a few dances, a carriage ride or two . . . enough to start a few tongues wagging until the rumors reach my father."

She regarded him as if he belonged in Bedlam. "Why in heaven's name do you think anyone would believe such a ruse? You and I are worlds apart. I cannot conceive of a more ill-suited pair."

"It's not all that unbelievable. A woman your age . . ." Andrew hesitated, considering the most tactful way to express himself.

"You are trying to say that since I am twenty-six years old, it naturally follows that I must be desperate to marry. So desperate, in fact, that I would accept your advances no matter how repulsive I find you. That is what people will think."

"You have a sharp tongue, Miss Hargreaves," he commented softly.

She frowned at him from behind her glinting spectacles. "That is correct, Lord Drake. I am sharp-tongued, I am a bluestocking, and I have resigned myself to being an old maid. Why would anyone of good sense believe that you have a romantic interest in me?"

Well, that was a good question. Just a few minutes ago Andrew himself would have laughed at the very idea. But as he sat close to her, his knees not far from hers, the stirring of attraction ignited in a sudden burst of heat. He could smell her fragrance—warm female skin and some fresh out-of-doors scent, as if she had just walked in from the garden. Cade had confided that his sister spent a great deal of time in the garden and the hothouse, cultivating roses and experimenting with plants. Caroline seemed like a rose herself—exquisite, sweetly fragrant, more than a little prickly. Andrew could scarcely believe that he had never noticed her before.

He flashed a glance at Cade, who was shrugging to indicate that arguing with Caroline was a hopeless endeavor. "Hargreaves, leave us alone for a few minutes," he said curtly.

"Why?" Caroline asked suspiciously.

"I want to talk privately with you. Unless . . ." He gave her a taunting smile that was guaranteed to annoy. "Are you afraid to be alone with me, Miss Hargreaves?"

"Certainly not!" She threw her brother a commanding glance. "Leave, Cade, while I deal with your so-called friend."

"All right." Cade paused at the threshold of the doorway, his boyishly handsome face stamped with concern as he added, "Just give a shout if you need help."

"I will not need help," Caroline assured him firmly. "I am capable of handling Lord Drake by myself."

"I wasn't speaking to you," Cade replied ruefully. "I was speaking to Drake."

Andrew struggled to suppress a grin as he watched his friend leave the room. Returning his attention to Caroline, he moved beside her on the settee, placing their bodies into closer proximity.

"Don't sit there," she said sharply.

"Why?" He gave her a seductive look, the kind that had melted many a reluctant woman's resistance in the past. "Do I make you nervous?"

"No, I left a paper of pins there, and your backside is about to resemble a hedgehog's."

Andrew laughed suddenly, fishing for the packet until he located it beneath his left buttock. "Thanks for the warning," he said dryly. "You could have let me find out for myself."

"I was tempted," Caroline admitted.

Andrew was amazed by how pretty she was, with amusement glimmering in her brown eyes, and her cheeks still flushed pink. Her earlier question—why anyone would believe he would be interested in her—abruptly seemed ludicrous. Why would he *not* be interested in her? Vague fantasies drifted through his mind . . . he would like to lift that dainty body in his arms right now, settle her on his lap, and kiss her senseless. He wanted to reach under the skirts of her plain brown cambric gown and slide his hands over her legs. Most of all he wanted to pull down the top of her bodice and uncover her pert little breasts. He had never been so intrigued by a pair of breasts, which was odd when one considered that he had always been interested in well-endowed women.

He watched as she turned her attentions back to the wooden frame. Clearly she was distracted, for she fumbled with the pins and managed to prick her fingers yet again as she tried to fasten the lace properly. Suddenly exasperated, Andrew took the pins from her. "Allow me," he said. Expertly he stretched the lace with just the right amount of tension and secured it with a row of pins, each miniature loop fastened exactly on the edge of the frame.

Caroline did not bother to hide her amazement as she watched him. "How did you learn to do that?"

Andrew regarded the lace panel with a critical eye before setting it aside. "I grew up as the only child on a large estate, with few playmates. On rainy days I would help the housekeeper with her tasks." He gave her a self-mocking grin. "If you are impressed by my lace stretching, you should see me polish silver."

She did not return his smile, but stared at him with new curiosity. When she spoke, her tone had softened a few degrees. "No one would believe the charade you propose. I know what kind of women you pursue. I have talked with

Cade, you see. And your reputation is well established. You would never take an interest in a woman like me."

"I could play the part convincingly," he said. "I've got a huge fortune at stake. For that I would court the devil himself. The question is, can you?"

"I suppose I could," she returned evenly. "You are not a bad-looking man. I suppose some might even regard you as handsome in a debauched, slovenly sort of way."

Andrew scowled at her. He was not vain, and rarely considered his own appearance other than to make certain he was clean and his clothes were decently tailored. But without conceit, he knew that he was tall and well proportioned, and that women often praised his long black hair and blue eyes. The problem was his way of life. He spent too much time indoors, too little time sleeping, and he drank too often and too long. More often than not, he woke up at midday with bloodshot, dark-circled eyes, his complexion pasty from a night of hard drinking. And he had never cared . . . until now. In comparison to the dainty creature before him, he felt like a huge, untidy mess.

"What incentive were you planning to offer me?" Caroline asked. It was clear that she would not consider his plan; she was merely interested to discover how he would have tried to entice her.

Unfortunately that was the weak aspect of his scheme. He had little to entice her with. No money, no social advantage, no possessions that would allure her. There was only one thing he had been able to come up with that might be sufficiently tempting.

"If you agree to help me," he said slowly, "I will leave your brother alone. You know what kind of influence I am on him. He is in debt up to his ears, and he is doing his best to keep pace with the pack of miscreants and degenerates I like to call friends. Before long Cade is going to end up exactly like me—rotten, cynical, and beyond all hope of redemption."

Caroline's expressive face revealed that this was exactly what she feared.

"How far in debt is he?" she asked stiffly.

He named a sum that astonished and sickened her. Reading the horror in her eyes, Andrew experienced a surge of predatory satisfaction. *Yes* . . . he had guessed correctly. She loved her younger brother enough to do anything to save him. Even pretend to fall in love with a man she despised.

"That is only the beginning," Andrew told her. "Before long Cade will be in a pit so deep that he'll never be able to climb out."

"And you would be willing to let that happen? You would simply stand by and let him ruin his life? And impoverish my mother and myself?"

Andrew responded with a casual shrug. "It is his life," he pointed out matter-of-factly. "I'm not his keeper."

"My God," she said unsteadily. "You don't care about anyone but yourself, do you?"

He kept his expression blank, and studied the scuffed, unpolished surface of his very expensive boot. "No, I don't give a damn who gets dragged down with me. But if you decide to help me, I'll take care of Cade. I'll make certain the others in our set don't invite him to their clubs or their favorite bawdy houses. I will ensure that all the listmakers I know—and believe me, that is a considerable number—will not extend him credit. He won't be allowed into any high-stakes games in London. Moreover, if I am reinstated in my father's will, I will assume all of Cade's financial obligations."

"Does Cade know about your plan?" Caroline was pale and intent as she stared at him.

"No. But it would prove his salvation."

"And if I refuse to accept your offer?"

A hard, somewhat cruel smile curved his lips. His father's smile, Andrew thought, with bitter self-awareness. "Then your brother is on the path to hell . . . right alongside me. And you will be left to pick up the pieces. I would hate to see your family's estate sold to pay off Cade's debts. Not a pleasant prospect for your mother, being forced to live off the charity of relatives in her old age. Or you, for that matter." He gave her an insultingly thorough glance, his gaze lingering on her bosom. "What skills do you have that would earn enough to support a family?"

"You fiend," Caroline whispered, visibly trembling, though it was impossible to discern whether her emotion was fear or anger, or perhaps a mixture of both.

In the silence, Andrew was aware of a twisting sensation somewhere in his chest, and suddenly he wanted to take it all back . . . reassure and soothe her . . . promise her that he would never allow a bit of harm to come to her family. He had a terrible feeling of tenderness that he struggled to thrust away, but it remained stubbornly lodged within him.

"What choice do I have?" Caroline asked angrily, forestalling any repentant words from him.

"Then you agree to my plan? You'll pretend to engage in a courtship with me?"

"Yes . . . I will." She sent him a simmering glare. "How long must this last? Weeks? Months?"

"Until the earl reinstates me in his will. If you and I are sufficiently convincing, it shouldn't take long."

"I don't know if I can bear it," she said, regarding him with patent loathing. "Exactly how far will this charade have to go? Words? Embraces? Kisses?" The prospect of kissing him seemed as enthralling as if she had been required to kiss a goat. "I warn you, I will not allow my reputation to be compromised, not even for Cade!"

"I haven't thought out the details yet." He kept his face unreadable, although relief shot through him in a piercing note. "I won't compromise you. All I want is the appearance of pleasant companionship."

Caroline sprang from the settee as if she had suddenly been released from the law of gravity. Agitation was evident in every line of her body. "This is intolerable," she muttered. "I cannot believe that through no fault of my own . . ." She whirled around to glare at Andrew. "When do we start? Let it be soon. I want this outrageous charade to be done with as quickly as possible."

"Your enthusiasm is gratifying," Andrew remarked, with a sudden flare of laughter in his eyes. "Let's begin in a fortnight. My half brother and his wife are giving a weekend party at their country estate. I will prevail on them to invite your family. With any luck, my father will attend as well."

"And then to all appearances, you and I will develop a sudden overwhelming attraction to each other," she said, rolling her eyes heavenward.

"Why not? Many a romantic liaison has begun that way. In the past, I've had more than a few—"

"Please," she interrupted fervently. "Please do not regale me with stories of your sordid affairs. I find you repulsive enough as it is."

"All right," he said agreeably. "From now on I'll leave the subjects of conversation to you. Your brother tells me that you enjoy gardening. No doubt we'll have enthralling discourses on the wonders of manure." He was satisfied to see her porcelain complexion turn mottled with fury.

"If I can manage to convince a single person that I am attracted to you," Caroline said through gritted teeth, "I vow to begin a career on the stage."

"That could be arranged," Andrew replied dryly. His half brother, Logan Scott, was the most celebrated actor of the day, as well as being the owner and manager of the Capital Theater. Although Andrew and Logan had been friends since childhood, they had only recently discovered that they were related. Logan was the by-blow of an affair the earl had conducted with a young actress long ago. Whereas

Andrew had been raised in an atmosphere of luxury and privilege, Logan had grown up in a hovel, frequently starving and abused by the family that had taken him in. Andrew doubted that he would ever rid himself of the guilt of that, even though it hadn't been his fault.

Noticing that Caroline's spectacles were smudged, he approached her with a quiet murmur. "Hold still."

She froze as he reached out and plucked the steel-framed spectacles from her nose. "Wh-what are you doing? I . . . *stop*; give those back . . ."

"In a minute," he said, using a fold of his soft linen shirt to polish the lenses until they gleamed brightly. He paused to examine them, and glanced at Caroline's face. Bereft of the spectacles, her eyes looked large and fathomless, her gaze slightly unfocused. How vulnerable she seemed. Again he experienced an odd surge of protectiveness. "How well can you see without them?" he asked, carefully replacing them on her small face.

"Not well at all," she admitted in a low voice, her composure seeming fractured. As soon as the spectacles were safely on her nose, she backed away from Andrew and sought to collect herself. "Now I suppose you are going to make some jest at my expense."

"Not at all. I like your spectacles."

"You do?" she asked with clear disbelief. "Why?"

"They make you look like a wise little owl."

Clearly she did not consider that a compliment, although Andrew meant it as one. He couldn't help imagining what she would look like wearing nothing *but* the spectacles, so prim and modest until he coaxed her into passionate abandonment, her small body writhing uncontrollably against his—

Abruptly aware that his erection was swelling again, Andrew shoved the images out of his mind. Damn, but he had never expected to be so fascinated by Hargreaves's spinster sister! He would have to make certain that she never realized it, or she would have even more contempt for him. The only way to keep her from guessing at his attraction to her was to keep her thoroughly annoyed and hostile. No problem there, he thought sardonically.

"You may leave now," Caroline said sharply. "I assume our business is concluded for the time being."

"It is," he agreed. "However, there is one last thing. Could you manage to dress with a bit more style during the weekend party? The guests—not to mention my father—would find it easier to accept my interest in you if you didn't wear something quite so . . ."

Now even the lobes of her ears were purple. "Quite so *what*?" she said in a hiss.

"Matronly."

Caroline was silent for a moment, obviously suppressing an urge to commit murder. "I will try," she finally said in a strangled voice. "And you, perhaps, might engage the services of a decent valet. Or if you already have one, replace him with someone else."

Now it was Andrew's turn to be offended. He felt a scowl twitching at the muscles of his face. "Why is that?"

"Because your hair is too long, and your boots need polish, and the way *you* dress reminds me of an unmade bed!"

"Does that mean you'd like to lie on top of me?" he asked.

He slipped around the door of the parlor and closed it just before she threw a vase.

The sound of shattering porcelain echoed through the house.

"Drake!" Cade strode toward him from the entrance hall, looking at him expectantly. "How did it go? Did you get her to agree?"

"She agreed," Andrew said.

The words caused a flashing grin to cross Cade's boyishly handsome face. "Well done! Now you'll get back in your father's good graces, and everything will go swimmingly for us, eh, old fellow? Gaming, drinking, carousing . . . oh, the times we're going to have!"

"Hargreaves, I have something to tell you," Andrew said carefully. "I don't think you're going to like it."

Chapter Two

CAROLINE SAT ALONE for a long time after Lord Drake left. She wondered uneasily what would become of her. Gossip would certainly abound once the news got out that she and Drake were courting. The unlikeliness of such a match would cause no end of jokes and snickers. Especially in light of the fact that she was notoriously particular in her choice of companionship.

Caroline had never been able to explain even to herself why she had never fallen in love. Certainly she was not a cold person—she had always had warm relationships with friends and relatives, and she knew herself to be a woman of very deep feeling. And she enjoyed dancing and talking and even flirting on occasion. But when she had tried to make herself feel something beyond casual liking for any one gentleman, her heart had remained stubbornly uninvolved.

"For heaven's sake, love is not a prerequisite for marriage," her mother had often exclaimed in exasperation. "You cannot *afford* to wait for love, Caro. You have neither the fortune nor the social position to be so fastidious!"

True, her father had been a viscount, but like the majority of viscounts, he did not possess a significant amount of land. A title and a small London estate were all the Hargreaves could boast of. It would have benefitted the family tremendously if Caroline, the only daughter, could have married an earl or perhaps even a marquess. Unfortunately most of the available peers were either decrepit old men, or spoiled, selfish rakes such as Andrew, Lord Drake. Given such a choice, it was no wonder that Caroline had chosen to remain unwed.

Dwelling on the subject of Andrew, Caroline frowned pensively. Her reaction to him was troubling. Not only did he seem to have a remarkable ability to provoke her, but he seemed to do it intentionally, as if he delighted in stoking her temper. But somewhere in the midst of her annoyance, she had felt a strange sort of fascination for him.

It couldn't possibly be his looks. After all, she was not so shallow as to be undone by mere handsomeness. But she had found herself staring compulsively at the dark, ruined beauty of his face . . . the deep blue eyes shadowed from too little sleep, the cynical mouth . . . the slightly bloated look of a heavy drinker. Andrew possessed the face of a man who was determined to destroy himself. Oh, what terrible company he was for her brother Cade! Not to mention herself.

Her thoughts were interrupted by the arrival of her mother, Fanny, who had returned from a pleasant afternoon of visiting with friends. Strangers were often surprised to learn that the two were mother and daughter, for they did not resemble each other in any way except for their brown eyes. Caroline and Cade had inherited their late father's looks and temperament. Fanny, by contrast, was blond and plump, with the mercurial disposition of a child. It was always disconcerting to try to converse with Fanny, for she disliked serious subjects and did not choose to face unpleasant realities.

"Caro," Fanny exclaimed, coming into the parlor after giving her frilly plumed hat and light summer wrap to the housekeeper. "You look rather displeased, dear. What has caused such a sour expression? Has our darling Cade been up to his usual pranks?"

"Our darling Cade is doing his best to ensure that you will spend your final years in a workhouse," Caroline replied dryly.

Her mother's face wrinkled in confusion. "I'm afraid I don't understand, dear. What do you mean?"

"Cade has been gambling," Caroline said. "He is going through all our money. Soon there will be nothing left. If he doesn't stop soon, we'll have to sell everything we own . . . and even *that* won't fully satisfy his debts."

"Oh, but you're teasing!" Fanny said with an anxious laugh. "Cade promised me that he would try to restrain himself at the hazard tables."

"Well, he hasn't," Caroline replied flatly. "And now we're all going to suffer for it."

Reading the truth in her daughter's eyes, Fanny sat down heavily on the pink brocade settee. In the grim silence that followed, she folded her hands in her lap like a punished child, her rosebud mouth forming an *O* of dismay. "It's all your fault!" she burst out suddenly.

"My fault?" Caroline gave her an incredulous stare. "Why on earth would you say that, Mother?"

"We wouldn't be in this predicament if you had married! A rich husband would have provided enough funds for Cade to indulge his little habits with his friends, and taken care of us as well. Now you've waited too long . . . your bloom has faded, and you're almost *twenty-seven* . . ." Pausing, Fanny became a bit tearful at the thought of having an unmarried daughter of such an advanced age. Pulling a lace handkerchief from her sleeve, she dabbed delicately at her eyes. "Yes, your best years are behind you, and now the family will come to ruin. All because you refused to set your cap for a wealthy man."

Caroline opened her mouth to argue, then closed it with an exasperated sound. It was impossible to debate with someone so inured to the concept of logic. She had tried to argue with Fanny in the past, but it had served only to frustrate them both. "Mother," she said deliberately. "Mother, stop crying. I have some news that might cheer you. This afternoon I received a visit from one of Cade's friends—Lord Drake . . . do you remember him?"

"No, dear. Cade has so many acquaintances, I can never keep them all straight."

"Drake is the Earl of Rochester's only legitimate heir."

"Oh, that one." Fanny's expression brightened with interest, her tears vanishing instantly. "Yes, what a fortune he will come into! I do indeed remember him. A handsome man, I recollect, with long, dark hair and blue eyes—"

"And the manners of a swine," Caroline added.

"With an inheritance like that, Caro, one can overlook a few tiny breaches in etiquette. Do tell, what did Lord Drake say during his visit?"

"He . . ." Caroline hesitated, galled by the words she was about to say. She did not dare tell Fanny that the courtship between her and Drake would be only a charade. Her mother was a notorious gossip, and it would be only a matter of days—no, hours—before she let the truth slip to someone. "He expressed an interest in courting me," Caroline said, stone-faced. "Toward that end, you and I will allow him to escort us to a weekend party given by Mr. and Mrs. Logan Scott, to be held within a fortnight."

The news was almost too much for Fanny to digest at once. "Oh, Caro," she exclaimed. "An earl's son, interested in *you* . . . I can scarcely believe . . . Well, it's nothing less than a miracle! And if you can bring him to scratch . . . what a fortune you will have! What land, what jewels! You would certainly have your own carriage, and accounts at the finest shops . . . Oh, this is the answer to all our problems!"

"So it would seem," Caroline said dryly. "But do not get your hopes too high, Mother. The courtship hasn't yet begun, and there is no guarantee that it will lead to marriage."

"Oh, but it will, it will!" Fanny practically danced around the room. Her blond curls fluttered and her well-rounded form jiggled with excitement. "I have a feeling in my bones. Now, Caro, you must heed my advice—I will tell you exactly how to set the hook and reel him in. You must be agreeable, and flatter his vanity, and give him admiring gazes . . . and you must never, never argue with him. And we must do something about your bosom."

"My bosom," Caroline repeated blankly.

"You will let me sew some quilted lining into the bodice of your chemise. You are a lovely girl, Caro, but you are in definite need of enhancement."

Assailed by a mixture of outrage and rueful laughter, Caro shook her head and smiled. "Quilted lining is not going to fool anyone. Especially not Lord Drake. But even if I did manage to deceive him, don't you think it would be a great disappointment on our wedding night to discover that my bosom was false?"

"By then it would be too late for him to do anything about it," her mother pointed out pragmatically. "And I would not call it a deception, Caro dear. After all, everyone must try to present herself or himself in the best light possible . . . that is what courtship is all about. The trick is to disguise all the unpleasant little faults that may put a man off, and maintain an air of mystery until you have finally landed him."

"No wonder I have never caught a husband," Caroline said with a faint smile. "I've always tried to be open and honest with men."

Her mother regarded her sadly. "I do not know where you have gotten these ideas, dear. Honesty has never fanned the flames of a man's ardor."

"I will try to remember that," Caroline replied gravely, fighting the temptation to laugh.

"THE CARRIAGE IS HERE," Fanny said with a squeal, staring out the parlor window at the vehicle moving along the front drive. "Oh, it is so fine! All that red lacquer and a Salisbury boot and crane neck, and what a fine large wrought-iron baggage rack. And no less than *four* outriders. Hurry, Caroline, do come and have a look."

"I had no idea you were so versed in the features of carriage construction, Mother," Caroline said dryly. She joined her mother at the window, and her stomach clenched with anxiety as she saw the Rochester coat of arms on the side of the carriage. It was time for the charade to begin. "Where is Cade?" she asked.

"In the library, I believe." Fanny continued to stare out the window, enthralled. "That dear, dear Lord Drake. Of all Cade's acquaintances, he has always been my favorite."

Amused despite her nervousness, Caroline laughed. "You didn't even remember who he was until I told you!"

"But then I recalled how much I liked him," Fanny countered.

Smiling wryly, Caroline wandered from the parlor to the small library, where her treasured collection of books was neatly stacked in the mahogany cases. Cade was at the sideboard, pouring a snifter of brandy from a crystal decanter.

"Are you ready to depart?" Caroline asked. "Lord Drake's carriage is here."

Cade turned with a glass in hand. His features, so like her own, were stamped with a scowl. "No, I am not ready," he said sourly. "Perhaps after I drink the rest of this bottle, I will be."

"Come, Cade," she chided. "One would think you were being sent to Newgate instead of attending a weekend party with friends."

"Drake is no friend of mine," Cade muttered. "He has seen to it that I am deprived of everything I enjoy. I'm not welcome at any hazard table in town, and I have not been invited to a single damned club for the past two weeks. I've been reduced to playing vingt-et-un for shillings. How will I ever earn enough to repay my debts?"

"Perhaps working?"

Cade snorted at what he perceived was a great insult. "No Hargreaves has occupied himself with trade or commerce for at least four generations."

"You should have thought of that before you gambled away everything Father left us. Then we wouldn't have to attend this dratted weekend party, and I would not have to pretend interest in a man I detest."

Suddenly shamefaced, Cade turned away from her. "I am sorry, Caro. But my luck was about to turn. I would have won back all the money, and more."

"Oh, Cade." She approached him and slid her arms around him, pressing her cheek against his stiff back. "Let us make the best of things," she said. "We'll go to the Scotts' estate, and I'll make calf eyes at Lord Drake, and you'll make yourself agreeable to everyone. And someday Lord Drake will be back in his father's will, and he will take care of your debts. And life will return to normal."

Suddenly they were interrupted by the housekeeper's voice. "Miss Hargreaves, Lord Drake has arrived. Shall I show him to the parlor?"

"Is my mother still in there?" Caroline asked.

"No, miss, she has gone upstairs to put on her traveling cloak and bonnet."

Wishing to avoid being alone with Drake, Caroline prodded her brother. "Cade, why don't you go welcome your friend?"

Evidently he was no more eager to see Drake than she. "No, I am going to show the footmen how I want our trunks and bags loaded on the carriage. You be the one to make small talk with him." Cade turned to glance at her, and a rueful grin spread across his face. "It is what you will be doing all weekend, sweet sister. You may as well practice now."

Giving him a damning look, Caroline left with an exasperated sigh and went to the parlor. She saw Andrew's tall form in the center of the room, his face partially concealed as he stared at a landscape that hung on the wall. "Good day, my lord," she said evenly. "I trust that you are . . ."

Her voice died away as he turned to face her. For a fraction of a second, she thought that the visitor was not Andrew, Lord Drake, but some other man. Stunned, she struggled silently to comprehend the changes that had taken place in him. The long, trailing locks of his dark hair had been cut in a new short style, cropped closely at the nape of his neck and the sides of his head. The alcoholic bloat of his face was gone, leaving behind a marvelously clean-lined jaw and hard-edged cheekbones. It seemed that he must have spent some time out-of-doors, for the paleness of his skin had been replaced by a light tan and the touch of windburn on the crests of his high cheekbones. And the eyes . . . oh, the eyes. No longer dark-circled and bloodshot, they were the clear, bright blue of sapphires. And they contained a flash of something—perhaps uncertainty?—that unraveled Caroline's composure. Andrew seemed so young, so vital, remarkably different from the man who had stood with her in this very parlor just a fortnight ago.

Then he spoke, and it became evident that although his outward appearance had changed, he was still the same insufferable rake. "Miss Hargreaves," he said evenly. "No doubt Cade has seen fit to tell you that I have upheld my part of the bargain. Now it is your turn. I hope you've been practicing your love-struck glances and flirtatious repartee."

Somehow Caroline recovered herself enough to reply. "I thought all you wanted was 'the appearance of pleasant companionship' . . . those were your exact words, were they not? I think 'love-struck' is a bit much to ask, don't you?"

"This past week I've gotten a complete accounting of Cade's debts," he returned grimly. "For what I'm going to have to pay, you owe me 'love-struck' and a damn sight more."

"You have yourself to blame for that. If you hadn't taken Cade along with you so many evenings—"

"It's not entirely my fault. But at this point I'm not inclined to quarrel. Gather your things, and let's be off."

Caroline nodded. However, she couldn't seem to make herself move. Her knees had locked, and she strongly suspected that if she took one step forward, she would fall flat on her face. She stared at him helplessly, while her heart thumped in a hard, uncontrollable rhythm, and her body flooded with heat. She had never experienced such a response to anyone in her life. Awareness of him pounded through her, and she realized how badly she wanted to touch him, draw her fingertips down the side of his lean cheek, kiss his firm, cynical mouth until it softened against hers in passion.

It can't be, she thought with a burst of panic. She could not feel such things for a man as immoral and depraved as Andrew, Lord Drake.

Something in her round-eyed gaze made him uncomfortable, for he shifted his weight from one leg to another, and shot her a baleful glance. "What are you staring at?"

"You," she said pertly. "I believe all your buttons have been fastened in the correct holes. Your hair appears to have been brushed. And for once you don't reek of spirits. I was merely reflecting on the surprising discovery that you can be made to look like a gentleman. Although it seems that your temper is as foul as ever."

"There is good reason for that," he informed her tersely. "It's been two weeks since I've had a drink or a wh—a female companion, and I've spent nearly every day at the family estate in the proximity of my father. I've visited with tenants and managers, and I've read account books until I've nearly gone blind. If I'm not fortunate enough to die of boredom soon, I'm going to shoot myself. And to top it all off, I have this damned weekend to look forward to."

"You poor man," she said pityingly. "It's terrible to be an

aristocrat, isn't it?" He scowled at her, and she smiled. "You do look well, however," she said. "It appears that abstinence becomes you."

"I don't like it," he grumbled.

"That is hardly a surprise."

He stared down into her smiling face, and his expression softened. Before Caroline could react, he reached out and plucked her spectacles from her nose.

"My lord," she said, unsettled, "I wish you would stop doing that! Hand those back at once. I can't see."

Andrew extracted a folded handkerchief from his pocket and polished the lenses. "It's no wonder your eyes are weak, the way you go about with your spectacles smudged." Ignoring her protests, he polished them meticulously and held them up to the light from the window. Only when he was satisfied that they were perfectly clean did he replace them on her nose.

"I could see perfectly well," she said.

"There was a thumbprint in the middle of the right lens."

"From now on, I would appreciate it if you simply *told* me about a smudge, rather than ripping my spectacles off my face!" Caroline knew she was being ungrateful and thorny-tempered. Some part of her mind was appalled by her own bad manners. However, she had the suspicion that if she did not maintain a strategic animosity toward him, she might do something horribly embarrassing—such as throw herself against his tall, hard body and kiss him. He was so large and irascible and tempting, and the mere sight of him sent an inexplicable heat ripping through her.

She did not understand herself—she had always thought that one had to *like* a man before experiencing this dizzying swirl of attraction. But evidently her body was not reconciled with her emotions, for whether she liked him or not, she wanted him. To feel his big, warm hands on her skin. To feel his lips on her throat and breast.

A flaming blush swept all the way from her bodice to her hairline, and she knew his perceptive gaze did not miss the tide of betraying color.

Mercifully, he did not comment on it, but answered her earlier remark. "Very well," he said. "What do I care if you walk into walls or trip over paving stones when you can't see through your damn spectacles?"

IT WAS THE most peculiar carriage ride Andrew had ever experienced. For three hours he suffered under Cade's disapproving glare—the lad regarded him as an utter Judas, and this in spite of the fact that Andrew was willing to pay all his debts in the not-too-distant future. Then there was the mother, Fanny, surely one of the most empty-headed matrons he had ever met in his life. She chattered in unending monologues and seemed never to require a reply other than the occasional grunt or nod. Every time he made the mistake of replying to one of her comments, it fueled a new round of inane babble. And then there was Caroline sitting opposite him, silent and outwardly serene as she focused on the everchanging array of scenery outside the window.

Andrew stared at her openly, while she seemed completely oblivious to his perusal. She was wearing a blue dress with a white pelisse fastened over the top. The scooped neck of her bodice was modest, not revealing even a hint of cleavage—not that she had much cleavage to display. And yet he was unbearably stimulated by the little expanse of skin that she displayed, that exquisite hollow at the base of her throat, and the porcelain smoothness of her upper chest. She was tiny, almost doll-like, and yet he was spellbound by her, to the extent of being half-aroused despite the presence of her brother *and* mother.

"What are you looking at?" he asked after a while, irritated by her steadfast refusal to glance his way. "Find the sight of cows and hedges enthralling, do you?"

"I have to stare at the scenery," Caroline replied without moving her gaze. "The moment I try to focus on something inside the carriage, I start to feel ill, especially when the road is uneven. I've been this way since childhood."

Fanny interceded anxiously. "Caroline, you must try to cure yourself of that. How vexing it must be for a fine gentleman such as Lord Drake to have you staring constantly out the window rather than participating in our conversation."

Andrew grinned at hearing himself described as a "fine gentleman."

Cade spoke then. "She's not going to change, Mother. And I daresay that Drake would prefer Caro to stare at the scenery rather than cast her accounts all over his shoes."

"Cade, how vulgar!" Fanny exclaimed, frowning at him. "Apologize to Lord Drake at once."

"No need," Andrew said hastily.

Fanny beamed at him. "How magnanimous of you, my lord, to overlook my son's bad manners. As for my daughter's unfortunate condition, I am quite certain that it is not a defect that might be passed on to any sons or daughters."

"That is good news," Andrew said blandly. "But I rather enjoy Miss Hargreaves's charming habit. It affords me the privilege of viewing her lovely profile."

Caroline glanced at him then, quickly, rolling her eyes at the compliment before turning her attention back to the window. He saw her lips curve slightly, however, betraying her amusement at the flattery.

Eventually they arrived at the Scotts' estate, which featured a house that was reputed to be one of the most attractive residences in England. The great stone mansion was surrounded with magnificent expanses of green lawn and gardens, and an oak-filled park in the back. The row of eight stone pillars in front was topped by huge sparkling windows, making the facade of the building more glass than wall. It seemed that only royalty should live in such a place, which made it rather appropriate for the family of Logan Scott. He was royalty of a sort, albeit of the London stage.

Caroline had been fortunate enough to see Scott perform in a production at the Capital Theater, and like every other member of the audience, she had found Scott to be breathtaking in his ability and presence. It was said that his Hamlet surpassed even the legendary David Garrick's, and that people would someday read of him in history books.

"How interesting that a man like Mr. Scott is your half brother," Caroline murmured, staring at the great estate as Andrew assisted her from the carriage. "Is there much likeness between you?"

"Not a farthing's worth," Andrew said, his face expressionless. "Logan was given a damned poor start in life, and he climbed to the top of his profession armed with nothing but talent and determination. Whereas I was given every advantage, and I've accomplished nothing."

They spoke in quiet murmurs, too low to be heard by Cade and Fanny.

"Are you jealous of him?" Caroline could not help asking.

Surprise flickered across Andrew's face, and it was clear that few people ever spoke so openly to him. "No, how could I be? Logan has earned everything he's gotten. And he's tolerated a great deal from me. He's even forgiven me for the time I tried to kill him."

"What?" Caroline stumbled slightly, and stopped to look up at him in astonishment. "You didn't really, did you?"

A grin crossed his dark face. "I wouldn't have gone through with it. But I was drunk as a wheelbarrow at the time, and I had just discovered that he had known we were brothers and hadn't told me. So I cornered him in his theater, brandishing a pistol."

"My God." Caroline stared up at him uneasily. "That is the behavior of a madman."

"No, I wasn't mad. Just foxed." Amusement danced in his

blue eyes. "Don't worry, sweetheart. I plan to stay sober for a while . . . and even if I weren't, I would be no danger to you."

The word *sweetheart*, spoken in that low, intimate voice, did something strange to her insides. Caroline began to reprove him for his familiarity, then realized that was their entire purpose for being here—to create the impression that they were indeed sweethearts.

They entered the two-story great hall, which was lined with dark wood paneling and rich tapestries, and were welcomed by Mr. Scott's wife, Madeline. The girl was absolutely lovely, her golden brown hair coiled atop her head, her hazel eyes sparkling as she greeted Andrew with youthful exuberance. It was clear that the two liked each other immensely.

"Lord Drake," Madeline exclaimed, clasping his hands in her own small ones, her cheek turned upward to receive his brotherly kiss. "How well you look! It has been at least a month since we've seen you. I am terribly vexed with you for remaining away so long."

Andrew smiled at his sister-in-law with a warmth that transformed his dark face, making Caroline's breath catch. "How is my niece?" he asked.

"You won't recognize her, I vow. She has grown at least two inches, and she has a tooth now!" Releasing his hands, Madeline turned toward Cade, Fanny, and Caroline, and curtsied gracefully. "Good morning, my lord, and Lady Hargreaves, and Miss Hargreaves." Her vivacious gaze locked with Caroline's. "My husband and I are delighted that you will be joining us this weekend. Any friends of Lord Drake's are always welcome at our home."

"You always despise my friends," Andrew remarked dryly, and Madeline gave him a quick frown.

"Your usual ones, yes. But friends like *these* are definitely welcome."

Caroline interceded then, smiling at Madeline. "Mrs.

Scott, I promise we will do our best to distinguish ourselves from Lord Drake's usual sort of companions."

"Thank you," came the girl's fervent reply, and they shared a sudden laugh.

"Wait a minute," Andrew said, only half in jest. "I didn't plan for the two of you to become friendly with each other. You had better stay away from my sister-in-law, Miss Hargreaves—she's an incurable gossip."

"Yes," Madeline confirmed, sending Caroline a conspiratorial smile. "And some of my best gossip is about Lord Drake. You'll find it vastly entertaining."

Fanny, who had been so in awe of their grandiose surroundings as to be rendered speechless, suddenly recovered her voice. "Mrs. Scott, we are so looking forward to meeting your esteemed husband. Such a celebrated man, so talented, so remarkable—"

A new voice entered the conversation, a voice so deep and distinctive that it could only belong to one man. "Madam, you do me too much honor, I assure you."

Logan Scott had approached them from behind, as large and handsome as he appeared on the stage, his tall form impeccably dressed in gray trousers, a formfitting black coat, and a crisp white cravat tied in an elaborate knot.

Looking from Andrew to his half brother, Caroline could see a vague likeness between them. They were both tall, physically imposing men, with strong, even features. Their coloring was not the same, however. Andrew's hair was as black as jet, whereas Logan Scott's was fiery mahogany. And Andrew's skin had a golden cast, as opposed to Scott's ruddier hue.

Watching them stand together, Caroline reflected that the main difference between the two men was in their bearing. It was clear that Logan Scott was accustomed to the attention that his celebrity had earned—he was self-confident, a bit larger than life, his gestures relaxed and yet expansive.

Andrew, however, was quieter, far more closed and private, his emotions ruthlessly buried deep below the surface.

"Brother," Logan Scott murmured, as they exchanged a hearty handshake. It was clear that there was deep affection between the two.

Andrew introduced Scott to the Hargreaves family, and Caroline was amused to see that the presence of this living legend had reduced her mother to speechlessness once more. Scott's penetrating gaze moved from one face to another, until he finally focused on Andrew. "Father is here," he said.

The brothers exchanged a look that was difficult to interpret, and it was obvious that the two shared an understanding of the man that no one else in the world did.

"How is he?" Andrew asked.

"Better today. He didn't need quite so much of his medicine during the night. At the moment he is conserving his strength for the ball tonight." Scott paused before adding, "He wanted to see you as soon as you arrived. Shall I take you to his room?"

Andrew nodded. "No doubt I have committed a hundred offenses he'll wish to upbraid me for. I should hate to deprive him of such entertainment."

"Good," Scott said sardonically. "Since I've already had to run through that particular gauntlet today, there is no reason that you should be spared."

Turning to Caroline, Andrew murmured, "Will you excuse me, Miss Hargreaves?"

"Of course." She found herself giving him a brief reassuring smile. "I hope it goes well, my lord."

As their gazes met, she saw his eyes change, the hard opaqueness softening to warm blue. "Later, then," he murmured, and bowed before leaving.

The intimacy of their shared gaze had caused warm flutters in the pit of her stomach, and a sensation of giddy lightness that floated all through her. Slightly bemused, Caroline reflected that Logan Scott was not the only man in the family with acting ability. Andrew was playing his part so convincingly that anyone would believe he had a real interest in her. She could almost believe it herself. Sternly she concentrated on the thought that it was all a pretense. Money, not courtship, was Andrew's ultimate goal.

ANDREW AND LOGAN crossed through the marble hall, its plasterwork ceiling embellished with mythological scenes and a mask-and-ribbon motif. Approaching the grand staircase, which curved in a huge gentle spiral, the brothers made their way upward at a leisurely pace.

"Your Miss Hargreaves seems a charming girl," Logan remarked.

Andrew smiled sardonically. "She is not *my* Miss Hargreaves."

"She's a pretty sort," Logan said. "Delicate in appearance, but she seems to possess a certain liveliness of spirit."

"Spirit," Andrew repeated wryly. "Yes . . . she has plenty of that."

"Interesting."

"What is interesting?" Andrew asked warily, disliking his half brother's speculative tone.

"To my knowledge, you've never courted a lady before."

"It's not a real courtship," Andrew informed him. "It's merely a ruse to fool Father."

"What?" Logan stopped on the stairs and stared at him in surprise. "Would you care to explain, Andrew?"

"As you know, I've been cut out of the will. To be reinstated I've got to convince Father that I've changed my wicked ways, or he'll die without leaving me a damned shilling." Andrew proceeded to explain his bargain with Caroline, and the terms they had struck.

Logan listened intently, finally giving a gruff laugh. "Well, if you wish to change Father's mind about his will,

I suppose your involvement with a woman like Miss Hargreaves is a good idea."

"It's not an 'involvement,'" Andrew said, feeling unaccountably defensive. "As I told you, it's merely a charade."

Logan slid a speculative glance his way. "I have a suspicion, Andrew, that your relationship with Miss Hargreaves is something more than a charade, whether you are willing to admit it or not."

"It's all for Father's benefit," Andrew said swiftly. "I am telling you, Scott, I have no designs on her. And even if I did, believe me, I would be the last man on earth whom she would take an interest in."

Chapter Three

"NOT IF HE were the last man on earth," Caroline said, glaring at her brother. "I am telling you, Cade, I feel no sort of attraction whatsoever to that . . . that *libertine*. Don't be obtuse. You know quite well that it is all a pretense."

"I thought it was," Cade said reflectively, "until I watched the two of you during that deuced long carriage ride today. Now I'm not so certain. Drake stared at you like a cat after a mouse. He didn't take his eyes off you once."

Caroline sternly suppressed an unwanted twinge of pleasure at her brother's words. She turned toward the long looking glass, needlessly fluffing the short sleeves of her pale blue evening gown. "The only reason he may have glanced my way was to distract himself from Mother's babbling," she said crisply.

"And the way you smiled at him this afternoon, before he left to see his father," Cade continued. "You looked positively besotted."

"Besotted?" She let out a burst of disbelieving laughter. "Cade, that is the most ridiculous thing I've ever heard you say. Not only am I *not* besotted with Lord Drake, I can barely stand to be in the same room with him!"

"Then why the new gown and hairstyle?" he asked. "Are you certain you're not trying to attract him?"

Caroline surveyed her reflection critically. Her gown was simple but stylish, a thin white muslin underskirt overlaid with transparent blue silk. The bodice was low-cut and square, edged with a row of glinting silver beadwork. Her dark, glossy brown hair had been pulled to the crown of her head with blue ribbons, and left to hang down the back in a mass of ringlets. She knew that she had never looked better in her life. "I am wearing a new gown because I am tired of looking so matronly," she said. "Just because I am a spinster doesn't mean I have to appear a complete dowd."

"Caro," her brother said affectionately, coming up behind her and putting his hands on her upper arms, "you're a spinster only by choice. You've always been a lovely girl. The only reason you haven't landed a husband is because you haven't yet seen fit to set your cap for someone."

She turned to hug him, heedless of mussing her gown, and smiled at him warmly. "Thank you, Cade. And just to be quite clear, I have *not* set my cap for Lord Drake. As I have told you a dozen times, we are simply acting. As in a stage performance."

"All right," he said, drawing back to look at her skeptically. "But in my opinion, you are both throwing yourself into your roles with a bit more zeal than necessary."

THE SOUNDS OF the ball drifted to Caroline's ears as they went down the grand staircase. The luminous, agile melody of a waltz swirled through the air, undercut by the flow of laughter and chatter as the guests moved through the circuit of rooms that branched off from the central hall. The atmosphere was heavily perfumed from huge arrangements of lilies and roses, while a garden breeze wafted gently through the rows of open windows.

Caroline's gloved fingertips slid easily over the carved marble balustrade as they descended. She gripped Cade's arm with her other hand. She was strangely nervous, wondering if her evening spent in Andrew's company would prove to be a delight or torture. Fanny chattered excitedly as she accompanied them, mentioning the names of several guests she had already seen at the estate, including peers of the realm, politicians, a celebrated artist, and a noted playwright.

As they reached the lower landing, Caroline saw Andrew waiting for them at the nadir of the staircase, his dark hair gleaming in the brilliant light shed by legions of candles. As if he sensed her approach, he turned and glanced upward. His white teeth flashed in a smile as he saw her, and Caroline's heartbeat hastened to a hard, driving rhythm.

Dressed in a formal, fashionable scheme of black and white, with a starched cravat and a formfitting gray waistcoat, Andrew was so handsome that it was almost unseemly. He was as polished and immaculate as any gentleman present, but his striking blue eyes gleamed with the devil's charm. When he looked at her like that, his gaze hot and interested, she did not feel as if this entire situation were an obligation. She did not feel as if it were a charade. The lamentable fact was, she felt excited, and glad, and thoroughly beguiled.

"Miss Hargreaves, you look ravishing," he murmured, after greeting Fanny and Cade. He offered her his arm and guided her toward the ballroom.

"Not matronly?" Caroline asked tartly.

"Not in the least." He smiled faintly. "You never did, actually. When I made that comment, I was just trying to annoy you."

"You succeeded," she said, and paused with a perplexed frown. "Why did you want to annoy me?"

"Because annoying you is safer than—" For some reason he broke off abruptly and clamped his mouth shut.

"Safer than what?" Caroline asked, intensely curious as he led her into the ballroom. "What? What?"

Ignoring her questions, Andrew swept her into a waltz so intoxicating and potent that its melody seemed to throb inside her veins. She was at best a competent dancer, but Andrew was exceptional, and there were few pleasures to equal dancing with a man who was truly accomplished at it. His arm was supportive, his hands gentle but authoritative as he guided her in smooth, sweeping circles.

Caroline was vaguely aware that people were staring at them. No doubt the crowd was amazed by the fact that the dissolute Lord Drake was waltzing with the proper Miss Hargreaves. They were an obvious mismatch . . . and yet, Caroline wondered, was it really so inconceivable that a rake and a spinster could find something alluring in each other?

"You are a wonderful dancer," she could not help exclaiming.

"Of course I am," he said. "I'm proficient at all the trivial activities in life. It's only the meaningful pursuits that present a problem."

"It doesn't have to be that way."

"Oh, it does," he assured her with a self-mocking smile.

An uncomfortable silence ensued until Caroline sought a way to break it. "Has your father come downstairs yet?" she asked. "Surely you will want him to see us dance together."

"I don't know where he is," Andrew returned. "And right now I don't give a damn if he sees us or not."

IN THE UPPER galleries that overlooked the ballroom, Logan Scott directed a pair of footmen to settle his father's fragile, tumor-ridden form onto a soft upholstered chaise longue. A maidservant settled into a nearby chair, ready to fetch anything that the earl might require. A light blanket was draped over Rochester's bony knees, and a goblet of rare Rhenish wine was placed in his clawlike fingers.

Logan watched the man for a moment, inwardly amazed that Rochester, a figure who had loomed over his entire life with such power and malevolence, should have come to this. The once-handsome face, with its hawklike perfection, had shrunk to a mask of skeletal paleness and delicacy. The vigorous, muscular body had deteriorated until he could barely walk without assistance. One might have thought that the imminent approach of death would have softened the cruel earl, and perhaps taught him some regret over the past. But Rochester, true to form, admitted to no shred of remorse.

Not for the first time, Logan felt an acute stab of sympathy for his half brother. Though Logan had been raised by a tenant farmer who had abused him physically, he had fared better than Andrew, whose father had abused his very soul. Surely no man in existence was colder and more unloving than the Earl of Rochester. It was a wonder that Andrew had survived such a childhood.

Tearing his thoughts away from the past, Logan glanced at the assemblage below. His gaze located the tall form of his brother, who was dancing with Miss Caroline Hargreaves. The petite woman seemed to have bewitched Andrew, who for once did not seem bored, bitter, or sullen. In fact, for the first time in his life, it appeared that Andrew was exactly where he wanted to be.

"There," Logan said, easily adjusting the heavy weight of the chaise longue so that his father could see better. "That is the woman Andrew brought here."

Rochester's mouth compressed into a parchment-thin line of disdain. "A girl of no consequence," he pronounced. "Her looks are adequate, I suppose. However, they say she is a bluestocking. Do not presume to tell me that your brother would have designs on such a creature."

Logan smiled slightly, long accustomed to the elderly man's caustic tongue. "Watch them together," he murmured. "See how he is with her."

"It's a ruse," Rochester said flatly. "I know all about my worthless son and his scheming ways. I could have predicted this from the moment I removed his name from the will. He seeks to deceive me into believing that he can change his

ways." He let out a sour cackle. "Andrew can court a mul-
titude of respectable spinsters if he wishes. But I will go to
hell before I reinstate him."

Logan forbore to reply that such a scenario was quite
likely, and bent to wedge a velvet-covered pillow behind the
old man's frail back. Satisfied that his father had a comfortable place from which to view the activities down below,
he stood and rested a hand on the carved mahogany rail-
ing. "Even if it were a ruse," he mused aloud, "wouldn't it
be interesting if Andrew were caught in a snare of his own
making?"

"What did you say?" The old man stared at him with
rheumy, slitted eyes, and raised the goblet of wine to his
lips. "What manner of snare is that, pray tell?"

"I mean it is possible that Andrew could fall in love with
Miss Hargreaves."

The earl sneered into his cup. "It's not in him to love
anyone other than himself."

"You're wrong, Father," Logan said quietly. "It's only
that Andrew has had little acquaintance with that emotion—
particularly to be on the receiving end of it."

Understanding the subtle criticism of the cold manner in
which he had always treated his sons, the legitimate one and
the bastard, Rochester gave him a disdainful smile. "You lay
the blame for his selfishness at *my* door, of course. You've
always made excuses for him. Take care, my superior fellow,
or I will cut *you* out of my will as well."

To Rochester's obvious annoyance, Logan burst out
laughing. "I don't give a damn," he said. "I don't need a
shilling from you. But have a care when you speak about
Andrew. He is the only reason you're here. For some reason
that I'll never be able to comprehend, Andrew loves you. A
miracle, that you could have produced a son who managed
to survive your tender mercies and still have the capability
to love. I freely admit that I would not."

"You are fond of making me out to be a monster," the earl remarked frostily. "When the truth is, I only give people what they deserve. If Andrew had ever done anything to merit my love, I would have accorded it to him. But he will have to earn it first."

"Good God, man, you're nearly on your deathbed," Logan muttered. "Don't you think you've waited long enough? Do you have any damned idea of what Andrew would do for one word of praise or affection from you?"

Rochester did not reply, his face stubbornly set as he drank from his goblet and watched the glittering, whirling mass of couples below.

THE RULE WAS that a gentleman should never dance more than three times with any one girl at a ball. Caroline did not know why such a rule had been invented, and she had never resented it as she did now. To her astonishment, she discovered that she liked dancing with Andrew, Lord Drake, and she was more than a little sorry when the waltz was over. She was further surprised to learn that Andrew could be an agreeable companion when he chose.

"I wouldn't have suspected you to be so well-informed on so many subjects," she told him, while servants filled their plates at the refreshment tables. "I assumed you had spent most of your time drinking, and yet you are remarkably well-read."

"I can drink and hold a book at the same time," he said.

She frowned at him. "Don't make light of it, when I am trying to express that . . . you are not . . ."

"I am not what?" he prompted softly.

"You are not exactly what you seem."

He gave her a slightly crooked grin. "Is that a compliment, Miss Hargreaves?"

She was slightly dazed as she stared into the warm blue intensity of his eyes. "I suppose it must be."

A woman's voice intruded on the moment, cutting through the spell of intimacy with the exquisite precision of a surgeon's blade. "Why, Cousin Caroline," the woman exclaimed, "I am *astonished* to see how stylish you look. It is a great pity that you cannot rid yourself of the spectacles, dear, for then you would be the toast of the ball."

The speaker was Julianne, Lady Brenton, the most beautiful and treacherous woman that Caroline had ever known. Even the people who despised her—and there were no end of those—had to concede that she was physically flawless. Julianne was slender, of medium height, with perfectly curved hips and a lavishly endowed bosom. Her features were positively angelic, her nose small and narrow, her lips naturally hued a deep pink, her eyes blue and heavily lashed. Crowning all of this perfection was a heavy swirl of blond hair in a silvery shade that seemed to have been distilled from moonlight. It was difficult, if not impossible, to believe that Caroline and this radiant creature could be related in any way, and yet they were first cousins on her father's side.

Caroline had grown up in awe of Julianne, who was only a year older than herself. In adulthood, however, admiration had gradually turned to disenchantment as she realized that her cousin's outward beauty concealed a heart that was monstrously selfish and calculating. When she was seventeen, Julianne had married a man forty years older than herself, a wealthy earl with a penchant for collecting fine objects. There had been frequent rumors that Julianne was unfaithful to her elderly spouse, but she was far too clever to have been caught. Three years ago her husband died in his bed, ostensibly of a weak heart. There were whispered suspicions that his death was not of natural causes, but no proof was ever discovered.

Julianne's blue eyes sparkled wickedly as she stood before Caroline. Her immaculate blondness was complemented by a shimmering white gown that draped so low in front that the upper halves of her breasts were exposed.

Sliding a flirtatious glance at Andrew, Julianne remarked, "My poor little cousin is quite blind without her spectacles . . . a pity, is it not?"

"She is lovely with or without them," Andrew replied coldly. "And Miss Hargreaves's considerable beauty is matched by her interior qualities. It is unfortunate that one cannot say the same of other women."

Julianne's entrancing smile dimmed, and she and Andrew regarded each other with cool challenge. Unspoken messages were exchanged between them. Caroline's pleasure in the evening evaporated as a few things became instantly clear. It was obvious that Julianne and Andrew were well acquainted. There seemed to be some remnant of intimacy, of sexual knowledge between them, that could have resulted only from a past affair.

Of course they had once been lovers, Caroline thought resentfully. Andrew would surely have been intrigued by a woman of such sensuous beauty . . . and there was no doubt that Julianne would have been more than willing to grant her favors to a man who was the heir to a great fortune.

"Lord Drake," Julianne said lightly, "you are more handsome than ever . . . why, you seem quite reinvigorated. To whom do we owe our gratitude for such a pleasing transformation?"

"My father," Andrew replied bluntly, with a smile that didn't reach his eyes. "He cut me out of his will—indeed a transforming experience."

"Yes, I had heard about that." Julianne's bow-shaped lips pursed in a little moue of disappointment. "Your inheritance was one of your most agreeable attributes, dear. A pity that you've lost it." She shot Caroline a snide smile before adding, "Clearly your prospects have dwindled considerably."

"Don't let us keep you, Julianne," Caroline said. "No

doubt you have much to accomplish tonight, with so many wealthy men present."

Julianne's blue eyes narrowed at the veiled insult. "Very well. Good evening, Cousin Caroline. And pray do show Lord Drake more of your 'interior beauty'—it may be your only chance of retaining his attention." A catlike smile spread across her face as she murmured, "If you can manage to lure Drake to your bed, cousin, you will find him a most exciting and talented partner. I can give you my personal assurance on that point." Julianne departed with a luscious swaying of her hips that caused her skirts to swish silkily.

Scores of male gazes followed her movement across the room, but Andrew's was not one of them. Instead he focused on Caroline, who met his scowling gaze with an accusing glare. "Despite my cousin's subtlety and discretion," Caroline said coolly, "I managed to receive the impression that you and she were once lovers. Is that true?"

UNTIL LADY BRENTON'S interruption, Andrew had actually been enjoying himself. He had always disliked attending balls and soirees, at which one was expected to make dull conversation with matrimonially minded girls and their even duller chaperones. But Caroline Hargreaves, with her quick wit and spirit, was surprisingly entertaining. For the last half hour he had felt a peculiar sense of well-being, a glow that had nothing to do with alcohol.

Then Julianne had appeared, reminding him of all his past debauchery, and the fragile sensation of happiness had abruptly vanished. Andrew had always tried to emulate his father in having no regrets over the past . . . but there it was, the unmistakable stab of rue, of embarrassment, over the affair with Julianne. And the hell of it was, the liaison hadn't even been worth the trouble. Julianne was like those elaborate French desserts that never tasted as good as they looked, and certainly never satisfied the palate.

Andrew forced himself to return Caroline's gaze as he answered her question. "It is true," he said gruffly. "We had an affair two years ago . . . brief and not worth remembering."

He resented the way Caroline stared at him, as if she were so flawless that she had never done anything worthy of regret. Damn her, he had never lied to her, or pretended to be anything other than what he was. She knew he was a scoundrel, a villain . . . for God's sake, he'd nearly resorted to blackmail to get her to attend the weekend party in the first place.

Grimly he wondered why the hell Logan and Madeline had invited Julianne here in the first place. Well, he couldn't object to her presence here merely because he'd once had an affair with her. If he tried to get her booted off the estate for that reason, there were at least half a dozen other women present who would have to be thrown out on the same grounds.

As if she had followed the turn of his thoughts, Caroline scowled at him. "I am not surprised that you've slept with my cousin," she said. "No doubt you've slept with at least half the women here."

"What if I have? What difference does it make to you?"

"No difference at all. It only serves to confirm my low opinion of you. How inconvenient it must be to have all the self-control of a March hare."

"It's better than being an ice maiden," he said with a sneer.

Her brown eyes widened behind the spectacles, and a flush spread over her face. "What? What did you call me?"

The edge in her tone alerted a couple nearby to the fact that a quarrel was brewing, and Andrew became aware that they were the focus of a few speculative stares. "Outside," he ground out. "We'll continue this in the rose garden."

"By all means," Caroline agreed in a vengeful tone, struggling to keep her face impassive.

Ten minutes later they had each managed to slip outside.

The rose garden, referred to by Madeline Scott as her "rose room," was a southwest section of the garden delineated by posts and rope swags covered with climbing roses. White gravel covered the ground, and fragrant lavender hedges led to the arch at the entrance. There was a massive stone urn on a pedestal in the center of the rose room, surrounded by a velvety blue bed of catmint.

The exotic perfumed air did nothing to soothe Andrew's frustration. As he saw Caroline's slight figure enter the rustling garden, he could barely restrain himself from pouncing on her. He kept still and silent instead, his jaw set as he watched her approach.

She stopped within arm's length of him, her head tilted back so that she could meet his gaze directly. "I have only one thing to say, my lord." Agitation pulled her voice taut and high. "Unlike you, I have a high regard for the truth. And while I would never take exception to an honest remark, no matter how unflattering, I *do* resent what you said back there. Because it is not true! You are categorically wrong, and I will not go back inside that house until you admit it!"

"Wrong about what?" he asked. "That you're an ice maiden?"

For some reason the term had incensed her. He saw her chin quiver with indignation. "Yes, that," she said in a hiss.

He gave her a smile designed to heighten her fury. "I can prove it," he said in a matter-of-fact tone. "What is your age . . . twenty-six?"

"Yes."

"And despite the fact that you're far prettier than average, and you possess good blood and a respected family name, you've never accepted a proposal of marriage from any man."

"Correct," she said, looking briefly bemused at the compliment.

He paced around her, giving her an insultingly thorough inspection. "And you're a virgin . . . aren't you?"

It was obvious that the question affronted her. He could easily read the outrage in her expression, and her blush was evident even in the starlit darkness. No proper young woman should even think of answering such an inquiry. After a long, silent struggle, she gave a brief nod.

That small confirmation did something to his insides, made them tighten and throb with savage frustration. *Damn* her, he had never found a virgin desirable before. And yet he wanted her with volcanic intensity . . . he wanted to possess and kiss every inch of her innocent body . . . he wanted to make her cry and moan for him. He wanted the lazy minutes afterward when they would lie together, sweaty and peaceful in the aftermath of passion. The right to touch her intimately, however and whenever he wanted, seemed worth any price. And yet he would never have her. He had relinquished any chance of that long ago, before they had ever met. Perhaps if he had led his life in a completely different manner . . . But he could not escape the consequences of his past.

Covering his yearning with a mocking smile, Andrew gestured with his hands to indicate that the facts spoke for themselves. "Pretty, unmarried, twenty-six, and a virgin. That leads to only one conclusion . . . ice maiden."

"I am *not*! I have far more passion, more honest feeling, than you'll ever possess!" Her eyes narrowed as she saw his amusement. "Don't you dare laugh at me!" She launched herself at him, her hands raised as if to attack.

With a smothered laugh, Andrew grabbed her upper arms and held her at bay . . . until he realized that she was not trying to claw his face, but rather to put her hands around his neck. Startled, he loosened his hold, and she immediately seized his nape. She exerted as much pressure as she was able, using her full weight to try to pull his head down. He resisted her easily, staring into her small face with a baffled smile. He was so much larger than she that any attempt on her part to physically coerce him was laughable. "Caroline," he said, his voice unsteady with equal parts of amusement and desire, "are you by chance trying to *kiss* me?"

She continued to tug at him furiously, wrathful and determined. She was saying something beneath her breath, spitting like an irate kitten. ". . . show you . . . make you sorry . . . I am *not* made of ice, you arrogant, presumptuous *libertine* . . ."

Andrew could not stand it any longer. As he viewed the tiny, indignant female in his arms, he lost the capability of rational thought. All he could think of was how much he desired her, and how a few stolen moments in the rose garden would not matter in the great scheme of things. He was nearly mad with the need to taste her, to touch her, to drag her body full-length against his, and the rest of the world could go to hell. And so he let it happen. He relaxed his neck and lowered his head, and let her tug his mouth down to hers.

Something unexpected happened with that first sweet pressure of her lips—innocently closed lips because she did not know how to kiss properly. He felt a terrible aching pressure around his heart, squeezing and clenching until he felt the hard wall around it crack, and heat came rushing inside. She was so light and soft in his arms, the smell of her skin a hundred times more alluring than roses, the fragile line of her spine arching as she tried to press closer to him. The sensation came too hard, too fast, and he froze in sudden paralysis, not knowing where to put his hands, afraid that if he moved at all, he would crush her.

He fumbled with his gloves, ripped them off, and dropped them to the ground. Carefully he touched Caroline's back and slid his palm to her waist. His other hand shook as he gently grasped the nape of her neck. Oh, God, she was exquisite, a bundle of muslin and silk in his hands, too luscious to be real. His breath rushed from his lungs in hard bursts, and he fought to keep his movements gentle as he urged her closer against his fiercely aroused body. Increasing the pressure of the kiss, he coaxed her lips to part, touched his tongue to hers, found the intoxicating taste of her. She started slightly at the unfamiliar intimacy. He knew it was wrong to kiss a virgin that way, but he couldn't help himself. A soothing sound came from deep in his throat, and he licked deeper, searching the sweet, dark heat of her mouth. To his astonishment, Caroline moaned and relaxed in his arms, her lips parting, her tongue sliding hotly against his.

Andrew had not expected her to be so ardent, so receptive. She should have been repelled by him. But she yielded herself with a terrible trust that devastated him. He couldn't stop his hands from wandering over her hungrily, reaching over the curves of her buttocks to hitch her higher against his body. He pulled her upward, nestling her closer into the huge ridge of his sex until she fit exactly the way he wanted. The thin layers of her clothes—and his—did nothing to muffle the sensation. She gasped and wriggled deliciously, and tightened her arms around his neck until her toes nearly left the ground.

"Caroline," he said hoarsely, his mouth stealing down the tender line of her throat, "you're making me insane. We have to stop now. I shouldn't be doing this—"

"Yes. Yes." Her breath puffed in rapid, hot expulsions, and she twined herself around him, rubbing herself against the rock-hard protrusion of his loins. They kissed again, her mouth clinging to his with frantic sweetness, and Andrew made a quiet, despairing sound.

"Stop me," he muttered, clamping his hand over her writhing bottom. "Tell me to let go of you . . . Slap me . . ."

She tilted her head back, purring like a kitten as he nuzzled the soft space beneath her ear. "Where should I slap you?" she asked throatily.

She was too innocent to fully comprehend the sexual connotations of her question. Even so, Andrew felt himself turn impossibly hard, and he suppressed a low groan of desire. "Caroline," he whispered harshly, "you win. I was wrong when I called you a . . . No, don't do that anymore; I can't bear it. You win." He eased her away from his aching body. "Now stay back," he added curtly, "or you're going to lose your virginity in this damned garden."

Recognizing the vehemence in his tone, Caroline prudently kept a few feet of distance between them. She wrapped her slender arms around herself, trembling. For a while there was no sound other than their labored breathing.

"We should go back," she finally said. "People will notice that we're both absent. I . . . I have no wish to be compromised . . . that is, my reputation . . ." Her voice trailed into an awkward silence, and she risked a glance at him. "Andrew," she confessed shakily, "I've never felt this way bef—"

"Don't say it," he interrupted. "For your sake, and mine, we are not going to let this happen again. We are going to keep to our bargain—I don't want complications."

"But don't you want to—"

"No," he said tersely. "I want only the pretense of a relationship with you, nothing more. If I truly became involved with you, I would have to transform my life completely. And it's too bloody late for that. I am beyond redemption, and no one, not even you, is worth changing my ways for."

She was quiet for a long moment, her dazed eyes focused on his set face. "I know someone who *is* worth it," she finally said.

"Who?"

"You." Her stare was direct and guileless. "You are worth saving, Andrew."

With just a few words, she demolished him. Andrew shook his head, unable to speak. He wanted to seize her in his arms again . . . worship her . . . ravish her. No woman had ever expressed the slightest hint of faith in him, in his worthless soul, and though he wanted to respond with utter scorn, he could not. One impossible wish consumed him in a great purifying blaze—that somehow he could become worthy of her. He yearned to tell her how he felt. Instead he averted his face and managed a few rasping words. "You go inside first."

FOR THE REST of the weekend party, and for the next three months, Andrew was a perfect gentleman. He was attentive, thoughtful, and good-humored, prompting jokes from all who knew him that somehow the wicked Lord Drake had been abducted and replaced by an identical stranger. Those who were aware of the Earl of Rochester's poor health surmised that Andrew was making an effort to court his father's favor before the old man died and left him bereft of the family fortune. It was a transparent effort, the gossips snickered, and very much in character for the devious Lord Drake.

The strange thing was, the longer that Andrew's pretend reformation lasted, the more it seemed to Caroline that he was changing in reality. He met with the Rochester estate agents and developed a plan to improve the land in ways that would help the tenants immeasurably. Then to the perplexity of all who knew him, Andrew sold much of his personal property, including a prize string of thoroughbreds, in order to finance the improvements.

It was not in character for Andrew to take such a risk, especially when there was no guarantee that he would inherit the Rochester fortune. But when Caroline asked him why he seemed determined to help the Rochester tenants, he laughed and shrugged as if it were a matter of no consequence. "The changes would have to be made whether or not I get the earl's money," he said. "And I was tired of maintaining all those damned horses—too expensive by half."

"Then what about your properties in town?" Caroline asked. "I've heard that your father planned to evict some poor tenants from a slum in Whitefriars rather than repair it—and you are letting them stay, and are renovating the entire building besides."

Andrew's face was carefully expressionless as he replied, "Unlike my father, I have no desire to be known as a slum lord. But don't mistake my motives as altruistic—it is merely a business decision. Any money I spend on the property will increase its value."

Caroline smiled at him and leaned close as if to confide a secret. "I think, my lord, that you actually care about those people."

"I'm practically a saint," he agreed sardonically, with a derisive arch of his brow.

She continued to smile, however, realizing that Andrew was not nearly as blackhearted as he pretended to be.

Just why Andrew should have begun to care about the people whose existence he had never bothered to notice before was a mystery. Perhaps it had something to do with his father's imminent demise . . . perhaps it had finally dawned on Andrew that the weight of responsibility would soon be transferred to his own shoulders. But he could easily have let things go on just as they were, allowing his father's managers and estate agents to make the decisions. Instead he took the reins in his own hands, tentatively at first, then with increasing confidence.

In accordance with their bargain, Andrew took Caroline riding in the park, and escorted her to musical evenings and soirees and the theater. Since Fanny was required to act as chaperone, there were few occasions for Caroline to talk privately with Andrew. They were forced instead to discuss seemly subjects such as literature or gardening, and their physical contact was limited to the occasional brush of their fingertips, or the pressure of his shoulder against hers as they sat next to each other. And yet these fleeting moments of closeness—a wordless stare, a stolen caress of her arm or hand—were impossibly exciting.

Caroline's awareness of Andrew was so excruciating that she sometimes thought she would burst into flames. She could not stop thinking about their impassioned embrace in the Scotts' rose garden, the pleasure of Andrew's mouth on hers. But he was so unrelentingly courteous now that she began to wonder if the episode had perhaps been some torrid dream conjured by her own fevered imagination.

Andrew, Lord Drake, was a fascinating puzzle. It seemed to Caroline that he was two different men—the arrogant, self-indulgent libertine, and the attractive stranger who was stumbling uncertainly on his way to becoming a gentleman. The first man had not appealed to her in the least. The second one . . . well, he was a far different matter. She saw that he was struggling, torn between the easy pleasures of the past and the duties that loomed before him. He still had not resumed his drinking and skirt chasing—he would have admitted it to her freely if he had. And according to Cade, Andrew seldom visited their club these days. Instead he spent his time fencing, boxing, or riding until he nearly dropped from exhaustion. He lost weight, perhaps a stone, until his trousers hung unfashionably loose and had to be altered. Although Andrew had always been a well-formed man, his body was now lean and impossibly hard, the muscles of his arms and back straining the seams of his coat.

"Why do you keep so active?" Caroline could not resist asking one day, as she pruned a lush bed of purple penstemons in her garden. Andrew lounged nearby on a small bench as he watched her carefully snip the dried heads of each stem. "My brother says that you were at the Pugilistic Club almost every day last week."

When Andrew took too long in answering, Caroline paused in her gardening and glanced over her shoulder. It was a cool November day, and a breeze caught a lock of her sable hair that had escaped her bonnet, and blew it across her cheek. She used her gloved hand to push away the errant lock, inadvertently smudging her face with dirt. Her heart lurched in sudden anticipation as she saw the expression in Andrew's searching blue eyes.

"Keeping active serves to distract me from . . . things." Andrew stood and came to her slowly, pulling a handkerchief from his pocket. "Here, hold still." He gently wiped away the dirt streak, then reached for her spectacles to clean them in a gesture that had become habitual.

Deprived of the corrective lenses, Caroline stared up at his dark, blurred face with myopic attentiveness. "What things?" she asked, breathless at his nearness. "I presume that you must mean your drinking and gaming . . ."

"No, it's not that." He replaced her spectacles with great care, and used a fingertip to stroke the silky tendril of hair behind her ear. "Can't you guess what is bothering me?" he asked softly. "What keeps me awake unless I exhaust myself before going to bed each night?"

He stood very close, his gaze holding hers intimately. Even though he was not touching her, Caroline felt surrounded by his virile presence. The shears dropped from her suddenly nerveless fingers, falling to the earth with a soft thud. "Oh, I . . ." She paused to moisten her dry lips. "I suppose you miss h-having a woman. But there is no reason that you could not . . . that is, with so many who would be willing . . ." Flushing, she caught her bottom lip with her teeth and floundered into silence.

"I've become too damned particular." He leaned closer, and his breath fell gently against her ear, sending a pleasurable thrill down her spine. "Caroline, look at me. There is something I have no right to ask . . . but . . ."

"Yes?" she whispered.

"I've been considering my situation," he said carefully.

"Caroline . . . even if my father doesn't leave me a shilling, I could manage to provide a comfortable existence for someone. I have a few investments, as well as the estate. It wouldn't be a grand mode of living, but . . ."

"Yes?" Caroline managed to say, her heart hammering madly in her chest. "Go on."

"You see—"

"Caroline!" came her mother's shrill voice from the French doors that opened onto the garden from the parlor. "Caroline, I insist that you come inside and act as a proper hostess, rather than make poor Lord Drake stand outside and watch you dig holes in the dirt! I suspect you have offered him no manner of refreshment, and . . . Why, this wind is intolerable, you will cause him to catch his death of cold. Come in at once, I bid you both!"

"Yes, Mother," Caroline said grimly, filled with frustration. She glanced at Andrew, who had lost his serious intensity, and was regarding her with a sudden smile. "Before we go inside," she suggested, "you may finish what you were going to say—"

"Later," he said, bending to retrieve her fallen shears.

Her fists clenched, and she nearly stamped her foot in annoyance. She wanted to strangle her mother for breaking into what was undoubtedly the most supremely interesting moment of her life. What if Andrew had been trying to propose? Her heart turned over at the thought. Would she have decided to accept such a risk . . . would she be able to trust that he would remain the way he was now, instead of changing back into the rake he had always been?

Yes, she thought in a rush of giddy wonder. *Yes, I would take that chance.*

Because she had fallen in love with him, imperfect as he was. She loved every handsome, tarnished inch of him, inside and out. She wanted to help him in his quest to become a better man. And if a little bit of the scoundrel remained . . . An irresistible smile tugged at her lips. Well, she would enjoy that part of him too.

A FORTNIGHT LATER, at the beginning of December, Caroline received word that the Earl of Rochester was on his deathbed. The brief message from Andrew also included a surprising request. The earl wanted to see her, for reasons that he would explain to no one, not even Andrew. *I humbly ask for your indulgence in this matter,* Andrew had written, *as your presence may bring the earl some peace in his last hours. My carriage will convey you to the estate if you wish to come . . . and if you do not, I understand and respect your decision. Your servant.*

And he had signed his name *Andrew,* with a familiarity that was improper and yet touching, bespeaking his distracted turn of mind. Or perhaps it betrayed his feelings for her.

"Miss Hargreaves?" the liveried footman murmured, evidently having been informed of the possibility that she might return with them. "Shall we convey you to the Rochester estate?"

"Yes," Caroline said instantly. "I will need but a few minutes to be ready. I will bring a maidservant with me."

"Yes, miss."

Caroline was consumed with thoughts of Andrew as the carriage traveled to Rochester Hall in Buckinghamshire, where the earl had chosen to spend his last days. Although Caroline had never seen the place, Andrew had described it to her. The Rochesters owned fifteen hundred acres, including the local village, the woods surrounding it, and some of the most fertile farmland in England. It had been granted to the family by Henry II in the twelfth century, Andrew had said, and he had gone on to make a sarcastic comment about the fact that the family's proud and ancient heritage would soon pass to a complete reprobate. Caroline understood that Andrew did not feel at all worthy of the title and the responsibilities that he would inherit. She felt an aching need to comfort him, to somehow find a way to convince him that he was a much better man than he believed himself to be.

With her thoughts in turmoil, Caroline kept her gaze focused on the scenery outside the window, the land covered with woods and vineyards, the villages filled with cottages made of flint garnered from the Chiltern hills. Finally they came to the massive structure of Rochester Hall, constructed of honey yellow ironstone and gray sandstone, hewn with stalwart medieval masonry. A gate centered in the entrance gave the carriage access to an open courtyard.

Caroline was escorted by a footman to the central great hall, which was large, drafty, and ornamented with dull-colored tapestries. Rochester Hall had once been a fortress, its roof studded with parapets and crenellation, the windows long and narrow to allow archers to defend the building. Now it was merely a cold, vast home that seemed badly in need of a woman's hand to soften the place and make it more comfortable.

"Miss Hargreaves." Andrew's deep voice echoed against the polished sandstone walls as he approached her.

She felt a thrill of gladness as he came to her and took her hands. The heat of his fingers penetrated the barrier of her gloves as he held her hands in a secure clasp. "Caro," he said softly, and nodded to the footman to leave them.

She stared up at him with a searching gaze. His emotions were held in tight rein . . . it was impossible to read the thoughts behind the expressionless mask of his face. But somehow she sensed his hidden anguish, and she longed to put her arms around him and comfort him.

"How was the carriage ride?" he asked, still retaining her hands. "I hope it didn't make you too uncomfortable."

Caroline smiled slightly, realizing that he had remembered how the motion of a long carriage ride made her sick. "No, I was perfectly fine. I stared out the window the entire way."

"Thank you for coming," he muttered. "I wouldn't have blamed you if you had refused. God knows why Rochester asked for you—it's because of some whim that he won't explain—"

"I am glad to be here," she interrupted gently. "Not for his sake, but for yours. To be here as your friend, as your . . ." Her voice trailed away as she fumbled for an appropriate word.

Her consternation elicited a brief smile from Andrew, and his blue eyes were suddenly tender. "Darling little friend," he whispered, bringing her gloved hand to his mouth.

Emotion welled up inside her, a singular deep joy that seemed to fill her chest and throat with sweet warmth. The happiness of being needed by him, welcomed by him, was almost too much to be borne.

Caroline glanced at the heavy oak staircase that led to the second floor, its openwork balustrade casting long, jagged shadows across the great hall. What a cavernous, sterile place for a little boy to grow up in, she thought. Andrew had told her that his mother had died a few weeks after giving birth to him. He had spent his childhood here, at the mercy of a father whose heart was as warm and soft as a glacier. "Shall we go up to him?" she asked, referring to the earl.

"In a minute," Andrew replied. "Logan and his wife are with him now. The doctor says it is only a matter of hours before he—" He stopped, his throat seeming to close, and he gave her a look that was filled with baffled fury, most of it directed at himself. "My God, all the times that I've wished him dead. But now I feel . . ."

"Regret?" Caroline suggested softly, removing her glove and laying her fingers against the hard, smooth-shaven line of his cheek. The muscles of his jaw worked tensely against the delicate palm of her hand. "And perhaps sorrow," she said, "for all that could have been, and for all the disappointment you caused each other."

He could not bring himself to reply, only gave a short nod.

"And maybe just a little fear?" she asked, daring to caress his cheek softly. "Because soon *you* will be Lord Rochester . . . something you've hated and dreaded all your life."

Andrew began to breathe in deep surges, his eyes locked with hers as if his very survival depended on it. "If only I could stop it from happening," he said hoarsely.

"You are a better man than your father," she whispered. "You will take care of the people who depend on you. There is nothing to fear. I know that you will not fall back into your old ways. You are a good man, even if you don't believe it."

He was very still, giving her a look that burned all through her. Although he did not move to embrace her, she had the sense of being possessed, captured by his gaze and his potent will beyond any hope of release. "Caro," he finally said, his voice tightly controlled, "I can't ever be without you."

She smiled faintly. "You won't have to."

They were interrupted by the approach of a housemaid who had been dispatched from upstairs. "M'lord," the tall, rather ungainly girl murmured, bobbing in an awkward curtsy, "Mr. Scott sent me to ask if Miss Hargreaves is here, and if she would please attend the earl—"

"I will bring her to Rochester," Andrew replied grimly.

"Yes, m'lord." The maid hurried upstairs ahead of them, while Andrew carefully placed Caroline's small hand on his arm.

He looked down at her with concern. "You don't have to see him if you don't wish it."

"Of course I will see the earl," Caroline replied. "I am extremely curious about what he will say."

THE EARL OF Rochester was attended by two physicians, as well as Mr. Scott and his wife Madeline. The atmosphere in the bedroom was oppressively somber and stifling, with all the windows closed and the heavy velvet drapes pulled shut. A dismal end for an unhappy man, Caroline reflected silently. In her opinion the earl was extremely fortunate to have his two sons with him, considering the appalling way he had always treated them.

The earl was propped to a semireclining position with a pile of pillows behind his back. His head turned as Caroline entered the room, and his rheumy gaze fastened on her. "The Hargreaves chit," he said softly. It seemed to take great effort for him to speak. He addressed the other occupants of the room while still staring at Caroline. "Leave, all of you. I wish . . . to speak to Miss Hargreaves . . . in private."

They complied en masse except for Andrew, who lingered to stare into Caroline's face. She gave him a reassuring smile and motioned for him to leave the room. "I'll be waiting just outside," he murmured. "Call for me if you wish."

When the door closed, Caroline went to the chair by the bedside and sat, folding her hands in her lap. Her face was nearly level with the earl's, and she did not bother to conceal her curiosity as she stared at him. He must have been handsome at one time, she thought, although he wore the innate arrogance of a man who had always taken himself far too seriously.

"My lord," she said, "I have come, as you requested. May I ask why you wished to see me?"

Rochester ignored her question for a moment, his slitted gaze moving over her speculatively. "Attractive, but . . . hardly a great beauty," he observed. "What does . . . he see in you, I wonder?"

"Perhaps you should ask Lord Drake," Caroline suggested calmly.

"He will not discuss you," he replied with frowning contemplation. "I sent for you because . . . I want the answer to one question. When my son proposes . . . will you accept?"

Startled, Caroline stared at him without blinking. "He has not proposed marriage to me, my lord, nor has he given any indication that he is considering such a proposition—"

"He will," Rochester assured her, his face twisting with a spasm of pain. Fumbling, he reached for a small glass on the bedside table. Automatically Caroline moved to help him, catching the noxious fragrance of spirits mixed with medicinal tonic as she brought the edge of the glass to his withered lips. Reclining back on the pillows, the earl viewed her speculatively. "You appear to have wrought . . . a miracle, Miss Hargreaves. Somehow you . . . have drawn my son out of his remarkable self-absorption. I know him . . . quite well, you see. I suspect your liaison began as a plan to deceive me, yet . . . he seems to have changed. He seems to love you, although . . . one never would have believed him capable of it."

"Perhaps you do not know Lord Drake as well as you think you do," Caroline said, unable to keep the edge from her tone. "He only needs someone to believe in him, and to encourage him. He is a good man, a caring one—"

"Please," he murmured, lifting a gnarled hand in a gesture of self-defense. "Do not waste . . . what little time I have left . . . with rapturous descriptions of my . . . good-for-naught progeny."

"Then I will answer your question," Caroline returned evenly. "Yes, my lord, if your son proposes to me, I will accept gladly. And if you do not leave him your fortune, I will not care one whit . . . and neither will he. Some things are more precious than money, although I am certain you will mock me for saying so."

Rochester surprised her by smiling thinly, relaxing more

deeply against the pillows. "I will not mock you," he murmured, seeming exhausted but oddly serene. "I believe . . . you might be the saving of him. Go now, Miss Hargreaves . . . Tell Andrew to come."

"Yes, my lord."

She left the room quickly, her emotions in chaos, feeling chilly and anxious and wanting to feel the comfort of Andrew's arms around her.

Chapter Four

IT HAD BEEN two weeks since the Earl of Rochester had died, leaving Andrew the entirety of his fortune as well as the title and entailed properties. Two interminable weeks during which Caroline had received no word from Andrew. At first she had been patient, understanding that Andrew must be wading through a morass of funeral arrangements and business decisions. She knew that he would come to her as soon as possible. But as day followed day, and he did not send so much as a single written sentence, Caroline realized that something was very wrong. Consumed with worry, she considered writing to him, or even paying an unexpected visit to Rochester Hall, but it was unthinkable for any un-married woman under the age of thirty to be so forward. She finally decided to send her brother Cade to find Andrew, bidding him to find out if Andrew was well, if he needed anything . . . if he was thinking of her.

While Cade went on his mission to locate the new Lord Rochester, Caroline sat alone in her chilly winter garden, gazing forlornly at her clipped-back plants and the bare branches of her prized Japanese maples. There were only two weeks until Christmas, she thought dully. For her family's sake, Caroline had decorated the house with boughs of evergreens and holly, and had adorned the doors with wreaths of fruit and ribbons. But she sensed that instead of a joyous holiday, she was about to experience heartbreak for the first time in her life, and the black misery that awaited her was too awful to contemplate.

Something was indeed wrong, or Andrew would have come to her by now. And yet she could not imagine what was keeping him away. She knew that he needed her, just as she needed him, and that nothing stood in the way of their being together, if he so desired. Why, then, had he not come?

Just as Caroline thought she would go insane from the unanswered questions that plagued her, Cade returned home. The expression on his face did not ease her worry.

"Your hands are like ice," he said, chafing her stiff fingers and guiding her into the parlor, where a warm fire blazed in the hearth. "You've been sitting outside too long—wait, I'll send for some tea."

"I don't want tea." Caroline sat rigidly on the settee, while her brother's large form lowered to the space beside her. "Cade, did you find him? How is he? Oh, tell me something or I'll go mad!"

"Yes, I found him." Cade scowled and took her hands again, warming her tense fingers with his. He let out a slow sigh. "Drake . . . that is, Rochester . . . has been drinking again, quite a lot. I'm afraid he is back to his old ways."

She regarded him with numb disbelief. "But that's not possible."

"That's not all of it," Cade said darkly. "To everyone's surprise, Rochester has suddenly gotten himself engaged—to none other than our own dear cousin Julianne. Now that he's got the family fortune in his possession, it seems that Julianne sees his charms in a new light. The banns will be read in church tomorrow. They'll be married when the new year starts."

"Cade, don't tease like this," Caroline said in a raw whisper. "It's not true . . . not true—" She stopped, suddenly unable to breathe, while flurries of brilliant sparks danced madly across her vision. She heard her brother's exclamation as if from a great distance, and she felt the hard, urgent grip of his hands.

"My God"—his voice was overlaid with a strange hum that filled her ears—"here, put your head down . . . Caro, what in the hell is wrong?"

She struggled for air, for equilibrium, while her heart clattered in a painful broken measure. "He c-can't marry her," she said through chattering teeth.

"Caroline." Her brother was unexpectedly steady and strong, holding her against him in a tight grip. "Good Lord . . . I had no idea you felt this way. It was supposed to be a charade. Don't tell me you had the bad sense to fall in love with Rochester, who has to be the worst choice a woman like you could make—"

"Yes, I love him," she choked out. Tears slid down her cheeks in scalding trails. "And he loves me, Cade, he *does* . . . Oh, this doesn't make sense!"

"Has he encouraged you to think that he would marry you?" her brother asked softly. "Did he ever say that he loved you?"

"Not in those words," she said in a sob. "But the way he was with me . . . he made me believe . . ." She buried her head in her arms, weeping violently. "Why would he marry Julianne, of all people? She is *evil* . . . oh, there are things about her that you don't know . . . things that Father told me about her before he died. She will ruin Andrew!"

"She's already made a good start of it, from all appearances," Cade said grimly. He found a handkerchief in his pocket and swabbed her sodden face with it. "Rochester is as miserable as I've ever seen him. He won't explain anything, other than to say that Julianne is a fit mate for him, and everyone is better off this way. And, Caro . . ." His voice turned very gentle. "Perhaps he is right. You and Andrew . . . it is not a good match."

"Leave me alone," Caroline whispered. Gently she extricated herself from his arms and made her way out of the parlor. She hobbled like an old woman as she sought the privacy of her bedroom, ignoring Cade's worried questions. She needed to be alone, to crawl into her bed and hide like a wounded animal. Perhaps there she would find some way to heal the terrible wounds inside.

FOR TWO DAYS Caroline remained in her room, too devastated to cry or talk. She could not eat or sleep, as her tired mind combed relentlessly over every memory of Andrew. He had made no promises, had offered no pledge of love, had given her no token to indicate his feelings. She could not accuse him of betrayal. Still, her anguish was evolving into wounded rage. She wanted to confront him, to force him to admit his feelings, or at least to tell her what had been a lie and what had been the truth. Surely it was her right to have an explanation. But Andrew had abandoned her without a word, leaving her to wonder desperately what had gone wrong between them.

This had been his plan all along, she thought with increasing despair. He had only wanted her companionship until his father died and left him the Rochester fortune. Now that Andrew had gotten what he wanted, she was of no further consequence to him. But hadn't he come to care for her just a little? She knew she had not imagined the tenderness in his voice when he had said, *I can't ever be without you . . .*

Why would he have said that, if he had not meant it?

To Caroline's weary amusement, her mother, Fanny, had received the news of Andrew's impending nuptials with a great display of hysterics. She had taken to her bed at once, loudly insisting that the servants wait on her hand and foot until she recovered. The household centered around Fanny and her delicate nerves, mercifully leaving Caroline in peace.

The only person Caroline spoke to was Cade, who had become a surprisingly steady source of support.

"What can I do?" he asked softly, approaching Caroline as she sat before the window and stared blankly out at the garden. "There must be something that would make you feel better."

She turned toward her brother with a dismal smile. "I suspect I will feel better as time goes by, although right now I doubt that I will ever feel happy again."

"That bastard Rochester," Cade muttered, sinking to his haunches beside her. "Shall I go thrash him for you?"

A wan chuckle escaped her. "No, Cade. That would not satisfy me in the least. And I suspect Andrew has quite enough suffering in store, if he truly intends to go through with his plans to marry Julianne."

"True." Cade considered her thoughtfully. "There is something I should tell you, Caro, although you will probably disapprove. Rochester sent me a message yesterday, informing me that he has settled all my debts. I suppose I should return all the money to him—but I don't want to."

"Do as you like." Listlessly she leaned forward until her forehead was pressed against the cold, hard pane of the window.

"Well, now that I'm out of debt, and you are indirectly responsible for my good fortune . . . I want to do something for you. It's almost Christmas, after all. Let me buy you a pretty necklace, or a new gown . . . just tell me what you want."

"Cade," she returned dully, without opening her eyes, "the only thing I would like to have is Rochester trussed up like a yuletide goose, completely at my mercy. Since you cannot make that happen, I wish for nothing."

An extended silence greeted her statement, and then she felt a gentle pat on her shoulder. "All right, sweet sister."

THE NEXT DAY Caroline made a genuine effort to shake herself from her cloud of melancholy. She took a long, steaming bath and washed her hair, and donned a comfortable gown that was sadly out of style but had always been her favorite. The folds of frayed dull green velvet draped gently over her body as she sat by the fire to dry her hair. It was cold and blustery outside, and she shivered as she caught a glimpse of the icy gray sky through the window of her bedroom.

Just as she contemplated the idea of sending for a tray of toast and tea, the closed door was attacked by an energetic fist. "Caro," came her brother's voice. "Caro, may I come in? I must speak with you." His fist pounded the wood panels again, as if he were about some urgent matter.

A faint quizzical smile came to her face. "Yes, come in," she said, "before you break the door down."

Cade burst into the room, wearing the strangest expression . . . his face tense and triumphant, while an air of wildness clung to him. His dark brown hair was disheveled, and his black silk cravat hung limply on either side of his neck.

"Cade," Caroline said in concern, "what in heaven's name has happened? Have you been fighting? What is the matter?"

A mixture of jubilation and defiance crossed his face, making him appear more boyish than his twenty-four years. When he spoke, he sounded slightly out of breath. "I've been rather busy today."

"Doing what?" she asked warily.

"I've gotten you a Christmas present. It required a bit of effort, let me tell you. I had to get a couple of the fellows to help me, and . . . Well, we shouldn't waste time talking. Get your traveling cloak."

Caroline stared at him in complete bewilderment. "Cade, is my present outside? Must I fetch it myself, and on such a chilly day? I would prefer to wait. You of all people know what I have been through recently, and—"

"This present won't keep for long," he replied, straight-faced. Reaching into his pocket, he extracted a very small key, with a frivolous red bow attached. "Here, take this." He pressed the key into her palm. "And never say that I don't go to trouble for you."

Stupefied, she stared at the key in her hand. "I've never seen a key like this. What does it belong to?"

Her brother responded with a maddening smile. "Get your cloak and go find out."

Caroline rolled her eyes. "I am not in the mood for one of your pranks," she said pertly. "And I don't wish to go outside. But I will oblige you. Only heed my words: if this present is anything less than a queen's ransom in jewels, I shall be very put out with you. Now, may I at least be granted a few minutes to pin up my hair?"

"Very well," he said impatiently. "But hurry."

Caroline could not help being amused by her brother's suppressed exuberance. He fairly danced around her like some puckish sprite as she followed him down the stairs a minute later. No doubt he thought that his mysterious gift would serve to distract her from her broken heart . . . and though his ploy was transparent, she appreciated the caring thoughts behind it.

Opening the door with a flourish, Cade gestured to the family carriage and a team of two chestnuts stamping and blowing impatiently as the wind gusted around them. The family footman and driver also awaited, wearing heavy overcoats and large hats to shield them from the cold. "Oh, Cade," Caroline said in a groan, turning back into the house, "I am not going anywhere in that carriage. I am tired, and hungry, and I want to have a peaceful evening at home."

Cade startled her by taking her small face in his hands, and staring down at her with dark, entreating eyes. "Please, Caro," he muttered. "For once, don't argue or cause problems. Just do as I ask. Get into that carriage, and take the deuced key with you."

She returned his steady gaze with a perplexed one of her own, shaking her head within the frame of his hands.

A dark, strange suspicion blossomed inside her. "Cade," she whispered, "what have you done?"

He did not reply, only guided her to the carriage and helped her inside, while the footman gave her a lap blanket and moved the porcelain foot warmer directly beneath her soles.

"Where will the carriage take me?" Caroline asked, and Cade shrugged casually.

"A friend of mine, Sambrooke, has a family cottage right at the outskirts of London that he uses to meet his . . . Well, that doesn't matter. For today, the place is unoccupied, and at your disposal."

"Why couldn't you have brought my gift here?" She pinned him with a doubtful glare.

For some reason the question made him laugh shortly. "Because you need to view it in privacy." Leaning into the carriage, he brushed her cold cheek with a kiss. "Good luck," he murmured, and withdrew.

She stared blankly through the carriage window as the door closed with a firm snap. Panic shuffled her thoughts, turning them into an incoherent jumble. *Good luck?* What in God's name had he meant by that? Did this by chance have anything to do with Andrew? Oh, she would cheerfully murder her brother if it did!

THE CARRIAGE BROUGHT her past Hyde Park to an area west of London where there were still large tracts of sparsely developed land. As the vehicle came to a stop, Caroline fought to contain her agitation. She wondered wildly what her brother had arranged, and why she had been such an idiot as to fall in with his plans. The footman opened the carriage door and placed a step on the ground. Caroline did not move, however. She remained inside the vehicle and stared at the modest white roughcast house, with its steeply pitched slate roof and gravel-covered courtyard in front.

"Peter," she said to the footman, an old and trusted family servant, "do you have any idea what this is about? You must tell me if you do."

He shook his head. "No, miss, I know nothing. Do you wish to return home?"

Caroline considered the idea and abandoned it almost immediately. She had ventured too far to turn back now. "No, I'll go inside," she said reluctantly. "Shall you wait for me here?"

"If you wish, miss. But Lord Hargreaves's instructions were to leave you here and return in precisely two hours."

"I have a few choice words for my brother." Straightening her shoulders, she gathered her cloak tightly about herself and hopped down from the carriage. Silently she began to plan a list of the ways in which she would punish Cade. "Very well, Peter. You and the driver will leave, as my brother instructed. One would hate to thwart his wishes, as he seems to have decided exactly what must be done."

Peter opened the door for her, and helped her off with her cloak before returning outside to the carriage. The vehicle rolled gently away, its heavy wheels crunching the ice-covered gravel of the front courtyard.

Cautiously Caroline gripped the key and ventured inside the cottage. The place was simply furnished, with some oak paneling, a few family portraits, a set of ladder-back chairs, a library corner filled with old leather-bound books. The air was cold, but a cheerful little fire had been lit in the main room. Had it been lit for her comfort, or for someone else's?

"Hello?" she called out hesitantly. "If anyone is here, I bid you answer. Hello?"

She heard a muffled shout from some distant corner of the house. The sound gave her an unpleasant start, producing a stinging sensation along the nerves of her shoulders and spine. Her breath issued in flat bursts, and she gripped the key until its ridges dug deeply into her sweating palm. She forced herself to move. One step, then another, until she was running through the cottage, searching for whomever had shouted.

"Hello, where are you?" she called repeatedly, making her way toward the back of the house. "Where—"

The flickering of hearth light issued from one of the rooms at the end of the hall. Grabbing up handfuls of her velvet skirts, Caroline rushed toward the room. She crossed the threshold in a flurry and stopped so suddenly that her hastily arranged hair pitched forward. Impatiently she pushed it back and stared in astonishment at the scene before her. It was a bedroom, so small that it allowed for only three pieces of furniture: a washstand, a night table, and a large carved rosewood bed. However, the other guest at this romantic rendezvous had not come as willingly as herself.

. . . the only thing I would like to have is Rochester trussed up like a yuletide goose, completely at my mercy, she had unthinkingly told her witless brother. And Cade, the insane ass, had somehow managed to accomplish it.

Andrew, the seventh Earl of Rochester, was stretched full-length on the bed, his arms tethered above his head with what seemed to be a pair of metal cuffs linked by a chain and lock. The chain had been passed through a pair of carved openings in the solid rosewood headboard, securely holding Andrew prisoner.

His dark head lifted from the pillow, and his eyes gleamed an unholy shade of blue in his flushed face. He yanked at the cuffs with a force that surely bruised his imprisoned wrists. "Get these the hell off of me," he said in a growl, his voice containing a level of ferocity that made her flinch. He was like some magnificent feral animal, the powerful muscles of his arms bulging against his shirtsleeves, his taut body arching from the bed.

"I am so sorry," she said with a gasp, instinctively rushing forward to help him. "My God . . . it was Cade . . . I don't know what got into his head—"

"I'm going to kill him," Andrew muttered, continuing to tug savagely at his tethered wrists.

"Wait, you'll hurt yourself. I have the key. Just be still and let me—"

"Did you ask him to do this?" he asked with a snarl as she climbed onto the bed beside him.

"No," she said at once, then felt scarlet color flooding her cheeks. "Not exactly. I only said I wished—" She broke off and bit her lip. "He told me about your betrothal to Cousin Julianne, you see, and I—" Continuing to blush, she crawled over him to reach the lock of the handcuffs. The delicate shape of her breast brushed over his chest, and Andrew's entire body jerked as if he had been burned. To Caroline's dismay, the key dropped from her fingers and fell between the mattress and the headboard. "Do be still," she said, keeping her gaze from his face as she levered her body farther over his and fumbled for the key. It was not easy avoiding eye contact with him when their faces were so close. The brawny mass of his body was hard and unmoving beneath her. She heard his breathing change, turning deep and quick as she strained to retrieve the key.

Her fingertips curled around the key and pried it free of the mattress. "I've got it," she murmured, risking a glance at him.

Andrew's eyes were closed, his nose and mouth almost touching the curve of her breast. He seemed to be absorbing her scent, savoring it with peculiar intensity, as if he were a condemned man being offered his last meal.

"Andrew?" she whispered in painful confusion.

His expression became closed and hard, his blue eyes opaque. "Unlock these damned things!" He rattled the chain that linked the cuffs. The noise startled her, jangled across her raw nerves. She saw the deep gouges the chain links had left on the solid rosewood, but despite the relentless tugging and sawing, the wood had so far resisted the grating metal.

Her gaze dropped to the key in her hand. Instead of using it to unlock the handcuffs, she closed her fingers around it. Terrible, wicked thoughts formed in her mind. The right thing to do would be to set Andrew free as quickly as possible. But for the first time in her entire sedate, seemly life, she did not want to do what was right.

"Before I let you go," she said in a low voice that did not quite sound like her own, "I would like the answer to one question. Why did you throw me aside in favor of Julianne?"

He continued to look at her with that arctic gaze. "I'll be damned if I'll answer any questions while I'm chained to a bed."

"And if I set you free? Will you answer me then?"

"No."

She searched his eyes for any sign of the man she had come to love, the Andrew who had been amusing, self-mocking, tender. There was nothing but bitterness in the depths of frozen blue, as if he had lost all feeling for her, himself, and everything that mattered. It would take something catastrophic to reach inside this implacable stranger.

"Why Julianne?" she persisted. "You said the affair with her was not worth remembering. Was that a lie? Have you decided that she can offer you something more, something better, than I can?"

"She is a better match for me than you could ever be."

Suddenly it hurt to breathe. "Because she is more beautiful? More passionate?" she forced herself to ask.

Andrew tried to form the word *yes*, but it would not leave his lips. He settled for a single jerking nod.

That motion should have destroyed her, for it confirmed every self-doubt she had ever possessed. But the look on Andrew's face . . . the twitch of his jaw, the odd glaze of his eyes . . . for a split second he seemed to be caught in a moment of pure agony. And there could be only one reason why.

"You're lying," she whispered.

"No, I'm not."

All at once Caroline gave rein to the desperate impulses that swirled in her head. She was a woman with nothing to lose. "Then I will prove you wrong," she said unsteadily. "I will prove that I can give you a hundred times more satisfaction than Julianne."

"How?"

"I am going to make love to you," she said, sitting up beside him. Her trembling fingers went to the neck of her gown, and she began working the knotted silk loops that fastened the front of her bodice. "Right now, on this bed, while you are helpless to prevent it. And I won't stop until you admit that you are lying. I'll have an explanation out of you, my lord, one way or another."

Clearly she had surprised him. She knew that he had never expected such feminine aggression from a respectable spinster. "You wouldn't have the damn nerve," he said softly.

Well, that sealed his fate. She certainly could not back down after such a challenge. Resolutely Caroline continued on the silk fastenings until the front of her velvet gown gaped open to reveal her thin muslin chemise. A feeling of unreality settled over her as she pulled her arms from one sleeve, then the other. In all her adult life, she had never undressed in front of anyone. Goose bumps rose on her skin, and she rubbed her bare upper arms. The chemise provided so little covering that she might as well have been naked.

She would not have been surprised had Andrew decided to mock her, but he did not seem amused or angry at her display. He seemed . . . fascinated. His gaze slid over her body, lingered at the rose-tinted shadows of her nipples, then returned to her face. "That's enough," he muttered. "Much as I enjoy the view, there is no point to this."

"I disagree." She slid off the bed and pushed the heavy gown to the floor, where it lay in a soft heap. Standing in her chemise and drawers, she tried to still the chattering of her teeth. "I am going to make you talk to me, my lord, no matter what it takes. Before I'm through, I'll have you babbling like an idiot."

His breath caught with an incredulous laugh. The sound heartened her, for it seemed to make him more human and less a frozen stranger. "In the first place, I'm not worth the effort. Second, you don't know what the hell you're doing, which throws your plans very much in doubt."

"I know enough," she said with false bravado. "Sexual intercourse is merely a matter of mechanics . . . and even in my inexperience, I believe I can figure out what goes where."

"It is *not* merely a matter of mechanics." He tugged at the handcuffs with a new urgency, his face suddenly contorted with . . . fear? . . . concern? "Damn it, Caroline. I admire your determination, but you have to *stop this now*, do you understand? You're going to cause yourself nothing but pain and frustration. You deserve better than to have your first experience turn out badly. Let me go, you bloody stubborn witch!"

The flare of desperate fury pleased her. It meant that she was breaking through the walls he had tried to construct between them, leaving him vulnerable to further assault.

"You may scream all you like," she said. "There is no one to hear you."

She crawled onto the bed, while his entire body went rigid.

"You're a fool if you think that I'm going to cooperate," he said between clenched teeth.

"I think that before long you will cooperate with great enthusiasm." Caroline took perverse delight in becoming cooler and calmer as he became more irate. "After all, you haven't had a woman in . . . how many months? At least three. Even if I lack the appropriate skills, I will be able to do as I like with you."

"What about Julianne?" His arms bulged with heavy

muscle as he pulled at the handcuffs. "I could have had her a hundred times by now, for all you know."

"You haven't," she said. "You aren't attracted to her—that was evident when I saw the two of you together."

She began on the tight binding of his cravat, unwinding the damp, starch-scented cloth that still contained the heat of his skin. When his long golden throat was revealed, she touched the triangular hollow at the base with a gentle fingertip. "That's better," she said softly. "Now you can breathe."

He was indeed breathing, with the force of a man who had just run ten miles without stopping. His gaze fixed on hers, no longer cold, but gleaming with fury. "Stop it. I warn you, Caroline, stop *now*."

"Or what? What could you possibly do to punish me that would be worse than what you've already done?" Her fingers went to the buttons of his waistcoat and shirt, and she released them in rapid succession. She spread the edges of his garments wide, baring a remarkably muscular torso. The sight of his body, all that ferocious power rendered helpless before her, was awe-inspiring.

"I never meant to hurt you," he said. "You knew from the beginning that our relationship was just a pretense."

"Yes. But it became something else, and you and I both know it." Gently she touched the thick curls that covered his chest, her fingertips delving to the burning skin beneath. He jumped at the brush of her cool hand, the breath hissing between his teeth. How often she had dreamed of doing this, exploring his body, caressing him. The surface of his stomach was laced with tight muscles, so different from the smooth softness of her own. She stroked the taut golden skin, so hard and silken beneath her hand. "Tell me why you would marry Julianne when you've fallen in love with me."

"I . . . haven't," he managed to choke out. "Can't you get it th-through your stubborn head—"

His words ended in a harsh groan as she straddled him in a decisive motion, their loins separated only by the layers of his trousers and her gossamer-thin drawers. Flushed and determined, Caroline sat atop him in a completely wanton posture. She felt the protrusion of his sex nestle into the cleft between her thighs. The lascivious pressure of him against that intimate part of her body caused a silken ripple of heat all through her. She shifted her weight until he nudged right against her most sensitive area, a little peak that throbbed frantically at his nearness.

"All right," he said in a gasp, holding completely still. "All right, I admit it . . . I love you, damned tormenting bitch—now get *off* of me!"

"Marry me," she insisted. "Promise that you'll break off the betrothal to my cousin."

"No."

Caroline reached up to her hair, pulling the pins loose, letting the rippling brown locks cascade down to her waist. He had never seen her hair down before, and his imprisoned fingers twitched as if he ached to touch her.

"I love you," she said, stroking the furry expanse of his chest, flattening her palm over the thundering rhythm of his heart. The textures of his body—rough silk, hard muscle, bone, and sinew—fascinated her. She wanted to kiss and stroke him everywhere. "We belong together. There should be no obstacles between us, Andrew."

"Love doesn't make a damn bit of difference," he almost snarled. "Idealistic little fool—"

His breath snagged in his throat as she grasped the hem of her chemise, pulled it over her head, and tossed the whisper-thin garment aside. Her upper body was completely naked, the small, firm globes of her breasts bouncing delicately, pink tips contracting in the cool air. He stared at her breasts without blinking, and his eyes gleamed with wolfish hunger before he turned his face away.

"Would you like to kiss them?" Caroline whispered, hardly daring to believe her own brazenness. "I know that you've imagined this, Andrew, just as I have." She leaned over him, brushing her nipples against his chest, and he quivered at the shock of their flesh meeting. He kept his face turned away, his mouth taut, his breath coming in hard gusts. "Kiss me," she urged. "Kiss me just once, Andrew. Please. I need you . . . need to taste you . . . kiss me the way I've dreamed about for so long."

A deep groan vibrated within his chest. His mouth lifted, searching for hers. She pressed her lips over his, her tongue slipping daintily into his hot, sweet mouth. Ardently she molded her body against his, wrapped her arms around his head, kissed him again and again. She touched his shackled wrists, her fingertips brushing his palms. He muttered frantically against her throat, "Yes . . . yes . . . let me go, Caroline . . . the key . . ."

"No." She moved higher on his chest, dragging her feverish mouth over the salt-flavored skin of his throat. "Not yet."

His mouth searched the tender place where her neck met the curve of her shoulder, and she wriggled against him, wanting more, her body filled with a craving that she could not seem to satisfy. She levered herself higher, higher, until almost by accident her nipple brushed the edge of his jaw. He seized it immediately, his mouth opening over the tender crest and drawing it deep inside. His tongue circled the delicate peak and feathered it with rapid, tiny strokes. For a long time he sucked and licked, until Caroline moaned imploringly. His mouth released the rosy nipple, his tongue caressing it with one last swipe.

"Give me the other one," he said in a rasping whisper. "Put it in my mouth."

Trembling, she obeyed, guiding her breast to his lips. He feasted on her eagerly, and she gasped at the sensation of being captured by his mouth, held by its heat and urgency.

Exquisite tension gathered between her wide-open thighs. She writhed, undulated, pressed as close to him as possible, but it was not close enough. She wanted to be filled by him, crushed and ravished and possessed. "Andrew," she said, her voice low and raw. "I want you . . . I want you so badly I could die of it. Let me . . . let me . . ." She took her breast from his mouth and kissed him again, and reached frantically down to the huge, bulging shape beneath the front of his trousers.

"No," she heard him say hoarsely, but she unfastened his trousers with unsteady fingers. Andrew swore and stared at the ceiling, seeming to will his body not to respond . . . but as her cool little hand slid inside his trousers, he groaned and flushed darkly.

Caroline brought out the hard, pulsing length of his sex, and clasped the thick shaft with trembling fingers. She was fascinated by the satiny feel of his skin, the nest of coarse curls at his groin, the heavy, surprisingly cool weight of his testicles down below. The thought of taking the entire potent length of him inside her own body was as shocking as it was exciting. Awkwardly she caressed him, and was startled by his immediate response, the instinctive upward surge of his hips, the stifled grunt of pleasure that came from his throat.

"Is this the right way?" she asked, her fingers sliding up to the large round head.

"Caroline . . ." His tormented gaze was riveted on her face. "Caroline, listen to me. I don't want this. It won't be good for you. There are things I haven't done for you . . . things your body needs . . . for God's sake—"

"I don't care. I want to make love to you."

She peeled off her drawers and garters and stockings, and returned to crouch over his groin, feeling clumsy and yet inflamed. "Tell me what to do," she begged, and pressed the head of his sex directly against the soft cove of her body. She lowered her weight experimentally, and froze at the intense pressure and pain that threatened. It seemed impossible to make their bodies fit together. Baffled and frustrated, she tried again, but she could not manage to push the stiff length of him through the tightly closed opening. She stared at Andrew's taut face, her gaze pleading. "Help me. Tell me what I'm doing wrong."

Even in this moment of crucial intimacy, he would not relent. "It's time to stop, Caroline."

The finality of his refusal was impossible to ignore.

She was swamped with a feeling of utter defeat. She took a long, shivering breath, and another, but nothing would relieve the burning ache in her lungs. "All right," she managed to whisper. "All right. I'm sorry." Tears stung her eyes, and she reached beneath her spectacles to wipe at them furiously. She had lost him again, this time permanently. Any man who could resist a woman at such a moment, while she begged to make love to him, could not truly be in love with her. Groping for the key, she continued to cry silently.

For some reason the sight of her tears drove him into a sort of contained frenzy, his body stiffening with the effort not to flail at his chains. "Caroline," he said in a shaking whisper. "Please open the damned lock. Please. God . . . don't. Just get the key. Yes. Let me go. Let me—"

As soon as she turned the tiny key in the lock, the world seemed to explode with movement. Andrew moved with the speed of a leaping tiger, freeing his wrists and pouncing on her. Too stunned to react, Caroline found herself being flipped over and pressed flat on her back. The half-naked weight of his body crushed her deep into the mattress, the startling thrust of his erection hard against her quivering stomach. He moved against her once, twice, three times, the pouch of his ballocks dragging tightly through her dark curls, and then he went still, holding her until she could hardly breathe. A groan escaped him, and a liquid wash of heat seeped between their bodies, sliding over her stomach.

Dazed, Caroline lay still and silent, her gaze darting over his taut features. Andrew let out a ragged sigh and opened his eyes, which had turned a brilliant shade of molten blue. "Don't move," he said softly. "Just lie still for a moment."

She had no other choice. Her limbs were weak and trembling . . . she burned as if from a fever. Miserably she watched as he left the bed, then glanced down at her stomach. She touched a fingertip to the glossy smear of liquid there, and she was puzzled and curious and woeful all at the same time. Andrew returned with a wet cloth, and joined her on the bed. Closing her eyes, Caroline flinched at the coldness of the cloth as he gently cleansed her body. She could not bear the sight of his impassive face, nor could she stand the thought of what he might say to her. No doubt he would berate her for her part in this humiliating escapade, and she certainly deserved it. She bit her lip and stiffened her limbs against the tremors that shook her . . . she was so hot everywhere, her hips lifting uncontrollably, a sob catching in her throat. "Leave me alone," she whispered, feeling as if she were going to fly into pieces.

The cloth was set aside, and Andrew's fingers carefully hooked under the sidepieces of her spectacles to lift them from her damp face. Her lashes lifted. He was leaning over her, so close that his features were only slightly blurred. His gaze traveled slowly down the length of her slender body. "My God, how I love you," he murmured, shocking her, while his hand cupped her breast and squeezed gently. His fingertips trailed downward in a lazy path, until they slipped into the plump cleft between her thighs.

Caroline arched wildly, completely helpless at his touch, while small, pleading cries came from her throat.

"Yes." His voice was like dark velvet, his tongue flicking the lobe of her ear. "I'll take care of you now. Just tell me what you want, sweetheart. Tell me, and I'll do it."

"Andrew . . ." She gasped as he separated the tender

lips and stroked right between them. "Don't t-torture me, please . . ."

Amusement threaded through his tone. "After what you've done to me, I think you deserve a few minutes of torture . . . don't you?" His fingertip glided in a small circle around the aching little tip of flesh where all sensation was gathering. "Would you like me to kiss you here?" he asked softly. "And touch it with my tongue?"

The questions jolted her—she had never imagined such a thing—and yet her entire body quivered in response.

"Tell me," he prompted gently.

Her lips were dry, and she had to wet them with her tongue before she could speak. To her utter shame, once the first words were out, she could not stop herself from begging shamelessly. "Yes, Andrew . . . kiss me there, use your tongue, I need you now, now *please*—"

Her voice dissolved into wild groans as he moved downward, his dark head dropping between her spread legs, his fingers smoothing the little dark curls and opening her pink lips even wider. His breath touched her first, a soft rush of steam, and then his tongue danced over her, gently prodding the burning little nub, flicking it with rapid strokes.

Caroline bit her lower lip sharply, struggling desperately to keep quiet despite the intense pleasure of his mouth on her. Andrew lifted his head as he heard the muffled sounds she made, and his eyes gleamed devilishly. "Scream all you like," he murmured. "There's no one to hear you."

His mouth returned to her, and she cried out, her bottom lifting eagerly from the mattress as she pushed herself toward him. He grunted with satisfaction and cradled her taut buttocks in his large, warm hands, while his mouth continued to feast on her. She felt the broad tip of his finger stroke against the tiny opening of her body, circling, teasing . . . entering with delicate skill.

"Feel how wet you are," he murmured against her slick

flesh. "You're ready to be taken now. I could slide every inch of my cock inside you."

Then she understood why she had not been able to accommodate him before. "Please," she whispered, dying of need. "Please, Andrew."

His lips returned to her vulva, nuzzling the moist, sensitive folds. Gasping, Caroline went still as his finger slid deeply inside her, stroking in time to the sweet, rhythmic tug of his mouth. "My God," she said between frantic pants for breath, "I can't . . . oh, I can't bear it, please, Andrew, my God—"

The world vanished in an explosion of fiery bliss. She sobbed and shivered, riding the current of pure ecstasy until she finally drifted in a tide of lethargy unlike anything she had ever experienced. Only then did his mouth and fingers leave her. Andrew tugged at the covers and linens, half lifting Caroline's body against his own, until they were wrapped in a cocoon of warm bedclothes. She lay beside him, her leg draped over his, her head pillowed on his hard shoulder. Shaken, exhausted, she relaxed in his arms, sharing the utter peace of aftermath, like the calm after a violent storm.

Andrew's hand smoothed over the wild ripples of her hair, spreading them over his own chest. After a long moment of bittersweet contentment, he spoke quietly, his lips brushing her temple.

"It was never a charade for me, Caroline. I fell in love with you from the moment we struck our infernal bargain. I loved your spirit, your strength, your beauty . . . I realized at once how special you were. And I knew that I didn't deserve you. But I had the damned foolish idea that somehow I might be able to become worthy of you. I wanted to make a new beginning, with you by my side. I even stopped caring about my father's bloody fortune. But in my arrogance I didn't consider the fact that no one can escape his past. And

I have a thousand things to atone for . . . things that will keep turning up to haunt me for the rest of my life. You don't want to be part of that ugliness, Caroline. No man who loves a woman would ask her to live with him, wondering every day when some wretched part of his past will reappear."

"I don't understand." She lifted herself onto his chest, staring into his grave, tender expression. "Tell me what Julianne has done to change everything."

He sighed and stroked back a lock of her hair. It was clear that he did not want to tell her, but he would no longer withhold the truth. "You know that Julianne and I once had an affair. For a while afterward, we remained friends of a sort. We are remarkably similar, Julianne and I—both of us selfish and manipulative and coldhearted—"

"No," Caroline said swiftly, placing her fingers on his mouth. "You're not like that, Andrew. At least not anymore."

A bleak smile curved his lips, and he kissed her fingers before continuing. "After the affair was over, Julianne and I amused ourselves by playing a game we had invented. We would each name a certain person—always a virtuous and well-respected one—whom the other had to seduce. The more difficult the target, the more irresistible the challenge. I named a high-ranking magistrate, the father of seven children, whom Julianne enticed into an affair."

"And whom did she select for you?" Caroline asked quietly, experiencing a strange mixture of revulsion and pity as she heard his sordid confession.

"One of her 'friends'—the wife of the Italian ambassador. Pretty, shy, and known for her modesty and God-fearing ways."

"You succeeded with her, I suppose."

He nodded without expression. "She was a good woman with a great deal to lose. She had a happy marriage, a loving husband, three healthy children . . . God knew how I was able to persuade her into a dalliance. But I did. And afterward, the only way she could assuage her guilt was to convince herself that she had fallen in love with me. She wrote me a few love letters, highly incriminating ones that she soon came to regret. I wanted to burn them—I should have—but I returned them to her, thinking that it would ease her worry if she could destroy them herself. Then she would never have to fear that one of them would turn up and ruin her life. Instead the little fool kept them, and for some reason I'll never understand, she showed them to Julianne, who was posing as a concerned friend."

"And somehow Julianne gained possession of them," Caroline said softly.

"She's had them for almost five years. And the day after my father died, and it became known that he left me the Rochester fortune, Julianne paid me an unexpected visit. She has gone through her late husband's entire fortune. If she wishes to maintain her current lifestyle, she will have to marry a wealthy man. And it seems I have been given the dubious honor of being her chosen groom."

"She is blackmailing you with the letters?"

He nodded. "Unless I agreed to marry her, Julianne said she would make the damned things public, and ruin her so-called friend's life. And two things immediately became clear to me. I could never have you as my wife knowing that our marriage was based on the destruction of someone else's life. And with my past, it is only a matter of time until something else rears its ugly head. You would come to hate me, being constantly faced with new evidence of the sins I've committed." His mouth twisted bitterly. "Damned inconvenient thing, to develop a conscience. It was a hell of a lot easier before I had one."

Caroline was silent, staring down at his chest as her fingers stroked slowly through the dark curls. It was one thing to be told that a man had a wicked past, and certainly Andrew had never pretended otherwise. But the knowledge made far more of an impression on her now that she knew a few specifics about his former debauchery. The notion of his affair with Julianne, and the revolting games they had played with others' lives, sickened her. No one would blame her for rejecting Andrew, for agreeing that he was far too tarnished and corrupt. And yet . . . the fact that he had learned to feel regret, that he wished to protect the ambassador's wife even at the expense of his own happiness . . . that meant he had changed. It meant he was capable of becoming a far better man than he had been.

Besides, love was about caring for the whole man, including his flaws . . . and trusting that he felt the same about her. To her, that was worth any risk.

She smiled into Andrew's brooding face. "It is no surprise to me that you have a few imperfections." She climbed farther onto his chest, her small breasts pressing into the warm mat of hair. "Well, more than a few. You're a wicked scoundrel, and I fully expect that at some point in the future there will be more unpleasant surprises from your past. But you are *my* scoundrel, and I want to face all the unpleasant moments of life, and the wonderful ones, with no one but you."

His fingers slid into her hair, clasping her scalp, and he stared at her with fierce adoration. When he spoke his voice was slightly hoarse. "What if I decide that you deserve someone better?"

"It's too late now," she said reasonably. "You have to marry me after debauching me this afternoon."

Carefully he brought her forward and kissed her cheeks. "Precious love . . . I didn't debauch you. Not completely, at any rate. You're still a virgin."

"Not for long." She wriggled on his body, feeling his erection rising against the inside of her thigh. "Make love to me." She nuzzled against his throat and spread kisses along the firm line of his jaw. "All the way this time."

He lifted her from his chest as easily as if she were an exploring kitten, and stared at her with anguished yearning. "There's still the matter of Julianne and the ambassador's wife."

"Oh, that." She perched on him, with her hair streaming over her chest and back, and touched his small, dark nipples with her thumbs. "I will deal with my cousin Julianne," she informed him. "You'll have those letters back, Andrew. It will be my Christmas gift to you."

His gaze was patently doubtful. "How?"

"I don't wish to explain right now. What I want is—"

"I know what you want," he said dryly, rolling to pin her beneath him. "But you're not going to get it, Caroline. I won't take your virginity until I'm free to offer you marriage. Now explain to me why you're so confident that you can get the letters back."

She ran her hands over his muscular forearms. "Well . . . I've never told this to anyone, not even Cade, and especially not my mother. But soon after Julianne's rich old husband died—I suppose you've heard the rumors that his death was not of natural causes?"

"There was never any proof otherwise."

"Not that anyone knows of. But right after Lord Brenton passed on to his reward, his valet, Mr. Stevens, paid a visit to my father one night. My father was a well-respected and highly trustworthy man, and the valet had met him before. Stevens behaved oddly that night—he seemed terribly frightened, and he begged my father to help him. He suspected Julianne of having poisoned old Lord Brenton—she had recently been to the chemist's shop, and then Stevens had caught her pouring something into Brenton's medicine bottle the day before he died. But Stevens was afraid to confront Julianne with his suspicions. He thought that she might somehow falsely implicate him in the murder, or punish him in some other devious way. To protect himself, he collected evidence of Julianne's guilt, including the tainted medicine bottle. He begged my father to help him find new employment, and my father recommended him to a friend who was living abroad."

"Why did your father tell you about this?"

"He and I were very close—we were confidantes, and there were few secrets between us." She gave him a small, triumphant smile. "I know exactly where Stevens is located. And I also know where the evidence against Julianne is hidden. So unless my cousin wishes to face being accused and tried for her late husband's murder, she will give me those letters."

"Sweetheart . . ." He pressed a gentle kiss to her forehead. "You're not going to confront Julianne with this. She is a dangerous woman."

"She is no match for me," Caroline replied. "Because I am not going to let her or anyone else stand in the way of what I want."

"And what is that?" he asked.

"You." She slid her hands to his shoulders and lifted her knees to either side of his hips. "All of you . . . including every moment of your past, present, and future."

Chapter Five

THE MOST DIFFICULT thing that Andrew, Lord Rochester, had ever done was to wait for the next three days. He paced and fretted alone at the family estate, alternately bored and anxious. He nearly went mad from the suspense. But Caroline had asked him to wait for word from her, and if it killed him, he would keep his promise. Try as he might, he could not summon much hope that she would actually retrieve the letters. Julianne was as sly and devious as Caroline was honest . . . and it was not the easiest trick in the world to blackmail a blackmailer. Moreover, the thought that Caroline was lowering herself in this way in an attempt to clean up a nasty mess that he had helped to create . . . it made him squirm. By now he should be accustomed to feeling the heat of shame, but he still suffered mightily at the thought of it. A man should protect the woman he loved—he should keep her safe and happy—and instead Caroline was having to rescue *him*. Groaning, he thought longingly of having a drink—but he would be damned if he would drown himself in the comforting oblivion of alcohol ever again. From now on he would face life without any convenient crutch. He would allow himself no more excuses, no place to hide.

And then, just a few days before Christmas, a footman dispatched from the Hargreaves residence came to the Rochester estate bearing a small wrapped package.

"Milord," the footman said, bowing respectfully. "Miss

Hargreaves instructed me to deliver this into your hands, and no one else's."

Almost frantically Andrew tore open the sealed note attached to the package. His gaze skittered across the neatly written lines:

My lord,
    Please accept this early Christmas gift. Do with it what you will, and know that it comes with no obligations—save that you cancel your betrothal to my cousin. I believe she will soon be directing her romantic attentions toward some other unfortunate gentleman.

                        Yours,
                        Caroline

"Lord Rochester, shall I convey your reply to Miss Hargreaves?" the footman asked.

Andrew shook his head, while an odd feeling of lightness came over him. It was the first time in his life that he had ever felt so free, so full of anticipation. "No," he said, his voice slightly gravelly. "I will answer Miss Hargreaves in person. Tell her that I will come to call on Christmas Day."

"Yes, milord."

CAROLINE SAT BEFORE the fire, enjoying the warmth of the yule log as it cast a wash of golden light over the family receiving room. The windows were adorned with glossy branches of holly, and festooned with red ribbons and sprays of berries. Wax tapers wreathed with greens burned on the mantel. After a pleasant morning of exchanging gifts with the family and servants, everyone had departed to pursue various amusements, for there were abundant parties and suppers to choose from. Cade was dutifully escorting Fanny to no less than three different events, and they would likely not return until after midnight. Caroline had resisted their entreaties to come along, and refused to answer their questions concerning her plans. "Is it Lord Rochester?" Fanny had demanded in mingled excitement and worry. "Do you expect him to call, dearest? If so, I must advise you on the right tone to take with him—"

"Mother," Cade had interrupted, flashing Caroline a rueful gaze, "if you do not wish to be late for the Danburys' party, we must be off."

"Yes, but I must tell Caroline—"

"Believe me," Cade said firmly, plopping a hat onto his mother's head and tugging her to the entrance hall, "if Rochester should decide to appear, Caroline will know exactly how to deal with him."

Thank you, Caroline had mouthed to him silently, and they exchanged a grin before he removed their inquisitive mother from the premises.

The servants had all been given the day off, and the house was quiet as Caroline waited. Sounds of Christmas drifted in from outside . . . passing troubadours, children caroling, groups of merry revelers traveling between houses.

Finally, as the clock struck one, a knock came at the door. Caroline felt her heart leap. She rushed to the door with unseemly haste and flung it open.

Andrew stood there, tall and handsome, his expression serious and a touch uncertain. They stared at each other, and although Caroline remained motionless, she felt her entire being reaching for him, her soul expanding with yearning. "You're here," she said, almost frightened of what would happen next. She wanted him to seize her in his arms and kiss her, but instead he removed his hat and spoke softly.

"May I come in?"

She welcomed him inside, helped him with his coat, and

watched as he hung the hat on the hall stand. He turned to face her, his vivid blue eyes filled with a heat that caused her to tremble. "Merry Christmas," he said.

Caroline wrung her hands together nervously. "Merry Christmas. Shall we go into the parlor?"

He nodded, his gaze still on her. He didn't seem to care where they went as he followed her wordlessly into the parlor. "Are we alone?" he asked, having noticed the stillness of the house.

"Yes." Too agitated to sit, Caroline stood before the fire and stared up at his half-shadowed face. "Andrew," she said impulsively, "before you tell me anything, I want to make it clear . . . my gift to you . . . the letters . . . you are not obligated to give me anything in return. That is, you needn't feel as if you owe me—"

He touched her then, his large, gentle hands lightly framing the sides of her face, thumbs skimming over the blushing surface of her cheeks. The way he looked at her, tender and yet somehow devouring, caused her entire body to tingle in delight. "But I am obligated," he murmured, "by my heart, soul, and too many parts of my anatomy to name." A smile curved his lips. "Unfortunately the only thing I can offer you is a rather questionable gift . . . somewhat tarnished and damaged, and of very doubtful value. Myself." He reached for her small, slender hands and brought them to his mouth, pressing hot kisses to the backs of her fingers. "Will you have me, Caroline?"

Happiness rose inside her, making her throat tight. "I will. You are exactly what I want."

He laughed suddenly, and broke the fervent clasp of their hands to fish for something in his pocket. "God help you, then." He extracted a glittering object and slipped it onto her fourth finger. The fit was just a little loose. Caroline balled her hand into a fist as she stared at the ring. It was an ornately carved gold band adorned with a huge rose-cut diamond. The gem sparkled with heavenly brilliance in the light of the yule log, making her breath catch. "It belonged to my mother," Andrew said, watching her face closely. "She willed it to me, and hoped that I would someday give it to my wife."

"It is lovely," Caroline said, her eyes stinging. She lifted her mouth for his kiss, and felt the soft brush of his lips over hers.

"Here," he murmured, a smile coloring his voice, and he removed her spectacles to clean them. "You can't even see the damned thing, the way these are smudged." Replacing the polished spectacles, he took hold of her waist and pulled her body against his. His tone sobered as he spoke again. "Was it difficult to get the letters from Julianne?"

"Not at all." Caroline could not suppress a trace of smugness as she replied. "I enjoyed it, actually. Julianne was furious—I have no doubt she wanted to scratch my eyes out. And naturally she denied having had anything to do with Lord Brenton's death. But she gave me the letters all the same. I can assure you that she will never trouble us again."

Andrew hugged her tightly, his hands sliding repeatedly over her back. Then he spoke quietly in her hair, with a meaningful tone that made the hairs on the back of her neck prickle in excitement. "There is a matter I have yet to take care of. As I recall, I left you a virgin the last time we met."

"You did," Caroline replied with a wobbly smile. "Much to my displeasure."

His mouth covered hers, and he kissed her with a mixture of adoration and avid lust that caused her knees to weaken. She leaned heavily against him, her tongue sliding and curling against his. Excitement thumped inside her, and she arched against him in an effort to make the embrace closer, her body craving the weight and pressure of him.

"Then I'll do my best to oblige you this time," he said when their lips parted. "Take me to your bedroom."

"Now? Here?"

"Why not?" She felt him smile against her cheek. "Are you worried about propriety? You, who had me handcuffed to a bed—"

"That was Cade's doing, not mine," she said, blushing.

"Well, you didn't mind taking advantage of the situation, did you?"

"I was desperate!"

"Yes, I remember." Still smiling, he kissed the side of her neck and slid his hand to her breast, caressing the gentle curve until her nipple contracted into a hard point. "Would you rather wait until we marry?" he murmured.

She took his hand and pulled him out of the parlor, leading him upstairs to her bedroom. The walls were covered with flower-patterned paper that matched the pink-and-white embroidered counterpane on the bed. In such dainty surroundings, Andrew looked larger and more masculine than ever. Caroline watched in fascinated delight as he began to remove his clothes, discarding his coat, waistcoat, cravat, and shirt, draping the fine garments on a shield-backed chair. She unbuttoned her own gown and stepped out of it, leaving it in a crumpled heap on the floor. As she stood in her undergarments and stockings, Andrew came to her and pulled her against his naked body. The hard, thrusting ridge of his erection burned through the frail muslin of her drawers, and she let out a small gasp.

"Are you afraid?" he whispered, lifting her higher against him, until her toes almost left the ground.

She turned her face into his neck, breathing in the scent of his warm skin, lifting her hands to stroke the thick, cool silk of his hair. "Oh, no," she breathed. "Don't stop, Andrew. I want to be yours. I want to feel you inside me."

He set her on the bed and removed her clothes slowly, kissing every inch of her skin as it was uncovered, until she lay naked and open before him. Murmuring his love to her, he touched her breasts with his mouth, licked and teased until her nipples formed rosy, tight buds. Caroline arched up to him in ardent response, urging him to take her, until he pulled away with a breathless laugh. "Not so fast," he said, his hand descending to her stomach, stroking in soothing circles. "You're not ready for me yet."

"I am," she insisted, her body aching and feverish, her heart pounding.

He smiled and rolled her to her stomach, and she groaned as she felt his mouth trail down her spine, kissing and nibbling. His teeth nipped at her buttocks before his lips traveled to the fragile creases at the backs of her knees. "Andrew," she groaned, writhing in torment. "Please don't make me wait."

He turned her over once again, and his wicked mouth wandered up the inside of her thigh, higher and higher, and his strong hands carefully urged her thighs apart. Caroline whimpered as she felt him lick the damp, soft cleft between her legs. Another, deeper stroke of his tongue, and another, and then he found the excruciatingly tender bud and suckled, his tongue flicking her, until she shuddered and screamed, her ecstatic cries muffled in the folds of the embroidered counterpane.

Andrew kissed her lips and settled between her thighs. She moaned in encouragement as she felt the plum-shaped head of his sex wedge against the slick core of her body. He pushed gently, filling her . . . hesitating as she gasped with discomfort. "No," she said, clutching frantically at his hips, "don't stop . . . I need you . . . please, Andrew . . ."

He groaned and thrust forward, burying himself completely, while her flesh throbbed sweetly around him. "Sweetheart," he whispered, breathing hard, while his hips pushed forward in gentle nudges. His face was damp, suffused with perspiration and heat, his long, dark lashes spiky with moisture. Caroline was transfixed by the sight of him—

he was such a beautiful man . . . and he was hers. He invaded her in a slow, patient rhythm, his muscles rigid, his forearms braced on either side of her head. Writhing in pleasure, she lifted her hips to take him more deeply. His mouth caught hers hungrily, his tongue searching and sliding.

"I love you," she whispered between kisses, her wet lips moving against his. "I love you, Andrew, love you . . ."

The words seemed to break his self-control, and his thrusts became stronger, deeper, until he buried himself inside her and shuddered violently, his passion spending, his breath stopping in the midst of an agonizing burst of pleasure.

Long, lazy minutes later, while they were still tangled together, their heartbeats returning to a regular rhythm, Caroline kissed Andrew's shoulder.

"Darling," she said drowsily, "I want to ask something of you."

"Anything." His fingers played in her hair, sifting through the silken locks.

"Whatever comes, we'll face it together. Promise to trust me, and never to keep secrets from me again."

"I will." Andrew raised himself up on one elbow, staring down at her with a crooked smile. "Now I want to ask something of you. Could we forgo the large wedding, and instead have a small ceremony on New Year's Day?"

"Of course," Caroline said promptly. "I wouldn't have wanted a large wedding in any case. But why so soon?"

He lowered his mouth to hers, his lips warm and caressing. "Because I want my new beginning to coincide with the new year. And because I need you too badly to wait for you."

She smiled and shook her head in wonder, her eyes shining as she stared up at him. "Well, I need you even more."

"Show me," he whispered, and she did just that.

Deck the Halls With Love

❧

LORRAINE HEATH

Chapter One

STANDING ALONE BESIDE a window a short distance away from the midst of the gaiety, Alistair Wakefield, the Marquess of Chetwyn, slowly sipped the Scotch that he had pilfered from his host's library on his way to the grand salon. He'd known that attending this holiday gathering at the Duke and Duchess of Keswick's new country manor would be unpleasant, but then he was not in the habit of shying away from the distasteful. It was the reason that on the morning he was to be married, he had encouraged his bride to seek out her heart's desire. He'd known his being abandoned at the altar would be cause for gossip, that he would be considered weak and inadequate, but he didn't much give a damn. He believed in love, and he'd recognized that Lady Anne Hayworth had given her affections to Lord Tristan Easton. So he'd willingly granted her the freedom to go, and then with as much dignity as possible he'd set about bearing the brunt of what many considered a humiliating affair.

From his shadowed corner, he now watched Lady Meredith Hargreaves dance with *her* betrothed, Lord Litton. Based on her smile and the way her gaze never strayed from his, she appeared to be joyous and very much in love with the fellow. Although perhaps she was simply imbued with the spirit of the season. He could always hope.

He knew he should look about for another dance partner. The problem was that she was the only one with whom he wished to waltz. Hers were the only eyes into which he longed to gaze, hers the only fragrance he yearned to inhale, hers the only voice he wanted whispering near his ear as passion smoldered.

It had been that way for some time now, but he had fought back his burgeoning desire for her out of a sense of obligation and duty, out of a misguided attempt to make amends regarding his younger brother, Walter, who had sacrificed his life in the Crimea. Chetwyn was destined to pay a heavy price for trying to assuage his conscience, unless he took immediate steps to rectify the situation. Lady Meredith was scheduled to marry a few days after Christmas. The decorated tree in the parlor, the sprigs of holly scattered about, and the red bows on the portraits that had greeted him upon his arrival had served as an unwarranted reminder that the auspicious morning was quickly approaching, and then she would be lost to him forever.

But if she loved Litton, could he deny her what he had granted Anne: a life with the man she loved?

It was a quandary with which he struggled, because he wished only happiness for Lady Meredith, but he was arrogant enough to believe that he could bring her joy as no one else could. No other gentleman would hold her in such high esteem. No other man would adore her as he did. Convincing her that she belonged with him was going to be quite the trick, as he suspected she'd rather see him rotting in hell than standing beside her at the altar.

Despite the fact that she was engaged to marry, he kept hoping that she would glance over, would give him a smile, would offer any sort of encouragement at all. Instead she waltzed on, as though for her he no longer existed.

LADY MEREDITH HARGREAVES, the Earl of Whitscomb's daughter, absolutely loved to waltz. Quite honestly, she enjoyed any sort of physical activity. She had loved running, jumping, skipping, and climbing trees until her father had sent her to a ladies' finishing school, where they had taught her that if she did not stifle her enthusiasm for the outdoors, she would never marry. So stifle she did with a great deal of effort and the occasional slap of the rod against her palm.

But dancing was acceptable, and because she was known for being charming—which was no accident—she never lacked for dance partners. She didn't care if they were married, old, young, bent. She didn't care if their eyes were too small, their noses too large, and they stammered. She didn't care if their clothes were not the latest fashion, their skills at interesting conversation nonexistent. When they swept her over the dance floor, she adored every single one of them. And well they knew it.

It showed in her eyes, her smile, and the way she beamed at them. She made them feel as though they mattered, and for those few moments they mattered a great deal because of the pleasure they brought her. But dancing with a lady did not mean that a gentleman wished to marry her. Because she was also known for being quite stubborn, strong-willed, and prone to arguing a point when most ladies would simply smile and pretend that they hadn't the good sense to know their own minds.

She did know hers, and therefore she knew without question that Lord Litton was the man for her. He often praised her strong points. He sent her flowers. He wrote her poetry. He danced with her, a daring four times the night they met. Four, when only two times was acceptable. He had told her that he simply couldn't deny himself the pleasure of her presence.

His inability to resist her was what had led to them being caught the night of Greystone's ball in the garden in a very compromising situation that had resulted in a rather hasty betrothal. Her father had managed to limit the damage done by ensuring that no one other than he and her brothers knew of the discovery. Litton had been quick to propose on the spot, but then her father could be quite intimidating. As they were discovered before they had moved beyond a kiss, the wedding was not being rushed. Meredith knew Litton was an honorable man. He could have run off, but he didn't. He stood by her and offered to marry her. She didn't like the little niggle of doubt that surfaced from time to time and made her wonder if he arranged to be caught. If he did, was it because he so desperately wanted *her* or her dowry?

As he smiled down on her now, she sent the irritating doubts to perdition and accepted that he was madly in love with her. They would be wondrously happy together. If only her heart would cooperate.

She did wish she hadn't noticed when Lord Chetwyn had strolled laconically into the room before the strains of the first dance had started. Based upon what had happened in the church earlier in the year, she hadn't expected him to make an appearance where he would be forced to encounter his former fiancée and her husband. Lord Tristan was, after all, the Duke of Keswick's twin brother, so Chetwyn had to know that he couldn't avoid them. But he had cut such a fine figure in his black tailcoat as he had greeted his host and hostess. His fair complexion stood out next to the duke's black hair and bronzed skin. His blond hair was perfectly styled, but even from a distance Meredith had seen the ends curling. She suspected by midnight the strands would be rebelling riotously, and he would no doubt be searching for some lady to run her fingers through them in order to tame them. She had once considered performing the service herself when they had taken a turn about a park. Thank goodness, she'd not been that foolish. It would have hurt all the more when he began to give his attentions to Lady Anne.

He was now standing in a corner, coming into view from time to time as though she were riding on a carousel, rather than swirling over a dance floor in Litton's arms. Even when she couldn't see him, she could sense Chetwyn's gaze lighting upon her as gently as a lover's caress. She had once thought that he might ask for her hand. But he had moved on, and so had she.

Litton was as fair, but his hair would not be misbehaving by the end of the evening. She rather wished it would. She longed for an excuse to run her fingers through it, although she suspected he might be rather appalled to know the direction of her thoughts. He did not have as easy a grin as Chetwyn, but his seriousness was endearing. She only wished he would reclaim the passion that had resulted in a near scandal.

"You've drifted away again," Litton said quietly.

"I'm sorry. I was just noticing how the snow is growing thicker beyond the windows." A small lie, but she rather doubted that he would welcome knowing that Chetwyn was occupying her thoughts.

"Yes, we're in for quite a storm tonight, I think. I hope we shall all be able to travel home when the time comes."

"I'm sure we will."

"You're such an optimist. It's one of the things I love about you."

Touched by his comment, she squeezed his shoulder. "We shall be happy together, won't we?"

"Immeasurably."

The music drifted into silence. He lifted her gloved hand to his lips. "As your card is filled and you're gracing other lords with your presence for a while, I'm going to the gaming room for a bit. Just remember the last dance is mine."

"I would never give it to anyone else."

Watching him walk away, she could not help but think that she was a most fortunate lady indeed. Then she looked over and saw her next dance partner approaching.

Lord Wexford smiled. He was a handsome enough fellow, recently returned from a trip to Africa. Bowing slightly, he took her hand. "My dance, I believe."

"Quite. I've been looking forward to it."

"Not as much as I have. The last lady with whom I danced is not yet spoken for, and she was quite adept at listing her wifely qualities as though she were delivering a shopping list."

Meredith was familiar enough with Lady Beatrix's habits to know that Wexford was speaking of her. Bless Lady Beatrix, but she seemed to think that if she didn't point out her good qualities, no gentleman would discover them. She had such little faith in the observational powers of the males of the species.

"Did you know that she is so talented with her sewing that she can weave twenty stitches into an inch of cloth?" Lord Wexford asked. "I am sure it is quite an impressive feat, but as I've never taken the time to measure and count stitches—"

"My lord?"

Wexford spun around. Lord Chetwyn stood there, extending a small slip of paper toward him, and Meredith's heart beat out an unsteady tattoo. She had vainly hoped with so many guests in attendance that she might avoid encountering him entirely. It wasn't that she was cowardly, but she reacted in the strangest fashion when he was near—as though she were on the cusp of swooning.

He smelled of bergamot, a scent she could no longer inhale without thinking of him. Thank goodness Litton smelled of cloves. Harsh, not particularly appealing, but it didn't matter. Nothing about him reminded her of Chetwyn, which made him perfect in every way.

"I'm sorry to interrupt you," Chetwyn murmured as music once again began to fill the ballroom, "but a lady asked me to deliver this to you as discreetly as possible. She said it was quite urgent."

Meredith couldn't help but think that Chetwyn didn't comprehend the term *discreet*. He should have secreted Wexford away or waited until the dance was over. She would have preferred the latter.

Wexford furrowed his brow. "Which lady?"

"She asked me not to say. I think she desired to remain a bit mysterious, but I was given reason to believe you were . . . well acquainted."

Wexford opened the note, then smiled slowly. "Yes, I see." He turned to Meredith. "I fear I must attend to this matter."

"Of course. I hope all is well."

"Couldn't be better."

And with that he was gone. Staring after him, she was certain he would be rendezvousing with the woman, whoever she was.

"I would be honored to stand in his stead," Lord Chetwyn said. Then, as though she had acquiesced, he was leading her onto the dance floor.

"I fear I'm no longer of a mind to dance. I thought to get some refreshment. Alone."

"Surely, you would not pass up your favorite tune."

"Greensleeves." He remembered. The first dance they'd ever shared was to this song. She had gazed up at his sharp, precise, patrician features and decided that he would age well, for there was nothing about him that would sag with time. He was one of those fortunate gentlemen upon whom the gods of heredity smiled kindly. She had been smiling upon him as well, giddy at his nearness, excited by his attentions. She thought she might have fallen a little bit in love with him during that first encounter. "Chetwyn—"

"One dance, Merry."

"Please don't call me that. It's far too personal, too informal." But she didn't object when he took her into his arms and glided her over the floor. She hated that he was such a marvelous dancer, that he exuded confidence, and that he made her feel as though only the two of them were moving about the room. Everyone else receded into the woodwork. Everyone else ceased to matter.

Giving herself a mental shake, she refused to succumb to his charms once again. She could be distant, pretend indifference, give the impression that he had never been more than a dance partner.

"Rather fortunate timing that Wexford received a note before this particular song started," she said pointedly. Did his eyes have to hold hers as though they were examining a precious gift?

"Not really. The note was from me, you see. Although he doesn't know that, as it was unsigned."

She didn't know whether to be angry or flattered. "You took a chance with that ploy. How did you know he would not question an unsigned note from a lady?"

"All gentlemen welcome notes from mysterious ladies suggesting a tryst in the garden."

Her eyes widened. "But it's storming out there."

"As I'm well aware, but I'm not familiar enough with the residence to know where else to send him."

"What if he freezes to death?"

"I don't think that's likely to happen. He strikes me as being fairly intelligent. I'm sure he'll head back in once he gets too cold and the lady doesn't show."

She studied him for half a moment before it dawned on her. "You purposely stole his dance."

"I did. I saw all the gentlemen circling you earlier, so I knew your dance card was filled. And if it wasn't filled, I rather doubted that you would take pleasure in scribbling my name—"

"I do not scribble."

He grinned. Why did he have to have such an infectious smile that begged her to join him?

"I'm sure you don't. Forgive me, Meredith, but I wanted

a moment with you, and I didn't think you would be likely to meet me in a garden. Not after our last meeting among the roses."

Inwardly she cringed at the reminder of when he had informed her that he would be asking Lady Anne to marry him. "I thought you should know," he'd said quietly, as though Meredith cared, as though he knew she'd pinned her hopes on him. When those hopes had come unpinned among the roses, her heart had very nearly shattered. Thank goodness she was made of stern stuff. She'd taken a good deal of satisfaction in the fact that her voice had not trembled when she'd replied, "I wish you the very best." Then she had strolled away with such aplomb that she had considered going onto the stage. What a scandal becoming an actress would cause, and the one thing her father could not abide was scandal.

Yet Chetwyn had found himself in the midst of one that still had the ladies wagging their tongues. Lord Tristan was seen as a heroic romantic for claiming his love on the day she was to marry another, and Chetwyn was viewed as that unfortunate Lord Chetwyn. She decided she could be gracious. "I'm sorry that things did not go as you'd planned for yourself and Lady Anne."

"I'm not sorry at all. I'm happy for her. Do you love him?" he asked, taking her aback with his abrupt question. They were supposed to be talking about him, not her. If he wasn't holding her so firmly, she thought she might have flown out of his arms.

"You say that, my lord, as though there is but one *him* in my life when there are several. My father, my brothers— there are five of them, you know—my uncles, cousins—"

"Litton," he cut in, obviously not at all enchanted by her little game.

"It seems a rather pointless question. I favor Viscount Litton immensely. I'd not be marrying him otherwise."

She could not mistake the look of satisfaction that settled into his deep brown eyes, as though she'd revealed something extraordinary. "Favoring is not love."

"I'll not discuss my heart with you." *Not when you'd once come so close to holding it, and then set it aside with so little care.*

"I don't know that you'll be happy with him."

She straightened her shoulders, angled her chin. "You're being quite presumptuous."

"You require a man of passion, one who can set your heart to hammering. Is he capable of either of those things?" His eyes darkened, simmered, captured hers with an intensity that made it impossible to look away. Her mouth went dry.

Ignoring his question, she released an awkward-sounding laugh. "You think *you* are?"

"I know I am. Within your gloves, your palms are growing damp."

Blast it! That was where all the moisture in her mouth had gone. How did he know?

"Your breaths are becoming shorter. Your cheeks are flushed." He lowered his gaze, her nipples tautened. Whatever was the matter with her? Then he lifted his eyes back to hers. "Correction. All your skin is flushed."

"Because I'm dancing. It's warm in here."

"It's the dead of winter. Most women are wearing shawls."

"Only the wallflowers."

"You would never be a wallflower. You are the most exciting woman here. Meet me later. Somewhere private so that we may talk."

"What do you call this current movement of the tongue? Singing?"

"It's too public. We need something more intimate."

An image flashed of him kissing her. She had often wondered at his flavor, but she would not fall for him again, she would not. "For God's sake, I am betrothed."

"As I'm well aware." She saw a flicker of sadness and regret cross his features. "You should know, Merry, that I am here only because of you."

"Your flirtation is no longer welcome, Chetwyn. I shall be no man's second choice."

"You were always my first." His eyes held sincerity and something else that fairly took her breath: an intense longing. Dear God, even Litton didn't look at her like that. Chetwyn's revelation delighted, angered, and hurt at the same time.

She released a bitter laugh. "Well, you had a frightfully funny way of showing it, didn't you?" She stepped away. "If you'll excuse me, I've become quite parched."

Before he could offer to fetch her a flute of champagne, she was walking away. His words were designed to soften her, but she wouldn't allow them to breach the wall she'd erected against him. She was betrothed now. Nothing he said would change that.

For Chetwyn, it was too late. Her course was set. She wished that thought didn't fill her with sorrow.

Chapter Two

CHETWYN DISCOVERED THAT being left at the altar wasn't nearly as humiliating or as infuriating as being abandoned on the dance floor. Or perhaps it simply seemed so because he cared a good deal more about Merry traipsing off without him than he did about Anne.

As people swirled around him, they gave him a questioning glance, an arched eyebrow, pursed lips. Then the whispers began, and he had a strong urge to tell them all to go to the devil.

Wending his way past ballooning hems and dancing slippers, he fought to keep his face in a stoic mask that revealed none of his inner thoughts. He suspected a good many of the women would swoon if they knew that he wanted to rush after Merry, usher her into a distant corner, and kiss her until the words coming from her mouth were sweet instead of bitter. It didn't lessen his anger that she had every right to be upset with him. But then the fury was directed at himself, not her. He'd handled things poorly. He needed to be alone with her to adequately explain, and furthermore to sway her away from Litton. But he could see now that he had misjudged her loyalty to Litton and her dislike of himself.

"Chetwyn?"

Turning, he smiled at the gossamer-haired beauty standing before him. "Anne."

"Is everything all right?"

"Yes, of course." Even as he spoke the words, he realized that had they married, he'd have spent a good deal of his time being untruthful with her, as he was now. He liked her, adored her, in fact, but he didn't love her. He doubted he ever would have fallen for her as Walter had before he left for the Crimea. And certainly not as Lord Tristan had.

"I'm so very glad you came," she said.

"Yes, well, I must thank you for sending me the list of guests who had accepted the invitation."

"I daresay that I needed to send only one name: Lady Meredith."

To imply he was taken aback by the accuracy of her words was an understatement. He thought he was so skilled at hiding his emotions. "How did you know?"

Taking his arm, she guided him over to an assortment of fronds that provided some protection from prying eyes. "While you were courting me, I noticed the way you looked at her with longing on a few occasions when our paths crossed with hers. I thought perhaps she had rebuffed you, which I certainly didn't understand, but after observing the drama on the dance floor, I don't think the rebuffing happened until tonight."

The *drama* that everyone had observed. He thought in public he'd be spared her wrath. Where Merry was concerned, he seemed destined to constantly misjudge. "I'm not quite certain *rebuffed* is the proper word. She is betrothed, after all. What sort of gentleman would I be to try to steal her away from Litton?"

Anne smiled. "A very determined one, I should think, and I would wager on your success." She glanced around as though fearing that she might be overheard. "As you know, my brothers are the worst gossips in all of England. Jameson tells me that Litton is up to his eyebrows in debt to Rafe. While I don't know my brother by marriage very well,

Tristan has assured me that Rafe is someone to whom I'd never wish to owe anything."

Chetwyn was of the same mind. Lord Rafe Easton owned a gambling establishment, and while it had a solid reputation, Chetwyn preferred one with a bit more class, better clientele, and no rumors of thuggery surrounding it. "You think Litton is marrying Meredith only for her dowry?"

"I've heard it's substantial. I wish Society would do away with the entire dowry business. It always leaves a lady wondering at a man's true motivations."

"Surely you have no doubt where Lord Tristan is concerned."

She laughed. "Oh, absolutely not. No, my concern is with Lady Meredith. One of my other brothers, and I can't remember which one now, hinted that this betrothal came about under unfortunate circumstances."

Chetwyn felt as though he'd taken a punch to the gut. "You think he compromised her?"

"I don't know. It was something about a garden and witnesses—" She held up her hands. "Dear God, I'm as bad as they are. Forgive me. I know not of what I speak, and so I should not be speaking. I just dislike seeing her with Litton—whom I don't much care for—when she could be with you, whom I favor a great deal."

Reaching out, Chetwyn squeezed her hand. "What matters, Anne, is that she is happy."

"Of course, you're right. It's just that she didn't look as happy with him as she did with you."

He chuckled. "Now I know you're biased. She was quite put out with me the entire time we were dancing."

"I was put out with Tristan a good bit of the time after I met him, but it didn't stop me from falling in love with him." Rising up on her toes, she bussed a quick kiss over his cheek. "I wish you luck with your endeavors here."

As she wandered away, Chetwyn decided that his best

course for the moment was to enjoy another glass of Scotch. He was heading toward the doorway when Wexford stepped into his path, his nose red, his cheeks flushed, his eyes radiating panic.

"Who the devil was she?" he asked. "I never saw anyone. She's no doubt wandered off and is in danger of freezing to death by now. We must cease the music, form search parties, call out the hounds."

"Steady, old chap," Chetwyn commanded, placing his hands on Wexford's shoulders, attempting to calm him before damage was done. "There was no woman."

Wexford blinked and stared at him as though he'd spoken in Mandarin. "Whatever do you mean?"

Obviously the man's ability to reason had frozen while he was outside. "I wrote the note. The entire thing was a ruse as I wished to dance that particular dance with Lady Meredith."

"You sent me out in the cold? For a dance? Why didn't you just ask, man?"

"Would you have stepped aside?"

"That is beside the point." Wexford held up a finger. "I shan't soon forget this, Chetwyn." With that ominous warning, he stormed off.

Considering Wexford had once shot a rhinoceros, Chetwyn considered himself fortunate that the veiled threat was quite mild. Then he saw a young lady grinning in the doorway. "I don't suppose it would be my good fortune to discover you're deaf."

With a giggle, she shook her head and disappeared into the hallway. Lovely. More fodder for the gossip mill.

"HE SENT LORD Wexford out into the storm so he could dance with you," Lady Sophia said.

Meredith had come to the retiring room to regain her calm because it was too early to retire to her chambers. She found herself surrounded by Ladies Sophia, Beatrix, and Violet.

"Terribly romantic," Lady Violet said.

"Terribly selfish," Lady Beatrix insisted. "Wexford could have died."

Meredith wondered if she was hoping for more than a dance from the fellow. She wondered if she should tell Lady Beatrix that she shouldn't strive so hard to impress men with her litany of accomplishments, then wondered if things might have been different if she, herself, had tried harder with Chetwyn—if she had thrown a fit in the garden instead of giving the impression that she could hardly be bothered by his change of heart. Was she as much to blame for their diverging paths as he?

"Perhaps we shall have a duel at dawn," Lady Sophia said, her voice rife with excitement.

"Between Chetwyn and Wexford?" Meredith asked.

"I was thinking more along the lines of Chetwyn and Litton. I daresay it is one thing to dance with a lady, an entirely different matter to go to such great lengths to do so."

"My dance card was filled. He wanted a dance. Make no more of it than that." Even now she should be in the ballroom fulfilling her obligations. Perhaps she would claim a headache.

"It's no secret his family coffers suffer for want of coin. His father made some ghastly investments, from what I hear. He needs an heiress with a substantial dowry. He lost Lady Anne—"

"You say that as though he misplaced her," Meredith interrupted, impatient with the conversation. Standing quickly, she shook out her skirts. She wanted to be more than her dowry to some man. Was she to Litton? She was no longer as sure. "I'm returning to the ballroom."

It was nearing midnight, the last dance would be soon, and she was anxious to see Litton, to have him wash away any lingering evidence that Chetwyn had danced with her. But she waited for him in vain, stood among the older matrons whose hips no longer allowed them the luxury of dance. Her only consolation was that Chetwyn wasn't about to witness her disappointment. She wondered if he'd taken his leave. She could only hope.

Chapter Three

THE RESIDENCE HAD grown quiet, the only sound the wind howling beyond the windows. Sitting alone in a chair by the fire in the billiards room, Chetwyn savored his Scotch and reminisced about the first time that he'd set eyes on Merry.

For more than a year he'd been in seclusion, grieving the loss of his brother. Finally, the Season before last, Chetwyn had taken the first step out of mourning by attending a ball. He had felt as though he were a stranger in a strange land. All the finery, the food, the laughter, the gaiety—did any of them deserve any of it when so many had died?

Suffocating in that overly flowered ballroom, attempting to talk about weather and theater and books, had made him feel as though his clothing were strangling him. He was merely going through the motions of being present, wishing he'd not been so quick to return to Society.

And then his gaze had landed on Lady Meredith. He was struck with the romantic notion that she was the sort over whom men fought wars. He'd desperately wanted to release her raven hair from its pins. The pink roses that adorned it matched the ones embroidered in her pale pink gown. It had draped off her alabaster shoulders, enticing a man to touch them. She was talking with three other ladies, and then she tilted back her head slightly and laughed. The glorious tinkling had wafted over to him, and for the first time in a good long while he didn't feel dead, didn't feel as though he had been buried alongside Walter. He was ever so glad that he was alive to hear such sweet music.

As though noticing his regard, she looked at him with eyes of clover green, and he had to take a step back to maintain his balance. The force of her was like nothing he'd ever experienced. Initially, he attributed it to being out of the ballrooms for so long, but he slowly came to realize that it was simply the power of her.

Throughout the Season, he danced with her at every opportunity, strolled with her through gardens and parks, sent her flowers and sweets. She returned to her father's estate for the winter. Chetwyn returned to his, but he'd been unable to forget her. She was more than a passing fancy.

Then in early spring a soldier delivered a letter from Walter, long after he was gone. The man hadn't posted it for fear it would become lost on the journey from the Crimea. Walter's words had shaken Chetwyn to the core. As he lay ill, he must have known that the Grim Reaper was hovering nearby, because he asked Chetwyn to promise to ensure that his betrothed was happy. Chetwyn, numbskull that he was, had thought the only way to ensure Lady Anne's well-being was to marry her himself, so he'd held his growing feelings for Lady Meredith in check. When the next Season was upon them, he turned his attentions to securing Lady Anne's happiness while Lady Meredith slipped beyond reach.

He had no right to ask her for forgiveness, no right to ask for a second chance. She had moved on with her life, she had found another. It was time for him to do the same, to stop living in the past, to stop focusing on what might have been—

If he'd not been so insistent on restoring his estates to their former glory.

If he'd not been hoarding his coins for that purpose rather than giving his brother an allowance so he could live the life of a gentleman.

If he hadn't purchased Walter a commission so he was forced to live the life of a soldier.

If he hadn't read Walter's final letter and allowed it to skew his perspective and overwhelm him with remorse.

It mattered little to him now that Walter had once commented that he enjoyed being in the army, had felt he had gained purpose. He had died as a young man, while Chetwyn would no doubt die as an old one. And without Merry at his side.

He downed the contents of his glass, reached for the bottle he'd set beside the chair, and refilled the tumbler. As the room was beginning to spin and his head was feeling dull, he knew he should be abed, where in sleep he would dream of Merry, of her raven hair and green eyes and the way she had once smiled at him as though he could do no wrong. Yet he had managed to do wrong aplenty.

He barely moved when he heard the door open. Slowly shifting his gaze over, he wondered briefly if he'd already fallen asleep, because there she was in a much simpler dress than she'd been wearing earlier. No petticoats. Possibly no corset. It was designed for comfort, not company. It could also be discarded in a flash if a man were to set his mind to removing it. He had imbibed a bit too much because he was already envisioning the joy he would experience in giving all those buttons their freedom.

Her braided hair fell past her hips, her slippers were plain. Nothing about her was intentionally enticing, and yet he was thoroughly beguiled.

She glanced around warily. He held still, waiting for the moment when she would see him. Only she didn't, and he realized the deep shadows and the angle of the chair hid his presence from her. She swept her gaze around the room once more before returning to the door and closing it with a hushed snick.

He wondered if she was waiting for Litton. Chetwyn

thought that if the viscount came through the door, he might very well lose any semblance he had of being a gentleman. He wouldn't stand for it, watching them behave as lovers. It could be the only reason for this late-night tryst, and dammit all to hell, she appeared to be anticipating it. Her eyes took on a glow, her smile was one of someone doing what she ought not to be caught doing. Dear God, help him, but he wanted to kiss those lips, he wanted to be doing things with them that *he* ought not to be doing.

She wandered over to the billiards table and scraped her fingers over the baize top as she slowly walked its length. Against the taut cloth, her nails made a faint raspy sound, and it was all he could do not to groan as he imagined her trailing those fingertips over his chest, circling around his nipples, pinching, leaning in—

She stilled, and his thoughts careened to a stop as though she'd heard them. She glanced over her shoulder, and he feared that he had made a sound. He wasn't quite ready for her to know that he was there. Again, he wondered if she was meeting Litton, if she was going to stretch out on the table for her lover. Would he unravel her hair and spread it across the green? Would he worship her as she deserved to be worshipped?

Chetwyn imagined removing her slippers, kissing her toes, then taking his mouth on a slow, leisurely journey up her calves, over her knees, along her thighs—

Christ! If he carried on with these imaginings, he was going to be unable to stand when Litton showed. If the rumors being bandied about were true, he'd compromised her once in a garden. He wouldn't hesitate to do so here, long after the stroke of midnight, when most were abed and no one was about to interrupt. Chetwyn flexed the fingers not holding the glass. He rather fancied the idea of introducing his fist to Litton's nose.

She fairly skipped over to the rack on the wall and selected a cue stick. Mesmerized, he watched as she tested its weight, twirled it between her fingers, and carried it over to the table. She gathered the balls, racked them; then, cue in hand, she leaned over, presenting him with a rather enticing view of her backside. A tiny voice urged him to stay where he was, to enjoy the unexpected gift of her arrival, but it was such a small voice, easily ignored, and he could enjoy her so much more if no distance separated them.

Unable to hold back his anticipation, he unfolded his body and crept over to where she was carefully positioning her cue. When he was near enough to smell her rose fragrance, he leaned in and whispered in a low, sensual drawl, "You're doing it all wrong."

With a startled yelp, she flung herself backward, her head smacking soundly into his jaw—

And the world went black.

WITH HER HEART pounding, her entire body quaking, Meredith dropped to her knees, more because of their weakened state than the man sprawled on the floor. Had she killed him? Dear God, her father abhorred scandal, and she couldn't think of anything that would set tongues to wagging faster than murder. She could envision herself traipsing toward the gallows with her father berating her the entire way for bringing shame upon the family.

"Chetwyn?" She placed her palm against his cheek, felt the stubble prick her tender flesh, and fought not to compare it to the stiff baize over which she trailed her fingers only moments before. She much preferred the warmth of his skin and the bristles that were thicker than she imagined and a shade darker than his hair. He should have appeared unkempt. Instead he looked very, very dangerous, and something that greatly resembled pleasure settled in the pit of her stomach. Why didn't she ever feel this liquid fire that spread into her limbs when she was in Litton's presence?

She leaned lower and inhaled Chetwyn's bergamot fragrance mingled with Scotch. She considered pressing her lips to his, just for a taste. How often—before he had shifted his attentions to Lady Anne—had she longed for a turn about the garden with him that would have resulted in an illicit kiss? It was her shameful secret, her dark fantasy that in a shadowed part of a garden he would cease to be a gentleman, and she would no longer act as a lady. She had wanted so much with him that she hadn't wanted with other admirers. She wished he hadn't come here, that his presence wasn't reminding her of all her silly imaginings. She wanted to marry Litton, to be his wife, his viscountess eventually—after his father passed.

Yet, if she were honest with herself, Chetwyn stirred something deep within her that Litton had yet to reach. And that acknowledgment terrified her. Would she make him happy if her thoughts could stray so easily to another?

As he groaned, Chetwyn opened his eyes wide, blinked, and rubbed his jaw. "You've got quite the punch," he muttered.

Now that she saw he was going to be all right, irritation swamped her. "You have a jaw like glass. None of my brothers would have gone down that easily or that hard. It's a wonder you didn't shake the foundation of the residence. What the devil were you doing here, sneaking up on me?"

"It's the gentlemen's room, so the question, sweetheart, is what are you doing here?"

She settled back on her heels, not quite ready to leave until she saw him firmly on his feet, although a small part of her was wishing she *had* killed him. "Not that it's any of your business, but I was having difficulty falling asleep. I was looking for the library so I might find a book to read."

He had the audacity to give her a wolfish grin that did nothing to settle her riotous thoughts. If anything, it only made her want to kiss him all the more. Whatever was wrong with her?

"But once you realized you weren't in the library, you didn't leave. I think you purposely came here."

"Think what you want." Rising to her feet, she turned to leave.

"Are you meeting someone?" he asked.

She spun back around. "Of course not. I'm a lady. I don't—"

She abruptly cut off her protest. She had been alone with a gentleman, was alone with one now. She knew she should leave, but the truth was that she *had* come here to play billiards. She was quite disappointed that she wouldn't have the opportunity to do so—because of his presence. He did little more than constantly bring disappointment into her life. "I hear that Lord Wexford is quite put out with you."

He shoved himself to his feet. In the shadowed room, he seemed larger, broader, more devastatingly handsome. "Facing his wrath was well worth the dance."

"Who do you think he *thought* he was going to meet?" she asked.

Chetwyn leaned his hip against the table and crossed his arms over his chest. "I haven't a clue. You seem to know more about the gossip than I. Who do you think?"

She shrugged, wondering why she was prolonging her visit. She had always felt most comfortable with him, even when her thoughts had turned down dark corners where they shouldn't. Even now she recalled the feel of him behind her, the warmth of his breath on her neck as he'd whispered in her ear. "I don't know, and I don't suppose it matters. I should go."

"Play billiards with me."

His eyes held a challenge that she knew had little to do with the actual game. He was daring her to stay, to risk being with him. Did he know how much she was drawn to him, how very dangerous he was to her?

"I'll teach you," he said.

She angled her chin haughtily. "I already know how to play. Litton taught me. What do I gain if I win?"

"What would you like?"

"For you to leave immediately."

He furrowed his brow. "The room?"

"The manor, the estate, the shire." She knew the challenge was now in her gaze, and she could see him considering it, perhaps wondering how truly skilled she was.

"And if I win?" he asked, his voice thrumming with an undercurrent that should have frightened her off. "What do I receive?"

"Our last night here there is to be another ball. A dance. Whichever one you want. I shall let you sign my card first."

He picked up her cue stick and studied it as though he were trying to determine how it had been made. "A kiss." He shifted his gaze over to her and captured her as though he'd suddenly wrapped his arms around her. "As soon as I sink my last ball."

"That would be entirely inappropriate."

He gave her a devilish grin. "Which is why I want it."

"You always struck me as quite the gentleman."

A shadow crossed his features. "Not tonight. I've spent too much time contemplating past mistakes. You were one of them, you know. If I had to do it over, I would not have hurt you."

Not exactly what she wanted to hear. If he had to do it over, she wanted him to kiss her madly, passionately in the garden, to court her properly, to perhaps ask for her hand on bended knee. But he had never declared any feelings for her, so she had little right to be hurt. "You overstate your importance to me. A kiss from you will have no effect upon me, so I accept the challenge."

His eyes darkened, and she was left with the impression that she'd made a terrible mistake.

"You may break," he said.

Yes, she thought, she very well might. Her heart, at least. Where he was concerned, it had once been close to shattering. Then she scolded herself. *Silly chit, he was talking about the balls.*

While he went to the wall to examine the selection of cue sticks, she picked up hers, moved to the end of the table, and began to position herself as Litton had taught her.

"Still not quite right," Chetwyn said, his voice coming from near enough that she realized he was no longer at the wall.

She didn't dare give him the satisfaction of glancing over her shoulder to discern exactly where he was, but when she took a deep breath she filled her nostrils with bergamot. Close then, very close indeed. "Oh?"

She was quite pleased that she didn't squeak like a dormouse. Her nerves were suddenly wrung tight, and she couldn't decide if she wanted the satisfaction of besting him or the gaining of the knowledge of what his kiss was like. She didn't know why she was suddenly obsessed with the thought of his mouth on hers. Litton had kissed her, so she knew very well that the pressing of lips left a great deal to be desired. She had always thought there would be heat, but all she'd felt was the cold. Perhaps it was because they had been outside, the evening had been cool, and the arrival of her father and brothers had abruptly ended any stirring of embers.

"Allow me to show you," Chetwyn said.

She was tempted to ignore him and smack the balls, but better to let him believe she knew not what she was doing so her victory would leave him flummoxed and feeling quite the fool. "All right."

She began to straighten.

"No, stay as you are."

She stilled as his arms came around her. Litton certainly hadn't taken this intimate approach to teaching her. He'd not touched her at all. He merely explained the rules in a serious, endearing manner as though he were preparing to submit them to *Hoyle's* to be included in an upcoming edition since the publication had yet to explain how billiards should be played.

As the length of his body nudged against hers, she became acutely aware of the fact that she was wearing little more than her chemise and drawers beneath the dress. After her maid had prepared her for bed and she'd had difficulty finding sleep, she'd wanted to slip into something that she could manage on her own. At home, she would have simply gathered her wrap about her, but one didn't traipse through a guest's home in her nightdress, although now she was questioning the wisdom of doing it with so little to separate her from Chetwyn. His warmth seeped through her clothing to heat her flesh. His large hands closed over hers, and she realized how capable they appeared. He possessed strong, thick fingers with blunt-tipped nails. His roughened jaw teased her neck. His hair tickled her temple. She had been correct with her earlier assessment. It was curling with wild abandon, and she ached to slip her fingers through the feathery strands.

"Relax," he murmured into her ear, and within her slippers her toes curled as though he were giving attention to them.

"I am relaxed." *Liar, liar.*

"You're as stiff as a poker. I'm going to position your hands, your stance."

"I think you're wrong. I think they are exactly as they need to be."

"Not if you wish to beat me."

Turning her head to the side, she met and held his gaze. "Why would you assist me in giving you a sound thrashing and miss out on your kiss? If you truly wanted it—"

"Oh, I truly want it," he said in a silken voice. "And I intend to have it."

Suddenly, one of his hands was cupping her cheek, while his fingers plowed through her hair. He somehow managed to twist and bend her slightly so she was cradled in his other arm. He lowered his head, and his mouth plundered. No soft taking this, but an urgency. He ravished with his tongue as though he would die if he didn't taste her, as though he would cease to exist if he left anything unexplored.

This was exactly what she had imagined kissing him would be like during the months when they had flirted, danced, and strolled about. She had expected heat and passion. She had instinctually known that within him was a smoldering fire that once set ablaze would be difficult to extinguish. Working one hand beneath his waistcoat, she felt the solidness of his muscles beneath the fine linen of his shirt. Wanton that she was, she wanted his coat, waistcoat, and shirt gone. She wanted the feel of his skin against her palms. She wanted to scrape her nails over his bare back.

Guilt slammed into her. She felt none of these things when Litton had kissed her. His had been pleasant, tame, proper. Nothing about Chetwyn was proper at that moment.

His guttural groans reverberated through his chest, vibrated into her. She ran her free hand through his golden locks, felt them wrapping around her fingers as though they intended to hold her captive as easily as his mouth did.

He dragged his lips along her throat, and she found herself arching up toward him, offering him more.

"You haven't won," she said breathlessly. They hadn't even started to play.

Raising his head, he gave her a dark grin. "Oh, but I have."

With as little effort as though she weighed no more than a pillow, he lifted her up and laid her on the billiards table. She was vaguely aware of the balls scattering. Leaning over her, he braced his arms on either side of her head, his gaze intent.

"Don't marry him," he urged, his voice low and sensual until it more closely resembled a caress.

"I have to."

"Because of the kiss in the garden?"

Her heart slammed into her ribs. "What do you know of the garden?"

"Only rumors. The rest of your life shouldn't be determined by a kiss."

Yet here she was thinking that if she weren't betrothed, the kiss he had just delivered would have been the guiding star for the remainder of her life. No one else's would ever measure up.

A broken betrothal . . . Litton would sue. Her father wouldn't allow that sort of scandal to happen. "You're being a bit hypocritical. You're asking me to change the direction of my life because you managed to steal a kiss that left me breathless. You had your chance with me, Chetwyn. You chose another. Now so have I."

"I can explain."

"It doesn't matter. You may be in the habit of hurting people, but I'm not." Rolling away from him, she scrambled off the table. "I was handling the cue properly. I would have beaten you, and I think you know it. Please accept that things are over between us."

"Things never really got properly started between us. If we had more time—"

She shook her head, grateful that was all that was required to silence him. So few lamps burned. The fire on the hearth cast dancing shadows around him as he stood tall and straight, but she was left with the impression of someone trapped in hell. "But we don't have the luxury of time, Chetwyn. Christmas is almost here, and then I'll be married shortly after."

Turning on her heel, she marched from the room before he could object. When the door was closed behind her, she raced down the hallway and up the stairs to her bedchamber. She flung herself across the bed and pressed her fingers to lips that still tingled from his ravishment. She had always believed that Christmas was a time for miracles, but at that precise moment she wasn't certain exactly what she wished for.

Chapter Four

WHEN MEREDITH ENTERED the breakfast dining room the following morning, her gaze immediately shot to Chetwyn. She didn't know why she noticed him first. The room was far from empty. Several round tables were filled with guests. He sat at one against the far wall, near a window that provided a view of the gloomy skies. Lady Anne and Lord Tristan were with him. It irritated her that Chetwyn looked as though he'd slept well after their parting, while she'd done little more than toss and turn.

After going to the sideboard and selecting a few sumptuous items for her plate, she turned and spotted Litton sitting in a corner alone. Contriteness snapped at her because she hadn't noticed him sooner. She strolled over. "Good morning."

He looked up at her with bloodshot eyes. "Don't know what's so good about it."

His being out of sorts was unusual for him, or at least she thought it was. She realized that courting was a strange ritual in which one always saw others only at their best for a few hours, never for any great length of time. "The storm's let up, for one thing," she said, as a footman pulled out her chair and assisted her into it. With a flick of her wrist, she settled her napkin on her lap. She realized he smelled of stale cigars and old whiskey. "I was disappointed not to have a final dance with you last night."

With a low groan, he slammed his eyes closed. "I'm

sorry, sweetheart. I was in the midst of a game of cards and lost track of the time."

"Were you winning?"

"No, luck wasn't with me." He twisted his lips into a sardonic grin. "To be honest, you're the only lucky thing to happen in my life of late."

"Lucky that we got caught in the garden, you mean?"

He gave her one of the smiles that had charmed her so many months earlier. "Simply lucky."

She sliced off a bit of sausage. "I don't suppose you told anyone about our encounter in the garden."

He appeared as flummoxed as she had been last night when Chetwyn had mentioned it. "Why would you think that?"

"It's just that there appears to be gossip going around about us and a kiss in the garden. As my father forbade my brothers to say anything—and they are quite familiar with his temper—I can't imagine how the rumors might have started."

"What does it matter? We're to be married in a little over a week."

"Yes, but we wanted people to believe that we were marrying because we wanted to, not because we were forced to as a result of my disgraceful behavior. My father is quite adamant that there be no scandal associated with our family."

Reaching across the table, he placed his hand over hers, where it rested beside her plate. "Be assured, my sweet, that I am marrying you because I *want* to. Scandal or no."

"Still, it's perplexing."

"People are always talking about one thing or another. Don't concern yourself with it."

"Yes, I suppose you're right." Although without the discovery in the garden, would she be marrying him? Choice had been taken away from her. It hadn't really mattered at the time because she liked Litton, and Chetwyn was involved with Lady Anne. But what if he hadn't been? What might have been was of no consequence. She would go mad if she focused on that rather than what was.

Shifting her gaze over to Chetwyn, she discovered him watching her. He would be about all day. Their paths might cross on occasion. Tonight a theater group would be performing *A Christmas Carol,* but until then she could find herself partnered with Chetwyn during a session of parlor games this afternoon. She could barely tolerate the thought.

"I was thinking of taking a walk," she told Litton.

"Where?"

She laughed lightly. "Outside, of course."

"My sweet, there's half a foot of snow out there."

"I have my boots. I thought you might care to join me."

Shaking his head, he rubbed his temples. "I feel as though my skull is about to split open."

"I'm so sorry. Why ever did you get out of bed, then?"

"I've not yet been to bed. I thought some coffee might help with the pounding in my head."

"You've been up all night?" She kept her horror at the thought contained. What if he'd decided that he wanted a game of billiards, if he and other gentlemen had walked in to see Chetwyn kissing her—or worse, her returning the kiss with equal fervor? The scandal would have ruined her, perhaps even her family. Her father would have never forgiven her.

"Cards do not run on a schedule, so yes, all night," he said.

"But you were losing. Why would you keep at it?"

He shrugged. "I didn't wager that much."

While he didn't say it, she couldn't help but think that her dowry, which would soon be his, would settle his debt.

"Besides," he continued, "I can't expect you to understand the thrill of acquiring the perfect hand."

"You won't continue to gamble like this when we're married, will you?"

He stood. "I'm off to bed." Leaning down, he pressed a kiss to the top of her head. "I'll see you this evening."

When she glanced over and saw Chetwyn still studying her, she wished Litton had taken her in his arms and given her a resounding kiss that would cause the windows to fog over. She also wished that she wasn't suddenly filled with misgivings.

CHETWYN WAS STANDING outside taking in some fresh air when he spied Merry traipsing off in the direction of the castle that had once been the official family residence. He hadn't meant to stare at her during breakfast, but he'd had a rough night of it, unable to forget the feel of her in his arms. Watching her with Litton—touching, talking, and smiling—had been torment. He wanted to begin his day with her at *his* breakfast table.

Bloody hell. He wanted to begin his day with her in his bed. Breakfast would come later.

As she disappeared, he glanced around. Surely she wasn't going off by herself. She must have arranged a meeting with Litton, but then where was he? He knew she probably wouldn't welcome his company, but if he just happened to be strolling in the same direction—where was the harm? How could she object?

With the thick blanket of snow muffling his footsteps, Chetwyn took off after her. He remembered how much she enjoyed the outdoors. Perhaps like him, she was simply starting to feel hemmed in. The last thing he wanted was to play a game of charades, and he seemed to recall that was first on the list of today's entertainments. As he quickened his pace, he closed the distance between them and caught glimpses of her through the trees. She trudged on with such determination and purpose. In one gloved hand, she held a pair of skates, and he realized she was hoping to find a pond frozen over. He waited until she'd gone far enough that he didn't think she'd contemplate returning to the residence in order to avoid his company. Then he lengthened his stride until he caught up to her.

"Bit brisk out for a walk, isn't it?"

She swung around, the fire of anger in her eyes, when he much preferred the fire of passion. He was surprised that all of the snow around them didn't melt. "Let me be, Chetwyn."

"You can't possibly think that I'm going to allow you to march off into the woods alone."

"I'm certain I'll be quite safe."

It wasn't a risk he was willing to take. "Why isn't Litton accompanying you? Did you have a squabble during breakfast?"

"It's none of your affair." She pursed her lips before blurting, "His head hurt. He was up for a good bit of the night."

Drinking and gambling, he thought, based upon what he'd heard. Tristan had told Chetwyn over their warm eggs and toast that Litton had ended his night with markers owed to several of the lords. He didn't know why he wanted her to feel better about the blighter. "Many were, from what I understand."

"We're just fortunate that they didn't walk into the billiards room during an inopportune moment."

"I wouldn't have allowed your reputation to be sullied."

"Sometimes it can't be helped. Please return to the manor, Chetwyn. I'm out here alone because I need solitude."

"Are you rethinking your plans to marry Litton?"

"I'm rethinking my decision not to knock my skates against your thick skull."

He couldn't help but smile. "At least you are thinking of me."

"Good God, but you are vexing," she stated before tromping off.

He should let her go. She didn't want his company. But he might never have another opportunity to be in her presence alone. He looked up at the sky. Gray, with heavy clouds, it had an ominous feel to it.

Falling into step beside her, he said, "I think we're in for some more nasty weather."

"I'm quite capable of dealing with a bit of snow."

Holding his thoughts, he simply watched her breaths turning white and fading away. Her cheeks were ruddy, her strides determined. He remembered his father telling him about a well-stocked pond on the estate where he'd fished with the previous Duke of Keswick. Chetwyn wondered if that was where she was heading. She certainly seemed to know where she was going. She also seemed to have given up on attempting to convince him to leave her alone.

The bare trees were laden with snow. Every now and then a stray breeze blew a dusting of white from its perch. A hushed silence surrounded them. It seemed the place to let anger go, or at the very least a place to share a special moment, to create a memory that would last a lifetime. If he could not have her forever, he could at least have her for now. He didn't know if it would soften or sharpen the regret with which he would live.

He took her elbow. She pivoted around, her arm swinging the skates toward his head. He ducked, and when they'd passed he grabbed her other arm and propelled her back against the nearest tree; then, releasing the hold on one arm, he touched his finger to her lips, striving not to give any reaction to how warm they were. Despite the cold, the heat seeped through his leather gloves. "Shh."

"How dare—"

"Shh. We're not alone."

Her green eyes widened. The leaves would match their shade come spring. He would never behold another tree without thinking of her.

Without panic, barely moving her head, she scanned the area. "Who?"

"To your right, below that scraggly bush there."

She looked down. He saw her expression soften, before she shored up her resolve not to enjoy a moment in his company and gave him a pointed glare. "A rabbit?"

He'd spotted the white fur just before he touched Merry. "A tad beyond is a deer."

She shifted her gaze and he took satisfaction in her curiosity. "I remember the interest you took in birds when we walked through the parks. You seem to know them all."

"I appreciate creatures, great and small. What I do not appreciate is your taking liberties. Please unhand me."

"Do you love him? You never truly answered my question last night. Tell me that much at least. Do you love him?"

She angled her chin. "With all my heart."

Hope soaring through him, he gave her a slow, triumphant grin. "You always were a poor liar, Merry."

Then he covered her mouth with his.

MEREDITH KNEW THAT she should knock her skates against the side of his skull, render him unconscious, and run for her life. Instead she released her hold on them and wound her arms around his neck. As he moved in, she welcomed the weight and warmth of his body pressing against her.

It was wrong, so very wrong for her to enjoy his kiss, to want his kiss. Without liquor flavoring his tongue, he still tasted marvelous. Rich and sinful. Decadent. His gloved hands came up, held her head, provided a cushion against the hard bark. He took the kiss deeper, his tongue swirling through her mouth, stirring carnal cravings to life.

There had been a time when she'd thought she'd die from wanting a kiss from him. She never felt that way with Litton. When he had kissed her, his lips upon hers had been pleasant. But she'd never thought that together they could melt snow.

With Chetwyn, she was fairly certain that when he was

done with her, she would find herself in a puddle of icy water. She stroked her hands over his shoulders. He was firm, strong. She knew he enjoyed the outdoors as much as she. His body reflected his passions. At one time, she'd hoped to become one of them.

He slid his lips from hers, nuzzling her neck, his mouth somehow finding its way beneath her collar, the heat of his breath coating dew along her skin. "Until Christmas, Merry, give me until Christmas to prove my affections are true."

Everything within her wanted to scream, *"Yes!"* But her heart, still bruised, whispered, *"No."*

"I'm afraid," she said, her voice as rough and raw as her soul.

Drawing back, he held her gaze, his rapid breaths visible in the cold air mingling with hers. "I won't hurt you again, I swear it."

He took her wrist. She wanted to wrench it free, but instead she was mesmerized watching as he brought it to his lips, crooked a finger beneath her cuff, and revealed a tiny bit of flesh. Gently, reverently, he placed his mouth there and closed his eyes as though he'd acquired heaven. Her breath caught, even as her heart sped into a wild gallop.

"Until Christmas, Merry," he whispered in a hoarse voice. "It's not so very long, and I'm a much better choice than Litton."

He opened his eyes, and the intensity she saw there almost dropped her to her knees. "It's too late, Chetwyn."

"Even if you were standing at the altar this moment, it wouldn't be too late. It's not too late until you exchange vows, until you sign the marriage register."

Shaking her head, she pushed him back and skirted away from him. She tugged down her cuff, yanked up her glove, but still she could feel the press of his lips against her wrist. She wanted to rub the sensation away, while at the same time she wanted to place it in a gilded box so she could keep it. "I trusted you with my heart once. I won't do it again."

"I know I bruised your feelings."

"You did nothing of the sort." Reaching down, she snatched up her skates.

"I won't give up," he said. "Not until Christmas."

"Why that particular day?"

"Because your love is the only gift I wish to receive."

Oh, how she truly wanted to believe the words, to bask in them, glory in them. But he had toyed with her affections once. She would not be so quick to fall for him again. "And with my love comes my dowry. How do I know it's not what you're truly after?"

"I don't give a damn about your dowry. I'll find a way to prove that to you as well."

"Even if you earn my love, you won't win my hand. Father promised it to Litton."

He narrowed his eyes. "Was it not your choice to marry him? Are the rumors true? Did he take advantage?"

"It was only a kiss, but we were caught. I wanted the kiss, and I want to marry him." Or at least she had convinced herself that she wanted to marry him, because in truth she had no choice. Her father would have it no other way. She wondered if a time would ever come when women didn't have to obey their fathers, when they would have the full freedom of adulthood. Although even her brothers, older than she, still obeyed their father. "The pond is just over the rise," she said, to steer them away from the conversation and a promise she didn't want to make.

She and Chetwyn carried on in companionable silence as the sky darkened and snow began to blow around them.

"Perhaps we should turn back," he said.

"Giving up so easily, Chetwyn?"

"Where you're concerned, never again."

She didn't want to admit that, with his words, something within her sang as clearly as the birds of spring.

THE SNOW WAS falling more thickly by the time they reached the pond.

"I wouldn't recommend we stay overly long," Chetwyn said. "Our tracks will soon disappear, and we'll have a difficult time finding our way back."

Something told her that they shouldn't stay at all. They'd walked quite a distance. The wind had picked up and was whining through the trees. Soon it would be howling. But the water was frozen and the ice inviting. "One trip around the outer edge, and we'll head back," she said.

She glanced around, striving to determine where she could sit without gaining a damp bottom.

"Lean against that tree there," he said. "I'll slip your blades onto your shoes."

After handing him her blades, she did as he suggested. With her back against the bark, she watched as he knelt in the snow. He lifted his gaze to hers, and a sharp pang ripped through her. She had dreamed of him in that position, only he was going to ask her to become his wife. She swallowed hard at the memory of how badly she had wanted it.

Chetwyn patted his knee. "Give me your foot."

With her hands to the side, gripping the trunk of the tree, she lifted her foot. Bending his head, he went to work securing the wooden blade to her shoe. Give him until Christmas to prove he was worthy of her affections? She didn't think he'd need more than a day. What of poor Litton? She knew what it was to be cast aside. He certainly didn't deserve such unkind treatment, but was it kinder to let him go when she longed for another?

When Chetwyn finished with one foot, she placed the other on his knee.

"A pity you didn't bring blades," she told him.

"I shall walk along beside you."

"On the ice?"

"On the bank."

"I shan't be able to skate very far."

He set her other foot aside and unfolded that long, lean body of his. "As you don't know how thick the ice is, you're better off staying close to shore, where the water is shallow. If you break through the ice, you'll only get your feet wet."

"I'm familiar with the dangers of ice skating. I've never had ice buckle beneath me."

"Then let's not have today be the first time."

She didn't think it would be. It was so terribly cold up here. If she didn't spend a good deal of her time outdoors, she'd no doubt be shivering. But her woolen riding habit and heavy cloak helped to keep her somewhat warm. Having Chetwyn nearby didn't hurt either.

With her hand on his arm, she cut a swathe through the snow until they reached the pond. It was strange, but the blue of the water viewed through the ice reminded her of the eyes of the Pembrook lords.

"Do you suppose it's possible that Keswick's ancestors studied this pond in winter for so long that it changed the shade of their eyes?" she asked.

"Are you trying to weave a fairy tale?"

"I guess I am being fanciful. I tend to do that from time to time. It's only that they have such unusual eyes."

"Not boring like mine."

She jerked her head around to stare at him. "They're not boring." They were the color of hot cocoa when there was more cocoa than milk. And they spoke volumes, which was the reason that she'd thought he would be asking for her hand. She had read so much into his words based upon what his eyes were saying. Now she was afraid to read too much, to believe that the affection she saw there was true.

He led her onto the ice. While he may have wished to

walk alongside her, she glided much faster than he walked. She slipped her hand away from his.

"Don't go out far, Merry."

"Honestly, Chetwyn, you worry too much. The duchess told me that the pond has been iced over for a couple of weeks now."

"That doesn't mean it's perfectly safe."

Safer than you, she thought. She welcomed the brisk air brushing over her face, the snow melting on her eyelashes. With the silence, she could almost imagine that she was completely and absolutely alone. It was what she'd thought she wanted.

Only now she realized that she wanted to be with him: walking, talking, her arm linked with his. She pirouetted to face him. She heard a crack of thunder. He was rushing toward her.

"Merry, don't move!"

Another crack, louder than the first, and she realized with horror that the storm wasn't above her, but beneath her.

"Chetwyn!"

Then the ice gave way.

Chapter Five

CHETWYN MANAGED TO grab her and haul her to the bank with enough force that they both tumbled onto the snow. Fortunately, not enough of the ice had given way that she was in danger of falling through, but still his heart was pounding. "Are you all right?" he asked.

She nodded, then released a breath that was more laugh than air. "I was terrified for a moment there. It sounded awful. I'm embarrassed that I screamed."

"I barely heard it because of my shout. But I think we should head back now."

"Yes, indeed. The weather seems to be worsening at an amazing clip."

The snowfall was heavier, damp and sticky. The wind was circling around in gales. He removed her skates, then shoved himself to his feet before pulling her up. He entwined his arm with hers, faced in the direction from which they'd come, and realized that a good bit of the visibility was lost to them. "Stay close," he ordered, and he felt her hold on him tighten.

They walked as quickly as possible, which wasn't fast enough, as far as he was concerned. Her strides were shorter than his, and she was having a difficult time keeping up. He could feel her trembling as the wind howled around them and the snow fell in a constant wash of thick, heavy flakes.

Barely breaking his stride, he shrugged out of his coat and draped it over her shoulders.

"Chetwyn, it's too cold."

"I'll be fine," he lied as the wind sliced through him.

Why had he not insisted that they head back? He had wanted more time with her, to speak with her, to try to make his case.

How far had they walked? Had he taken a wrong turn? It was as he'd anticipated. The snow had begun filling in their tracks, and he could no longer be sure they were on the right path. Tiny shards of ice sliced at him. Where the devil were they?

Looking around, striving to get his bearings, he saw the crenellated outline of Pembrook Castle, the original holding. The recently built manor would be on the other side, up a rise that he didn't know if she'd have the strength to climb. He could carry her, but even then it was so far. If he stumbled, what would become of her? It didn't bear thinking about. He wasn't going to let anything happen to her.

"We'll take refuge in the old castle," he said.

"No, I don't want to go there."

"Merry, we don't have much choice. The manor is still a good distance away."

"I didn't realize we'd gone so far."

"My charms distracted you."

She laughed. It was so good to hear her laugh. "How can you be pompous at a time like this?"

Because he needed to distract her again, to give her something to focus on other than their dire circumstances. He pushed them forward, slogging through the drifts of snow. How could such a fierce storm have come upon them so quickly? He was more familiar with the weather in the south, in Cornwall. He'd always heard that the north was brutal, but until now he hadn't understood what that meant.

By the time they reached the old manor and slumped

against the stone wall, he realized it was madness to try to get her to the new residence. He had to get her dry and warm. "We've no choice. We're going to stop here."

"We can . . . carry on," she stammered, her teeth chattering with such force he was surprised they didn't crack.

"Perhaps we'll give it a try after we've warmed up and gathered our strength."

She didn't argue as they made their way along the side of the building. He fought the strong gale that wanted to smash him into it, into her. As much as possible, he was trying to shield her from the fury of nature. Finally, he saw a door. Reaching out, he closed his fingers over the handle, released the latch, and felt relief swamp him when it gave way.

Nearly torn from its hinges by the wind, the wooden door banged against the wall. He ushered her into the kitchen and staggered in after her. Closing the door, he took stock of their surroundings. Although the building had been abandoned, not everything had been taken. There was a stove, a table, a stack of wood. He didn't think it likely that he would find food, but for now it gave him hope that he had found a shelter from the storm.

"Come along, let's see what we've got."

With Merry in his wake, he stalked down a darkened hallway and then another, a bit of light coming through a window at the end guiding him. Then he walked into what had once been a great hall. The fireplace was massive, the sort where the master of the household might have roasted deer.

He knelt before it, grateful to find more wood, kindling, and matches. He set himself to the task of getting a fire going. It wasn't long before the flames were blazing, sending out welcomed warmth.

"Oh, th-that's l-lovely," she whispered as she moved closer to the fire.

Glancing around, he noticed the draperies. They would

have to do. He rushed across the room, grabbed a handful of the fabric, and with a sharp tug, brought them down. Dust motes kicked up around him, but at least the curtains were dry.

He hurried back over to her and dropped them at her feet. "Take off your clothes."

Merry stared at him as though he'd gone mad. "I beg your pardon?"

"Yours are damp, mine are drenched. We have to get warm before I lose my senses, and you are truly alone. Body heat is the fastest way. You'll have some privacy while I see what else I can find. Wrap those draperies about you."

He made his way through a good portion of the residence, tearing down more moth-eaten draperies. He located a half-full bottle of rum.

Returning to the great room, he strove to ignore the pile of clothes near the fire and what that signified. Merry sat on the floor, the draperies pulled in close about her. He fashioned a crude pallet with what he'd found. Then he handed her the bottle of rum. "Drink this. It'll warm you."

Although not as much as I plan to. Turning away from her, he began removing his own clothes. He tore off his jacket, but his fingers were too stiff with the cold to loosen the buttons. He was going to have to rip—

"Here," she said, suddenly standing in front of him. The drapery was wrapped around her, gathered in front of her. With just a shrug of her shoulders, it would pool on the floor. "You drink now."

His fingers were so numb he thought he might drop the bottle, but he managed to hold on to it and take deep swallows. He was aware of her fingers working his buttons free.

"I've dreamed of you doing this," he said.

She jerked her gaze up to his, and he was surprised that his facial muscles were warm enough to grin.

"Remove my clothes," he explained in case his meaning

wasn't clear. "I would have liked to have removed yours, but you seemed rather alarmed by the notion of what I was suggesting."

"It's scandalous. I was brought up to avoid scandal at all costs, and yet I seem to find myself slipping into the quagmire of it once again." She helped him out of his waistcoat, then slowly unraveled his neckcloth.

"How long do you think we'll be here?" she asked, and he heard the trepidation mirrored in her voice.

"Only until the storm passes."

"That could be days."

"Could be years."

She grinned at him. He was grateful for that. "I don't know where I'd be now if you hadn't gone on the walk with me."

"I doubt you'd have stayed out as long if I hadn't been serving as a distraction."

"Probably not." She peeled his shirt up over his head. He welcomed the warmth from the fire finally dancing over his skin.

"You're like ice," she said.

"Unfortunately."

"Can you manage your trousers?"

"If I must."

She laughed lightly. "Yes, in this instance I think you must."

Moving away, she sat on the mound of draperies, her back to him. He wasn't as cold or shaking as he had been. They probably no longer needed the warmth of each other's bodies. The fire would suffice. But it seemed a shame to waste the opportunity of having her so near when it might never come again.

BEYOND THE GLASS and stone, it sounded as though demons trapped in hell howled.

"It's only the wind, Merry."

They were enclosed in a cocoon of warmth provided by the ragged draperies. Their clothes were resting near the fire. They appeared to be somewhat dry. She should probably gather up her things and get dressed, but she didn't want to move. She thought she might like to stay here forever.

"I've heard this manor is haunted."

"Is that why you hesitated to stop here?"

She nodded. "I know it's silly to believe in ghosts, but there you are."

"Nothing about you is silly."

She couldn't deny the pleasure his words brought. "They'll have noticed I'm missing by now—have noticed we both are, no doubt."

"They won't come looking yet. Their visibility is no better than ours."

"When my father finds us here, he'll insist that we marry. Being alone with a gentleman in an abandoned manor during a storm is more scandalous than being discovered in a man's arms near a trellis of roses in a dark corner of the garden."

With his finger trailing along her neck, he slid her hair over her shoulder and pressed his lips to her nape. In spite of their warmth, she shivered. "But does he hold your heart? You captured mine from the beginning."

Twisting around, she looked sharply at him. "Then why did you give your attentions to Lady Anne?"

Cradling her face with one hand, he stroked his thumb along her cheek. "Out of a misguided notion that I owed it to my brother." He held her gaze, and she found herself swimming in the depths of his brown eyes. "He wrote me a letter as he was dying and asked me to see to her happiness."

"But he died long before you gave me any attention."

"Unfortunately, the officer who had the letter did not deliver it until this past spring. He feared it getting lost, and so he brought it himself. If not for me, Walter would not be dead."

Her heart went out to him at the fissure of guilt that ran through his voice with his words. "You did not make him ill."

"No, but he'd have not been there had I possessed the funds for him to live like a gentleman. The income from my estates is dwindling. I couldn't support him in the manner in which he wished to live, so we agreed that a commission in the army was best. Not an hour passes by that I don't miss him, not a day goes by that I don't regret not finding another way. I could have married any number of women with dowries that would have provided me with the means to live more luxuriously. Instead, I was holding out for love. I was waiting for you."

She did not move away when his lips joined hers. His tongue stroked the seam of her mouth, urging her to open it for him. She shouldn't have, but she did, because if she was honest with herself, she would admit that she had been waiting for him as well. She'd had offers for marriage during her first Season, but she'd turned them all away, had thought perhaps she would be more content as a spinster. Until the ball when she spied him across the room, that is. When their eyes had met, it was as though he were standing right in front of her, touching her, gazing into her soul, weaving some sort of spell over her. When he'd asked her to dance, she'd thought she'd arrived in heaven.

Then this Season when he'd informed her that he would be pursuing Lady Anne, she'd wondered what she had done to douse the passion that had trembled on the edge between them.

Yet here it was again, blazing to life.

She twisted around completely, giving him easier access to her mouth, and with a deep growl he deepened the kiss, threading the fingers of one hand through the tangled mess of her hair and holding her in place, while the other hand stroked her back, squeezed a shoulder, skimmed down her side, and came around to cup her breast.

She knew she should be incensed with the liberties he was taking. Instead, she moaned softly and took both her hands over a similar journey, noting the corded muscles of his back, the flatness of his stomach, the breadth of his chest. Smooth. Silk over steel. It was as though he'd been forged by the gods. His clothing hid well his attributes, and she felt as though she were discovering little buried treasures.

Dragging his mouth along the arch of her throat, he rasped, "I want you, Merry. You can't imagine how much I want you."

Oh, she could imagine it very well, because she wanted him. As wrong as it was, she wanted him with an intensity that fairly threatened to destroy her. When Litton had kissed her in the garden, she hadn't wanted to melt into him, to meld her body with his. With Chetwyn, all rational thought scattered away like dried leaves before an autumn breeze. She couldn't think, didn't want to think, wanted only to feel the eager press of his hands, the hunger of his mouth against her flesh.

Shifting his weight, he carried her down to their make-shift velveteen bed. She thought the thickest of mattresses could not be more welcoming. Rising above her, he stared down on her. She combed her fingers through his unruly locks before bringing her palms down to cradle his jaw. The rough bristles tickled her tender skin.

"I was a fool, Merry," he whispered. "Misguided, trying to do right by my brother, putting my own wants, needs, and happiness aside. I want you. I *need* you. You bring me happiness such as I've never known. Let me show you how much I can love you."

She swallowed hard. She knew he wasn't speaking of flowers or poetry or chocolates. He wanted to give of himself, completely and absolutely. He wanted her to freely accept what he was offering. When they were discovered here, the scandal would be insurmountable. Alone with him through the storm. Litton would let her go. Her father would insist Chetwyn marry her. She would be ruined. She might as well be ruined in truth.

Besides, she desired him with a fervor that she thought would be her undoing. If she didn't have him at that moment, she would probably die anyway. Reaching up, she placed her hand on the nape of his neck and brought him down.

He latched his mouth onto hers with a fierceness that matched the storm. Hot, heavy, and passionate as though walls existed that needed to be torn down. He made short work of removing the covers that separated them, and then they were bare flesh against bare flesh from top to toe. Velvety warmth that could have melted the thickest pond surrounded them. She felt her heart's resistance giving way inch by inch as his hands and fingers explored her, while hers did the same with him. Broad shoulders, strong back, taut buttocks.

He had rescued her from the pond, guided her through the storm, and created a haven for them to wait out the screeching winds. He had managed to hold her fears at bay, and she'd known that somehow he would save her.

A small part of her wondered if he was saving her now as well.

She couldn't marry Litton after this. She wouldn't marry him. One night he had pursued her with purpose. But once her hand and dowry were secured, passion, desire, whatever it was that had led them into the garden had taken refuge, never to be seen again. With Chetwyn, it always hovered near the surface, threatened to join them, promised to carry them to exalted heights.

Here she was, clamoring up those heights, unafraid as Chetwyn's mouth trailed over every inch of her, exploring, enticing, kissing provocatively. The bend of her elbow, the back of her knee, the turn of her ankle, the tip of her tiny toe. Down, up, over, and around. He left no part of her untouched.

His mouth returned to hers as he nestled himself between her thighs. She felt the pressure of him, the weight, the heat. She lifted her hips to receive him. Holding back her cry at the sharp pain as he sank fully into her, she concentrated on his mouth, its texture, its flavor. She focused on his hair, the strands that were never tamed for long.

His movements were slow, leisurely. The pain eased, and pleasure slipped in to replace it, sweet and ripe, like a new bud feeling the sun coaxing it up. With each petal unfurled, the pleasure increased. Thrashing her head from side to side, she anchored herself to him as he took her on a journey for which there were no words.

She cried out as the release slammed into her, as her world darkened, then exploded into light. With a rough groan, he gave a final thrust and stilled, his arms closing more tightly around her. Lethargy worked its way through her.

The last thing she heard was his whispered, "I love you," before sleep claimed her.

Chapter Six

Iᴛ ᴡᴀꜱ ᴛʜᴇ baying of the hounds that woke her. Nestled against Chetwyn beneath the draperies, her cheek against his chest, she became acutely aware of his stiffening.

"It's morning. The storm's passed," he said before throwing back the covering and coming to his feet.

In fascination, she watched his bare backside as he strode to the window. The light from the dying fire was enough to give her an impressive view. He was quite marvelously carved of flesh, muscle, sinew, and bone.

"A search party," he continued before turning about and heading back toward her.

Did it make her a wanton because she couldn't help but smile at the sight of him?

"Is my father among them?" she asked.

"Afraid so. Your brothers, too, from the looks of it. Litton and both Pembrook lords."

After gathering up his clothes, he knelt beside her and cradled her face. "Tell them you made your way here, but the storm prevented you from going farther, and you've been waiting it out."

"I don't understand. You'll be here."

He stroked her cheek, and the sadness in his eyes almost made her weep. "No. I won't have your reputation dragged through the mud by having us found together."

She flattened her hand against his chest. "But the discovery of us together will ensure that we marry. My father will very well insist."

He brought her in close, then tucked her beneath his chin. "I want you, Merry, more than I've ever wanted anything in my life, but not at the risk of bringing you shame or more pain than I've already caused. Nor will I do as Litton and force you into marriage." Dipping his head, he kissed her short and sweet, but in the tenderness of the moment she heard volumes: love, caring, goodbye.

Then he was rushing out of the room as though the hounds of hell were nipping at his heels, while the duke's hounds were barking more loudly with their approaching nearness. Feeling lost and bereft, she went through the motions of slipping back into her stiff but dried riding habit. She was buttoning up the last of the pearl disks when she heard a door slam open and the stomp of feet.

Her father was the first to come barging through the doorway. "Meredith, thank God. What in the blazes happened, girl?"

"I . . . I got caught in the storm. I wanted to go ice skating."

Litton approached and swept his coat around her. "You must have been terrified."

"Only of the ghosts. I've heard the manor is haunted."

"The tower and the dungeon," the duke said, studying her carefully. "Not the manor itself."

"Well, then, I had nothing to fear."

"I don't suppose you've seen Lord Chetwyn," Lord Tristan asked. "We've not been able to find him."

Her mouth dry, she shook her head. "No, our paths didn't cross, but I'm certain he's all right. He probably just went for a walk. But he's familiar enough with the outdoors that he would have taken shelter."

Litton placed his arm around her shoulders. "Come, we must get you back to the residence. You must be famished."

"Quite."

She allowed him to lead her from the room but she couldn't help glancing back over her shoulder. Lord Tristan had a speculative gleam in his eyes as he studied the mound of draperies. He had a reputation for being quite the rogue, and she hoped he couldn't guess what had truly transpired here.

FROM THE MASTER'S bedchamber upstairs, Chetwyn watched as the search party headed back toward the manor. For a few hours, he held in his arms every dream he'd ever dreamed, and once again he'd let her go.

To have her, he would have to ruin her, and he loved her far too much for that. But neither could he bear the thought of her with Litton.

"Thought I'd find you somewhere about."

He spun around at the sound of Lord Tristan's voice.

"Trying to protect the lady's reputation?" Lord Tristan asked.

Chetwyn sighed. "I seem to recall your doing a very similar thing for Anne."

"And it almost cost me a life of happiness."

"I could never be happy if Meredith suffered because of scandal."

Lord Tristan ambled over, leaned against the window casing, and looked out. "Suppose I could say that I found you in the tower."

Chetwyn shook his head. "Too close."

"The abbey ruins then. We shall have to wait here for an hour or so to make that believable."

With a nod, Chetwyn pressed his back to the wall and slid down to the floor. He glanced up as Tristan offered him a silver flask. He said nothing as he took it and drank deeply. Rum. It might warm the coldness that had settled in his chest when he'd watched Meredith walk away without looking back.

Chapter Seven

MEREDITH AWOKE IN a fog. She remembered the warm bath, the tray of food, and the bed covers slipped over her. She'd fought off sleep, wanting to wait until Chetwyn returned, but exhaustion had claimed her. Rolling onto her side, she stared at the burgundy draperies, thinking of others that she'd recently encountered. They were drawn aside, and through the windowpane she could see the darkness. She'd slept through the day. They'd missed the play. Tonight was the ball. She needed to get dressed and see how Chetwyn was. She knew Lord Tristan had stayed behind to continue searching for him. She wondered if he'd found him or if Chetwyn had made his own way here.

Reaching over, she yanked on her bell pull to summon the maid who had been assigned to her. When the door opened, however, it was Lady Anne who walked through.

"Oh, finally, you're awake."

"Lord Chetwyn?"

"Doing remarkably well. Tristan announced that he found him at the abbey ruins, although I shall eat my favorite bonnet if Tristan truly found him there and not at the castle."

Meredith felt the heat suffuse her face. While she didn't know Lady Anne well, they shared a common interest: Chetwyn. Meredith felt as though she could trust her with anything involving him. "He didn't want us to be found together."

"No, he wouldn't have, now, would he?"

"Why do you say that?"

"Because I know him well enough to know that he would give to you what he once gave to me."

With her brow furrowed, Meredith stared at her. "What was that?"

"The gift of choice."

AS MEREDITH DESCENDED the stairs, she could hear the orchestra playing a quadrille, the first dance of the night, according to the dance card that the duchess had given her. She much preferred the waltz. She considered going to the grand salon. Instead, she turned into the parlor and walked over to the small decorated tree that sat on a table near a window. Tiny boxes were gathered beneath the boughs. Meredith had little doubt that they contained treats that the duchess would pass out to her guests tomorrow upon their parting. She would return home to spend the holiday with her family, and a few days afterward she would be moving into the residence she would share with Litton. Where she would share his bed. Where he would touch her and kiss her and bring her pleasure, and she would do the same with him.

And all the while she would think of Chetwyn, who could have stayed by her side this morning. Then she would be marrying him. In the years to come, would each have wondered if the person sitting across the table was the one they would have chosen—if given a choice?

Only she had a choice. Chetwyn had ensured it by leaving.

"Oh, there you are. I'd heard you were finally up and about."

Turning slightly, she smiled at Litton. "Yes, I had quite the lovely nap."

"Let's go have our dance, shall we?"

"How many?" she asked.

"Pardon?"

"How many dances?"

"Well, two, of course. The first and the last."

"And in between?"

"You shall dance with others, and I shall play cards."

Four dances the night they met. She wondered how long it would be before he desired only one . . . and then none.

She swallowed hard, considering if she really wanted to know the truth, but she had to put the niggling doubts to rest. "The night when we were discovered kissing in the garden, during Greystone's ball—I heard my father and brothers coming."

He stared at her as though she'd lost her senses. "As did I."

"I tried to slip away, so we wouldn't be caught. You held me tight and whispered that it would be all right."

He smiled. "And it did turn out all right, didn't it?"

"Would you have held me so tightly if I had no dowry?"

He laughed. "Now you're being silly. Let's go join the merriment."

He took her arm, and she shook him off. "I'm serious, Litton. We had time *not* to get caught."

"I wanted to marry you," he said impatiently. "Is that suddenly a crime?"

"Not a crime, but not entirely right, either." She thought of the kiss that Chetwyn had bestowed upon her in the billiards room. Then again when they were walking. At the castle. It was as though he couldn't get enough of her, would never have enough of her. "Do you know that we have not kissed once since that night? Not once."

"I took liberties that night I should not have taken. I've been trying to spare you any further gossip."

She narrowed her eyes. "So you did tell people about the kiss in the garden."

He shrugged. "Only as a precaution."

"Against what?"

"Your father changing his mind and thinking that it didn't matter, that our marriage was not in order."

She gave a light laugh. "Since he's withdrawn the dowry, that's not likely to happen, as he knows no one else will have me now."

He grabbed her arms, jerked her. "What are you talking about?"

Not a lie, she told herself, but a small test. "My father has decided, based upon the recent worry I caused him, that I shall not come with a dowry."

Releasing her, he plowed his hands through his hair. "I won't have it. We discussed the settlement. Granted, we haven't signed the papers, but I was depending on that dowry to cover my gaming debts. I shall have a word—"

"Don't bother," she said. "I shan't be marrying you, with or without the dowry."

He narrowed his eyes. "Have you been testing me? You silly girl, I'll tell everyone what happened in the garden. Your reputation will be ruined. No one will have you."

"I think you may be wrong on that score." At least she hoped he was. But even if he wasn't, as she walked from the room, she realized that she'd been spared making a grave mistake.

"—TWENTY STITCHES PER INCH."

Chetwyn tried to look impressed with his present dance partner's sewing skills, but the truth was that Lady Beatrix's words merely collided together as they bombarded his ears and made no sense. He'd heard that Merry had recovered from her ordeal and would be coming to the ballroom before the night was done, so he was trying to distract himself. A part of him wished desperately that he had stayed by her side at the castle. It would have ensured she became his wife.

But he didn't want her forced into something she might not want. He just didn't know where he would find the strength to stay away from her once she married Litton. But stay away he would, because the last thing he wanted was her unhappiness.

"Pardon me."

At the tap on his shoulder, he came to an abrupt halt and almost forgot to breathe. Merry stood there in a striking red velvet dress with white trim. She smiled at him, and this time his heart nearly forgot to beat. Then she turned her attention to Lady Beatrix.

"Forgive me for interrupting, but a gentleman asked me to give this to you," she said, holding out a slip of paper.

"Oh." Lady Beatrix took it, unfolded it, and read it. She blinked her eyes. "Who gave this to you?"

"He asked me not to say. He wanted to remain a bit mysterious, I think. But I am given to understand that he is quite impressed with your sewing skills."

Lady Beatrix brightened. "Indeed. I knew some gentleman would eventually appreciate them." She looked at Chetwyn. "If you will excuse me, my lord, I must see to this."

"By all means. Who am I to stand in the way of true love?"

Lady Beatrix gave a tiny squeal before hurrying from the room.

Chetwyn studied Meredith. "What have you done, Merry?"

"I wanted to dance with you."

"Well, then, allow me the honor."

Taking her in his arms, he swept her over the dance floor. "Who was the note from?"

She smiled. "Me, of course. It said only, 'Meet me in the library.'"

"At least she'll be warm."

Her smile grew. "And not alone. I saw Lord Wexford going in there on my way here."

He laughed. "Jolly good."

She blushed. "Who knows? Perhaps something will come of it."

Tightening his hold on her, he asked, "And what of us? Will anything come of us?"

"I'm not quite sure. It depends on you, I suppose. You should know that within my pocket I have a slip of paper for every lady you intend to dance with tonight. I want all of your dances."

"You shall have them."

"You should also be aware that Father threatened to take away my dowry if I didn't marry Litton. I suppose he knew I had reservations and thought to dispense with them. I don't know if he'll carry through on his threat."

"I've told you before that I don't give a damn about your dowry."

She took a deep breath. "I don't love Litton. I never did, but he seemed a pleasant enough sort, and he made me feel appreciated. I thought I would be content with him, but then I discovered something I wanted more. Just a few moments ago, I cried off with him. He plans to tell everyone about the tryst in the garden. I shall be ruined."

"Lovely chap. I shall introduce him to my fist later. But right this moment you do know that the best way to stop gossip is to give people something far more interesting to talk about."

She nodded. "I never stopped loving you."

His heart contracted, then expanded, and he thought it might burst through his chest. "That's good, because I have loved you from the night we met, and I shall love you until the day I die."

"Then kiss me now."

And he did. He stopped dancing, folded his arms around her, and lowered his mouth to hers. He heard the slowing of feet, a few gasps, some chuckles, a clap or two. Yes, they would be the talk of high society. But he wasn't quite done.

Breaking off the kiss, he held her warm gaze for but a moment before going down on bended knee and taking her hand.

All dancing halted. The music stopped.

"Merry, will you do me the honor of becoming my wife, my marchioness, the mother of my children? Will you be my love for as long as I draw breath?"

Tears welled in her eyes, as she pressed a trembling hand to her lips. "Oh, Chetwyn, yes, of course."

Taking from his pocket a ring with small emeralds that matched her eyes, he slipped it onto her finger. At her stunned expression, he couldn't help but smile. "I told you, Merry, that first night that you were the reason I was here. Happy Christmas, my love."

Standing, he kissed her again as a rousing cheer went up from those who surrounded them. As her arms closed around his neck, he pulled her in against the curve of his body and held her tighter. It was going to be a very lovely Christmas for them both. The first of many.

No Groom at the Inn

MEGAN FRAMPTON

Agamist:

1. A person opposed to the institution of matrimony.

2. A thick fog specific to bodies of fresh water.

3. A compound of iron and salt.

Chapter One

1844
A coaching inn
One lady, no chickens

"Poultry."

Sophronia gazed down into her glass of ale and repeated the word, even though she was only talking to herself. "Poultry."

It didn't sound any better the second time she said it, either.

The letter from her cousin had detailed all of the delights waiting for her when she arrived—taking care of her cousin's six children (his wife had died, perhaps of exhaustion), overseeing the various village celebrations including, her cousin informed her with no little enthusiasm, the annual Tribute to the Hay, which was apparently the highlight of the year, and taking care of the chickens.

All twenty-seven of them.

Not to mention she would be arriving just before Christmas, which meant gifts and merriment and conviviality. Those weren't bad things, of course, it was just that celebrating the season was likely the last thing she wanted to do.

Well, perhaps after taking care of the chickens.

The holidays used to be one of her favorite times of year—she and her father both loved playing holiday games, especially ones like Charades or Dictionary.

Even though he was the word expert in the family, eventually she had been able to fool him with her Dictionary definitions, and there was nothing so wonderful as seeing his dumbstruck expression when she revealed that, no, he had not guessed the correct definition.

He was always so proud of her for that, for being able to keep up with him and his linguistic interests.

And now nobody would care that she was inordinately clever at making up definitions for words she'd never heard of.

She gave herself a mental shake, since she'd promised not to become maudlin. Especially at this time of the year.

She glanced around the barroom she was sitting in, taking note of the other occupants. Like the inn itself, they were plain but tidy. As she was, as well, even if her clothing had started out, many years ago, as grander than theirs.

She unfolded the often-read letter, suppressing a sigh at her cousin's crabbed handwriting. Not that handwriting was indicative of a person's character—that would be their words—but the combination of her cousin's script and the way he assumed she would be delighted to perform all the tasks he was graciously setting before her—that was enough to make her dread the next phase of her life. Which would last until—well, that she didn't know.

Sophronia was grateful, she was, for being offered a place to live, and she didn't want to seem churlish. It was just that she had never imagined that the care and feeding of poultry—not to mention six children—would be her fate.

She hadn't been raised to think too highly of herself, an impoverished earl's daughter couldn't, no matter her bloodlines. But she'd thought her father had put by enough money to see her through to find a cottage somewhere, somewhere to live with her books, and her wit, and her faithful maid, after he'd left this mortal coil. But while her father had been very specific when it came to ordering which text of ancient Greek poems would suit his needs the best, he had been less so when it came time to providing for his daughter's future after his eventual, and inevitable, demise.

He'd left her with practically nothing, in fact.

Hence the chickens.

Which was why she had spent a few precious pennies on a last glass of ale at the coaching inn where she was waiting for the mail coach to arrive and take her to the far reaches of beyond. A last moment of being by herself, being Lady Sophronia, not Sophy the Chicken Lady.

The one without a feather to fly with.

Chuckling at her own wit, she picked her glass up and gave a toast to the as yet imaginary chickens, thinking about how she'd always imagined her life would turn out.

There were no members of the avian community at all in her rosy vision of the future.

Not that she was certain what her rosy vision of the future would include, but she was fairly certain it did not have fowl of any kind.

She shook her head at her own foolishness, knowing she was giving in to self-pity by bemoaning her lot. It was more than many women had, even ladies of her station. She might have to take care of children and chickens—hopefully in that order—but she would have a roof over her head, food to eat, and clothing to wear. Perhaps the holiday season would be one of celebration. Celebrating a roof over her head, for one thing.

"All aboard to Chester," a voice boomed through the room. Immediately there were the bustling sounds of people getting up, gathering their things, saying their last goodbyes.

Sophronia didn't have anyone to say goodbye to. Her maid, Maria, had found another position, even though she'd wept and clung to Sophronia until the very last minute. But Sophronia's cousin had made it very clear the invitation was for one lady in distressed circumstances—namely, Sophronia—and there was no room nor salary for a lady's maid.

So she drained her ale and stood, rising up on her tiptoes for one last stretch. As tall as she was, it was difficult for her to retain any kind of comfort in a crowded coach for any period of time, and she knew the journey would be a long one.

That she would be cramped and uncomfortable for longer than the actual coach journey was a truth she was finding very hard to ignore.

"Excuse me, miss," a gentleman said in her ear. She jumped, so lost in her own foolish (fowlish?) thoughts that she hadn't even noticed him approaching her.

She turned and looked at him, blinking at his splendor. He was tall, taller than she, even, which was a rarity among gentlemen. He was handsome in a dashing rosy-visioned way that made her question just what her imagination was thinking if it had never inserted him—or someone who looked like him—into her dreams.

He had unruly dark brown hair, longer than most gentlemen wore. The ends curled up as though even his hair was irrepressible. His eyes were blue, and even in the dark gloom, she could see they practically twinkled.

As though he and she shared a secret, a lovely, wonderful, delightful secret.

Never mind that all those words were very similar to one another. Her word-specific father would reprimand her, if that gentle soul could reprimand someone, that is, and if he heard how cavalierly she was tossing out adjectives that all meant nearly the same thing.

But he wasn't here, was he, which was why she was here, and now she was about to find out why this other he was here.

Far too many pronouns. Her attention returned to the tall, charming stranger.

Who was talking to her. Waiting for her response, actually, since she had spent a minute or so contemplating his general magnificence. And words, and her father, and whatever other non-chickened thoughts had blessedly crossed her mind.

"Can I help you, sir?" Sophronia asked. He was probably lost on his way to the Handsome Hotel where they only allowed Exceedingly Handsome guests.

That he might think she'd know where the Handsome Hotel was gave her pause. Because she was not handsome, not at all.

But what he said next was even more unexpected than being asked to provide directions to some establishment where one's appearance was the only requirement for entry.

"Would you marry me?" he said in a normal tone of voice, as though he hadn't just upended Sophronia's entire world.

Cachinnator:

1. One who cashes in on an opportunity.

2. A loud or immoderate laugher.

3. The element of a spinning wheel that feeds the wool through.

Chapter Two

"IT WILL BE two weeks. At most, three." His mother beamed at him, as though the prospect of a house party in the country during the holiday season with people he did not know was some sort of rare treat.

It most definitely was not.

Jamie began to walk around the room, unable to stay seated for longer than a few minutes, at least when he was at his mother's house. Which usually made him regret being so generous to her, since she had most of the things he'd sent her on display, which made walking around even harder. "And who will be in attendance?" There had to be a reason she was so insistent he accompany her. It wasn't just that she didn't get to see him enough; he knew that look in her eye. The one that said, "I've got plans for Jamie, and they are probably going to bring him very little joy." Not that she thought that, of course. She only thought about what she thought he might like, and he always felt like the worst kind of ungrateful wretch when it turned out he did not like what she'd presented, whether it was a special meal, or a new watch, or a house party when he'd rather just stay in London, when everyone else was gone.

He'd gotten very good at pretending to be pleased when that was not what he was at all. But that was better than watching her face fall in disappointment.

He'd seen how his father hadn't been able to pretend,

how it ate away at him. How he compromised what he truly wanted in order to keep someone else happy. Jamie was determined not to let that happen to him.

She shrugged, as though it wasn't important. Which only meant that it absolutely was. "The Martons, the Viscount Waxford and his family, and Mrs. Loring and her daughter. Oh, plus the hosts, of course. The Greens are the loveliest people."

"And how many of them have unmarried daughters?"

She shifted in her seat.

Jamie stopped pacing to look at his mother. "That many, hm?"

She couldn't seem to quite meet his eyes. "Well, I have heard that Lady Marigold Waxford is a beauty. All golden curls and bright blue eyes. The Greens' daughter is apparently quite studious, she is usually away at school, but has returned home for the holidays. She has quite a tidy fortune, and is said to be a good conversationalist. And the other two, well yes, they have daughters who are friends with the Green girl."

Jamie swallowed through a suddenly thick throat. "Four young ladies, then?" Could just the thought of four young women at a house party make a person choke to death?

It felt like that, even though he desperately hoped not.

But his mother wasn't paying attention to how difficult it was for him to breathe, nor could she know how her words seemed to wrap themselves around his neck. "You never know, James, when you might find someone you like. When are you going to settle down?"

Jamie opened his mouth to reply, but snapped it shut as he thought about her question. *When are you going to settle down, Jamie?*

It was a question she had been asking, off and on, since the first time he had left England to go on one of his "funny trips," as she called them.

That his funny trips were as necessary to him as breathing wasn't something they discussed. He'd tried to, once, but she'd merely grabbed her handkerchief and sobbed quietly into it as he told her how he felt as though he might explode if he stayed in one place too long.

He had seen the same thing play out when he was a child, when his father tried to change the way things were. It just wasn't done. Which was why Jamie had to do it.

It wasn't as though he didn't love his mother; he did. And it wasn't as though he needed the money that his funny trips brought. His father had left him more than enough money, even if all the elder Mr. Archer had done was sit on a sofa and drink wine. No, Jamie lived for the adventure of it, the finding of a treasure that was hidden in plain sight, something that only he could discern. He was doing the thing his father, he thought, had always wanted to do himself. Finding treasures.

Jamie always brought the treasure back to England and sold it to someone who craved adventure as much as he did, but had to be content with experiencing it through objects, not actual living. He rarely kept a treasure, not for himself.

If Jamie ever stopped, he thought he might die.

And yet—and yet sometimes, when he was lying awake at night in another place that wasn't England, he wondered if it was enough.

Of course it is, his mind would go on to assert.

But his heart begged to differ.

"Actually, Mother, I have something to tell you," he began, knowing he was making possibly the stupidest decision he'd ever made—and that included the purchase of something he'd thought was an ancient papyrus that turned out to be a creative child's way of demonstrating how annoying she thought her parents were—but unable to stop himself once he'd started. "I am betrothed."

For once, his mother had nothing to say.

AS SOON AS the proposal left his mouth, Jamie had the urge to punch himself in the face.

Judging by the expression on the lady's face, she felt the same way.

At least they were in agreement.

He closed his eyes and grimaced. "That wasn't exactly what I meant," he said, letting out a deep breath as he spoke.

"So you're saying you don't wish to marry me?" At least she wasn't screaming or hitting him. That was something.

"No, I mean, yes, I mean—" He gestured at the chair she'd just risen from. "Could we sit down and discuss this?"

She glanced over his shoulder, a concerned look knitting her brows together. "I am supposed to get on the mail coach, the one leaving in a few minutes."

"This will take only a few minutes to explain," Jamie replied, hoping to God it was true.

She tilted her head and gave him a look of appraisal, then nodded her head. "Very well. Only a minute, mind you. I can't be late for the chickens."

Jamie opened his mouth to ask about that, but snapped it shut again as she sat. He didn't have time to ask questions about what she might possibly mean, not when his future as an unencumbered bachelor was at stake.

He sat down, as well, scooting his chair forward so he could speak quietly to her. *Speaking in a low voice will not make this any less outrageous*, a voice in his head reminded him.

But it could perhaps persuade her that he was not actually insane. Or remarkably presumptuous.

"The thing is," he said, speaking both quickly and quietly, "I am in need of a fiancée, but just for a short time." Judging by the expression on her face, he was not doing any better at explaining himself. "The thing is," he said again, wishing he could just snatch her up and present her to his mother without having to bother about explanations and such, "I might have just told my mother I am engaged to be married."

"And you are not." It seemed she understood a bit of it, at least.

"No. Nor do I wish to be."

"Despite what you just asked me." Now she sounded amused, and he allowed himself to feel a little hope that she would understand him, at least, even if he failed to convince her to help him.

He had to admit he hadn't planned on asking a random stranger to marry him—few people did—but when he'd burst out of his mother's house, having told her he was engaged, of all things, he'd known that a drink was in order, and he also knew where the nearest place to obtain said drink was.

And then he'd strode in, desperate and thirsty, and had seen her. A slender woman sitting by herself, looking off in the distance like some wise goddess, Athena or Minerva or whatever she was called, a simple traveling bag at her feet, a worn cloak wrapped around her against the cold.

She was entirely alone. Alone and traveling during one of the coldest months of the year, close to the holidays when families got together. Only he didn't think she was going to her family—her expression would have been expectant, not resigned. Unless she had an unpleasant family, in which case perhaps she would be just as happy to leave with him as on the mail coach.

He liked to think he was a better choice than an unpleasant family, especially given what he had to offer her.

"My mother is here, living in London, only she's taken it in her head to go to a house party in the country, and there are many unattached young ladies there. And, and you haven't met my mother—"

"I haven't even met you," she interrupted in a tart tone.

"Right, well, Mr. James Archer at your service." He held

his hand out and she regarded it with one arched eyebrow, as though contemplating what he might do if she allowed him to take her hand.

It honestly hadn't occurred to him to do anything, but now that she had that eyebrow raised, and her manner seemed to waver between entertained and aghast, he wondered just what she'd do if he took her hand and walked her out of the inn.

Probably scream. So that was not a good idea.

Thankfully, she did allow him to grasp her hand for a brief handshake. "I am Lady Sophronia Bettesford," she replied. She spoke in a measured way, as though every word was held up for examination before being released from her lips.

"It is a pleasure to make your acquaintance, Lady Sophronia." Jamie tried to summon up his most charming smile, but even with his ingenuity with women, he was at a loss when confronted with this situation—how did one behave toward a woman one might have deliberately not proposed to?

"And yours, Mr. Archer." She glanced to the door, where people were lining up to board the coach, presumably. "But I do have to be on that coach, and while I appreciate the opportunity not to marry you, I cannot take any more time."

She had a title—he hadn't anticipated that; he'd just seen she was Quality. She was well spoken, she seemed to take things in stride, and she was relatively attractive.

He was not going to find a better potential bride-not-to-be anywhere.

"What would it take for you to do this? It would last a month, at most, and then you could get on your coach and go to wherever you are planning to go." He heard the desperation in his voice, and hoped it would sway her toward him, rather than making her want to run away.

She knitted her brow and stared at him, so intently he

had the feeling she could see inside to his soul. Hopefully she'd see how much he wanted his mother to be happy, not any of the things he knew might make him seem to be a bad person—his ability to talk a potential seller into letting go of that treasure for a lower price than the seller had asked for, his equal ability to persuade women to give up their treasures in bed, his need to be on the go, constantly.

His selfish wish to live the life he wanted even though it might—it did—hurt his mother.

"I would want enough to purchase a cottage somewhere. I have no idea what that would cost, and it is likely far more than you'd want to pay for a pretend betrothed," she said, lifting her chin as though in defiance. As though now he was the one who might run away screaming. "And I would want your assurance that this is all the time you would require of me, that you wouldn't need me to return and pretend to be your wife or anything later on." She took a deep breath. "If you can give me those things, I will do this for you."

"Last call to Chester!"

They both glanced to the door, to where the stable boy was calling.

"Well?" she asked, reaching down to her valise.

"Done," he said. His happiness and his mother's happiness—in opposition to one another—were worth whatever he'd have to pay.

"Then we have a bargain, Mr. Archer," she replied, raising her hand from the valise's handle and holding it out to him.

"A bargain," he repeated, shaking her hand.

Otosis:

1. A skin affliction that causes discoloration.

2. Mishearing; alteration of words caused by an erroneous apprehension of the sound.

3. Remaining in a state of suspension.

Chapter Three

"YOUR PURCHASING CLOTHING for me is not part of our bargain," Sophronia said as she walked hurriedly after Mr. Archer—her new betrothed.

He turned to look at her, a roguish smile on his lips. He had a remarkably lovely mouth for someone who appeared so otherwise masculine. Not that lovely mouths weren't masculine, but she had never actually noticed a gentleman's mouth before.

Now it seemed that was all she could think of. Well, that and that he was determined to buy clothing for her, when she was perfectly capable of buying her own.

Except she really wasn't. She hadn't even tried to get her money back for the coach. She knew that would be a fruitless endeavor, and what with the ale she'd bought and the rest of the money she'd carefully secured away so she could eat on the journey—she might have had enough for one sleeve.

And, her new betrothed told her, they were on their way to a house party. One where getting appropriately dressed was one of the ladies' primary activities.

So while she could object, she knew he was right. She just didn't want to make him spend more than he already had to—she was fairly certain that fake betrotheds, if there was a market price for them, cost far less than what she had demanded.

Who was to say he wouldn't find another, less expensive betrothed somewhere?

But meanwhile, as soon as they'd shaken hands, he'd taken her from the inn and began walking, very quickly, toward a place he assured her would have gowns suitable for her, and that could be made in time so they could make the journey the day after next.

"Excuse me, Mr. Archer?" she ventured, wondering how he could walk so fast without it seeming to be a strain. Likely something to do with his long legs.

And now here she was thinking about his legs, and the long strength of them, in addition to his mouth.

Perhaps by the time their month together was complete she would have inventoried his entire self.

Although that was not something she should be contemplating.

"If we are to persuade people as to our relationship, Lady Sophronia, you should call me James. Or Jamie, that is what my mother calls me," he said, flinging the words over his shoulder without losing his speed. "And I will call you— Sophy? My lamb? Sophycakes?"

"Sophronia will do just fine," Sophronia replied, as stiffly as she could manage given that she wanted to laugh— Sophycakes?

"Sophronia is not nearly as much fun," he returned.

He had a point.

"But what did you want to ask, Sophronia?" She didn't have to see his face to know he was smiling—he spoke as though they were both in on the joke, whatever the joke was.

She hadn't felt as though she'd been included in anything even close to a joke for a long time. It felt—lovely. Nice. Wonderful.

Again, she heard her father chastising her for saying basically the same thing three different times, but "lovely" was sufficiently different from "nice" and "wonderful," wasn't it? And now she felt all three.

"I don't have a place to stay this evening. If you know of a respectable hotel," *and can pay my bill*, "I can stay there this evening, and then join you on the journey to"—and she didn't even know where they were going—"to the house party."

He stopped and spun around to face her, so abruptly it made her gasp. But then again, that could be because she was struck, again, by just how handsome he was. Would anyone believe he had chosen her? It wasn't that she thought ill of herself—she didn't—but she did know that while nobody would bat an eye at his taking up residence in the Handsome Hotel, they would likely quibble if she were to attempt to book a room at the female equivalent—the Pulchritudinous Pub, for example, or perhaps the Ideal Inn.

Somewhere, she heard her father cheering her expansive language.

"You can stay at my house," he began, only to hold his hands out to her as he saw her reaction. "That is, at my mother's house. I am staying there as well, but she will be a more than suitable chaperone. Besides," he added, his mouth quirking up in a rueful smile, "she will have many questions to ask you." He frowned, as though struck by something. "We need to get you a lady's maid, however. Mother will know something is awry if you just appear alone."

Sophronia's heart leapt. Of course, she would be able to be reunited with Maria, who was spending her last night of freedom at her sister's house in Cheapside. "I have a lady's maid I can obtain, that is no worry at all."

"Good, good," he said distractedly. "You can send a note to retrieve her while you are being fitted at Madame Fairfax's establishment. And then we can return to my mother's house, and I can introduce you. We will need to better acquaint ourselves with one another so as to make our story plausible."

The enormity of what she—what they—were doing struck Sophronia so sharply she gasped again, and this time it was not in appreciation of his pulchritude.

"It will be fine, you will see." It was as if he had read her mind, even though not a moment ago it had seemed he had been thinking of something else entirely.

"Yes, I just—" She paused, then blurted it all out. "I just want to be certain you will not regret this, we don't even know how much it will cost for a cottage, and then there's the expense of the clothing, and my maid, and the travel, and—" She heard her words roll faster and faster, and her heart sped up in rhythm.

"Breathe, Sophronia," he replied, taking her hands in his. She gazed down at his fingers, noting how large they were, but still shapely, sprinkled with hair on the back of his hand.

She had moved on from his mouth and legs, it seemed. She heard herself laugh, a breathy, nearly hysterical laugh, and felt the rush of what this could mean for her—for her whole future.

She couldn't ruin this, either for him or for herself. The rest of her life depended on it.

Taking a deep breath, she lifted her head and looked into his eyes. "I am breathing, James," she said in a measured tone. Close-ish to the way she normally spoke, at least. "Thank you for the kind offer," she said, feeling her mouth curl up in a half smile. "I promise you, I will do my best to be the betrothed you require."

He lifted her hand to his mouth and kissed it, keeping his gaze on her face. "We are in this together, Sophronia. I promise you in return, I will uphold my end of the bargain and will also do my best to be the betrothed you are worthy of."

Her throat got thick at hearing the obvious sincerity in his voice. And then she wondered if she was getting into even more than what she'd expected.

JAMIE TOOK HIS betrothed's arm—Sophronia, not Sophycakes or even just plain Sophy—as they walked up the stairs to his mother's house. They'd spent two hours at the dressmaker's shop, and thankfully Madame Fairfax had exercised discretion, not commenting on how this young lady was so markedly different in looks and style than the other ladies Jamie had brought to her shop before.

He glanced over at her as they waited for the door to be opened. She was remarkably tall, so tall he would guess her to be only five or so inches shorter than he. It was refreshing not to have to bow his head down to look at her. And he found he did want to look at her—something in her face, something in her dark brown eyes, in her expression, made him want to discover who she was, why she was in that coaching inn, what made her needs so modest that a remote cottage would suit her.

He hadn't been in London or among Society so much as to have the breadth of English aristocracy at his command, so he had no idea who her father the earl had been, or where she had lived before arriving at the inn. He knew, however, that she was a lady, in more than just the titled sense; there was something so elegant about her, her movements, her way of speaking, that was both appealing and off-putting. As though she were a beautiful diamond who would cut you if you got too close.

Jamie should remind himself of that, he thought—not to get too close. She wasn't at all like any of the women he'd found intriguing before, but for some reason, she intrigued him.

"Ah, Mr. James," his mother's butler said, a welcoming smile on his face. Taylor had been with his mother for years and treated Jamie as someone to be tolerated for her sake. Jamie knew the warmth of Taylor's smile was in direct correlation to how many times his mother must have sent Taylor outside to see if her son had returned yet.

He was surprised there wasn't a path on the carpet in the hallway indicating the poor man's footsteps.

"Yes, we are back. If you could inform my mother—"

"You're back!"

"Never mind, Taylor, I see she is here." Jamie took a deep breath before turning to face his mother. This was it. He had to persuade her that not only was he betrothed, but that he was deeply in love with his bride-to-be. He knew Sophronia's favorite color was green, she preferred novels to poetry, she liked ale, and she had a way of pausing before she spoke that made him think she was truly considering her words.

He hoped his mother would keep her questions to those important topics so they wouldn't be found out.

"Allow me to introduce my betrothed," he said, drawing Sophronia forward. Her hand trembled. "Mother, this is Lady Sophronia Bettesford. Sophronia, this is my mother, Mrs. Archer."

She withdrew her hand from his arm and held it out to his mother, who gaped at it, then stepped forward and gathered Sophronia into a hug, which meant the much taller woman had to stoop to be embraced. "I am so delighted to meet you, my dear. Jamie kept you such a secret, I didn't even know he was acquainted with any lady who might be worthy of him, much less you!" She released Sophronia but kept hold of her arms, gazing up at her with an expression something close to rapture. "You are so lovely, I am certain we will be as close as though I was your own mother," she said, her words coming out in a sob.

Sophronia darted a startled look at Jamie, but her expression was serene when she looked back at his mother. "I am delighted to meet you as well, Mrs. Archer. This was all rather unexpected," she said, in such a dry tone Jamie nearly choked on his laugh, "so it is not surprising to hear this is the first time you have heard of me."

"Come into the sitting room, dear, and let me hear all about you."

His mother took Sophronia's arm and led her into the room, chattering nonstop about her general delight at Jamie having brought her home. "Even though an indication that this was happening would have been nice," she said, with a sharp look directed at Jamie. He followed them, feeling some of the knot of tension in his chest untie, just a bit, that the first encounter seemed to be going well.

Now they just had to get through the next two, perhaps three, weeks without anyone realizing they'd met only earlier in the day, and that neither one of them had any intention of marrying the other.

Jamie had once successfully negotiated the purchase of artifacts that were reportedly the only things keeping the town from being destroyed by angry gods, so he thought he could handle the relatively minor endeavor of persuading his mother and the guests at a house party that he was, indeed, engaged to be married.

Even though he rather wished he were back facing those superstitious villagers rather than attempting this subterfuge.

Vecordy:

1. Senseless, foolish.

2. A harmonious sound.

3. The change of seasons.

Chapter Four

"MY LADY!" MARIA shrieked as she was shown into Sophronia's bedroom. She'd been given the best bedroom, according to her new not-yet mother-in-law, and Sophronia had to admit it was substantially better than the place she'd lived in most recently, when she'd still held out hope that something could keep her from her cousin, and his chickens.

And now, just when she had given up and was resolutely headed to become an unpaid chicken-and-children herder, he'd appeared.

"Maria, how lovely to see you, and isn't this incredible?"

Maria hugged her, and Sophronia felt immediately better—she had spent only a day or so on her own, without any kind of human discourse (beyond the purchasing of the coach tickets, not to mention the ale), and she hadn't realized just how bereft she had felt without anyone to connect to. Until Maria wrapped her in an embrace.

"Now, now, my lady, why are you crying?" Maria sounded perturbed, as she should—Sophronia never cried, not even when she'd come to the conclusion that her father had, indeed, left nothing for her. "Why are you here? Is there anything I can do?"

Sophronia drew back from her friend's embrace and shook her head. "I am fine, this is really an amazing story, I just—I think I am just overwhelmed."

Maria nodded toward the bed. "Let's just sit down and

you'll tell me all about it. I have to say, you could have knocked me over with a feather when the note arrived, telling me to come here posthaste."

Thankfully I will not be knocked over by any kind of feather, not if I do this properly, Sophronia thought to herself. It seemed she could leave the chickens behind, but they would not leave her.

"SO YOU JUST have to pretend to be engaged to the gentleman?" Maria said after Sophronia had related the details. Put that way, it did sound rather easy.

"Yes, and I have to persuade his mother that I am a suitable bride for her son, which is the most important element." The lady was so sweet, and obviously adored her son. Already Sophronia felt bad about her part of the deception, at fooling the woman who only wanted her son to settle down and have a family. A fact she had repeated no fewer than a half dozen times while they were having tea and getting "better acquainted."

If all the people she was to meet in the ruse were as talkative as Mrs. Archer, there would be no concern about having the lie discovered—she had barely gotten a word in edgewise, and the words were limited to "yes, please" and "just milk."

"You will do fine. And then—and then you'll have enough for us to go to the country?" Maria's tone was hopeful and wistful; they'd talked about what they wished they could do when they knew there was no chance of it. That Maria was still hesitant about the possibility made Sophronia's heart hurt, even as she was thrilled their dream could become reality.

And then what? a voice asked in her head. *You buy a cottage, you and your maid go to live there, and then what? You spend the rest of your life alone?*

She had to admit the voice had a point. She hadn't thought

much past leaving London and being able to survive without having to become a poor relation. What if that was all there was to her life? Things that were less bad than something else?

Was that a way to live? Now it was her father's voice talking to her, and she frowned. It was because of his daydreams, his refusal to settle for less than the best, to look to the future, that she had been landed here in the first place. He didn't have a say in what she was going to do for the rest of her life, given how he hadn't thought of it at all while he was alive.

She would just have to adopt her father's viewpoint, ironic though that felt; she would get to the point where she was in the cottage, but wouldn't think beyond that.

"Yes, we'll be able to go to the country, and buy a little cottage, and live there. Forever." Even to her own ears, she didn't sound delighted at the prospect, but thankfully Maria was focusing on the words, not how she said them.

"Thank you, my lady," Maria said in a fervent tone. "We will persuade all of them. We have to."

And that was the truth of it, wasn't it? "Yes, we will." Sophronia walked to the wardrobe in the corner of the room, opening the doors to reveal a few gowns that Madame Fairfax happened to have on hand. The rest she'd promised for the following day. Sophronia hated to think of what the workers would have to do to make that happen, but she needed the clothing in order to make this work, so she couldn't spare sympathy for a tired dressmaker. Hopefully the women there would be compensated. She'd tell her betrothed of her concern, perhaps ask him to send them some of what he had promised to give her. "And here are some of my disguises, so you can help me dress for dinner."

Maria followed her, her hand reaching in to touch the gowns with a near palpable reverence. "Oh, my goodness, these are lovely. Not only will we get our cottage, you'll have these gorgeous gowns, as well."

"And no chickens to waste them on," Sophronia muttered under her breath.

JAMIE WASN'T PREPARED for the sight he saw as Sophronia walked down the stairs for dinner. He'd known she was tall, and slender, but beyond that, he hadn't noticed much except her suitability for the task.

But now, dressed in one of Madame Fairfax's gowns, she was a different word than "beautiful"—she was glorious. The amber sheen of the silk brought out the gold highlights in her brown hair, and made her brown eyes glint gold, as well. The gown was simply adorned, something Madame Fairfax had insisted on, since Sophronia was so tall, and any kind of furbelow would make her look awkward.

Jamie had to admit that Madame was correct. Sophronia looked like she was a goddess in truth, descended from Mount Olympus to take pity on mere mortals by blessing them with her presence. Her figure was flattered by the cut of the gown, the soft swell of her breasts showing above the fabric, the center dipping down in a V that made him want to see what was underneath.

Her waist was tiny, and then the gown flared out below, no doubt hiding long, lissome legs. She met his gaze, a hesitant look in her eyes, and he felt his chest tighten that she didn't know, that she didn't enter the room knowing what she looked like, and the effect she was having on him.

But given that this was an entirely fake betrothal, perhaps it was good that she didn't realize any of it. He was intrigued, of course, but he most definitely did not want to become entangled—that was the whole purpose of this deception, to keep his way of life and make his mother happy.

Although the thought did cross his mind that they were technically betrothed, after all, so he might have to do some of the things one did with one's betrothed.

If one were quite, quite intrigued.

And not determined to leave the country at the earliest possible moment.

"You look lovely, Sophronia," he said, taking her hand in his and raising her fingers to his mouth. Her eyes widened as his lips made contact with her skin, and he wondered for a moment what she would do, how she would react, if he were to turn her hand over and press a kiss into her palm.

And then immediately vowed to himself he absolutely should not satisfy his curiosity. It would not be fair, either to her or to himself, to mix that possibility into their business agreement.

They were to be intimately acquainted for less than a month, and then they would leave one another, him to travel, knowing his mother was pleased, and her to her cottage, wherever that might be.

"Let us go in to dinner. Mother is waiting," he said, retaining her hand in his and leading her to the dining room.

"Just one moment, please." She sounded shaky, and he had to wonder if she was having second thoughts.

"I don't—I just wanted to say thank you for this." She uttered a little snort. "Thank you for the opportunity to pretend to be someone I am not so I can avoid having to deal with poultry for the rest of my life."

That explained the chickens—somewhat. "You are welcome," he said.

"Only," she asked, "what will you tell your mother later on? I won't be in London when this is over. How will you explain that?"

"Easy," he said smoothly. "I will make some excuse about why we have to get married elsewhere, then we will leave to do just that, and then when I return, you will be staying there, taking care of our numerous children."

She blanched. "Numerous—?"

He exhaled. "Well, that part probably isn't wise. Mother will wish to see her grandchildren. I might have to kill you off, I hope you don't mind."

Her eyebrows rose up, her eyes wide. "Kill me off? How are you going to do that?"

He waved his hand in the air. "An inconvenient snake, a village uprising. Don't be concerned, you will be far away by the time you die."

"Good to know," she replied dryly.

He hadn't quite worked out all the details, honestly, but he had to deal with the situation one step at a time. Or, rather, one false betrothal at a time. He knew well enough he could persuade his mother of anything; she had believed him when he'd told her he had developed a sudden, but not fatal, illness that could only be cured by eating an entire apple pie. He'd been five at the time. He hadn't eaten apple pie since.

"Now, let us go persuade my mother we are hopelessly in love."

He held his arm out for her, and she looped her arm through his, fitting perfectly to his side.

Her skirts rustled as they walked into the dining room, and Jamie detected a faint floral scent—he couldn't identify which flower, just that it wasn't overpowering and he found he liked it more than he might have originally thought.

Or was that just her?

Laetificate:

1. To make joyful, cheer, revive.

2. A portrait done in miniature.

3. The lower level of a raised garden.

Chapter Five

"Allow me to present my son's intended, Lady Sophronia Bettesford." Mrs. Archer spoke to an older woman with a faintly disapproving air. That was probably due to Mr. Archer having arrived with a betrothed in tow. Given what he'd said about the available ladies, and his desire to escape them.

Sophronia dipped into a curtsy, feeling her muscles protest at the movement. Six hours in the coach with Mr. Archer and his mother had resulted in her feeling like she'd been wrapped around herself and tied into a few knots—she couldn't imagine how Mr. Archer felt, given that he was so much taller. He stood next to her, not showing any sign of travel strain. But then again, perhaps that was because he traveled so frequently—his mother had spent nearly an hour listing, to comic effect, the various countries her son had been to in the course of his work, something Sophronia vaguely understood to be the buying of things from one place to sell to people from another.

She had to pretend to cough when Mrs. Archer announced her son had been in Paws Hill when she meant Brazil, and then couldn't stifle her laughter at her saying Jamie had found the most wonderful cotton in Eyesore—meaning Myosore.

Thankfully, the lady herself was well aware of how she

muddled things, and laughed the longest and loudest when her son gently corrected her.

"Sophronia, this is our host, Mrs. Green, and her daughter, Miss—?"

The disapproving woman drew a younger version of herself forward. "Miss Mary Green."

"How do you do, Mrs. Green, Miss Green?"

"And you hadn't met my son yet, had you? Of course when I first accepted your kind invitation to spend the holidays together, I had no idea we would be bringing his future bride! I do so appreciate your making room for dear Sophronia. She is the best Christmas present." The Green ladies' expressions indicated that, indeed, they were not quite so pleased as Mrs. Archer at this development.

"Thank you for the invitation, Mrs. Green." Sophronia kept her voice as pleasant as she could, given the looks in the other ladies' eyes.

Mrs. Green looked as though she were about to sniff in disdain, but merely said, through a pursed mouth, "You are welcome, Lady Sophronia." She regarded all three of her newly arrived guests as though they were things to be allocated somewhere, not people to interact with. Sophronia hoped Mrs. Green's guests were not as severe as their hostess, or she would be longing for the chickens.

Or forced to spend hours with Mr. Archer.

She darted a glance over at him, wishing that her pretend betrothed wasn't quite so impossibly good-looking. And charming. And intelligent. And patient with his somewhat scatterbrained mother.

She let out an involuntary sigh, and felt his elbow touch her arm. "Are you all right?" he whispered, as his mother was engaged in a long description of the carriage ride to the house, which was apparently far more interesting than Sophronia had experienced.

"Yes, I am fine," she replied softly. *And observant*, she would have to add in her assessment. Her father had often told her he could see what she was thinking, she was that easy to read, and she would have to guard her expressions here, among all these strangers. And Mr. Archer.

Who was no stranger, not now, not when she'd seen the amused smirk on his face as he recited the list of possible nicknames. Or seen his expression as she'd descended the staircase in her new gown, the one that made her feel like a princess, not a lady who was down on her luck and (hopefully) would not have to pluck. Or cluck.

And now she was allowing her mind to wander, to practically gallop through the forest of her imagination, where she was witty, and not alone, and had a future that wasn't one that just featured her and her maid off in a small house somewhere.

That was dangerous, especially since a distinctly tall, handsome, and observant gentleman was lurking nearby in her imagination as well, now doing whatever it was he would do after looking at her like that.

She shivered, just thinking about it.

"Lady Sophronia is chilly," Mr. Archer announced, taking her arm. "Perhaps you could take her up to her room, and she could lie down before dinner?"

"I'm not—" Sophronia began, only to snap her mouth shut as she realized she was about to contradict him, her betrothed, and she didn't want anyone—particularly the Green-Eyed Monster ladies—to think there was any kind of discord between them. "Ah, yes, thank you, that would be lovely," she said in a stronger tone.

"You will meet the rest of the party at dinner," Mrs. Green said, waving her hand over her head to summon the housekeeper who'd apparently been waiting in the shadows. "The Martons have had to cancel"—a swift glance to Sophronia revealed why—"but the Viscount Waxford and his family will be here later on. Dinner is at eight o'clock. We keep country hours, you see."

"This way, my lady," the housekeeper said.

"Rest well, my dear," Mrs. Archer called as Sophronia began to walk up the stairs. "And do you know, Jamie met his bride-to-be at an exhibition of Arty Facts?" Sophronia heard her pretend future mother-in-law say.

"Artifacts, Mother," Jamie replied. She wished she had been down there to see his expression at his mother's colorful language.

THREE HOURS LATER, Sophronia was wearing the most lovely gown she'd ever seen in her entire life, Maria had outdone herself with her coiffure, and yet she knew she was the most despised person in the room.

"My lady," the Viscountess Waxford asked, leaning past the vicar, who'd arrived to round out the table, Mrs. Green explained, with yet another look toward Sophronia, "how did you meet Mr. Archer?"

Her words asked how they had met, but her tone implied, "How did you dare?" A young lady with light blond hair and the most enormous blue eyes sat two seats down from the viscountess, and also appeared to want the answer to the question. Perhaps the viscountess's daughter? Goodness, there were certainly an enormous number of unwed girls here. No wonder James had been so desperate.

Mr. Archer answered before she had the chance to. "My beloved Sophy and I first found a commonality of spirit in our shared love of hieroglyphics."

Sophronia blinked, realizing she wasn't quite certain what hieroglyphics were. Or was. She didn't even know if they were singular or plural.

But no matter, nobody was questioning the veracity of Mr.

Archer's—James's—words. Not when he was sitting at the table, all tall, charming, roguish self of him, his entire manner setting out to charm, to persuade, to convince, to deceive.

For goodness' sake, she nearly believed his words, and she knew full well they hadn't met because of hieroglyphics. And she hoped she wouldn't be asked to repeat the word, because she was imagining she would mangle it as thoroughly as Mrs. Archer would.

"What are your favorite ones, Mr. Archer?" Miss Green asked. She was apparently studious, judging from what her mother said. She blinked myopically in the candlelight, her youth and petite self and protective mother all making Sophronia stupidly, ridiculously jealous. And too tall.

Or that could be because of the way Mr. Archer was looking at Miss Green. As though she was the only woman in the world he wished to gaze upon. Sophronia hated herself for wondering if Miss Green could even see it, since he was across the table.

And then wondered what she would do, how she would feel, if he were to look at her like that.

She felt suddenly hot and restless, as though there was a heat storm about to roll through her general vicinity. Not that she knew what a heat storm was as much as she didn't know what hieroglyphics were, but that was how she felt.

"I find it so hard to choose, Miss Green," James replied. He shot a quick glance toward Sophronia with an accompanying curl of his lips.

Yes, the same lips she couldn't seem to get her mind off of. And somewhere her father was yelling at her about ending a sentence with a preposition, not the fact that she could not stop thinking about a man's mouth.

Father's priorities were always off.

"I think I like whichever one my Sophy likes," he continued. Sophronia had to concentrate not to let her mouth drop open. What was he doing? Was he trying to reveal the falsehood? Could he just not help himself? Or was he being so clever at trying to make it appear that they were truly and well acquainted that no one would question them?

Which was a lot of words that basically meant, "I am not certain what hieroglyphics are, much less which ones are my favorite, and I don't know why he had to possibly expose the reality of our situation to all these people who are at this moment wondering who I think I am."

Instead of saying any of that, however, she pretended for a moment she was him, and thought of what he might say in reply. She glanced toward him and gave him as warm a smile as she could manage, given that she wanted to strangle him. "My favorites are the ones you showed me when we first met," Sophronia replied, imbuing her tone with as much honey-cloying sweetness as she could.

His answering grin, the spark of recognition in his blue eyes, caused that heat storm to flare up into something almost tangible—as though he were touching her, running his fingers down her neck, onto her spine, making her tingle everywhere.

All of that didn't mean she wasn't still aggravated with him, and worse, for jeopardizing their subterfuge, but it did mean that she wished she could find out what his mouth felt like. Firsthand. Or firstlips, so to speak.

All of the other ladies in the room, even the married ones, appeared to feel the effects of his charm. Mrs. Green had shed some of her haughty demeanor to ask his opinion on the epergne in the middle of the table, while the viscountess had told him she was interested in finding candlesticks that would suit her Oriental sitting room, keeping her hand on his sleeve as she described in exact detail what the room looked like.

Meanwhile, Mrs. Archer just observed, smiling widely, seeming blissfully unaware of all the currents of want flowing through the room—the ladies wanting Jamie, Jamie wanting (apparently) to irk Sophronia, Sophronia finding she wished to discover a way to disturb his casual charm.

"My lady, you are the Earl of Lunsford's daughter, are you not?" It was the vicar—Mr. Chandler, she thought—addressing her, thankfully taking her attention away from the current conversation between James and the girl who was indeed the viscountess's daughter, who seemed to believe she had been an African princess in a previous life.

"Yes, I am. That is, I was. Father passed away two years ago." Leaving behind a massive amount of books, little debt, but even fewer funds for his daughter.

"I am so sorry, my lady. I was a great admirer of your father's, I might even go so far as to say we were acquaintances. He and I exchanged a few letters on etymological issues several years ago. I keep those letters still."

"Ah," Sophronia replied. "Father was an avid correspondent." He rarely left the house, in fact, preferring to live his life through books and letters rather than venturing outside. In hindsight, perhaps it was just as well; if he had gone out more, he would have spent more money, and Sophronia would have been among the chickens much earlier than this. There definitely would not have been the opportunity Mr. Archer had presented.

"Do you share his love of words?"

Sophronia opened her mouth to respond in the negative, but realized that wasn't the case. "I do," she said, feeling a fragment of warmth at the memory of her father. She'd lost her mother too young for her to recall, so it had been just her and him for as long as she had awareness. "Father made the very startling decision not to hire a governess for me, so he oversaw my instruction. He was an engaging teacher, even if his skills at maths left something to be desired." That went a long way toward explaining his financial difficulties. She didn't know if he was even aware of just how dire their straits were. Although he would know for certain that it was "straits," not "straights."

"You were so lucky to have the benefit of a mind like that," the vicar said in an admiring tone of voice.

"I suppose so," Sophronia replied with a smile, unable to deny his enthusiasm.

"Would you—do you suppose you would be so gracious as to visit my rectory and see some of the books I've collected? I know your father approved of some of my purchases, he was very helpful in advising me about them." He seemed to realize what he'd asked her, and turned a bright shade of red. "That is, with your betrothed, of course, and perhaps others of the party who would like to visit."

Sophronia suppressed a giggle at Mr. Archer being forced to go look at someone's musty collection of books when, from what she had gathered, he was a collector of remarkable and often dangerous artifacts, nothing nearly so prosaic as books. Written in English, no less. "We would love to, Mr. Chandler, thank you for the invitation."

It would serve him right for the whole hieroglyphics incident.

Wheeple:

1. The handled end of a sword.

2. Melancholy; prone to sadness.

3. To utter a somewhat protracted shrill cry, like the curlew or plover; also, to whistle feebly.

Chapter Six

His pretend betrothed was ending up being far more bothersome to his state of mind than he would like, Jamie thought sourly. He glanced down the table to where she was in an animated conversation with a youngish gentleman that Jamie thought might be the curate, or one of the young ladies' brothers. He was gazing at her with what looked like near adoration.

And Jamie couldn't blame him. Just as she had the previous evening, Sophronia was wearing a lovely gown that seemed as though it had been specifically designed to make her look as beautiful and goddesslike as possible.

Its lines were simple, in stark contrast to the gowns the other women were wearing—this gown had one frill trailing from her waist diagonally to the other side, ending up at the bottom, serving to highlight just how tall and willowy she was. The bodice was simple as well, fitted perfectly to her frame, showcasing the slope of her elegant shoulders and the strength of her slim arms.

But the color was what made it hers. The gown appeared to be either brown or purple, the colors shifting depending on how she moved and where the light caught the fabric. It was daring, unusual, and distinctive—like, he was coming to understand, his fake betrothed herself.

And he did not like the way the young man was looking

at her, still. He wanted to be the one gazing into her dark brown eyes, the recipient of her quick, shy smile.

More than that, however, he wanted to hold her in his arms and find out what it would be like to kiss a lady who was nearly his height.

It was purely the jealousy of a male who was accustomed to being the center of female attention, he assured himself. While also feeling like a spoiled child.

But no matter why he felt the way he did, he knew one thing—the gift he wanted most for this holiday season was a kiss from her. Despite what he'd vowed before. A kiss, just one kiss, couldn't do any harm, could it? And if it brought joy to both of them—holiday joy, the joy of the season, and he knew it would bring joy to her, he had been told often enough of his kissing prowess—then it would make the season brighter.

One gift, that was not so wrong to wish for, was it?

And he was going to do his damnedest to get it.

"SOPHY," HE SAID, striding toward her as the men returned to the drawing room where the ladies sat, drinking their tea after dinner.

He'd met the man who'd so engrossed her during dinner. The vicar, who apparently had known Sophronia's father and chattered on about some sort of book collection he had that she had agreed they would both go see. Not a threat, then.

She looked up at him, arching her eyebrow in a faintly dismissive manner, which only served to make him want to fluster her even more. "Yes, James?"

Good. She was addressing him by his first name now. He smirked at the thought of suggesting she call him by a nickname—"lord and master," perhaps, or "future perfection." He knew that would irk her as much as it would amuse him.

"Mrs. Green was telling me about some of the items she's collected, and she wanted me to take a look at them. I was wondering if you would like to accompany us?"

"My daughter is just as knowledgeable about the collection as I am, Mr. Archer," Mrs. Green said, raising her voice as she spoke over the distance between them. "Lady Sophronia has just gotten a fresh cup of tea, we wouldn't want to disturb her."

Jamie met Sophronia's eyes, and he saw perfect understanding there. Thank goodness.

She placed her teacup on the table next to her, then rose in one elegant movement. It looked like water flowing upstream, or a tree nymph emerging from her woodland home.

Or a tall, lovely woman standing. When had he ever been poetic like that before? He'd have to say never. Not that backwards-running water sounded like anything Wordsworth or any of his cohorts would say, but it was definitely more colorful than he had ever been before.

"I would love to see your collection, Mrs. Green, thank you so much for thinking of James and his interests in these things. I share his interest, that is but one of the things we have in common." She walked to where he stood and took his arm, gazing up at him with an adoring glance.

Bravo, he wished he could say, only that would totally give the game away, wouldn't it?

"My son has always been interested in old things," his mother said. From the spiteful glint in Mrs. Green's eye as she heard the comment, Jamie knew the woman was thinking of Sophronia's age, and he wished he could deliver some sort of cutting response.

But they were spending at least two more weeks here, and he wouldn't do anything to disturb his mother's pleasure, even if it meant enduring looks and comments for the entire time they were there.

Plus it would just mean he would find more reasons to escape to be alone with his betrothed, and perhaps he'd get his Christmas present early.

"JAMES, A WORD, PLEASE." It was the end of the evening—the very long evening—and Sophronia was exhausted, as much from being on her guard as from having traveled all day.

He, she thought grumpily, looked as fresh and handsome as he had that morning when they'd gotten into the coach. His charming smile remained in effect, hours into the excruciating evening, although perhaps it wasn't quite as excruciating for him as it had been for her. Or a different kind of excruciating; he was wanted by nearly all the ladies in the general area, whereas she . . . was not.

She'd dutifully accompanied him to view what appeared to be some old, dingy pieces of tin, the "collection" of which Mrs. Green was so proud. Mr. Green seemed to not have an opinion about anything whatsoever, merely nodding in reply to any question posed him and devoting all of his interest to his dinner and later, his brandy.

Miss Green refused to be daunted by Sophronia's presence, clinging to James's arm as they walked the hallway to the room where the collection was kept, Sophronia trailing along behind like a tall afterthought.

Until James paused and waited for her to come alongside him, then took her arm on his other side so the three of them were walking abreast. Sophronia couldn't help but be touched by that courtesy, even though it also proclaimed his marital intentions, and thus served his purpose in bringing her along in the first place.

"What is it, my dear?" He grinned at her, as though fully aware just how his epithet would make her feel, and delighted by the prospect of her reaction—whether annoyance or amusement, she wasn't sure. A mingling of both, likely as not.

"Could we step outside for a moment?"

His grin got deeper. "You are aware, are you not, that it is December? And therefore likely to be quite cold?" He glanced around at the rest of the company. "Unless you know I can keep you warm."

"Jamie!" his mother exclaimed. "You'll embarrass Sophronia!"

And Mrs. Archer was right. Although now her cheeks felt as though they were burning, and heat was spreading through her body so she knew she would not be cold outside at all.

So he had managed to keep her warm after all.

His eyes were laughing as he took her arm and guided her toward the door to the hallway. "We'll be just a moment, not long enough to cause a scandal," he called as they walked.

"Do you enjoy doing that?" she asked exasperatedly, then answered her own question. "Of course you do, or you wouldn't do it."

"Do what?"

They reached the door, at which a surprised footman waited. "Yes, we're going outside just for a moment," James said.

"Can I fetch the lady's wrap?" the footman asked.

"I won't need it," Sophronia replied, still feeling as though she were burning from the inside out.

"Excellent, my lady," the footman replied, unable to keep the dubious tone from his voice.

The night was cold, but not frigid, and it felt entirely refreshing after being in the stifling—in all ways—atmosphere of the drawing room.

They stood on the stairs, a light showing from the stables to the right of them, the moon casting a glow over the driveway and the gardens in the distance.

It was so blessedly and wonderfully quiet. It seemed he appreciated that as well, since he didn't speak, just kept hold

of her arm as he guided her down the stairs, across the driveway, and just up to the gardens, which had a light dusting of
snow.

Sophronia hadn't seen snow in its natural state perhaps
ever—her father rarely wanted to go to the country, and
even when he did go, it was in the fall or spring. A snow in
London quickly turned to slush, the only remnants of the
real thing lingering on the trees for a day or two after. Until
that, inevitably, melted to join the slush on the streets and
the sidewalks.

"What did you want to speak to me about?" His voice
was quiet, as though he was reluctant to break the silence.

"I don't even know." Well, she did, but she didn't want to
ruin the stillness. "Or I do, but it seems so silly, given what
we're doing."

"Let me guess—the hieroglyphics?" His words sounded
amused again. What must it be like to walk around continually amused? She wished she knew. Then again, if she did
know, she would likely be insane, and she did not wish for
that.

"Yes. That. You could have warned me."

"And missed the look of surprise and outrage on your
face? You are very expressive, Sophy."

"Sophronia," she corrected.

He leaned into her, and she felt the warmth of him, his
solid shape at her side. It would be so easy to lean into him
as well, to take this moment for what it was, to relish perhaps
the only instance—depending on what her future held—to
spend time and flirt with a handsome gentleman who was
just what he said he was.

Which was a man entirely determined to remain unencumbered by a woman, who was so desperate to avoid said
entanglements that he would go so far as to fake a betrothal,
to run the risk of having his much beloved mother find out
that he was lying, in outrageous fashion, to her.

To be known as the kind of man who would do such a thing in order to avoid walking down the aisle.

So perhaps she would not lean back.

"It is my turn to thank you," he said, startling her.

"Why?" *Because I have just vowed to stay immune to your charms? Good luck with that, Sophronia,* she thought to herself.

"Because if you were not here, if I was forced to face this situation on my own, it would be far more dreadful, even without adding in the possibility that I would find myself engaged to a woman I did not want at the end of the holiday." He paused as Sophronia was parsing out what he was saying. "That is likely why I chanced discovery." He shrugged, as though embarrassed. "It isn't something I seem to be able to help. If there is a worse thing than being stagnant, than being immobilized by one's life circumstances, I don't know it."

"Hence the traveling," Sophronia replied. She was starting to feel the cold, and felt herself shiver.

"Here." He must have felt it, too, which wouldn't be surprising, given their arms were touching and she could almost swear she felt his hand hovering somewhere behind her, not quite on her body but not quite not on it, either. "You can wear my jacket. I just wish to stay out here a little longer." He removed his jacket before she could protest, then draped it around her shoulders, tucking it in at her waist with a frown of concentration drawing his eyebrows together.

The jacket was warm from his body, and was redolent of his scent, a mix of soap and something that smelled spicy and faintly exotic.

Of course, faintly exotic to Sophronia was anywhere outside London, so perhaps his cologne or whatever it was came from York or Devon or something.

"I don't know when it first began, but I just remember having to sit still while being given some lesson or another, and feeling as though I wanted to burst out of my skin."

He stared up at the sky, his breath showing visibly in the cold air. "My father used to talk about how much he wished he could just escape, but he had us, and my mother is not a good traveler." He shrugged, as though it didn't matter, when Sophronia could tell it absolutely did. "I don't think it's fair to ask someone to live a life they don't want to live." His voice sounded almost lost. As though it was the young Jamie speaking, not the adult one standing beside her. "If I could move all the time, I think I would. Unfortunately," he said with a laugh, his tone audibly changing, "there are such essential things as sleep, and visiting with one's mother."

"You love her very much, don't you?" Even in his jacket, she was shivering, but she didn't want to go back in, not when she had the chance to speak with him out in the open—in so many ways.

"I do. I would do anything to keep her happy." He paused, then continued. "Anything, that is, except marry someone when I'm not ready to."

They were both silent for a time, each looking up at the sky. The one place, Sophronia mused, that he hadn't been yet.

"My father and I were on our own, much as you describe with your mother." They did have things in common, Sophronia realized. Just not hieroglyphics. "It often felt to me as though it were us against the world." She shook her head, burrowing herself further into his jacket. "Not that we were against anything, but we were on our own. Just us."

"You have no other family?" he asked, a surprisingly soft tone in his voice.

She thought of her cousin, and her cousin's children, and the chickens. "Not precisely. I do, but none I wish to be with. That is why I was so willing to take you up on your offer. Or non-offer," she said with a laugh.

He didn't reply. He seemed content to be still here, just standing beside her, his head flung back, the strong lines of his throat showing fierce and strong.

Add throat to the list of body parts she was now thinking about.

"We should go in, you're freezing," he said after a bit. He took her arm without waiting for her reply—something characteristic of him, she was coming to realize—and walked her back into the house, her mind jumbled up with cold, and Christmas, and what home meant, and why someone would find it impossible to stay in one place, even though that one place held people who loved him.

Gyrovague:

1. Loss of freedoms.

2. One of those monks who were in the habit of wandering from monastery to monastery.

3. The outside circle of a compass.

Chapter Seven

"TODAY WE THOUGHT the young people in the company would take the carriages and visit the abbey. It remains as it was when Henry II reigned, and I am certain Mr. Archer and my own dear girl will find plenty to admire." Mrs. Green issued her words like a proclamation, leaving no possibility of declining. "As well as the rest of the party," she added, even though it sounded as if "the rest of the party" was an afterthought to Mr. Archer and her own dear girl.

Sophronia looked to where Mr. Archer—James—sat at the breakfast table, a bleary look on his face as though he were still sleeping. Perhaps he did not like the mornings as she did—she found she did her best thinking at that time, much to her night-owl father's chagrin.

She felt her lips curve into a smile as she recalled just how many times he wanted to discuss some new discovery he'd made after a long evening of reading, only to get exasperated because she was so tired.

"Something amusing, my dear?" He was so observant, even when looking as though he were still lying in bed, the covers tangled about his—

Oh, no. Now she was thinking about his torso. Who knew the study of anatomy was so fascinating to her?

"Nothing in particular, my dear," she replied, stressing the last two words. He grinned back at her, his eyes lighting up with a shared amusement.

He was altogether too charming, even when half-asleep. Especially when half-asleep.

"The visit to the abbey sounds delightful, Mrs. Green," Jamie said, turning to speak to their hostess. "My Sophy was just saying the other day that she hadn't visited enough ancient abbeys in her lifetime." He spoke without a hint of amusement in his voice, as though he were entirely serious.

How did he do that? Sophronia had to bite her lip to keep from giggling, and meanwhile, he had an entirely serious mien.

And yet—and yet when she met his gaze he winked at her, which just made her want to laugh and smack him at the same time.

Or do something else entirely.

Oh, dear. She had known him for no more than a few days, and she was already entranced by his charm. Not really a surprise, given how charming in general he was. But dangerous—her father had been equally charming, albeit in an entirely different way, and she couldn't trust charm like that. What was it hiding? The inability to plan ahead? A need to do what one wanted—read books or travel to exotic lands—rather than taking care of one's responsibilities?

Rather than choose to live a compromised life?

Fine. She could admire him, even find him charming, but she could not trust him. In the time she'd known him, he'd come up with an elaborate ruse to avoid matrimony, risked discovery by teasing her, and nearly made her give herself away through laughter.

Although she could admire him, as she'd said, and she most definitely did that. She hadn't known before that a gentleman's appearance could have such a—*visceral* effect on her, even though that was likely entirely the wrong word.

Sorry, Father.

Disturbing. Enchanting. *Beguiling.* He was fascinating, and she teased herself now with the thought that perhaps it would not be so bad to allow herself some harmless fun and flirtation while she was inhabiting this disguise.

It would be entirely expected, would it not? After all, a distant betrothed would be seen as even less of an impediment to a marriage-minded miss (or her mother) than one who was constantly hanging around her beloved.

So she would constantly hang around him, if only to satisfy their bargain, and to ensure he wasn't trapped by someone else while they were here.

It would be a lovely Christmas present to give herself, something she hadn't even known she wanted, but now that she knew about it, it was all she could think about.

Thus settled, Sophronia listened as Mrs. Green laid out the very exact details of their day.

MORNINGS, JAMIE INVARIABLY found, came far too early. Especially when one's hostess insisted on speaking very stridently before one had had one's full complement of coffee.

He'd discovered the beverage while traveling in Turkey, and while English people didn't make the drink with as much ferocity as the Turks did, he found it essential to his ability to remain awake during the first few hours of the day.

"Did you sleep well, Jamie?" His mother patted his hand as she spoke, and he covered it with his own in an almost unconscious gesture. It had always been this way—her worrying about him even though she usually had no resources to solve what might have been bothering him, and often exacerbating the problem.

Such as arranging his presence at a house party with a veritable cricket team's worth of eligible young ladies. His gaze darted to his betrothed, looking alert and untroubled at the other side of the breakfast table, her entire self exuding a quiet composure that settled him, somehow. Quieted his restless spirit.

She truly was lovely. He didn't think he would call her

beautiful, necessarily, and "pretty" was far too mundane a word for how she glowed. She was striking, like a lush tree standing by itself in the middle of a green field. At the moment, all of her attention appeared to be on her breakfast, her gaze lowered to the plate in front of her, so he could look at her as much as he liked.

And he found he liked to. The viscountess's daughter, seated beside her, was pretty, definitely, but her looks seemed immature and insignificant when compared with Sophronia's. Even Mrs. Green's pleasant—and intelligent enough—daughter seemed less by comparison.

Sophronia, his betrothed, was a woman, a strong, smart, capable woman. One who quaffed ale in a public house as easily as she did tea in a gentleman's breakfast room. One who spoke of her childhood with a quiet solemnity, who found a way to soothe him through their common experience.

That was far more alluring than the most beautiful girl.

He was very much looking forward to his self-prescribed Christmas gift, and he hoped it wouldn't take him too long to receive it.

"I slept well enough, Mother," Jamie replied at last. It was only while sleeping, actually, he found he could remain still for longer than a few moments.

Being unconscious would do that to a person.

"Mrs. Green, may I compliment you on the softness of your pillows?" Jamie said, taking the last swallow of coffee and gesturing to the footman to refill his cup. "I have slept in some remarkably unpleasant places, and it is a treat to sleep in a proper English bed." He paused, then something entirely wicked within him made him add, "I only wish I'd had someone with whom to revel in the comfort."

Sophronia had just taken a bite of something, but choked at his words, a whoosh of crumbs flying up from her plate as she coughed. She raised her head and glared at him, as much as saying, "how dare you," and he wanted to laugh aloud.

It was entirely too much fun to irk her, to watch the pink flow into her cheeks as he ruffled her feathers.

"I order the bedding from a fine establishment in London," Mrs. Green replied, apparently ignoring both Jamie's words and the fact that her guest was choking on one of her breakfast offerings. "I do find that English goods are so much better than foreign ones, don't you?"

Mrs. Green, Jamie decided at that moment, was an actively obnoxious person. It was as though she were setting out to be deliberately unpleasant. Or at the very least, exceedingly protective of her own country's goods. "Mrs. Green, I am not certain I can agree with you," Jamie replied. "After all, my vocation is the purchasing of items outside of England that British people are desirous of." He spread his hands. "If I did not believe that things outside of our fine country were valuable, I would be wasting my own time, wouldn't I?"

Mrs. Green's mouth pursed, and her expression faltered, as though she was warring within herself to argue with him because she didn't agree with him, or allow the point to pass, because she still had hopes for her daughter, regardless of Sophronia's presence.

She chose the latter course, and he had to say at least she was stubborn, as well. "Perhaps, Mr. Archer, that is so."

Jamie glanced over at Sophronia, who had gotten her breathing under control, and met her gaze, feeling the reassuring warmth of her understanding practically radiating out from her.

There was something so addictive about that comfort, something he'd never experienced in another person's presence in his entire life.

With certain objects, yes—there was a carved statue of some ancient god or another he'd found while in Africa, and he'd kept the statue for longer than he normally would because of how he felt when he looked at it.

He had felt it almost like a tangible loss when he'd finally let it go, but he didn't want to be encumbered by anything—not an object, or a person, or anything that could tie him down, make him stay still for longer than a few moments.

Or two to three weeks, depending on the circumstances.

It felt as though he had the statue back in his possession, in fact, because of the way he felt when he looked at her. Knowing she understood, at least partially, some of what he was going through, what he was enduring in this enforced holiday.

Speaking of which, at least he was being given opportunities to explore, to move, to see things that would engage his interest.

Well, things that were in addition to the thing—the person—most engaging his interest, his pretend betrothed. Whom he didn't have to pretend to find entirely engaging.

Queem:

1. The first bud of a flower; more generally, the first indication of Spring; behold, the queem of Spring.

2. Pleasure, satisfaction. Chiefly in *to (a person's) queem*: so as to be satisfactory; to a person's liking or satisfaction. To take to queem: to accept.

3. To consider oneself higher than another; conscious of one's position in life.

Chapter Eight

"I DIDN'T EXPECT THIS." James spoke in a different tone of voice than any Sophronia had heard before; he sounded almost reverent as he gazed around the small chapel in the abbey.

He had insisted she sit beside him in the carriage, and she'd been acutely conscious of his body—those legs she couldn't seem to stop thinking about—just next to hers, his large hands clasped on his knees, the scent of him seeming to seep into her skin.

Miss Green and the viscountess's daughter also joined them, sitting opposite. When not guided by her mother, Miss Green was a very pleasant conversationalist, if shy. The viscountess's daughter was much more talkative, and most of her talk revolved around what people thought of her— namely, that she was the most lovely girl in the room at any moment.

Sophronia spent a few joyful moments pondering what it would be like if Mrs. Archer and the viscountess's daughter were left alone in a room together, neither showing much ability to listen to another person.

But that was mean to Mrs. Archer, who was likely just lonely. It sounded as though James was away far more often than he was here, and it was clear her life revolved around her son, and the vast amount of concern and love she had for him.

Sophronia promised herself she would spend some more time with Mrs. Archer. That is, before the holiday was over and James killed her off in some horrific way.

Wouldn't that be more upsetting to Mrs. Archer than to have him just tell her he did not wish to be married?

Although telling her would be to confront his problem head-on, and she had the feeling he was unaccustomed to that, being far more used to using his vast amount of charm to wriggle out of a situation.

Like her father. Another reminder to keep her guard up.

"Look, here," James said, startling her out of her thoughts. He had taken her hand and was leading her to a dark corner of the chapel. A table was placed there, several items gleaming dully in the darkness on its surface.

He paused before the table and dropped her hand, reaching out to lift up one of the items. A large vessel, it appeared to be, with whorled edges and a wide lip.

"What is that?" Sophronia asked, interested in spite of herself. There was something so contagious in his manner, in how he held the vessel with a near reverence but still caressed its curves.

Sophronia felt her eyes roll at herself as the imagery made her think of things she should absolutely not be thinking of, in a chapel, no less.

"It is a pitcher," he said in a less reverent voice.

Sophronia uttered a snort, surprised by the mundane plainness of his words. "So nothing special? A goblet for holy wine or an offering of flowers to pagan gods or something?"

"I didn't say that," he replied, setting the pitcher back on the table. His movement was graceful and cautious, revealing his attitude toward the pitcher and whatever it might be. "It was used by the people who worshipped here. To serve their water, or wine, or whatever they were drinking, during celebrations." He turned to look at her, his eyes riveting in his handsome face. "Just imagine what it was like to be here, all that faith and love and family in one room. Maybe they were honoring a fallen family member, or celebrating a successful harvest or something. Like when we celebrate the holidays. And they'd be sharing the feelings and also sharing something to drink, something to sustain them. Something to bond them in this time of togetherness."

She felt shaky as she met his gaze. "That is—that is amazing," she said, speaking of how he'd described things, the moment in this room a few hundred years ago, rather than the pitcher itself. "No wonder you are so successful in your work."

He smiled, but it was a rueful smile, one tempered by some sort of—loss? Longing? "I used to wish I could have lived back in those times, where one remained in one place for one's entire life. Not to have the opportunity to travel, unless it was to wage war, and I certainly did not wish to do that. To be constrained by circumstances rather than open to opportunity."

She stepped forward and touched his arm. "Why?"

He shook his head, not meeting her gaze, looking at the ground. "It seems I've always wished to belong somewhere, even though I chafe against it." He raised his head and looked into her eyes. She felt the force of that blue stare all the way through to her feet. He was charming, and unreliable, and was even now telling her he would never settle down, never live up to his responsibilities.

And yet she wanted to savor him in this moment, in these few weeks they had together during their pretense.

She stepped forward again, not even knowing what she was planning, only fairly certain of what she was about to do.

"Lady Sophronia," Miss Green called from the back of the chapel, "and Mr. Archer, do come look at this marvelous triptych." And just like that, the moment was gone, and whatever she'd thought about doing was swept away by the duty of going to view a triptych, which sounded nearly as indecipherable as whatever hieroglyphics were.

But the fragment of the emotion she'd felt radiating from him—that feeling of wanting something, of yearning—remained, and she was left with the desire to help him. Or if she were to be entirely honest with herself, she was left with the desire for him. She recognized the inherent loneliness in him—she had it herself—and she knew, with even more resolution, that it wouldn't do any harm for them to assuage their loneliness together, if only for a few weeks.

That, more than mild flirtation or even a stolen kiss or two, would be her gift to him. He deserved it, especially since soon enough he would be rid of her and back to his nomadic ways.

JAMIE CURSED MISS Green's interest, at least at that very moment. He had gotten good at discerning when a lady was about to do something less than circumspect, and he'd seen the determination in Sophy's eyes as she regarded him. The determination and the desire, along with perhaps a spark of mischief.

That definitely intrigued him. He wouldn't have said, upon first meeting her, that she had a mischievous spark. She had too much of her goddess mien on display, which of course made sense since when they first met he'd proposed. Falsely.

But now that he'd spent some time in her company, he'd glimpsed things about her he wondered if she even knew about herself—that she had a sense of humor, that she was capable of deception, but even more, that she was an understanding soul, someone who seemed to sympathize with his situation, though he knew full well he could be derided for it—after all, what relatively young man wouldn't want to be the focus of female attention, especially when the females were all just as young, comely, and had their respective attractions? If it weren't him in the situation, he would mock the man who bemoaned that particular fate.

But not her. She'd gauged the situation and offered acceptance, and assistance, and even, he thought, a sense of commonality, though he had no idea what her own difficult position was.

Except that of course there must be one, or else he wouldn't have found her in a coaching inn drinking ale on her way . . . somewhere, with no family and no objection, after the usual reasonable ones, to embarking on this charade with him.

He wanted to know more about her, about why she had family, but had decided not to be with them, but had instead taken a great leap of faith in agreeing to their bargain; but he was also keenly aware that the more he knew, the more entangled he would become. He couldn't afford entanglements, at least not emotionally. He could afford them literally, which was why he was willing to give her so much for just a few weeks of her time.

But the cost of an emotional entanglement—that was far more than he was willing to pay. Which made her understanding and sympathy even more dangerous to his peace of mind.

But meanwhile, he couldn't resist the urge to find out more about her. To give in to the pull he felt to be with her, to see what it would be like to kiss a goddess.

He would just have to stay on his guard, which he'd been doing his whole life.

"What have you found, then, Miss Green?" he asked, following Sophy as she headed toward the back of the chapel. He'd found a treasure, he thought, and not just the pitcher on the table—a treasure he could keep for just a bit, just long enough to soak in its warmth, and feel the calming stillness, if only for a moment.

Peragrate:

1. A half measure.

2. To travel or pass through (a country, stage, etc.).

3. The closure to a teapot.

Chapter Nine

"And after dinner, we will play games, as we always do during the holidays." Again, Mrs. Green didn't make a suggestion so much as issue a command.

Sophronia wondered if the woman would take it amiss if she saluted in response.

And then wanted to laugh, because of course she would.

They'd spent another hour at the abbey, Jamie walking around the place with great strides and gazing at each of the objects in the gallery for far longer than Sophronia would have deemed possible.

For a man who claimed to be so restless, he was definitely able to be still when he was engrossed in something.

Sophronia shifted in her chair as the ramifications of that thought crossed her mind. She couldn't seem to help it, she immediately looked his way, something she had done for most of the dinner. She'd barely concentrated on the food, actually, since her mind was swimming with images of him, his expression as he looked at yet another ancient dusty object, how intent he seemed.

There was something so moving about it, and yes, something so intriguing, as though she weren't already intrigued.

(She was entirely intrigued.)

What would she do if he were to turn that attention, that specific, engaged attention to her?

He had somewhat already, but it was nothing like the way

he had looked as he'd stalked around, picking something up and just holding it in his hand—that large, strong hand, *for goodness' sake, Sophronia, think of something else*— regarding it with a keen interest that sent shivers down her spine.

What could she do to incite and engage his interest? Why was she even thinking about it?

Well, that last one she could answer—because she couldn't seem to stop being intrigued by him, and she wanted to feel what it would be like to be the object of his scrutiny.

To have him hold her the way he'd held one of those items, to look at her with that intense interest.

"Lady Sophronia, are you interested?"

Sophronia gulped at all the ideas that put into her head, but didn't think Mrs. Green meant to ask any of what Sophronia was mentally answering.

Although the answer to all the questions was "Yes."

"Yes, Mrs. Green, I am."

Mrs. Green smiled thinly, as though wishing Sophronia had said she was too old and tired and determined to remain a spinster for the rest of her life to play any holiday games.

Or it could be that Sophronia was imagining all that.

"I am delighted you feel you can participate in these humorous games, my lady. I would not have thought someone with your interests would want to do something so frivolous."

Or she wasn't imagining it at all.

"My Sophy is quite playful, actually," James said. "She has too intricate a personality to be understood at first or even second meeting. It took me many weeks before I was able to peel back the layers and expose the woman underneath."

Sophronia felt her cheeks—and lots of other parts of her—start to heat at his words. *Peel back the layers and expose her.*

Well, so much for not thinking about all of that. About all of him.

The worst part was she wanted him to peel back her layers and expose her, even though it would only be for a short time, and they both understood that.

Did that make it possible? That it was by necessity short-lived? And how did one broach such a topic? *Excuse me, my pretend betrothed, but do you think we could pretend we were actually betrothed, so we could engage in things that actual betrothed couples do?*

It would take someone far better with words to formulate that thought without seeming like an idiot.

Even her father wouldn't have been able to do it, not that she would have asked for his help with *that*. He was a tolerant parent, but she had to guess he would draw the line at finding the right language so that she could embark on a meaningless but also meaningful limited-time relationship.

Now her head hurt with it all. She hoped they weren't playing Dictionary tonight; she'd probably end up with definitions like "Thingy that does things" or "The opposite of dumb."

Or "Inappropriately obsessed with a tall charming man."

JAMIE HAD TO restrain himself, not for the first time, from just taking his fake betrothed and his mother and leaving. But his mother would be disappointed, and what was more, these were the people with whom she socialized—he'd be long gone, but she'd be here to deal with the aftermath of his behavior.

So he did what he could, but felt the prickles of disdain Mrs. Green shot toward Sophronia. All the young ladies, including Miss Green, seemed to understand that he was no longer available, but it appeared that Mrs. Green took it as a personal affront—and perhaps a challenge—that he had arrived encumbered with a wife-to-be.

Although that just gave him more of an excuse to be alone with her, so perhaps he should thank Mrs. Green and her unpleasant behavior.

Meanwhile, he'd be damned if he or Sophronia would be forced into an uncomfortable situation.

"Mrs. Green, if I may, I have a suggestion for a game we could play." He donned his most charming smile, as though he didn't wish her to hell.

"Yes, Mr. Archer?"

"It has been a few years since my mother and I celebrated the holidays together, and one game we used to play is You're Never Dressed Without a Smile. I thought that would be fun."

"Oh, excellent suggestion, Mr. Archer," Mrs. Green's daughter said, making him less annoyed she'd interrupted the potential kiss he had yet to get. "Mother, I do love that one."

"You'll have to tell us how to play," the vicar whatever-his-name said. "I am not familiar with it."

"Mr. Archer?" Mrs. Green's tone, as usual, made it clear what she wanted to happen. In this case, for him to explain the directions.

"Yes, well, one person is It, and tries to make everyone else in the room smile. The first person to smile then becomes It. At the end, the last remaining person who hasn't smiled wins the game. Simple, really."

He allowed himself to glance over at Sophronia, intrigued to see her cheeks flushed pink and a bright light in her eyes. Ah, so it seemed his Sophy liked to play games, as well.

That added yet another layer to his depth of knowledge about her. Layers, like the ones he'd said he'd peeled away from her, just a few moments ago.

And he would like to do that. Very much.

It wasn't just the missed kiss opportunity that was piquing his interest; it was how she asked him what he felt about the objects in the abbey, and how she paid attention to him as he spoke about what he saw. As though she were truly engaged and interested, not merely being polite.

Even though she was, absolutely, and perfectly, polite.

Perhaps he should have suggested Hide and Go Seek, and then he could have found out for himself just how impolite she was willing to be.

Or no; perhaps later on in the visit, when they had gotten to know one another better. That would be something to look forward to, a prickle of anticipation to help steady his course.

"That sounds delightful," Mrs. Green replied in a voice that indicated it was anything but. Perhaps she just always spoke that way? That would make him very sorry for Mr. Green, although that gentleman didn't seem to mind things one way or the other.

IT WAS AFTER DINNER, and the party had all moved into the drawing room, which was arranged for general entertainment—a piano in one corner, several couches scattered about, and a few shelves of books. They hadn't yet started playing the games since there was tea to be had first.

"My Jamie is so clever, don't you think?" Mrs. Archer leaned over to speak in Sophronia's ear, as though sharing a secret, and not something that everyone in the room knew Mrs. Archer thought.

She really was a sweet woman. "He is."

"I am so pleased you'll be joining our family. It's just been me and Jamie for years now, and he deserves some happiness."

And now she felt like the worst kind of lowly worm, fooling this lovely, gentle woman.

"James isn't in town that often, is he?"

Mrs. Archer shook her head regretfully. "No, he is always going off to one place or another. It's been the same ever since he was small. I'd send him out to play, and then he'd end up in the village, or down at the lake, or in the fields. We lived in the country until Jamie was about twelve years old. Then his father—Mr. Archer, that is—found he was required to be at his place of business every day, and so he moved us into London." She sighed. "Jamie takes after his father. My late husband was always off doing things until we got married."

It was on the tip of Sophronia's tongue to ask if James had any brothers and sisters, but she had to think that a normal about-to-be-married couple would have discovered that kind of information about one another already, and while Mrs. Archer did not appear to be a suspicious type of person, her suspicions would certainly be aroused if the topic of family hadn't come up already.

She could, however, safely ask Mrs. Archer questions about herself. "Do you like living in London?"

Mrs. Archer glanced around as though to ensure nobody was listening in. They weren't; prior to the start of the games, Mrs. Green had insisted that James examine yet another artifact—or "arty fact"—and Miss Green had dutifully brought it out from one room or another for him to see, as well as for the guests, presumably, to admire.

To Sophronia's eyes, it appeared to be a misshapen drab piece of pottery. She would not be sharing her opinion with Mrs. Green.

"I don't really enjoy London," Mrs. Archer said. "That is, I do like the conveniences, and when Jamie returns to England he invariably has business in London, so there is a greater chance I will be able to see him. I do miss him." She sighed and looked over to where her son was staring intently at the misshapen drab. "I did always hope—well, it's foolish."

"What did you hope for?" Sophronia asked, wanting to know even as she was dreading the answer—it would likely be something involving her son staying nearby with his wife and their brood of not-yet-existing children.

"I always hoped that when Jamie settled down he would truly settle down. Like his father did with me. Perhaps in the country, a town like this one, or like the one where we lived before. A place where I could see him, and his wife," she added, with a warm smile toward Sophronia, "and where it was less of a commotion."

She was right to have dreaded the answer. It was precisely what she would have imagined the woman wanted, and precisely opposite what her son was determined to do.

She did feel terrible for the deception, but on the other hand, she could feel just how bound up and stifled it made him feel to be in one place for too long.

"I understand that," she replied. "I've always lived in London, and so I am accustomed to it, but I am finding it quite pleasurable to be here in a much quieter place for a while. Even though of course there are plenty of things to do, and plenty of entertainment. But it feels more peaceful, despite the party."

Mrs. Archer beamed at her, as though she had said something entirely clever. When Sophronia had just spoken what was in her heart—she did like it out here, she liked the quiet, and the soft stillness that settled over the place in the evening.

"It is time for the game," James said, addressing them. The misshapen drab seemed to have been put away. He stood in front of them, his expression soft and warm as he looked at his mother. Sophronia felt her heart ache, just a little. She couldn't look at her father anymore, even though for some months after he'd died and she'd discovered how he'd left things, she'd wished he were there she could rail at him.

But as time had gone on, she'd realized she would be fine, no matter that he hadn't quite taken care of her that way. He had taken care of her by letting her know she was loved, and cared for (at the time), and he respected her opinions and feelings.

She missed him. And she felt regretful that Mrs. Archer would not be her mother-in-law in truth, since she wished she could have that again.

"I will just watch, you know I laugh immediately anyway," Mrs. Archer said, waving her hand at her son. "You are so clever, I was just saying that to your beloved Sophronia here."

His gaze traveled to her, a knowing smile quirking his lips. "My beloved Sophronia has yet to discover just how clever I can be," he said, and it sounded as though he were talking about far more than just a game. Sophronia's breath caught, and she felt her cheeks flush—again—and her heart flutter just a bit in her chest.

He held his hand out as he spoke, and she took it, nearly gasping as she felt the strength of his grip and the heat of his fingers through his gloves. She stood on shaky legs, and smoothed her gown, him keeping hold of her hand all the while.

"Let us play," he said, that grin deepening.

Tuant:

1. Cutting, biting, keen, trenchant.

2. A meringue flavored with almond.

3. Careful, precise.

Chapter Ten

JAMIE WON, OF COURSE, as she could have predicted. He'd been so infectiously charming everyone had to laugh, even Mrs. Green, eventually.

And no one had been able to get him to even crack a smile. Sophronia was surprised to find how competitive she'd been at the game, trying her best to make him at least smile.

But no. He remained implacable, a startling change from the charming man she'd come to expect.

She would have to challenge him to a private game of it sometime, perhaps, to see if she could break his composure.

And wasn't that a thought she should absolutely not be having.

"What are you thinking about, my lady?" Maria asked her, pausing midstroke as she was brushing her hair.

Sophronia felt her cheeks immediately begin to burn, and she swallowed. "Nothing. Not a thing." *No need to say it again, Sophronia*, she heard her father's voice say. "Why do you ask?"

Maria shrugged, beginning to brush her hair again. "Because you made this funny noise, and then you looked all different for a second."

Wonderful. So when she thought about things like that, she made funny noises and faces. Maybe that would be the thing to make him laugh.

"What are you doing tomorrow?"

Whatever Mrs. Green wants, Sophronia thought. "I believe we are spending the day at the house, making plans for Christmas. The Greens host a party for the villagers, and so everyone comes and has wine, and food, and there is singing and some dancing."

It sounded delightful, especially since Sophronia had attended very few parties in her life. But also sad, since it meant the visit and the charade would be almost over, and she would be heading to her cottage with Maria, taken care of, but not cared for.

"That sounds a treat," Maria said, her tone showing only delight at the prospect. "And there is that one gown that is perfect for the party—it is cream-colored, with dark green ribbons, and you will look perfect for the season."

"Thank you, Maria, I have no doubt you will make me look lovely." She had to admit to enjoying the look in her pretend betrothed's eye when she appeared dressed in one of her new gowns. She'd never realized before just how much some fabric, buttons, and stitching could alter a person's appearance. Yet another benefit to this whole lying-to-a-perfectly-nice-woman-because-her-son-couldn't-tell-her-the-truth thing.

And with that depressing thought, Sophronia dismissed Maria and took herself off to bed, trying not to count the remaining days.

"DO YOU EVER LOSE?" Sophronia—his Sophy—sounded entirely disgruntled. They had been at the Greens for close to a week, with only a week and a few days left to go in the visit.

Jamie didn't think he'd ever spent so much time just socializing. And since it was with all the same people, he'd run out of things to say by about the third day, which meant he was reduced to playing games so he wouldn't die of boredom.

Plus he was, as his pretend betrothed had soon discovered, very good at games.

They had escaped the drawing room after dinner, when Mrs. Green had decided anyone with musical talent had to perform. Jamie had none, and was delighted to discover that neither did Sophy. Another thing they had in common.

They'd told their dismissive hostess that they would prefer to read, so here they were in the library.

Not reading.

Instead, they sat at either end of one of the sofas in the room, him with his legs crossed and leaning back against the sofa, while she sat perfectly straight, her hands placed just so in her lap.

He'd thought he might have tired of looking at her—he tended to tire of things far more quickly than other people did. But he hadn't. If anything, he wanted to look at her more, to see the range of emotions that flittered across her face in the course of minutes.

"I've lost," he said, knowing his saying it so self-righteously would irk her.

She rolled her eyes. "You might have lost, once, but it wasn't to me." She lifted her head in that goddess pose he was coming to adore. "I am not accustomed to losing." Then she shrugged. "Although to be fair, these are not the games I've played in the past. Still," she said, and he wanted to laugh at her aggrieved expression, "it does not seem fair that I have lost each and every game we have played."

"You were so close when we were playing Similes." He shook his head mockingly. "But then you had to say it was strong as a mule, when it's an ox. Mules are the stubborn ones."

She frowned, twisting her mouth up in an expression of disgruntlement. "I could have sworn it was a mule, not an ox."

"What games are you accustomed to playing?" he asked, tilting his head to look at her.

He could hear the strains of music coming from the drawing room, and knew they had some time before anyone would notice they hadn't returned with their books. He was finding that a good thing—perhaps the only good thing—about a house party was that the rules were just slightly more relaxed out here, so chaperones weren't always required, and besides, he was engaged to be married.

That is, he was purportedly engaged to be married.

Her expression got dreamy, as though she were recalling a memory. "My father and I played Similes, but we usually made ourselves extend beyond England. In fact, it was a rule that we couldn't use any similes that were in the common vernacular."

"Sounds . . . edifying." He couldn't keep himself from sounding skeptical.

She rolled her eyes again. "Of course it wasn't that, it wasn't as though we deliberately sat around and made ourselves seem important because of our obscure knowledge."

"Good to know," he replied, sounding dubious.

She was about to roll her eyes again, he could tell, but then she paused, and instead, she got a wicked smile on her face.

That smile promised many things, and he hoped he would be the recipient of at least a few of them.

Actually, of all of them.

"I have thought of a game we could play where I will win." She sounded so certain he couldn't help but be intrigued. As though he weren't entirely intrigued already.

"What game?"

"You're Never Dressed Without a Smile." She accompanied her words with, of course, a smile. That same wicked one that promised all sorts of things, probably three-quarters of which she wouldn't know herself.

He would like the chance to teach her, however.

"We played that, and I won. We played a few times, didn't

we?" He tapped his mouth with his index finger. "And I believe I won every time." He lowered his hand and looked at her, lifting one eyebrow as he spoke. "Why would tonight's game be any different?"

WHY WOULD TONIGHT'S game be any different? She hoped he wouldn't regret asking that, since the game she intended to play—that she intended to play with him—would be very different indeed.

She swallowed, feeling her eyes flutter closed for a moment as she braced herself. Not that what was about to occur was unpleasant—it would hopefully be the opposite of that—but that she had never been so forward before. And she was planning on it this evening.

"Because the game will be played with just us," she replied. She scooted closer to him on the sofa, keeping her eyes on his face. His handsome, commanding, far-too-gorgeous-for-her face, only it was also his clearly-interested-she-wasn't-stupid face.

She just hoped the interested section of him trumped the out-of-her-league section.

Now she definitely had his interest. She felt herself exhale, just a bit, out of relief. His expression had tightened, sharpened somehow, and she was keenly, even more so, aware that they were in the library alone, that Mrs. Green and her group of Somewhat Talented Musicians were still playing away in the other room, and this—whatever this was—was going to happen.

One way or the other.

"And how do you think to make me smile, much less laugh?" he asked in a serious tone. She could tell he was schooling himself not to smile, but the glint in his blue eyes belied his sober mien.

"I will just have to say a few words," she said in a low voice.

"And if I don't smile? What then?"

She shrugged, a far more casual gesture than her internal emotions warranted. "Then you may claim a forfeit. What-ever you want, I will do. If you win, that is."

"Oh, that sounds promising." The combination of his low, sensual tone and the serious expression on his face made something inside of her warm, as though he were touching her all over, a caress that was heating her up from the inside.

But perhaps he didn't mean the way he sounded—she couldn't assume, it wasn't as though she had ever been in this dangerous flirting situation before. For all she knew, he was like this with every lady, regardless of how he thought of her.

Actually, he was like this with every lady. She'd seen it for herself, only there was something slightly different, more intense, about him now. She continued. "For example, I could ensure Miss Green was occupied for a few hours so her mother wouldn't require you to escort her to view more arty facts." She pronounced it as his mother would, and he nearly broke then, as well. "Or if you wanted me to gaze at you in rapt adoration as you expounded on the history of one of those odd jugs you seem to find entrancing. I could do that."

His lips twitched, but he didn't break. "Or I could ask for something else entirely." She shivered at the low promise in his tone.

"What would you want?"

He paused, his expression still serious, but the light in his eyes was fierce and wild. Thrilling her, even though she had no idea what it meant.

"I want a kiss."

She nearly laughed aloud at the irony of it, but merely nodded and thrust her hand out. "We have a deal."

He took her hand, sliding his fingers over her palm, making her heart race with just the merest touch.

Imagine what would happen to her when they did kiss. Because they would be kissing, of that she was now certain.

"You mentioned you could beat me with just a few words." He still held her hand, his tone teasing, his expression entirely somber. "What words would those be?"

She paused and licked her lips, which had suddenly gone dry. His gaze fastened on her mouth and she felt it as though it was an almost palpable touch.

"I want a kiss."

Smicker:

1. The collar of an apron.

2. To look amorously.

3. The spines of a fish.

Chapter Eleven

OF COURSE HE had to smile at that, but it didn't matter, since—since now it was a moot point. "Well, then who is the winner here?" he asked, moving forward to put his hand on her waist.

Drawing her to him, as he'd wanted to do from the first time—well, no, the first time he saw her she'd been sitting down in a pub drinking ale, and he hadn't been thinking about what he wanted to do to her, or with her, until a few hours later.

Still, it was fairly close to the first time they'd met.

She gazed at him, and once again, he had cause to be grateful she was such a tall woman. He would only have to lower his mouth to hers a few inches, especially if she rose up on her toes. Kissing could be damned hard on the spine, he'd found, if the two participants were upright.

"Why, I have won, of course. You smiled." And then she did the same, her lips curling up into the most provocative, compelling smile he'd ever seen.

Or that could be just her.

"So will you claim your reward, my lady?" Jamie said, sliding his palm to the small of her back and pulling her closer.

She raised her hands and put them at his shoulders, pushing him back. The immediate words of apology began to come from his mouth, but she shook her head, keeping her gaze locked on his face. "*I* wish to claim my reward, sir," she replied, stressing the first word. "*You* will just have to give it."

Oh, well then. He wanted her to take it more than he'd wanted anything in his entire life. He'd never been with a woman like her before, one who knew what she wanted, even though he was fairly certain she wasn't entirely aware of what she wanted, being an unmarried woman and all. And since he had been with experienced unmarried women before, he knew she wasn't experienced, not at all.

"Will this be your first kiss?" The words popped out of his mouth before he could even think about them.

Her cheeks pinked, and he knew the answer before she spoke. "Yes," she said in a soft voice, her fingers beginning to caress his shoulders.

"Good." He couldn't help the note of masculine pride in his voice. "I will just allow you to take it." He stilled himself, letting his hands go down by his side, watching her as she prepared herself.

God, her face was so expressive. He could watch it for hours, and still find new emotions revealed there. Her eyes swept down his body, almost as though she were touching him everywhere she looked. She allowed her hands to slide down his arms, to his waist. When they came to rest there, she bit her lip, and he had to restrain himself from bending down to bite it, as well.

And then she looked up at him, the frank desire in her eyes making him feel as though he were lit from inside. An odd way to put it, to be sure, but it felt as though only she could make him warm. Could soothe him with her kiss.

Even though he doubted very much that kissing her would be a soothing activity. Exciting, sensual, and an entirely new experience, yes, but not soothing.

"Well?" he said at last. It was speak or claim her mouth, and he knew she didn't want that.

"Don't rush me," she said in nearly a growl. That made him laugh, too—that his polite goddess could be so transformed by the prospect of a mere kiss.

But it wouldn't be just mere, would it. This would be an epic kiss, if he knew his goddess.

He saw her throat work, and she lifted her face to his, raising herself up with the hands at his waist. That necessitated her to move in closer, and he felt the points of contact between them—her hands, his waist, her breasts, his chest.

Their feet.

But he stopped thinking about any of that when she placed her mouth on his. Her kiss was soft and warm, just a simple pressing of their mouths together.

And then she opened her mouth, just a bit, and he did as well, hoping that while she didn't have direct experience with the act, she would have investigated what could happen when one person kissed another.

And, thankfully, it seemed she was a studious person.

Her tongue touched his mouth hesitantly, just the slightest touch, but it was enough to make him groan. Which seemed to encourage her, since she slid her tongue inside his mouth, widening her lips.

The sensation of getting lost in her kiss grew, and it felt as though that was all he could think about, her there, and him here, and them kissing. At that moment, he couldn't say he wanted anything more.

Well, he did—he was a man, after all—and if this was all it ever was, it would be enough.

But he did want more, he had to admit.

Which was why he was the one to eventually draw back, knowing if he didn't that he would reach the point of no return, and he didn't want her first kiss to be also her first other things.

Well, he did, he was a man, after all, but it wouldn't be right.

All of which meant that he was entirely and thoroughly befuddled.

"How was it?" He had to ask; he was a—well, damn it, he knew what he was.

Her eyes were soft and dreamy, but held a sensual glint that made his breath catch. "It was excellent." Her mouth—that mouth he'd just been kissing—twisted into a smirk, as though she were sharing a private joke. With herself. "Delightful. Incredible. *Sensational*, even. An excellent gift," she added in a lower voice.

"All those things, all together?" Jamie leaned in close to whisper in her ear. "Imagine just how stupendous it will be when we do it again."

WHEN WE DO it again. Goodness, she wanted to do it again, and she wished she could do it again right now, only that would lead, she well knew, to all sorts of improprieties, improper even if they were actually betrothed and not fakely betrothed.

"Fakely" is not a word, Sophronia, her father muttered somewhere inside her head.

Now is not the time to be offering word critique, Father, she replied.

"Shall we return to the party?" James glanced over her shoulder. "We've been away long enough to miss the music, I believe. Let's just hope they don't ask us what books we've been reading."

She grinned, and turned her head to look at the books on the shelves. "I'll tell them I read a few husbandry guides, paying particular attention to the *Husband Husbandry Guide*."

He spun and looked at the shelves, his mouth dropping open. "There is no such thing—is there?"

She burst out laughing at his expression, which was equal parts nonplussed and bemused. She shook her head and patted him on the arm. "No, there is no such thing. Although

I imagine if there were such a guide, Mrs. Green would have a say in writing it."

"The woman does like to offer pronouncements, doesn't she?" he replied in a rueful tone.

"And potential brides. Thank goodness you had the fore-thought to provide yourself with a betrothed, or else you would be addressing Mrs. Green as Mother."

She laughed even more when she saw him shudder.

"For that, I should buy you two cottages."

He took her arm and led her out of the library, the glow of the kiss fading as she thought about what he'd said. Of course. There was only this, this brief period of time. An interlude during the holidays. It wasn't as though this was anything more than what it was—two people entering into a bargain to save their respective futures. Their separate respective futures.

At least she now knew he was justified in going to such lengths to prevent an accidental betrothal—she had no doubt but that Mrs. Green, or one of the other ladies, would have him plighting his troth by the time Christmas came around.

And after the holiday, long after the Yule log was burnt down, and the kissing bough had given up all its berries, when the mistletoe had shriveled, and the snow was just a distant memory, she would be snug in her cottage with Maria, with memories of this night, and that kiss, to warm her through the ensuing years.

That should be enough. It would be enough. And perhaps, if she was patient, and open, she would find someone who would truly wish to be betrothed to her. To marry her, and stay in one place, and always be reliable, and have enough money to keep her in books and ale. That was all she wanted. Just someone to belong to in a place she felt she belonged.

If she were to receive that Christmas gift one year—not this year, of course, but someday—she would rejoice and try to forget about the tall, restless man who offered her a chance at escape. As well as her first kiss.

"You're not regretting this, are you?" he asked in a low voice as they walked down the hall to the drawing room.

"No, of course not, why?" She glanced up at him, noting the concern in his eyes. "Are you?" *Dear God, please don't let him regret this.* That would be the worst Christmas gift, the anti-Christmas gift, and she herself would regret not making her way to her cousin and his children and all the chicken iterations, and if she—

"That kiss was the best thing to occur since my mother informed me we'd be attending a house party." She couldn't doubt the sincerity in his tone. "It is just—you sighed, just then, as though something were weighing on you." Right. She had forgotten how observant he was.

I was just thinking about how this would all come to an end, and Cinderella would get a cottage, not a prince, at the end of the story.

"I think I was just dreading more of Mrs. Green's orders. Imagine what else she might want us to do while we're here."

He grinned, with such a devilish look in his eye she nearly swooned. "We'll have to excuse ourselves to go play some of our own games."

Forget thinking beyond now, when she'd be off with Maria in a simple cottage paid for with his money. For once, she was going to live in the moment. She would enjoy what this time now would bring, and figure out the rest later.

She could return to being a responsible woman who looked to the future in a week or so; for now, she was as careless and headstrong and impulsive as the next person.

Who happened to be him.

Matutinal:

1. Of, relating to, or occurring in the morning.

2. Feeling nauseated.

3. An acrimonious parting.

Chapter Twelve

He DIDN'T KNOW what he had done, just that he had done something. Besides being kissed by her, that is.

He wanted to inquire more, but they had only a few moments between the library and the drawing room, and he didn't want to get into a discussion where anybody could see them.

It worried him; he couldn't tell what she was thinking now. Her face looked as though someone had drawn a curtain down, her usual lively expression dimmed.

They stepped back into the drawing room, her slightly ahead of him, his hand at the small of her back, just grazing the fabric of her gown with his knuckles. He wished they hadn't ever left the library, that they were still there, kissing, or her teasing him about books and their laughing together.

"Jamie, you have been an age! What could you and Sophronia have gotten up to for so long?"

His mother didn't mean to be shocking, of course; she never did. But all the same, most of the rest of the party smothered chuckles, except for Mrs. Green, who glowered.

She might be the most unpleasant woman he had ever met, but at least she was consistently unpleasant.

"As you are well aware, Mother, I am fascinating when I want to be." He assisted Sophronia into a chair beside his mother. "And my betrothed finds me infinitely fascinating. Don't you, Sophy?"

He grinned at her, hoping she would burst out laughing or say something cutting in response. But she merely lifted a brow and nodded, biting her lip. To stifle a laugh, or a rebuttal? And why was he feeling so torn up about what her reaction might possibly be?

"We were just discussing the plans for tomorrow," the viscountess said. "Mrs. Green has suggested we make a game of finding a suitable tree for decorating. The team who finds the best tree has the honor of—well, what does the team have the honor of doing, Mrs. Green?"

The lady surveyed the house party with a considering air. "The winning team members will be allowed to stand under the mistletoe with the person of their choosing."

Not bad, Mrs. Green, not bad at all. He would have to make sure he or Sophy won, just so he would have the privilege of kissing her in front of all these people.

Of staking his claim to her, even though they both knew—and only they knew—that the claim was a temporary one.

But meanwhile, he didn't know if he could wait until tomorrow to kiss her again, now that he'd tasted the sweetness of her lips, and felt how she responded to him.

Actually, he did know if he could wait. And the answer was no, he couldn't.

THE KNOCK CAME just after Maria had gone, leaving Sophronia in blissful anticipation of a comfortable book, a warm fire, and an hour before she thought she should try to be in bed.

Thankfully, Mrs. Green's dictatorial ways extended to telling her guests when they should be tucked up in their rooms, and the lady insisted everyone get a good night's sleep since the holiday tree-hunting expedition was likely to be strenuous.

Sophronia didn't argue since it meant more time away from the lies they were telling, and Mrs. Archer, whom

Sophronia found she liked more each time they were together.

Yes, the woman was talkative, and somewhat silly, but she had such a good heart, and she loved her son so much, even if she didn't entirely understand him.

It made Sophronia feel even more terrible that she and Mrs. Archer's son were lying to her face, and she knew that Mrs. Archer would be devastated when she learned that Sophronia had died. Even though it hopefully wouldn't be true.

But that wasn't answering the door, was it?

Of course she knew who it was on the other side; it wasn't as though there was anyone else at the house who would be knocking at eleven o'clock at night. She walked to the door, tightening her wrapper but still feeling dangerously underdressed.

Not because he would necessarily get carried away, but because she would. She definitely had not expected that kiss to be so . . . meaningful. Important. Wonderful.

Yes, many words for describing one thing. As seemed to be the case when she thought about him, or that, or how this holiday was both the most wonderful and the most painful one she'd ever had.

She pulled the lock and opened the door, stepping aside to let him in. He wasn't dressed for sleeping, as she was, but he was more casually clothed than before—he had removed his cravat and coat, and wore only his shirt and trousers. He had his hands full with something, but she didn't notice that, because she was too distracted—now that his cravat was off, she could see his strong neck and a few tufts of hair peeking over the collar of his shirt.

Those hairs made her feel all sorts of new and strange feelings.

"What are you doing here?" Because she was fairly

certain he wasn't here so she could admire the hair on his chest.

He grinned and held up what was in his hands—two glasses and a bottle of wine. "I'm here to strategize how we're going to win the tree-finding contest tomorrow."

She gave him a skeptical look. "And for that we need wine?"

He shook his head and strode past her to place the wine and glasses on her bedside table, then sat down on the bed. Her bed. "The wine isn't for strategizing, Sophycakes, it's for fun." He paused, then a sly grin twisted his lips. "We do know how to have fun together, don't we?"

Sophronia immediately felt her face turn not pink, but thoroughly and absolutely red. She doubted a sunset at the end of a summer day was more red than she was at this moment.

He was watching her, and his grin turned into full-out laughter, but not as though he was enjoying her discomfiture, but as though he was gleeful about it all. About his being here, and them together, and their kiss from earlier before.

She could do this. Hadn't she vowed to give herself permission to have fun? She went and plopped next to him on the bed, the motion pushing them together. "Well, open that bottle, then, and let's strategize."

HE DIDN'T THINK he had ever laughed so much in his entire life. His Sophronia—not Sophycakes, she'd informed him in a mockingly supercilious tone—turned out to be even more fun when he was alone with her.

That is, even more fun when he was alone with her and not kissing her. He still thought kissing her was just slightly more fun than making elaborate plans to lure their competitors to a sparse bit of forest. Not that they knew where said sparse bit of forest was, nor how they would succeed in luring the others there, but they had a stupidly fun time talking about it.

"And then, when you've done your job and brought them to where they're all somewhere else, I'll fell the best tree and drag it back to the house."

She looked at him askance. "All by yourself?"

Jamie felt the sting of masculine pride. "You don't believe I can handle a tree on my own?"

She took the last swallow of her wine, and he poured her another glass. "No, I don't."

He reached for her glass and set it on the table, then took her hand and put it on his bicep. And flexed.

At which point, her eyes widened, and his masculine pride was assuaged. But now other parts of him wished to be assuaged—namely, to have her run her hands all over him, not just on his arm.

"Uh," she said, not letting go. If anything, squeezing harder.

It was difficult to keep his muscle flexed for so long, but if it kept that wondrous look on her face, he'd do it.

"Have I rendered you speechless?" he asked, feeling rather at a loss for words himself. Mostly because his mouth would prefer to be doing something else.

She scowled and dropped her hand from his arm, but then launched herself at him, knocking them both over onto the bed. She lowered her mouth to his and kissed him, this time with much more finesse than the first time.

His Sophycakes was a fast learner, it seemed.

He allowed her to take what she so obviously wanted, opening his mouth to let her tongue in, reaching his arm across her body and letting his hand rest just below her breast on her rib cage. Although that was not, technically, what she wanted, but he figured that if he wanted it, it was a likely thing she did, as well.

And oh, how he wanted it.

Clothed in her sleepwear, she was less unapproachable goddess and more . . . approachable. Although that was an inane thought, given that they were each doing plenty of approaching at this very moment.

She twisted so she was nearly underneath him, her hand caressing his back, her other hand in his hair. He felt her softness everywhere, and it was more amazing than he would have imagined.

So amazing, in fact, that he had to stop before it was too late, and they were betrothed in truth.

He reluctantly broke the kiss, hearing their gasping breaths in the otherwise silent room.

"What is it?" she said, a dazed look in her eye.

He knew how she felt.

"If we don't stop, we might never stop, and then—" He paused, not quite sure how to phrase it.

"You'll feel worse about killing me off?" she said in a dry voice.

He laughed, albeit somewhat uncomfortably. Being with her had ameliorated his restless spirit, for certain, but he still felt the pull of the unknown, of continually moving so he didn't have to settle down. Or be anything more than he was.

Was that enough? Would it always be enough?

Or was there something more? Something . . . different that was possible?

Images of his father, how he'd just sat on the sofa and drunk wine—rather as Jamie was doing tonight, although on a bed, not a sofa—crowded his brain, making him acutely aware that this might lead him to that very same dissatisfied spot.

He rolled over onto his back, his body immediately regretting the loss of her. Well, his brain did as well, but his brain also shied away from that fact.

"It's just I don't wish to—" he began, only to have her cut him off.

"I know. I wouldn't think you meant anything by it." She gave a half laugh. "Besides which, it was me who made the first charge. None of this," she said, and waved her hands in the air, "means anything. I know that. It's just"—and he heard how her breath caught, and his throat thickened—"it's just that it feels so wonderful." She laughed softly. "And wondrous, and amazing, and all sorts of other words I've likely never heard of."

He rolled onto his side, propping his head in his hand. She turned her head to look at him, and they were so close, he could see her brown eyes had flecks of green and gold within, and there was a very faint mole on her eyelid.

He wanted to kiss that mole. And everywhere else on her face.

"I feel the same way," he said softly, surprised to find it was true. He'd never been with a woman who intrigued him as much when he was not doing inappropriate things with her as when he was.

"But I know I can't have you forever," she said. "Nor would I want to," she added quickly, once again stirring up Jamie's masculine pride. "I know you are restless, and I—I just want a place to belong."

He wished he could give that to her. But he knew himself, and what's more, he knew what she wanted—a cottage somewhere, a cottage he'd promised he'd give her when they'd entered into their bargain.

That sounded like slow death to him—staying in the same place, knowing the same people, seeing the same things.

It was better this way. It *was*.

He looked at her for a moment longer, then got off the bed and stood, gazing down at her. Her face was still flushed, her lips red and swollen, and he wished he were enough of a cad to take what she would likely give him, if he coaxed her.

But he wasn't, and so she wouldn't, and therefore he should go before the temptation of her outweighed the honor of him.

"Good night, Sophronia," he said, then turned on his heel and walked quickly out the door, before he had the chance to change his mind.

Uhtceare:

1. The next-to-last toe.

2. The combination of juniper and mint, used as a remedy for toothache.

3. Anxiety experienced just before dawn.

Chapter Thirteen

Sophronia flopped back on the bed, feeling all sorts of new, interesting, and very difficult emotions. At the same time.

Why did he have to be so honorable? Why couldn't he just make the decision for her, push her to where she secretly wished to be?

The one man with whom she wanted to be inappropriate, and he turned out to be an honorable, considerate man. Of all the stupid luck.

She had to laugh at herself, of course, because if she didn't—well, if she didn't, she'd cry. And she did not want to cry. Not only because crying felt so maudlin, but also because it would make her eyes puffy, and her nose red, and Mrs. Green would likely notice and comment and send her daughter scurrying after Jamie to try and comfort the poor dear.

And then he'd end up compromising Miss Green, and have to really marry her, not just be pretend betrothed to her.

So crying was not on the agenda.

It had felt so wonderful, being kissed by him. She'd liked how he felt, as well, his muscles, his back, his mouth on hers.

And now she was back to wishing he weren't so honorable.

But if he were so honorable he wouldn't have thought of this devious plan in the first place—she wouldn't be here, they wouldn't have met, and she'd be in the country tending children and chickens. So maybe it was her?

No, she knew it wasn't that. He seemed to have a perverse sense of honor, one that made him try to please his mother (in the short term, at least), but not have to do anything unpleasant for himself. And it was clear he thought being tied down permanently was thoroughly unpleasant.

Whereas she had to admit that if the person tying her down permanently was him, she would find it very pleasant indeed.

And that was what she had decided earlier, wasn't it? Even if it was temporary—and that wasn't an if, it just was a fact—she would very much like to find out what it would all be like. She could be a respectable spinster when she and Maria were at the cottage.

During this most festive season, she wanted to be festive. She knew now she couldn't depend on him to do the wrong thing, so she was going to have to.

She was going to have to seduce him.

Happy Christmas, indeed.

THERE WOULD BE no seduction today, however. For one thing, it was too cold outside to engage in any proper seduction, and secondly, Jamie was too competitive to get sidetracked by anything that might prevent him from winning.

"Over here, Sophy," he called. They had been the first into the forest, and he'd had the foresight to equip himself with a sturdy saw and some rope so they wouldn't waste time getting help to drag the tree in.

"Sophronia," she muttered, following the sound of his voice. The wardrobe he'd gotten for her didn't include clothing suitable for tramping about in the cold and the snow, so she was already damp and cross.

And since she couldn't achieve her own ends, now that she'd decided on them, she was even more cross. But it wasn't as though she could say, *Excuse me, James, but would you mind taking advantage of me over by this tree here? Yes, it is inappropriate and scandalous and cold, but I've come to realize that this is what I want for Christmas, and you are the only one who can give it to me.*

She *wished* she could say that, but she also suspected that the aforementioned cold and snow would reduce the pleasure she found in it, and if she were going to ruin herself, she wanted it to be enjoyable, at least.

"Look, this has to be the best tree out here," he said in an enthusiastic tone of voice as she made her way to him.

It was definitely a tall tree. Perhaps twice his height, and that was saying something. Its branches were thick and full, and it didn't take much imagination to see the tree would be gorgeous decorated with garland, candles, and ribbon.

Or whatever Mrs. Green deemed appropriate to decorate a tree with. Thank goodness she didn't take issue with Prince Albert's importation of the custom, since Sophronia did love the tradition.

She'd have to keep it up next year, when it was just her and Maria.

Although she wouldn't have six feet plus worth of strong male to haul her tree back for her. She'd have to get a gentle shrub or something.

"Are you certain we can bring it back by ourselves? Oughtn't I go get some help?" Sophronia couldn't keep the skepticism from her voice. It was a very tall tree.

"And risk someone else finding something that would suit just as well, and they would win the contest?" He sounded outraged. "No, we can do it, didn't I prove that last night?"

Oh, right. By taking her hand and placing it on his bicep, which was hard and large and made her feel all sorts of prickly things inside.

"You did." No need to express her continued doubt. He would likely just hoist the tree over his shoulder to prove her wrong.

"Bring the saw over, I'll have the tree down in no time."

Sophronia handed him the saw, then watched as he started the process.

A half hour later, he was in only his shirtsleeves, his hair was tangled and damp, and he was still sawing.

She didn't think she'd ever seen such a gloriously visceral sight in her life.

"There," he said at last, just in time for her to jump out of the way. The tree landed with a thump, sending whirls of snow flying up into the air.

"Now all we have to do is get it back to the house."

"Good thing that's all we have to do," Sophronia commented dryly.

But she had to admit she was wrong—gloriously, sweatily, strenuously wrong.

He dragged the tree while she walked alongside, holding his jacket and cravat. She felt awash in his scent, a warm, strong aroma that just seemed essentially him.

He'd rolled his sleeves up, and she couldn't stop darting glances at his forearms—strong, of course, and sprinkled with brown hair.

"Let's sing, shall we?" he said, startling her out of her perusal of said arms.

"What? But don't you need your breath to—?"

He shook his head in mock outrage. "You doubt me, Sophycakes. I can drag a tree and sing at the same time. I am very talented."

She had to laugh at that. "Fine, then. What shall we sing?"

"A holiday carol, of course. Have you no imagination?"

I've got plenty, she wanted to reply. *Enough to think about what it would feel like if you wrapped me in those strong arms of yours and kissed me senseless. And did other things I know about, but am too embarrassed to discuss even in the confines of my own brain.*

"Good King Wenceslas looked out, on the Feast of Stephen," he began to sing, and of course he had a lovely voice, all resonant and rich and thrilling.

She joined him, not nearly as shy about singing out loud because it was with him, and he just made her feel so comfortable, even though he also made her feel all prickly and odd and wanting.

"YES, YOUR TREE is definitely the best, Mr. Archer." For once, Sophronia didn't begrudge the woman's definitive way of speaking. It was a few hours later, and Jamie had unfortunately had a bath and gotten properly dressed again. The rest of the party had returned, each team having retrieved a tree for Mrs. Green's inspection.

None were as large or as robust as theirs. Of course. Because none of the team members was as large or as robust as Jamie himself.

"And you may take anyone you wish under the mistletoe," Mrs. Green continued. Jamie glanced her way, a mischievous look in his eye. "Except for your own team member," she added, and Sophronia wanted to laugh at how startled he looked at that, and he looked at her again, only this time it was in shock and with a mild expression of horror.

"Mrs. Archer, do come and stand just here," Sophronia said, taking the older woman by the arm and guiding her under the mistletoe.

Jamie met her gaze and smiled, a thankful, relieved smile that made her feel all warm and useful.

"Oh, but what about the other young ladies?" Mrs. Archer expostulated, even though she went to the correct spot willingly enough.

"None are as deserving of a holiday kiss as you, Mother," Jamie replied smoothly, looking down at her fondly. He leaned down and kissed her on the cheek, then shot one last thankful look at Sophronia.

"And now that is done, we will all go rest for a bit and

then meet again at dinner. We will have the tree decorated, and then we can play some more games and sing carols." Mrs. Green looked directly at Sophronia. "We all need to look our best."

Thus commanded, Sophronia returned to her bedroom, thinking about strong forearms, what she wanted to do, and the best way to go about it.

"NOT THAT GOWN, Maria. The gold one."

Maria's hand stilled in the wardrobe and she darted a glance back at Sophronia. "Are you certain? That one seems rather grand for a house party."

"It isn't as though I will have occasion to wear it any other time, Maria," Sophronia replied in a dry tone of voice. "After this, the most I'll be dressing up for is maybe a village dance, and then only to keep watch over the young ladies."

Maria shook her head. "You never know, my lady. You could be in our cottage and a handsome stranger would stop by, needing something all of a sudden, and there'd you be, and he'd be struck by you, and then you could wear that gown on your wedding day."

Wearing a gown bought by the man who had engaged her to act as his pretend betrothed to marry a stranger she had yet to meet, and doubted existed, didn't sound like the kind of thing she wanted to be doing. Especially since she'd rather be doing all the marrying in the gold gown with the man who had actually purchased the gown in the first place.

She was a hopeless wreck, she knew that. But at least, at the end of it, she would be on her own, beholden only to herself. Ensuring she and Maria had a reasonable future ahead of them.

Huzzah.

But she also had a seduction to accomplish, hence the gold gown. Huzzah!

IT WAS WORTH all of Maria's shaking her head and concern that she was overdressed to see the expression on his face when she entered the dining room. He had been speaking with Mr. Green, but turned as the door opened, and his mouth dropped open, as well.

He walked quickly to her, taking her elbow in his hand and guiding her to her seat. "You look lovely, Sophy," he murmured, and she knew it wasn't for show, he really meant it, since he'd said it too quietly for anyone else to hear.

"You do, too," she replied. He did, of course; he was dressed in his evening clothes, and his hair was as smooth and well brushed as she'd ever seen, so she was better able to see his face. There was something appealing about how dangerously rakish he looked when his hair was unruly, but there was also something appealing about him when he was well groomed, the clean lines of his face showing the result of a close shave, his features standing out in their stark beauty.

In other words, there was something appealing about him no matter what he did to himself. She should just admit that and stop fussing about it.

DINNER WAS ENJOYABLE, even though Sophronia spent far too much time darting glances at him rather than what was on her plate, so she didn't notice what she'd actually eaten.

Hopefully this was not the time Mrs. Green decided to poison her.

"We will be decorating the trees after dinner, and then we will play some games. The townsfolk will come tomorrow afternoon to partake of holiday refreshments and we must present them with the best Christmas trees they have ever seen." Mrs. Green's normally disapproving expression was practically beatific. "As happens every year."

Jamie leaned over to whisper in her ear. They were seated in the large room the trees had all been brought to, theirs occupying the place of honor right in front of the fireplace. "If it happens every year, then how can they be the best they've ever seen?"

Sophronia stifled a giggle. "Perhaps you should be the one to bring up that incongruity to her. I don't think she thinks very well of me, given our circumstances."

"For which I am devoutly grateful," Jamie replied, a sincere look in his eye.

The servants, under Mrs. Green's watchful eye—and commanding voice—dragged in all the decorations deemed essential for the trees: candles, ribbons, apples, colored paper, dolls, sweetmeats, and walnuts. At first it seemed as if there were far too many things to fit on the trees, but since their tree was so enormous, it was just enough.

"Goodness," Sophronia breathed, as she stood back and looked at the sight.

It was impressive. The candles had all been lit, casting a golden glow that seemed as bright as the sun. The trees' branches were bedecked with all the treasure, and Sophronia glanced around at the other guests, all of whom were wearing the same enchanted expression.

It was lovely. She couldn't, she wouldn't, think that in half an hour or so the candles would be snuffed. For right now, this was enough. Enough that she was here, drinking in the sight, feeling the charm and the warmth of the season.

Not to mention the charm and the warmth of her fake betrothed, who looked even more gorgeous in the candlelight, the flickering lights making shadows on his face, highlighting the strength of his cheekbones, the dark intensity of his gaze.

Oh, Sophronia, you are in so much trouble. And this

will all be a distant memory in a few months, and then next Christmas you'll recall it, hopefully with a warmth and a pang of something to be cherished.

"WHAT GAMES WILL I be winning at this evening?" Jamie said, viewing the company. Mr. Green was tucked in the corner, drinking a second or third glass of port; the viscountess and her daughter were seated on the sofa, talking about a ball they'd been to where the viscountess's daughter had been, as usual, the prettiest thing there; the vicar had buttonholed Sophronia and was talking animatedly about her father and his own collection of books; and Mrs. Green and her daughter were discussing what to serve to the villagers the next day.

"I like the game Alphabet Minute," Miss Green offered with a hesitant smile. Jamie returned the smile, thinking how difficult it must be to be Mrs. Green's daughter.

"I do, as well," he said. He glanced around the room. "Does everyone who wishes to play know how to play?"

Sophronia shook her head. "I do not, but I don't have to play."

"Don't be silly," he replied. "It's simple. We choose a topic, and then we begin to discuss it, only we have to start each sentence with the next letter in the alphabet. So if we start at the letter G, the next person has to say something beginning with H, and so on."

She still looked puzzled, but shrugged. "I will figure it out, I suppose."

"Yes, you will." His Sophy was clever, she would catch on quickly.

And when had he come to think of her as his Sophy?

"What topic shall we choose?"

Mrs. Green had the answer, of course. "Christmas, naturally. Mr. Archer, you shall begin. The choice of letter is yours."

"Merry Christmas, everyone," he said. He nodded to Miss Green. "The next letter is N. "

" 'No room at the inn' is what Mary and Joseph heard on their journey."

"Or was it that there was no *groom* at the inn," Sophy said, shooting him a mischievous glance.

Well played, he thought, smothering a grin.

"Perhaps we will all get our heart's desire," the viscountess's daughter said with a sly look.

"Queen Victoria might issue a proclamation," the viscountess said.

"Really?"

That was his mother. He was proud she had come up with something so quickly.

"So when you mention the queen, you should also mention her husband."

"That's Prince Albert, is it not?"

"Undoubtedly."

Now it seemed everyone was joining in the game, without regard for whose turn it was. It was actually fun to watch their faces as they thought of a sentence for the letter, and Jamie felt as though he finally understood why a house party of this sort was enjoyable. Not that he wished to do it all the time, but it had its appeal—the camaraderie of good conversation, company, and an overriding belonging to the season that made him feel relaxed, and as though he might not jump out of his skin at any moment.

Or, he thought as he glanced over at her, that was just Sophy's influence.

He had been a gentleman the night before, and while he wasn't precisely regretting that—well, never mind, he was, but he knew it was the right thing to do.

But if she said she wanted to explore further, then who was he to stand in the way of adventure?

He'd just have to let her make the next move in the game.

Cunctation:

1. Procrastination; delay.

2. The inability to pronounce certain consonants.

3. A confused state of mind.

Chapter Fourteen

WHAT WAS THE protocol for visiting a gentleman by yourself in his bedroom?

Scratch that, there wasn't any such thing. At least not that she knew of; perhaps she should have befriended the viscountess's daughter. It seemed as though she knew far more about such things, the male and female thing, than Sophronia did.

Although nearly anybody would know more than Sophronia, so that didn't signify.

She drew her wrapper around her, tying the knot to close it as she slid her feet into her slippers.

It was nearly one o'clock, and the house had been quiet for over an hour. The games had continued all evening, and they had been fun, she had to admit, but she kept wishing everyone would just get tired so she could get on with what she wanted to do.

With him.

Even thinking about it made her breath catch—and here she was thinking about actually doing it? What if she was unable to breathe entirely? What if she expired in his bedroom from lack of oxygen, and he had to explain to everyone how she came to be there and then she really would be dead, and Mrs. Archer would be sad and Mrs. Green would be delighted and—and—

"Breathe, Sophronia." He'd said that to her when they

were just embarking on this masquerade. It was good advice then and it was good advice now.

She stepped into the hallway, thankful that his bedroom was only a few doors down from hers. It was dark, and she didn't want to end up sprawled on the floor because she'd missed her footing.

That would be even awkwarder—for her, at least—than expiring in his bedroom. And yes, she knew that wasn't a word.

She reached his door without either fainting or falling, and counted it as a victory already. And then she raised her hand to knock, but the door whooshed open, and she was pulled inside.

"I was hoping," he began, before lowering his mouth onto hers.

She twined her arms around his neck, remembering to breathe through her nose, wanting to burrow up into his skin and get submerged in him, his warmth, his scent, his size.

He ran his hands down her back, then right under her buttocks, lifting her off her feet and pressing her to his chest. She gasped, and he chuckled, walking backward before lying down on the bed with her still on his body. As though she weighed nearly nothing.

"I'll smush you," she said, when she was able to lift her mouth.

He smirked at her, his hands still on her arse, his blue eyes alight with what she very much thought was delighted pleasure. "Of course you won't," he said. "Haven't you learned by now that I am much stronger than I look? And if I do say so myself, I already look awfully strong."

His tone was so smug and sure of himself she had no choice but to be amused. And to be certain she wouldn't crush him in her ardor.

"Now what are you doing visiting my bedroom at such a late hour?" He grinned, and she couldn't help but grin back.

"Maybe that is the topic for an Alphabet Minute game." He kissed her briefly. "What are you doing here, Miss Sophronia?"

X. The next letter was X, which he knew, the competitive wretch. "Ex-amining the betrothed," she replied.

He shook his head, but didn't challenge her. "You like what you see, then?"

Zed. Whose idea was it to play this game when she could be kissing him? "Zounds, how could I not?" She shifted so she could splay her hand on his chest. His remarkably broad chest.

"A wise choice, my lady," he replied.

"But why are you still talking when you could be kissing me?" There, it was out in the open.

"Consider it done," he replied, pulling her to him so their bodies touched nearly everywhere.

SHE WAS HERE. He'd nearly given up hope that she would come, but here she was. He was relieved he had decided not to chase after her—this would be her choice, not his, just as her wanting a cottage in a small village somewhere was her choice, as well, and it was within his means to give it to her.

But meanwhile, before all that, there was this. The gift of her.

He relished her kiss, plundered her mouth with his tongue as his hands roamed over her curves—she was slender, yes, but she had all the right curves, and those curves fit perfectly in his hands.

She was caressing his chest, running her palm over his nipples, making him want to groan and laugh all at the same time.

And have wonderful sublime sexual relations with her, but that went without saying.

Only he should say something, shouldn't he? It wouldn't

be honorable to just assume something because a dressed-for-bed woman had appeared at one's door in the middle of the night?

Damn it. "Are you sure about this?" he said, murmuring into her ear.

She stilled and buried her nose in his neck. *Please say yes, please say yes*, he thought.

And then she licked his skin as her palm continued her travels on his chest, down his side, and at his waist. So close to right there it was maddening and wonderful and excruciating all at the same time.

"Does that answer your question?" she said, accompanying her words with a low laugh.

"Absolutely," he replied, taking her and flipping her onto her back, swallowing her noise of surprise with his mouth.

Part of him—no surprise which part—wanted to just take her, slide his hand up her leg, taking her night rail with it, exposing what he fully anticipated to be long legs.

He'd never been with a woman who was this tall before. In fact, he'd never been with a woman who was this smart, who was this remarkable, who was able to soothe him while at the same time making his heart race and his throat tighten and do other things to other parts of his body.

No surprise which part there, either.

But this wasn't just about him, and it would all be so much sweeter if he took his time.

She was gazing up at him, a warm, sensuous look on her face, less like a goddess now and entirely like a woman. A woman who knew what she wanted, and thankfully, what she seemed to want was him.

"What are you thinking about?" she asked in a husky voice.

Well, he could answer that. "You."

She laughed and swatted his arm. "We have so much in

common, I was thinking about you, too. Namely," she continued, arching an eyebrow, "when you were going to get on with it."

That was so entirely unexpected he burst out laughing. He didn't think he'd ever laughed while engaged in all of this sort of activity—a new experience for him, as it would be a new experience for her. Albeit not the same new experience.

"Get on with it?" he repeated. "If you have somewhere to be, please do let me know, and I will hasten the activity." He waggled his eyebrows meaningfully, and she grinned.

"I don't have anywhere to be, but I believe you do," she said, winking at him. *Winking!* That was even more unexpected than her urging him to just get on with it.

And he didn't know if he should get on with ravishing her, as he dearly wished to do, and it seemed she did, as well, or if he wanted to stop and laugh until he cried.

Definitely a new experience.

SOPHRONIA HAD NEVER felt more daring in her life. Which made sense, since she had never *been* so daring in her life. Not just coming to his room clad in her night rail and wrapper, but encouraging him to—to *do* things she very much wanted him to do to her.

His expression when she urged him to get on with it was delightful—so surprised, and almost affronted that she would dare to issue a command.

"You appear to be this—this regal vision, all elegance and, and regality."

She was touched by his compliment, even though he'd repeated himself.

"But you're not that at all," he continued, leaving Sophronia to wonder just what he was going to say. "You're"—he put his hand on her cheek, his thumb on her mouth, his gaze on her face—"you're clever and impudent and ready for an adventure." He smiled and stroked her mouth. "And I am happy to provide it for you."

And then he kissed her, but he didn't just kiss her, because that would be too weak a word for what he was doing to her. He was imprinting her, claiming her body as his own with every touch. And currently he was touching her waist, his fingers splayed so they were nearly touching her breast, an occurrence she didn't realize had been entirely lacking in her life but now she didn't know how she had lived without it.

Touch me there, she wanted to say, only her mouth was occupied, kissing him back, learning his taste and smell and feel.

She had somehow wrapped her arms around him and was stroking his strong, solid back, pulling him into her, even though he was practically on top of her already.

His—that part was pressed into her, a hard, quite fervent reminder of what was going to happen, or else she would actually expire.

She heard herself moan, low and deep in her throat, her whole body feeling as though it had been zapped with an electric current. Only the electric current was named Jamie, and she hadn't been thoroughly zapped quite yet.

This was the Christmas gift she had really wanted when she thought she wanted a kiss. This—this *ownership*, this entire subsumption into feeling, not thinking at all.

Even though she was thinking. But all she was thinking about was him.

Oh, God, and now his hand was on her breast, his finger rubbing her nipple, causing spirals of a slow, sensuous heat to curl through her body. And his other hand—well, that was drawing her night rail up, his palm on her shin, her knee, her thigh, and then—

She couldn't help but gasp as his fingers reached there, and he broke the kiss, the expression in his eyes both fiercely desiring and concerned. "Are you—is this all right?" he asked, speaking in a ragged voice.

"Mm-hm," she replied, knowing that actual speech might be beyond her. At this moment, at least.

"You're so ready for me," he murmured, his fingers touching her, finding her wet, which would have embarrassed her if she hadn't been so thoroughly determined not to be embarrassed.

Not at this moment, at least; later on, then she could be embarrassed, when she was an old spinster living with her chatty maid in a cottage somewhere. But she would also be able to look back at this whole thing and be delighted that she had been bold enough to say what she wanted, and to get it.

"I am ready." She spoke against his mouth. "So why don't you get on with it?"

He half laughed, half groaned, and she stopped being able to think as he pushed her legs apart and something that was not his hand was at her entrance, and it felt wonderful, if entirely frightening, and made her breathless in all sorts of ways.

Aubade:

1. A jelly made with quince.

2. To lean back.

3. A song or poem greeting the dawn.

Chapter Fifteen

HAD SHE THOUGHT before she might die if he didn't do all this to her?

Now she had to wonder if she would die because he had—of pleasure, of overwhelming emotion, of just feeling glorious and as though the first part of her life was in muted shades of gray, and now the world was colored in the most vivid of hues.

Yes, it hurt at first, and it definitely felt as though it wouldn't entirely fit, but Jamie was patient, even though she could tell it was a strain.

And then, eventually, he thrust home, and she felt him all the way inside, sending echoes of pleasure through her body.

It wasn't just mindless pleasure, either; that is, she felt mindless, but he was mindful, moving carefully and clearly concentrating on how she was feeling, and what felt good.

My goodness, did it feel good.

And it felt as though it were building to something even better.

"That's it, love." He kissed her hard and fierce, and then lowered his head to her neck, his grasp tightening as he continued to thrust, in and out, in a maddeningly wonderful rhythm.

She felt it start to pick her up and sweep her away, knowing it was impossible to stop, not that she would be idiotic enough to stop it at all.

"Ohhh," she said as she felt the escalation making its inexorable way to somewhere, she had no idea.

And then it was as though that same electric current sparked through her, shooting tendrils of pleasure through her entire body, making her boneless and subject to all her feelings and emotions.

She half opened her eyes and saw his smirk of satisfaction, and then he got a look of intense concentration on his face as he increased his rhythm, pushing harder and faster until all she could feel was him, thrusting deep, hearing the sound of their bodies crashing together, his grunts and moans which managed to sound intriguing and not ridiculous.

Until finally, he thrust in and stayed there, his whole body shaking, his hair falling on her face, their bodies touching completely everywhere.

She never wanted to move.

And it seemed, after a few moments, that neither did he.

That would be uncomfortable after an hour or so.

She wriggled a bit under him and he withdrew, rolling onto his side and gasping. "Oh, my lord, Sophycakes." He had his eyes closed, but his face bore a smile.

She had done that to him. Or more accurately, they had done that together and this was the result. "Sophronia," she corrected, hearing the laughter in her voice.

She wasn't expecting his next words.

"If there is a—a result from this, you will let me know, won't you?" He placed his palm on her stomach, and she gaped at him, not quite sure what he meant, until she did.

Well, that was hardly romantic. Although it was her fault for engaging in it without thinking of the consequences—the result, as he'd put it.

"Yes, of course," she said in a stiff tone of voice.

"Did I upset you?" And now, damn it, he sounded concerned. And she felt like she'd been irresponsible and pettish, where only a few minutes ago she'd had the most blissful experience of her life.

Well, and that was life after all, wasn't it? Blissful experience followed by mundane idiocy. Namely, hers.

"I'm fine, I should go back to my room."

"You can stay for a bit, can't you?" It sounded as though he really did wish she would stay, and she wanted to exclaim at how remarkable it was, that this handsome, strong, smart man was wanting her to stay for a bit longer when all she wanted to do was run off.

"I shouldn't, because if we fall asleep and someone finds us, then we will actually have to get married."

A part of her wanted him to say that it would be fine if that happened, that now that they'd done all this, they should get married. Of course the other part was in vehement disagreement with that, because she'd come to his room without any kind of expectation, and she would never want him to regret this moment.

A long silence during which the two parts warred inside Sophronia's head about what she wanted. No accord had been reached when he finally spoke.

"And I know you don't want that," he said at last. What did he mean? Did he want her to argue with him about it? Tell him she did want it?

She wasn't the one who should be arguing about anything right now. It wasn't as though she went around doing this kind of thing all the time, and knew what to say and do afterward.

Even if she were absolutely and totally in love with the person in question.

Oh no. *Oh no.*

"I have to go," she said hurriedly, pushing herself up off the bed and shaking her night rail back down to her feet. Because if she stayed she might tell him how she felt, and then he would feel obligated to marry her, and then he would eventually resent her, and that was not at all the bargain they'd made.

He stood also, a dazed expression on his face. "Fine, yes. I'll see you tomorrow," he said, his words getting more clipped as he spoke.

"Good night, James," she said, turning to give him one last look.

"Good night, Sophronia," he replied.

WHAT THE HELL just happened? He'd had the best sex of his life, he'd been in a post-coital bliss when responsibility made him speak, and apparently he'd done the wrong thing.

He thought the men in this situation were the ones who didn't want to discuss such things as contraception and prevention. And what if there was a child? He would want to know, and he would want to do the right thing.

Which he would want to do anyway.

That was the reality of it, wasn't it?

He flopped back on the bed, letting his arms drop to the side, a wash of what might have been heartbreak flooding his senses.

Because he'd never felt like this before—this devastation at the thought of not seeing her after this, of knowing she was out there on her own, in her little cottage that he'd bought for her.

Was it possible he'd gone and fallen in love with her? His pretend betrothed? The one person from whom he didn't wish to escape? The one person who knew that his reckless spirit made it impossible for him to commit to anything—or anyone?

Damn it, he had. He was in love with her, his Sophy, his Sophronia. Who wasn't his at all.

Well, if it were possible to have a more ludicrously appalling situation, he didn't know what it would be.

But what he did know was that now that all this had happened, he did not want to let this go. He couldn't let her go.

He would just have to find a way to convince her he meant it.

THE NEXT MORNING he woke up surprisingly alert—probably because he had a woman to persuade he loved her. He'd thought about it for at least an hour, and finally settled on something, something that would hopefully be enough.

Or he'd have to head off into the wilds alone, and he did not want to do that. Not now, not ever again. Not now that he knew what it might be like to be with her.

Thank goodness he'd paid attention when she was speaking—not that he wouldn't have, if he hadn't thought it important, but he hadn't recalled ever paying so much attention to a woman before. When he wasn't in bed with her, at least.

That's how he knew she was different, that she was the one who would intrigue him until they were old and doddering. And until they were old and doddering, he wanted to be with her, to hear her soft moan as he kissed her, feel her curves and skin and watch her descend staircases dressed in fabulous gowns.

"Good morning, everyone." He addressed the room, his gaze alighting—of course—on her. The house was bustling with activity; the villagers were to come gaze on the Greens' magnanimous splendor and perhaps drink a cup of wine before returning home.

She looked startled as he spoke, perhaps because of what they'd done the night before, but also perhaps because he wasn't usually so . . . *sprightly*, if he could call it that, this early in the morning.

He grinned at her, loving how her cheeks pinked up. She had to be thinking about what they had done. If she weren't, then he had seriously misjudged his skill in the bedroom.

"I am planning to go to the vicar's today to view his collection of rare books." He paused. "Sophronia, you needn't accompany me, I think it would be lovely if you stayed here with my mother. I'll return when the party is to occur. Four o'clock, is it?"

Mrs. Green nodded, not looking pleased, but likely too busy to argue or to try to send her daughter along to accompany him.

Sophronia just blinked, and her face froze. He knew she was likely thinking he didn't want to be with her, not after what had happened the night before. He wished he could reassure her, but there was no way to say that without letting his plans for later slip. That is, perhaps there was, but he wasn't confident he could do it.

"Fine, that sounds pleasant." She spoke in a tight tone of voice, and he wanted to laugh at how prickly and goddess-like she was being, only he really didn't think that would do anything for what he wanted from her.

Namely, forever. He wanted forever from her, and he hoped he had thought of the best way to do it.

"WHERE ARE YOU and Jamie planning on settling down?" Mrs. Archer looked hopefully at Sophronia, who wished Jamie—James—Mr. Archer—had not put her in this position. Actually, she was starting to regret she'd been in any kind of position with him, especially the one last night where he was—well, suffice to say she was feeling irked.

Had he planned on that? So it would be easier to say goodbye when this was all over?

It wasn't as though she expected anything, but she had hoped he would seek her out and let her know how he was feeling. Unless he didn't want to let her know what he was feeling, which was why he had gone to Mr. Chandler's house to look at books she knew he had no interest in, for goodness' sake.

And he'd made it impossible for her to go with him, encouraging her instead to stay here with his mother. The mother he was even now duping with her presence, and Sophronia didn't even want to think how the woman would react when she heard Sophronia had died.

And so, though she was angry and hurt and disappointed, she had to admit it wasn't his fault. And she was absolutely and totally in love with him. Still.

Oh, and here she was leaving Mrs. Archer just blinking at her, holding her teacup and regarding Sophronia with a patient look.

"That is something we have to discuss," she replied at last.

Mrs. Archer nodded as though that actually came close to answering her question. Which it did not.

"I was speaking with your lady's maid, Maria she said her name was?" Mrs. Archer didn't wait for a reply. "She is a lovely girl, I was asking her for ideas for—well, never mind that," she said with a knowing look, "but she did say she always hoped to live in a small cottage somewhere, away from the bustle of London." Mrs. Archer sighed. "And I told her that's what we had talked about, and how much I would love to do that. Only if Jamie could find his way to visit, of course, but I would dearly love to have some peace and quiet."

"Yes, that would be lovely." Although the more she thought about it, the more Sophronia wished for some adventure—she'd spent most of her life indoors with her father going through books and reading and visiting. She wanted to go somewhere, just be active and engaged, and not observing.

Perhaps she would find that in her cottage? She didn't hold out much hope for it, but it was definitely better than the poultry she'd anticipated just a few weeks ago. So there was that, at least.

SHE DIDN'T HAVE any thoughts that hadn't revolved around her fake betrothed and the long endless stretch of loneliness that was to be her future for the next few hours. The house party had dispersed, and Sophronia had seized on the excuse to go up to her room to write some letters.

That she had no one to write to was depressing in and of itself.

She found she was looking forward to the villagers' arrival—she did love seeing people enjoying the holidays, even if the people weren't her.

And wasn't she the most maudlin person ever? She did have a future, thanks to him, that ensured her independence. She wouldn't have to be a poor relation, and next year at this time she would perhaps have found a few friends with whom she could share the spirit of the season.

So when she heard the first arrivals, she descended the staircase from her room, feeling a warmth that was very different from the warmth she'd had in Jamie's arms, in his bed, the night before.

"Welcome, everyone!" Mr. Green seemed to have roused himself, as well, and was greeting the townsfolk at the entrance, a huge smile on his face. Even Mrs. Green looked festive, albeit still disapproving when someone was a bit too cheery.

Sophronia took a cup of wine from a sideboard in the hallway and walked to the large room where the trees were decorated.

She smiled as she heard the audible gasps from the visitors as they caught first sight of them.

And they truly were impressive—all of them were lit, the afternoon sun competing with the glow of the candles for which could be the brightest. There were tables laden with food ringing the edges of the room, and in one corner stood a pianoforte with someone playing a variety of holiday carols.

It gave her a lump in her throat. This, this was truly the spirit of the season, the emotion that she wished she could keep in her heart all year long, even after this magical time was over, because this was what made people joyous. The company of others, simple, quiet beauty, and delightful music. Perhaps accompanied by some food and some wine, always accompanied with the satisfaction of being at peace with oneself.

No matter what would happen from now on, she would be at peace, she promised herself as she gazed around the room. "Merry Christmas, Sophronia," she whispered softly under her breath.

"MRS. GREEN, IF you don't mind, I would like to propose a game for the evening." She hadn't gotten a chance to speak with him, not privately, and despite her earlier feelings she was currently vacillating between utter despair that it seemed he didn't care about what they had done the night before and triumph at herself that she had initiated it in the first place. She was not proud of that, but she knew she would return to that earlier, peaceful place eventually.

He, of course, looked the same. Not as though he'd done anything but be solidly mobile Jamie, although she'd been surprised he'd spent so long at Mr. Chandler's house. He'd arrived halfway through the holiday party and then had left before it was entirely over, returning only when it was time for dinner. She'd caught him glancing at her a few times, a knowing look on his face.

Knowing because he knew what she was like during intimacy? Knowing because he knew the charade they were engaged in? Knowing because that's just who he was?

"Of course, Mr. Archer," Mrs. Green replied. "What do you have in mind?"

They were all in Mrs. Green's capacious sitting room, now comfortable enough with one another after the past weeks that there was none—well, hardly any—of the over-stated politeness of new acquaintances. The holiday party had been a success, with the children running around and shooting Christmas crackers at one another, all the food having been consumed, and more than a few bottles of wine, as well.

They'd sung a few carols toward the end, and Sophronia had felt her heart swell even more at hearing the various voices raised together in song.

And there were only a few more nights left. She felt her throat grow tight as she looked around at the company that had been her constant companions for the last few weeks. Soon it would only be her and Maria.

Sophronia and Mrs. Archer were seated together on one sofa, while Miss Green and the viscountess's daughter were to the side in chairs, their heads close together as they whispered. Mr. Green was in the corner, a book on his lap, but his eyes suspiciously closed, while the vicar was standing looking at a bookshelf, his back to the group.

Mrs. Green was also standing, overseeing the disposition of tea.

And Jamie. He was the focus of the room, even for those people who hadn't seen what he looked like without his nightshirt.

"Excellent, Mrs. Green." It was so fast if she had blinked she would have missed it, but he did dart a glance at her. And then returned to looking at the group in general.

"Someone has remarked to me that I win almost all the games." Another quick look in her direction. "And since we are nearly at the end of this delightful visit, I thought I would give others a chance to triumph." He looked at each of them in turn; all of the group, with the exception of Mr. Green, were paying attention to him. "So tonight I would like us to play Dictionary, only I will be the only one supplying the definitions. I cannot vote on the correct one, since I will know it already, and that will give all of you"—and this time he definitely looked her way, and what's more, she thought he winked—"a chance to excel."

"That's hardly fair to you, Mr. Archer," Miss Green said in a hesitant voice.

He smiled at her, and Sophronia felt a stab of something—fine, it was jealousy—enter into her ricocheting gallery of emotions.

"On the contrary, it is unfair for me to keep winning all the games." He shrugged. "This way, I get to give all of you a chance."

"That's settled, then," Mrs. Green declared. She spoke to one of the servants who was still in the room, arranging the tea things. "Bring paper and pencils here, and please send Mr. Hotchkiss to the library to retrieve the dictionary."

The servant made some sort of incomprehensible sound of agreement, then scurried out of the room.

Jamie's expression was—sly, mischievous, and nearly delighted. She wondered just what they were in for, since she didn't think this would be a simple game of Dictionary.

"YOU ALL KNOW how to play, don't you?" Mrs. Archer shook her head, and Jamie rolled his eyes. "Of course you do, Mother, you and I used to play many years ago."

"Many years ago, Jamie," she said. "Keep in mind I am old, I forget things."

"You're not that old," he said. A brief look of concern crossed his features, and she felt his conflict—to stay a bit longer to please his mother, or to follow his instinct to roam, leaving his mother behind?

She was glad she didn't have to worry about anything like that.

"Since my mother asked, I will remind you all of the rules." He was a born speaker, commanding the room with his handsome presence, his deep, compelling voice, and his—well, she had already mentioned his handsomeness, but he was so handsome perhaps it was deserving of a second mention.

"I will choose a word none of you know—if you know, you have to confess it—and then you will all write a definition for the word. We'll vote on which definition is the right one, and whoever gets the most votes for either submitting the best definition or who votes the most often on the correct definition will win."

Miss Green smiled in delight, and Sophronia was struck again by what a pretty girl she was when she wasn't glancing anxiously at her mother. The viscountess's daughter looked bored, but that was probably because it wasn't likely her beauty was going to be the focus of a word. Unless she wrote her own definition.

Sophronia had to stifle a snort at that thought, a brief moment of lightness that showed her that no matter what had happened, no matter what would happen, she was better off than she had been a few weeks ago, when her prospects were poultrylike in nature.

He had done all that for her. And he had done other things for her, too, but she shouldn't be thinking of those things in public, or she knew her expressive face would give her away, and then she and Jamie would be even deeper into the deception.

"The first word is 'agamist.'" Jamie's mouth twisted up in a smirk as he followed with, "Something I no longer am."

"That is not fair, giving hints. The people who know you the best, your mother and Lady Sophronia, will have an undue advantage." Mrs. Green—of course it was Mrs. Green—raised her voice in protest, but nobody else seemed to mind the possible disadvantage.

"Nobody knows that word, correct?" Jamie continued. At everyone's silence, he nodded. "Then you know what to do."

All the people who were playing (Mr. Green had fallen

asleep, and was tacitly being allowed to slumber) gathered their pencils and paper and began writing.

Agamist. Sophronia tapped her pencil against her mouth and caught Jamie looking at her, much as he had looked at her the night before. She lowered her gaze to her paper, but not before she felt her face nearly burst into flame.

She thought of something, thankfully something other than an unclothed Jamie, and began to write, smiling as she recalled how zealously her father had attacked the game of Dictionary. As though it were crucially imperative that he devote all of his remarkable brain power to fictitious definitions.

She missed him.

"Is everyone ready?" Jamie didn't wait for everyone to respond, he just began to walk around the room, putting each person's slip of paper into a basket Mrs. Green had thought to provide.

He cleared his throat and began to read. "'Agamist: A thick fog specific to bodies of fresh water.'" There were a few murmurs around the room as people thought about the word, and its possible definition. Sophronia knew, or at least she thought she knew, that wasn't the correct one, since it was too obvious, the definer using "mist" as the inspiration for the definition.

He continued, reading a few she definitely knew were incorrect. Something about ribbons and books, so likely written by the viscountess's daughter and Mr. Chandler, respectively.

He drew out another piece of paper and cleared his throat. "'Agamist: A compound of iron and salt.'" That was hers, so that wasn't the right one.

The next one must be it. She tensed, waiting for him to speak. Why it seemed so important she didn't know, just perhaps that she had been wondering where he had gotten to all day, and what he thought about the night before, and if it were possible for them to engage in the activity again before this whole charade was over.

"'Agamist: A person opposed to the institution of matrimony.'" And her heart stuttered in her chest, because then he met her gaze and raised an eyebrow as though in a challenge, but his mouth was smiling, so she didn't know what to think.

Except that he'd found a word that might mean more than its definition, even though that sounded absolutely odd, and her father would be frowning right now.

But Jamie wasn't frowning. Now he was regarding her with that dashing twinkle in his blue eyes, and now he was grinning at her as though daring her to read into his word.

"Who votes for the first definition?" He didn't take his eyes off her as he spoke.

The viscountess's daughter raised her hand.

Nobody voted for the ribbons and horses definition, and then it was time for hers to be up for voting. "The ore compound definition?"

The Green ladies and the viscountess raised their hands. He still kept his eyes locked on her face, and she felt as though she wanted to squirm in her seat.

"The last definition?"

She met his gaze and raised her chin as she raised her hand. Mr. Chandler and Mrs. Archer raised their hands, as well, and his eyes darted over to them before returning to Sophronia.

"Excellently done. The last definition—the person who is no longer afraid of marriage—is the correct one. Mother, you, Mr. Chandler, and Sophronia each win a point. Sophronia gets three extra points for submitting a definition three people voted on. Well done."

She nodded, wondering if a simple game of Dictionary was meant to be so—so loaded with meaning. That is, it was a game about meaning, but she didn't think it was meant— ha!—to be interpreted as a real life thing. Only what if she was reading more into it than was there? What if his choosing of that word was coincidental?

"Time for the next word," he said, thankfully interrupting her ridiculous musings. They were ridiculous, weren't they? It couldn't be—it couldn't be that—her mind couldn't even go there, it felt so wonderful, and her chest hurt at the thought that it couldn't be, it wasn't, true.

" 'Gorgonize.' "

All the players immediately bent to their definitions, the rustling of pencil on paper the only noise in the room. Sophronia tried to think of something, anything, that would be able to fool the room, and eventually settled on something she knew wouldn't fool anybody—well, maybe it would fool the viscountess's daughter, but that didn't count—and waited as the rest of the room finished up, and Jamie collected the papers.

" 'Gorgonize.' " He paused and glanced around the room. " 'To have a paralyzing or mesmerizing effect on someone.' "

Her breath caught.

" 'Gorgonize: To turn into stone.' " He grinned, and shot a quick look at the vicar. Of course that was his definition.

" 'Gorgonize: To organize all the things that begin with the letter G.' " He looked at Sophronia with a skeptical look on his face and she returned it with a shrug.

No, she couldn't think of anything right now, not with her head in such a whirl.

He read out the rest of the definitions, and they voted; Sophronia's definition didn't even get the viscountess's daughter's vote, and she had to admit her brain had taken a break since her heart was currently the only organ she seemed to be listening to.

"The definition is to have a paralyzing or mesmerizing effect on someone." Murmurs as everyone exclaimed, and he looked at her, speaking again. "Sophronia gorgonizes me, each and every day."

Oh. She couldn't speak, she could barely breathe. Thankfully, there was no need to since Mrs. Archer made cooing sounds, and even Mrs. Green seemed to smile a tiny bit.

"And now we have another word." A pause as everyone in the room waited, pencils poised above papers. " 'Appentency.' "

A silence ensued as everyone got to work on their definitions, their heads lowered to their paper. Sophronia didn't look down immediately, still too caught up in the tumult of what he might be doing to concentrate.

Thank goodness, because then he winked at her, as if to confirm her suspicions, and her heart went from stuttering to fluttering, and she had to take a few deep breaths to keep from bursting out with a question, or several questions, in fact: *Are you an agamist now? Does that mean you wish to make this falsehood into a reality? Did you feel the same way I did last night?*

Do you love me?

She didn't even bother trying to write a definition, she knew it would result in that "Thingy that does things" definition she'd thought of a previous time he'd managed to fluster and bewilder her.

" 'Appentency: A longing or desire.' " Again, he met her gaze, and there just was no mistaking the look in his eye now. She had just barely stopped herself from leaping up and rushing into his arms when Mrs. Archer spoke.

"Jamie, I feel as though this game is for more than just sport." She nodded significantly to Sophronia. "You are so clever, to woo her like this." She waved her hand in the air. "But don't you know, son, you already have her?"

Jamie looked at her and her breath caught.

"Do I?" he asked softly.

She almost couldn't speak, but she managed to eke out a soft "yes" and a nod of her head.

"Excellent," he replied, his expression looking relieved.

And still charming, of course. "And if I may, I would like to break from the game for a moment to osculate my be-trothed." A pause. "That means to salute a person on the lips." His eyes met hers. "Namely, to kiss her."

And then he strode toward her as she rose from her chair, guiding her to where the mistletoe hung and kissing her thoroughly on the mouth.

"I love you, Sophronia," he murmured at last.

"I love you, as well, Jamiecakes," she replied. "I am so glad I got my present," she added, a sly, wicked smile on her face, which just made him have to kiss her senseless.

Epilogue

"WHEN WILL YOU two be leaving?" Mrs. Archer, as Jamie frequently noted, had her questions reversed; she'd ask them when they were leaving when they'd just arrived, and ask when they'd be returning when they were about to leave.

But now his mother's tone didn't have the same plaintive note from before—now that she and Sophronia's maid Maria had discovered a shared love of small villages and gossip, they'd settled happily into their cottage by the sea, which was close enough to the house he'd found for himself and Sophronia. They still traveled, but the house was an anchor, something he knew he'd be returning to eventually.

He'd found, anyway, that he didn't have the same need to be constantly on the go, now that he had Sophronia. He still enjoyed it, and he liked showing his wife new things, but they were spending more time in England.

And soon, quite soon, in fact, they would be home permanently, since Sophronia was expecting, and neither one of them wanted to deprive Mrs. Archer of seeing her grandchild grow up.

He glanced over to where Sophy sat, his Sophy, the only one who'd been able to soothe him, the one who challenged him, as well, who made him want both to be and to become a better man.

And knew that his reckless taking on of a fake betrothed had been one of the best decisions of his life.

Author's Note

Correct definitions:

Agamist: A person opposed to the institution of matrimony.

Cachinnator: A loud or immoderate laugher.

Otosis: Mishearing; alteration of words caused by an erroneous apprehension of the sound.

Vecordy: Senseless, foolish.

Laetificate: To make joyful, cheer, revive.

Wheeple: To utter a somewhat protracted shrill cry, like the curlew or plover; also, to whistle feebly.

Gyrovague: One of those monks who were in the habit of wandering from monastery to monastery.

Queem: Pleasure, satisfaction. Chiefly in *to (a person's) queem*: so as to be satisfactory; to a person's liking or satisfaction. To take to queem: to accept.

Peragrate: To travel or pass through (a country, stage, etc.).

Tuant: Cutting, biting, keen, trenchant.

Smicker: To look amorously.

Matutinal: Of, relating to, or occurring in the morning.

Uhtceare: Anxiety experienced just before dawn.

Cunctation: Procrastination; delay.

Aubade: A song or poem greeting the dawn.

The Duke's Christmas Wish

VIVIENNE LORRET

For Heather

Chapter One

Ivy Sutherland grimaced at the sight of *another* long, winding corridor inside Castle Vale. She might never reach her room. Worse, she might never stop regretting the second cup of tea she'd drunk before leaving the inn this morning. "Do you suppose we're still in Hertfordshire?"

From beside her, Lilah Appleton lifted a gloved finger to her pursed lips. Silently, she shook her head and gestured to the imperious Lady Cosgrove, who walked ahead of them. It was a well-known fact that Lilah's aunt Zinnia did not possess a single shred of humor.

Of course, Lilah's disapproval might have been more believable if not for the subtle lift of her cheeks. Amusement brightened her brown eyes and caused her dark lashes to tangle at the corners. "I'm certain the view from our windows will be of the incomparable grounds of this estate."

That notion still did not appease Ivy. The Duke of Vale's estate reached as far as Bedfordshire. Upon their arrival, they'd been given ample time to admire the vast grounds with the queue of carriages extending nearly a mile. At the time, a light dusting of snow had begun to settle upon the rolling hills and stands of evergreens, creating a portrait backdrop for the duke's party, leading up to a Christmas Eve Ball. Even so, while Christmas was only a sennight away, Ivy wasn't entirely sure they would reach their rooms by then.

As it was, she and her friend, along with Lady Cosgrove

and a pair of footmen, followed a maid down another corridor within this stone fortress. Truly, the place was immense. Ivy wished there were benches lining the arched walls instead of battle scene tapestries and empty suits of armor. Then again, stopping for a rest wasn't the best idea. The sooner she reached her room, the sooner she could stop regretting that second cup of tea.

"I wonder if His Grace hired extra servants to find guests who might become lost," Ivy said, only partly in jest. "They might call themselves *The Rescue Brigade,* equipped with food rations and blankets for the long journey."

The comment earned Ivy a snicker from one of the footmen and a laugh from Lilah. Her friend covered the amused outburst with a cough, but not quickly enough. Lilah's aunt Zinnia turned her head, snapped her fingers, and glared—all without missing a step or altering her clipped stride. While Lady Cosgrove was a handsome woman in her middle years, she was also a master of quick, censorious glances.

When that look was turned on her, Ivy imagined that a sense of discomfiture might make most young women blush. She, however, had been told by several people that a blush turned her milky complexion to an unbecoming shade of scarlet and made her pale blue eyes rather dull. Because of that, she refused to be embarrassed whenever possible. Therefore, Ivy answered the look with an innocent lift of her brows. To which Lady Cosgrove responded with a smile . . . *of sorts.* Not many women could affect such a formidable countenance when dressed in a cheerful cerulean traveling costume. An unexpected shudder coursed through Ivy at the skilled display of such a severe smile. It must have taken years of practice.

When Lady Cosgrove faced forward again, Lilah composed herself, brushing wisps of brown hair away from a sloped brow, then silently mouthed to Ivy, "You are incorrigible."

Ivy grinned, tucking a limp lock of her own, whitish-blond hair behind her ear. She'd rather be incorrigible than spend any more of her life trying to be perfect. Those years had been fruitless and exhausting. Even when Jasper—Lilah's brother—had been alive, Ivy still hadn't been enough for him.

More than two years had passed since then, and now, at five and twenty, Ivy was firmly *on the shelf* and not interested in marriage in the least. Well, not her own. She was, however, interested in helping her friend find the perfect match. While Lilah might be willing to marry any man who could satisfy the stipulations of her father's will, Ivy wanted her friend to find a man who loved her, as well. And their bachelor host might be that man. After all, there was rampant speculation about the reason the duke was hosting the party. Many wondered if he might be in search of a bride. That was the sole reason Ivy was here at Castle Vale.

That, *and* to find the nearest chamber pot. *For mercy's sake, they'd been walking corridors for an age!*

Ivy shortened her stride to quick, small steps. She also curled her fingers into her palms and squeezed, hoping to send the signal to the rest of her body. *Stay clenched,* she begged, *and do not think about tea.*

"Here we are, my lady," the mobcapped maid said as she turned the key in the door. Bobbing a curtsy, she gestured them inside the elegant room furnished with rose-colored silk wallpaper, bedding, draperies, and accented in peridot-green pillows and upholstered chairs. "Your ladyship's suite is the larger chamber. Miss Appleton and Miss Sutherland share the smaller one on the other side of the dressing room."

The maid led the way past the white stone hearth in the corner, then through a shorter, arched doorway. The dressing chamber was more like a parlor, large and elegant, equipped with velvet-cushioned chairs, a low table for tea, and a vanity table near a slender window. The view overlooked an inviting garden path lined with snow-speckled topiaries. Further inward, the doorway to the smaller bed-chamber waited. But in between the vanity and the door, a slender, square stone outcropping stood. Ivy imagined it must have been a garderobe at one time.

In her youth, Ivy had toured a few older castles and found similar structures built against outer walls. Typi-cally, the inside would hold a stone bench with a hole cut out of the center, nothing more than a festering pit beneath it. Although it seemed primitive to her, years ago, people would hang their clothes in such rooms, believing that the stench would ward off insects and whatnot. *The stench on the clothes likely warded off people as well,* she thought.

Thankfully, that practice had been abandoned. From what she'd witnessed, the old garderobes were sealed off or transformed into closets, *sans* festering pits, of course.

When the maid opened the door to the small stone room, Lady Cosgrove let out a gasp. "What is this—this *thing* in the closet? Where are the chamber pot and the washbasin?"

Blocked by the maid and Lady Cosgrove, Ivy could not see the *thing* that had earned such censure. She shuffled to the side in order to peer between the pair. First she saw only sprigs of lavender hanging from the ceiling in front of a window slit. Then, following the line of Lady Cosgrove's shoulder down to the hand she had pointed at the offend-ing object, Ivy saw what resembled a large copper cauldron, fixed to the floor.

"It is a *plunger toilet,* my lady," the maid said with obvi-ous pride, standing straighter. "His Grace has installed these in three of the castle's former garderobes. The dowager duchess wishes for your ladyship to have every luxury and convenience. Her Grace placed you in the finest chamber."

With the mention of the dowager duchess, a friend of Lady Cosgrove's, her ladyship's visible disdain gradually dissipated. She lowered her arm and cleared her throat.

"You may inform Her Grace that it is a fine room, indeed—though to my mind, a chamber pot is far simpler and less offensive. Nevertheless, I'm certain we can all adapt to this modern . . . *contraption.*"

Ivy knew that these *plunger toilets* had been around for decades, but they had not yet gained in popularity. Only the most affluent houses had them, and sometimes not even then. While she'd heard of them, this was Ivy's first time seeing one in person.

Rumor stated that the duke was a modern-thinking man and something of a scientist, naturalist, and mathematician. In fact, his latest *Marriage Formula*—it had been said—was designed to obliterate the need for courtship before marriage. His proposal had both intrigued the gentlemen of the *ton* and earned the disdain of the women.

Ivy didn't care a whit either way. Because, with all of Lady Cosgrove's talk about chamber pots, Ivy was all too aware of her current state of discomfort. She shifted from one foot to the other and tried not to think of chamber pots. Of course, not thinking about chamber pots made her *really* think about chamber pots.

"It would, however," Lady Cosgrove continued, unwittingly and *mercifully* interrupting Ivy's train of thought, "ease my mind somewhat to know where the washbasin was located." Turning her back on the *toilet,* she gave it one last cursory flip of her fingers before stepping aside.

The maid sighed in relief and gestured to the cabinet on the opposite side of the spacious dressing chamber. "Right this way, my lady."

Now that Ivy had an unobstructed view of the *toilet,* she realized it was far more oval-shaped than a cauldron. To her, it looked like a giant copper egg, hollowed out and served up on an ornate, curvaceous dish.

"I've never seen one before," Lilah said, sidling up to her. "It's rather large and somewhat off-putting. Imagine stepping in here in the middle of the night. You might hit your leg on it and trip, bashing your head against the wall, while losing a slipper inside, and there it would go, down to . . . places unknown. Oh, but what if it did *not* go down all the way? Then it could be trapped and—"

"You worry too much." Ivy bumped Lilah's shoulder with her own. Although understandingly, it was no wonder that Lilah worried, with all the weight on her shoulders, the urgent need to find a titled husband to satisfy the codicil to her father's will. Still, Ivy was determined that her friend would enjoy the next week and find a husband, even in the unlikely instance of a ruined slipper.

Lilah leaned forward on her toes and peered down into the shallow water as if it had been the great abyss. "Mother says that I haven't been worrying enough. Which is precisely the reason I have begun to think of every terrible thing that could occur."

As they spoke, Lady Cosgrove finished perusing the cabinets and returned to the first bedchamber, maid in tow. The sound of other voices drifted into the dressing room, likely Lilah's aunt directing the footmen where to place the luggage.

"If you ask me, it's all a matter of perception," Ivy said, pointing toward the bowl. "Let's say you do trip, bash your head, *and* lose a slipper."

Lilah straightened her spine and frowned. "Aren't you supposed to be allaying my fears?"

"*Pfft,*" Ivy said with a shooing motion of her hand. "Not when they are preposterous. Now play along. What is the worst thing that could happen?"

"I don't know, Ivy," Lilah said on a breath, her exasperation clear in the way she lifted her brows, shoulders, and hands in one simultaneous twitch. "I suppose the worst thing would be that the duke would discover that I've *ruined* his *plunger toilet* with my slipper."

"Precisely."

Lilah's slender brow furrowed. "And why are you grinning as if this would be good news?"

"Because then the duke would notice you, *obviously*. Not only would he know your name and face but he would think of you every time he went to his own garderobe." Ivy nodded in encouragement, only to have Lilah shake her head.

"That is not how I would wish him to think of me."

Ivy dismissed her friend's concern with a half shrug and a tilt of her head. "You could work on that later. Alter his perception."

Lilah sighed, but there was a hint of a smile on her lips. "You truly are incorrigible, you know."

"Surprisingly, that doesn't discourage me in the least." Ivy reached out and embraced her longtime friend.

Then, suddenly, a twinge speared through her with great urgency. Ivy shifted. Standing back on her heels, she crossed one foot over the other. The second cup of tea forced her to study the *toilet* with an even more critical eye. "It appears sturdy enough, don't you think? Far more resilient than a porcelain chamber pot. In fact, the more I think on it, this large copper *egg* makes perfect sense. It's rather brilliant."

Of course, her judgment might have been influenced a bit by a need to use it *tout de suite*.

"I quite agree, Miss Sutherland," someone said from just outside the dressing room. "The Duke of Vale only wishes that the *plunger toilet* were his own invention."

Ivy turned to see the Dowager Duchess of Vale step through the archway. In that instant, Ivy realized that Lady Cosgrove had not been directing the footmen after all. Instead, she spoke with a gentleman who was partially hidden from view by the door. Ivy could not identify him from his profile. All she could glimpse from here was a crop of short, dark hair, the edge of a thick eyebrow, a well-formed ear, and the shadows lining the underside of his cheek and jaw.

"Your Grace," Ivy and Lilah said in unison to the dowager duchess, and each dipped into a curtsy. With Ivy's legs still crossed, however, rising gracefully proved to be a challenge.

"Miss Lilah Appleton," the dowager duchess began, directing her smile to Lilah first. "I'm thrilled that your mother could spare you over the holiday for this party. I do believe you were introduced to my nephew at the Ruthersfield Ball last May."

In the exact moment that the dowager duchess said the word *nephew,* the gentleman in the other room inclined his head toward Lady Cosgrove and pivoted on his heel. Out of the corner of her eye, Ivy watched as Lilah bowed her head and dipped once more. However, quite inexplicably, the majority of Ivy's attention fixed upon the Duke of Vale. His perfunctory gaze skimmed past the dowager duchess to Lilah, and he bowed his head once more.

Strangely, Ivy couldn't breathe. Her breath was caught somewhere between an inhale and an exhale, in the same manner that a sudden fierce wind stole one's breath. Yet there was no breeze. There was, however, the rushing swish of her pulse in her ears. She couldn't imagine what was causing this peculiar reaction.

It certainly couldn't have been due to her first glimpse of the duke. After all, he was not a handsome man. Not the way Jasper had been, with a face sculpted by angels and fleece-like waves of golden hair upon his head. No, the duke was too angular, as if forged by a blacksmith. His aquiline nose and square jaw were too harsh. His shoulders, too broad for his tall, narrow frame. In fact, if she were to trace his silhouette from head to toe, he would look exactly like one of those suits of armor in the hall.

Yet there was something arresting about him. Something that kept her staring at him, waiting for the moment when his eyes would rest on hers. The notion, and the waiting, were as disconcerting as they were absurd.

"And Miss Ivy Sutherland," the dowager duchess continued, "I'm simply delighted by your presence, as well. You abandoned soirees and society all too soon, and I don't believe I've had the pleasure of introducing you to my nephew."

"No, ma'am," Ivy said, garbling the words as she fought to breathe properly. Then, expecting the exchange to follow immediately, Ivy dipped into a curtsy. Only she forgot that her legs were crossed and ended up teetering slightly. With all of her weight balanced on one foot, she wobbled. For an instant, she must have looked like a teapot tipping over. Or worse, she must have appeared a *trifle disguised*. Yet there was no polite way to explain her lack of grace. With the garderobe in such close proximity, she'd just as soon confess to imbibing spirits as say she'd drunk far too much tea.

Needing an excuse, she quickly added, "Your Grace, please excuse my clumsiness. These slippers ... *er* ... pinch."

Regrettably, between the words *slippers* and *pinch*, Ivy lifted her gaze from the duke's camel-colored waistcoat and white cravat to his darkly intense eyes. Those eyes resembled two hematite stones and drew her in like a flake of iron to a blacksmith's magnet. Those eyes, fringed with thick, black lashes, seemed to swallow any surrounding light, but while reflecting it at the same time. She felt as if she were wobbling again, or that the room was tilting beneath her feet. She did not like the sensation in the least. It made her impatient to end this introduction.

Yet the duke said nothing, to either end it or begin it. Instead, he furrowed his brow and stared at Ivy as if she were a madwoman.

"You are fortunate, indeed, Miss Sutherland," the dowager duchess said, her voice sounding distant through the din in Ivy's ears. "My nephew has invented a device to assist with such a problem. How serendipitous it is that you should have tightly fitting slippers."

Slippers. At once Ivy recalled her conversation with

Lilah from a moment ago. The sole reason for attending the duke's party was to find a husband for Lilah. And who better than their host? With great relief, an idea sprang to mind that would potentially rescue both *her*—from this dreadful situation—*and Lilah*—from being too easily forgotten by gentlemen, as she had in the past.

"Then the fortunate one is Miss Appleton, because I'm wearing her slippers, ma'am," Ivy said in a rush. Everyone knew that if you told a lie quickly, your voice wouldn't waver and give you away. Not only that, but Ivy counted on Lilah's good breeding to keep her secret. She knew that Lilah wouldn't put forth an argument until they were alone. Even with this announcement, however, the duke's gaze did not waver from Ivy's. And oh, how she wished it would, because she remained ensnared by those magnets. "Miss Appleton has quite the inquisitive mind. I'm certain she would be delighted to see such an invention, sir."

The duke frowned. Then, from the doorway, a feminine throat cleared.

"Forgive the interruption, ma'am, but you wished to know immediately if any circumstances arose that would require your attention," said the woman, who was likely the housekeeper. "Lady Granworth has arrived."

The dowager duchess gasped. "How delightful! I must welcome her at once. And my dear Lady Cosgrove, as her relation, you must accompany me. I'm certain you are as curious as I about what prompted her return to society after so many years away."

"What a coup, Duchess! Not even I have been able to draw her out of Bath," Lady Cosgrove exclaimed. "I daresay the tongues will wag, and you will be the envy of all."

"Zinnia, you flatter me," the dowager duchess answered, adding a trill of laughter, "but I am not opposed to such an honor. No, indeed. And when Lady Harwick arrives, we shall all have tea in my sitting room and—*Good gracious!*

I nearly forgot. Miss Appleton and Miss Sutherland, I regret to cut our visit short. I will see to it that a tea tray is brought up to your room at once."

"Thank you, ma'am," Lilah said as she moved out of Ivy's peripheral vision.

Ivy parroted her friend, albeit distractedly, because she was still caught by the duke's gaze. Even though it likely had been fewer than two minutes from when she'd first spotted his profile—and less than a minute since they'd been introduced—it felt like substantially more. Even more peculiarly, she'd apparently incurred his disapproval. She could think of no other reason why he would stare at her so intently.

"Nephew," the dowager duchess called from the other room, "I wonder if you would be so good as to accompany us?"

Then, without any hint that he'd heard his aunt at all, the duke brusquely nodded his head, turned, and strode out of the room.

The moment the door clicked shut, Ivy doubled over, clutching her middle as she fought for breath and balance.

"The fortunate one is Miss Appleton because I'm wearing her slippers? Miss Appleton has quite *the inquisitive mind?"* Lilah scoffed as she stormed into view. Coming to a sudden halt, the hem of her fawn redingote swirled around her ankles, revealing the unpolished toes of her half boots. "We both know those are your slippers on your feet. In addition, I haven't the least desire to see the duke's slipper-stretcher."

"Whyever not?" Having caught her breath, Ivy straightened and hurriedly moved toward the garderobe. "I think the invention sounds interesting."

"Of the two of us, you are the inquisitive one. After all, you were the one who wanted to see how fast the gardener's flower cart would roll down the hill . . . with you inside of it, no less."

Ivy closed the door and started to lift her redingote and

skirts, talking to Lilah from the other side. "I was twelve years old. *Of course* I wanted to know how fast the cart would roll. Besides, Jasper dared me. And I don't recall hearing your words of warning before I climbed in it—only your peals of laughter."

Oh! Ivy gasped as her backside and legs met the cold toilet. Then . . . nothing happened. That demanding second cup of tea was being stubborn. After trying for so long to stay clenched, she was now facing the real possibility that she'd forgotten how to *un*clench.

"Shortly thereafter, we all knew better," Lilah said, the annoyance fading from her tone. "You were lying in a heap on the ground, your head bleeding from the stone that you hit. Even my brother was frightened."

"Don't be dead, Ivy. Don't be dead," the thirteen-year-old Jasper had whispered over and over as he'd knelt beside her in the grass. *"I promise I'll never dare you to do another foolish thing as long as we live. Just don't be dead."*

The moment Ivy had opened her eyes and seen the worried tears streaking through the dirt on his cheeks, she'd fallen in love with him. She'd known right then that she would never love anyone else the way she'd loved Jasper. And until he'd died three years ago, she'd done everything she could to prove it to him. Sadly, it had never been enough.

She sighed, weary from thinking about how difficult it had been to pretend that she was careful and perfect for all those years. That was over now. She needn't worry about garnering anyone's approval in order to appear marriageable, because she wasn't going to marry. She wasn't even going to worry about what the duke might think of her. All that mattered was what he thought of Lilah.

"At least our introduction was a success," Ivy said, her voice echoing around her. "Surely the duke will think of you often."

Lilah laughed with more mockery than mirth. "Indeed,

whenever his shoes pinch. Such is the dream of every debutante."

"Then we shall wish ill-fitting shoes upon him for the duration of the party." Ivy grinned, and with that thought, felt at ease for the first time since meeting the duke. Perhaps her reaction to him had been nothing more than a product of an overactive imagination and that second cup of tea.

NORTHCLIFF BROMLEY KNEW he wasn't going mad. There was no record of insanity in his lineage. His own parents had been of sound mind. While he had no siblings to provide further study, his cousins were seemingly reasonable individuals. Even his uncle, from whom he'd inherited the dukedom, had been perfectly sane.

Knowing this, however, did not explain why his logical mind had suddenly abandoned him. Or why his thoughts were as unpredictable as a wooden cube tripping down a spiral staircase.

Alone in his private study, he flattened his hands on his desk and glared down at the ledgers spread before him. Not one of them held the answer.

"Nephew, have you heard a single word I've said?"

North jerked his head up at the sound of his aunt's voice. He glanced around to find the room virtually the same as it always was, in orderly disorder. Towers of books teetered on tables. Unfiled patent papers were strewn about. Gadgets, inventions, and more books littered the shelves. There was a rather comfortable chair and hassock beside the hearth, but it was currently serving as the foundation for a scale bridge he was designing for the stream that cut through his land. Most importantly, however, the door to his small sanctuary was closed. It was always closed because he did not like interruptions when he was thinking. Yet for some reason, his aunt was now standing on the opposite side of his desk, and he hadn't heard her approach.

"Aunt Edith, how long have you been in here?"

"I've been scolding you for the past five minutes," she answered, the fine wrinkles around her mouth drawn tight as she pursed her lips. Her silver-lashed eyes flashed in annoyance.

Since she rarely scolded him, and rarely disturbed him in his study, he supposed he owed her the courtesy of listening. At least for a moment. "Pray tell, what have I done to earn this reprimand?"

"Weren't you listening?" She tsked, glaring at him. Then, on a heavy exhale, she shook her elaborately coiffed head in a manner that suggested she'd answered her own question. "I've never seen you so distracted as you were when we met with Juliet Granworth earlier. Not to mention, directly before that, you were quite rude to Miss Appleton and Miss Sutherland."

"Rude? I've never been rude in my life." He followed the rules of society with exactitude. In fact, he engaged in most introductions by rote, all the proper words spilling from his lips without fail, even while his mind was engaged elsewhere. To him, most people fit into two categories: dull or wholly uninteresting. During these introductions, he allowed his mind to move on to matters of estate business, familial obligations, weekly schedules, and, more importantly, to ideas for inventions.

"You didn't say a word to either of those young women," Edith claimed.

"Of course I did." With a father who had been ostracized from the family because he'd married a commoner, North had encountered opposition when his late uncle, the former Duke of Vale, had named him as the heir apparent. Since the duke had had no children of his own, no surviving brothers, and North was the eldest of the nephews, the title had naturally fallen to him. Even so, North had always felt the need to prove that he was the rightful heir. Therefore, his manners were always impeccable.

"Not a single word. Not even a murmur of acknowledgment," Aunt Edith continued. "I thank Mrs. Humphreys for saving us all by coming to the door when she did."

This news was odd indeed. He thought for sure that he'd made an obligatory greeting. His brain was like a machine in perfect working order. Yet even he had to admit that he'd felt something inside of him go drastically wrong the moment he'd heard Miss Sutherland speak.

It was as if his entire world had come to a sudden, grinding halt. He could think of no matter of estate business that needed attention. No familial obligations had come to mind. His weekly schedule had suddenly gone blank. Worse, a keen sort of panic had assailed him in regard to his invention of the *Marriage Formula*. And when he'd looked at her, his brain—the machine he relied upon the most—had failed him. The only part that remained working was a voice that kept asking one question over and over again: *Why isn't Miss Ivy Sutherland's name in one of the ledgers?*

In order for his formula to work, he needed to know every marriageable person in polite society. One single error or miscalculation could risk his Fellowship with the Royal Society. He was hosting this party for one purpose—to reveal the validity of his *Marriage Formula*. Not only to his guests but to two persons who could assist him in gaining the Fellowship he wanted more than he'd ever wanted anything before. In fact, he'd purposely invited Lord Basilton and Lord Pomeroy from the Royal Society in order to calculate matches for their unwed offspring. If everything went as planned, Basilton and Pomeroy's approval—by way of their votes in the new year—would earn him a Fellowship.

Gazing at his aunt, who was ineffectively attempting to tidy the corner of his desk, North swallowed his pride. "Forgive me. I was distracted earlier. Though it is no excuse, I'd realized suddenly that I had an unmarried guest at my party whose name was, until that moment, unknown to me. Under the current circumstances, surely you can understand my appearance of rudeness."

Surprise lifted his aunt's penciled brows before her expression fell to something of a disappointed pout. "Oh, is that all? For a moment, I'd thought Miss Sutherland's understated beauty had you tongue-tied."

If one could call blue eyes that resembled the pale perfection of a winter sky *understated*. Or a complexion as flawless as moonlight. Or hair the white-blond color of a candle flame. Or lips tinged pink as if brushed by madeira. *Understated?* No, her beauty was quite evident.

He meant to laugh, but more of a growl came out instead. "I am not a man ruled by baser impulses. If I were, then my formula would mean nothing and every hope I have of becoming a *Fellow* would be for naught."

"Nephew, I had no idea that Miss Sutherland's attendance at this party could jeopardize so much. When Zinnia wrote and asked if her niece's friend could attend, I saw no harm in it. *Clearly* I underestimated the power of one unmarried young woman."

North eyed his aunt. There was more than a trace of mockery in her tone and expression. "Miss Sutherland holds no power over me. You give her far too much credit. Besides, she cannot be overly marriageable if I'd never met her."

"She has been out of society for the past two years," she said, appearing distracted by her attempts to straighten the papers on the corner of his desk. "Which, as it happens, was when you garnered interest in society in order to begin your formulaic calculations."

He opened a drawer and pulled out a fresh sheet of parchment before dipping a quill pen into the inkpot. "Then Miss Sutherland must be at least four and twenty."

"Five and twenty."

He jotted that down. "Of noble birth?"

"Her father is a country gentleman. He earned a knighthood in the war, years before he married. Her mother is a cleric's daughter. They reside in Surrey. Norwood Hill."

"Such a meager connection to earn Miss Sutherland the opportunity to marry into the aristocracy." Still, it was more of a connection than his own mother had had, he mused, dipping his pen once more. "Has she a fortune, a wealthy relation, or dowry property?"

"None. She is educated, however. Her parents employed a tutor and a dance master for her instruction before her debut."

"Perhaps she descends from a hearty lineage—multiple sons born on both her father and mother's side? How many brothers does she have?"

Edith clasped her hands and offered him a patient stare. "Like you, she is an only child, as were her parents."

Huh. Studying the parchment, he released a breath he didn't realize he'd been holding. He felt . . . relieved. Beyond relieved, actually—*elated* was more precise. "Then she is of no consequence. Her presence will not disrupt my ability to prove my formula in the least."

Eager now, he opened one of the fresh ledgers, which he'd begun solely for this party, and scribbled her name on the page. MISS IVY SUTHERLAND OF NORWOOD HILL—NO CONSEQUENCE. Then he underlined the last two words for good measure.

Aunt Edith huffed in obvious exasperation, drawing his attention. From that disapproving purse of her lips, he already knew what she was going to say.

"Nephew, I wish I could admire your uncanny ability to write down a name and summarily disregard the person who carries it."

"I do not disregard either the person or the name," he argued, while softening his tone. "The names in each of my ledgers are the means that will gain me a Fellowship. I value them a great deal."

She pointed down to his disorderly desk. "If only you'd spent as much time figuring love and happiness into your equation."

"A man should be happy on his own without needing another to spoon-feed it to him. As for love," he said while sprinkling sand over the fresh ink in the ledger so that it wouldn't smear, "it is an emotion invented by the idle-minded."

When he heard no response, he lifted his gaze from Miss Sutherland's name and saw his aunt's disappointed frown.

He released an exhale. "Very well. Will it soothe your ruffled feathers if I promise not to ignore Miss Sutherland or her friend with the pinching slippers for the duration of the party?"

Appearing to mull this over, Edith took a moment before nodding curtly. "Dinner will be in one hour."

North had other plans for this evening, such as organizing his ledgers and making sure every person here was accounted for. He felt the flesh between his brows furrow. "This morning, you'd said that we would not be having a formal dinner this first night, since so many of our guests would be tired and want trays taken to their rooms."

"Yes, but we must think of those who are not tired. Besides, we have many more guests in attendance than we'd originally anticipated. Perhaps you have finally earned a measure of acceptance from those dreaded purists."

"It is more likely that they believe I aim to make one of their daughters a duchess."

"Then let them think what they will." As if the matter had been settled, she made her way to the door. "Tonight's gathering will be an informal dinner in the Great Room. The footmen will carry trays of cheeses, tarts, and hors d'oeuvres, allowing you the freedom to move about, thereby giving you the perfect opportunity to make amends to Miss Appleton and Miss Sutherland."

As the door clicked shut, leaving him to his solitude, North's gaze drifted down to the name in the ledger. As before, all other thoughts stopped, suspended like a pendulum in a clock paused at the crest of the oscillation. It was unnatural. Illogical.

The only reason for his current state of mind had to stem from the inordinate pressure he was under to prove his formula. *Yes, that must be the reason.* And with that reassuring thought, he bent down, blew the dust from the page, and closed the book.

North was certain that his next encounter with Miss Sutherland would be a matter of rote behavior and nothing more.

Chapter Two

"For an informal dinner, this is quite the crush," Ivy said from beneath the wide stone archway of the Great Room.

There were at least one hundred guests, she surmised. The finest array of satins, silks, and lace crowded elbow to elbow in the vast space. If not for the green and gold brocade draperies along the far wall, and the wide tapestries adjacent, the clamor of conversation likely would echo to deafening proportions. Instead, prattling, laughter, and the occasional clink of glassware all rose overhead to the vaulted wood-beamed ceiling.

Beside her, Lilah nodded. "It's a veritable sea of coiffures, tiaras, and feathers."

"Yes, and beware the waves of gossip," Ivy said, charting a course toward the footman with the red wine on his tray. She needed something to settle her unexpectedly raw nerves. For some reason, she could not stop mulling over her encounter with the duke and wondering if the next would unsettle her just as much. From this vantage point, however, she hadn't spotted him yet.

"Gossip, I can take. It's the wine I'm worried about." Lilah smoothed her gloved hands down her pristine white dress.

As a woman on the shelf, Ivy's wardrobe wasn't restricted to a muted palette. This evening she wore her favorite red satin petticoat beneath a gauzy silk tulle sheath.

Earlier, she'd had the maid prepare the blue muslin, trimmed in velvet, yet blue was too calming a color. Inside, Ivy was anything but calm. Therefore, she needed to wear something that made her feel confident, and even a bit pretty.

Belying her self-assuredness, however, she caught herself fidgeting with the cuff of her long white glove. Abruptly, she stopped. "If you do happen to encounter a spill of wine, just be sure it is from the duke's glass."

"I do not know why you are fixed on seeing me married to the duke. As you well know, any titled gentleman of noble birth will do," Lilah whispered.

To Ivy, the answer was obvious. "Yes, but one can easily assume that the duke invited unwed debutantes to his party for the sole purpose of finding a bride for himself. The same cannot be said of the other gentlemen in attendance."

"After your performance earlier, the duke is likely to see me and then instantly glance down to my feet and inquire about the comfort of my shoes."

"I fail to see the problem in a man recalling you from a previous encounter."

Lilah sighed. "Because his recollection would be of my shoes, not of me, Ivy. You don't know how many times Aunt Zinnia has reintroduced me to a gentleman within minutes of a first introduction, only for him to behave as if the second time was new to him. Just once, I'd like a gentleman to remember *me*."

Ivy threaded her arm through her friend's and squeezed her companionably. "And I am here to make certain that your wish comes true."

From the far corner, Lady Cosgrove lifted an arm and beckoned both Ivy and Lilah to her. As they entered the room, the crowd seemed to undulate, each group of attendees moving to and fro. If the center of the room could be compared to a tidal pool—filled with the shiniest of stones—then the cluster of society's premier elite fit there perfectly. Their ostentatious display of jewels gleamed beneath the light of an immense wrought-iron chandelier. Chaperones and their pastel-clad charges formed the first ring, turning their ears toward the center of the room while their eyes followed the unmarried gentlemen. In groups of only two or three, those gentlemen caused surges, altering the form of the gathering as many angled for their attention. Along the outer rim were the matrons. It was no surprise that this group positioned themselves to oversee the entire room at a glance. Everyone knew that these women held the most power. The dowager duchess and Lady Cosgrove were among them.

Also within their midst was a woman too old to be a debutante but far too young to be considered a matron. Her hair was silken gold—a shade darker than Ivy's—the thick waves styled into an elegantly simple twist. Her peach silk gown was the same, elegant and simple. As was the diamond pendant she wore. In her slender carriage, she possessed a regal quality that one could never learn. One had to be born with it. Ivy, unfortunately, had not been.

"Miss Appleton, Miss Sutherland," the dowager duchess began the instant they arrived. "I should like to introduce you to an honored guest, Lady Granworth."

The name sparked a recollection for Ivy as both she and Lilah offered the obligatory curtsies. This time, Ivy managed to be somewhat graceful.

"Of course, since Lady Cosgrove and Lady Granworth are cousins through—Zinnia, is it your mother's side?" The dowager duchess turned to her friend. In receiving a nod, she continued. "No doubt you have heard mention of her, Miss Appleton."

"I have, Your Grace," Lilah said. "In fact, Aunt Zinnia, Lady Granworth, and I have exchanged letters during the past year."

It was in this moment that Ivy recalled hearing Lady Granworth's name in conversations with Lilah. Juliet Granworth was Lilah's third cousin. Apparently, there had been a split at one time in their family. When Lady Granworth's husband had passed a year ago, however, Lady Cosgrove had reached out with an olive branch.

"After so many letters, you must call me Juliet. It is a true pleasure to meet you in the flesh, at last, cousin." Extending a gloved hand to Lilah, Juliet Granworth smiled. When the light caught her sapphire-jeweled eyes, her delight was evident. Then she turned to Ivy. "Miss Sutherland, please call me Juliet, for I am certain we will be friends as well. From Lilah's letters, I feel as if you and I are already acquainted."

"I assure you that I'm not nearly as wayward or impulsive as Lilah has likely expressed," Ivy said with a grin.

This comment earned a cough from Lady Cosgrove and a silent smirk from Lilah.

"I believe the descriptions I read were quite complimentary of an admirable determination to live by one's own rules," Juliet replied with all the appearance of sincerity.

Even though Ivy was touched by the compliment, at the same time she noted Lady Cosgrove's disapproving glance toward Lilah. Deciding it was best to save her friend, Ivy added, "A careless endeavor on which only a woman resolved never to marry should embark." She managed the words without the slightest of grins. *Contrition, thy name is Ivy,* she thought, congratulating herself.

"A truth well spoken, Miss Sutherland," Lady Cosgrove said, her stern agreement a clear warning to her niece. "Gentlemen of noble birth prefer accomplished, genteel brides."

Lilah laughed wryly. "What good are accomplishments or manners if there is not a single gentleman interested in them? We are tutored to speak French, to read Latin, to dance, to exhibit poise, to draw, and to sew, but none of that matters if . . ." Her words trailed off as her eyes widened.

Surprised by her friend's outburst, Ivy couldn't speak. Lilah often spoke her mind to Ivy when they were alone, but this was the first time she'd ever said anything in direct contradiction to her aunt. As Ivy watched her, Lilah's lips parted and her gaze darted to her aunt as if she'd just realized the same thing.

"That is to say—"

"I quite agree, cousin," Juliet interrupted. "I've met no gentleman who has any real interest in needlework. Otherwise they would all be dressed in coats with thistle flowers embroidered on the cuffs, and keep a ready needle tucked away in a waistcoat pocket."

Ivy laughed, liking Juliet Granworth despite her enviable beauty. "Indeed. Now, whenever I see a gentleman with a monogrammed handkerchief, I will not assume he has a sister but more so that he embroidered the square himself."

"That must be the true reason gentlemen do not want ladies in their clubs," the dowager duchess said cheekily, stunning the group. "They fear the competition."

This time they all laughed, even Lady Cosgrove.

"I wonder what has become of my nephew," the dowager said after a moment, searching the crowd. "Regrettably, he is often late when distracted by a new invention. I do believe that his *Marriage Formula* is currently occupying his mind."

"A formula for marriage, ma'am?" Juliet asked, her wispy brows lifting. "I don't believe I've heard of such a thing. Are men and women so easy to enter into an equation?"

The dowager duchess tsked. "I am not in full agreement with my nephew on this notion of his. However, he did alter his original title for my sake—which was *The Matrimonial Goods Exchange*— therefore, I feel obligated to support him."

"Ghastly title, Duchess," Lady Cosgrove said under her breath.

"I concur," the dowager duchess answered. "His former title made it sound as if marriage were part of a bartering system, which—of course—it has been for centuries. I believe, however, we've risen above that archaic notion. In our modern day, more and more marriages are decided on by matters of mutual regard and fondness, as they should be. I'm sure you would agree, Zinnia."

Lady Cosgrove was silent for a moment. Ivy imagined that at any moment, she would employ another infamous look. Instead, a wistful smile graced her lips.

"You and I were fortunate, Duchess," Lady Cosgrove said with an uncharacteristic softness. Then, looking to Lilah, she cleared her throat. "Though not all young women can afford romantic notions."

Perturbed, Ivy spoke up in defense of her friend. "Everyone deserves a chance to find love, no matter their circumstance."

She would have said more, too, but suddenly, a wave of dizziness spiraled through her. She closed her eyes for an instant to recover. Then her gaze swept to the door, as if instinct directed her to the cause of the ailment. She didn't understand how she knew the duke would be standing there. But he was.

And he was looking directly at her.

"At last, there is my nephew," the dowager said, lifting a hand to beckon him forth. "You were good to spot him first, Miss Sutherland. Had I not noticed the shift of your attention, his arrival might have escaped my notice."

Ivy wanted to deny that her attention had shifted in any way. She wanted to think of a lie to excuse her sudden absorption in the area surrounding the archway. At the very least, she wanted to be able to turn away. Yet she could do none of those.

The duke hesitated, reluctance etched on his features in the way his dark brow furrowed. Then his nostrils flared as he drew in a breath, deep enough to expand those broad shoulders and the wide chest beneath a dark gray coat and silver satin waistcoat.

And when he took his first step, Ivy was certain she felt the quake of it beneath her feet.

"For his tardiness," the dowager duchess continued, "we should question him ceaselessly about his formula."

"Duchess, I fear we should not antagonize your nephew," Lady Cosgrove said, likely in the hopes of making a favorable impression for Lilah's sake.

Earlier, it had seemed that neither Ivy nor Lilah had made any impression on the duke at all. He hadn't spoken a single word of acknowledgment. In contrast, Ivy had spoken far too much. While she'd blamed that dratted second cup of tea before, now she was beginning to wonder if it was something else. She tended toward verbosity when she was nervous. Yet what reason could she have for being nervous? She didn't care what the duke thought of her. All she wanted was to ensure a match for Lilah.

"If there is any person used to criticism, it is my nephew. And he is a stronger man for it." The dowager duchess's voice lilted with obvious pride.

Criticism? From what Ivy had heard, he'd inherited the title at the age of fifteen. And from what she saw, he wore the ducal title like a second skin. His stride was sure and direct, his hematite gaze disarming. Who would dare criticize such a man?

That thought aside, however, Ivy wished he would look away, or that a footman would offer him a glass of wine, a wedge of cheese, a fig tart . . . *Anything.* A frisson of fear dowsed the dizziness, though fear of what, she wasn't certain. All she knew was that her heart was beating faster now. Moreover, she had the uncanny desire to bolt from the room.

"Ivy, I beg you not to mention my shoes or spill wine on my gown," Lilah whispered from beside her.

He would be upon them any moment. Even from half the distance of the room away, he stared at Ivy as if she were completely insane. Or possibly as if she'd offended him in some manner. Truly, he looked entirely too bothered by her presence.

"Of course I won't," Ivy said, her voice thready and quivering. She was in a state of panic now. "Lilah, please tell me that you see a friend in the crowd—someone with whom you must visit this instant."

Lilah released a quiet, sardonic laugh. "Whyever for?"

"Pray, do not ask me, because I do not know." Then, like an answer to a prayer, a footman crossed in front of Ivy, breaking the spell she'd fallen under. Hastily, she took Lilah's hand, turned, and curtsied to their party. "Forgive me, ma'am, but I only now spied a drop of wine on Lilah's gown. We must make haste to the retiring room before it stains."

Even before being dismissed, Ivy hauled her friend away in the opposite direction. She had no idea where she was going, but she started to feel better immediately.

It wasn't long before Lilah wrenched out of their clasped hands. "What has come over you today, Ivy? And more importantly, why must *my* dress be the one with the stain? Yours would be equally ruined by an imaginary splash of wine."

"But not as noticeable." Ivy smoothed her hands down the front of her gown, more out of a need to calm herself than to make her point. Her left glove had slipped down her arm again. Drawing it up, she fought the urge to glance over her shoulder to see if the duke had noticed their abrupt departure. "Besides, I needed to ask you what topics you would like to discuss with the duke. There must be certain things you'd want to know about your future husband."

"Have you gone mad?" Lilah squinted, her brown eyes flashing daggers. "Please tell me now before your *assistance* in seeing me wed goes any further."

Ivy drew in a breath. She knew her actions of this day were questionable. Not even she could guess how to explain herself. All she knew was that she needed to keep her distance from the duke until she figured it out.

She drew in a breath, preparing to exhale a slight fabrication of the truth. "I'm almost entirely positive that I'm not mad. However, I have realized, quite suddenly, that I have been neglecting to consider the other gentlemen in attendance. Given the freedom of an informal dinner, we really must take advantage and mingle around the room."

Lilah's eyes softened somewhat as she studied Ivy. After a moment, she nodded. "That is perfectly sound reasoning— though perhaps you could have used that as your excuse for our departure instead."

"If you'll recall, that was my first attempt when I asked you to find a friend," Ivy pointed out, lifting a finger as she adjusted her glove once more.

"You gave me *two seconds* to examine the entire room."

Ivy offered a half shrug and a grin. "Very well, I forgive you."

"You are lucky that I am fond of you, otherwise I might accidentally spill an entire glass of wine over your head," Lilah said all too sweetly.

"Tut tut. No need for theatrics, dearest. From this moment forward, I shall be perfectly sensible." *As long as I stay far away from the duke,* Ivy thought. The only problem was, if she continued to avoid the duke, then how could she steer him in Lilah's direction?

NORTH SPENT THE next hour mingling, just as Aunt Edith had intended. He welcomed nearly all of his guests—all except two. Thus far, Miss Sutherland and her friend with the pinching slippers remained elusive. However, not so elusive that he was unaware of their placement in the room at any given moment.

Even so, while his mind was diverted, he displayed the proper amount of interest in various topics of conversation. During this time, he heard no fewer than four dozen castigating reports on the state of the roads. At least thirty criticisms regarding the inconvenience of house parties at such a time of year. And yet, an unending list of the accomplishments possessed by the debutantes in attendance.

The reason for the last was that many assumed this party was for the purpose of finding a bride for himself. Whether or not they thought his half-commoner blood was inferior to theirs, his title made him irresistible. Once he revealed his true purpose—the final proof of his *Marriage Formula*—he would soon prove his worth on his own terms.

His guests would be more than delighted. Well, at least the men would be. They were, after all, the ones put upon by all this Season nonsense and pointless courting rituals.

Two years ago, at the club, North had overheard Basilton and Pomeroy speaking of the expenses and inconveniences of each Season. That was what had first given North the idea for the formula. He knew there had to be a simpler method for a gentleman to find a bride whose person and dowry appealed to him. And once North proved his formula, he would finally earn his Fellowship.

To his mind, the formula and his plan provided a universal benefit to society. Edith, however, was not at all convinced that women would want to be partnered by way of a formula instead of a series of parties and balls. He hoped his aunt's sentiments were not shared by too many others of her sex. He knew that if women gave his formula a chance, they would soon see the brilliance of his plan.

"Why does Aunt Edith appear so cross with you, cousin?" Beside him, Liam Cavanaugh, Earl of Wolford, plucked a fig tart from the tray and ate it in one bite, leaving time enough to reach for another before the footman could get away.

North glanced over a half dozen heads to Edith. Her narrow-eyed gaze was already upon him, and it abruptly snapped to another person in the room—or persons, rather—before it returned to him. This was Edith's way of pointing out that he'd neglected to greet Miss Sutherland and her friend.

He offered his aunt a nod of understanding. Then, as his gaze skimmed over the crowd, it lingered for a moment on Miss Sutherland, standing not two strides from him. She was turned away, but only just. From his vantage point, he noted the tension in her jaw and the way her eyes darted around the room, searching. He wondered if there was cause for her restlessness, or if she was forever in motion, unable to be still.

While he pondered this, she shifted. The line of her shoulder tilted, drawing his attention to the movement of her arm at her side, and to the glove that slipped down her slender arm. His gaze fixed on the small expanse of milky flesh it revealed.

The tips of his fingers tingled, making him aware that he'd left his chamber before taking his gloves from his valet. Typically, an idea for a new invention made him absent-minded. This time, however, his preoccupation had been Miss Sutherland's fault entirely.

After a moment, he forced himself to turn back to Liam. "How do you know Edith isn't glaring at you instead?"

His cousin failed to subdue the amused smirk that creased one side of his mouth. North and Liam resembled each other enough for one to presume a familial connection. Both were of the same height, build, and age. Both had the same dark brows and dark hair, but that was where their similarities ended.

Liam wore his hair at a length befitting a man of leisure and overindulgence. More than that, his reputation for excess was well earned. He was fortunate that dissolution had not marred his more refined features. Or dulled the glint of mischief ever-present in his green eyes.

Most important, however, was their final dissimilarity—if Liam had been born just one month sooner, he would have become the Duke of Vale without the barest hint of disapproval.

"Because she likes me better," Liam said, nudging North with his elbow.

North had always suspected as much. After all, he did not possess what some might call a warm, engaging personality. "Where is your usual coterie? I thought both Thayne and Marlowe expressed an interest in the ascending room I've built in the east wing. Of course, with Burton and Hormer's design marginally flawed, I felt the need to modify the pulley system to my standards."

"Had I half your brain, all of London would be my playground." Liam shook his head and tsked as if in regret.

North lifted his brows. "You mean to say that it isn't already?"

"*Hmm* . . . a third, perhaps," Liam said with a thoughtful nod. "As you might have guessed, Marlowe will not attend. Once he learned that the Earl of Dovermere was due to attend with the eldest of his eight daughters, he changed his plans."

It was common knowledge that Jack Marlowe was Dovermere's illegitimate son. Born on the wrong side of the blanket, Marlowe had never had the acceptance of society. Criticism over a less-than-acceptable birth was something both he and North had in common. "An oversight, though I'm sure Edith meant well. Since Dovermere was a friend of our late uncle's, she merely wants father and son to reconcile."

"As for the *estimable* Marquess Thayne, he and his mother will arrive on the morrow. As of yet, he does not know that Lady Granworth has chosen your party to re-emerge into society. Something tells me that Thayne will be quite surprised. After all, everyone remembers the scandal between the two of them . . ."

North barely heard his cousin speaking. Like earlier today, his mind abruptly stopped. Everything around him slowed, voices merged into a collective murmur, the room seemed to darken everywhere but where Miss Sutherland stood. And for an instant, he caught her staring in his direction.

Even from this distance, he saw her shocked expression clearly—a delicate movement in her throat, the widening of her pale eyes, and the first tinge of bright red to her cheeks. In the way her lips parted, he saw rather than heard her small gasp.

All of a sudden, he wanted to hear that sound. Taste it. Feel her breasts rise on a swift intake of air as he hauled her into his embrace. The weight of arousal dropped swift and low inside him, like the sudden plummet of a sandbag at the end of a rope. She turned away quickly, but the result didn't alter. He still felt that inexplicable, heavy desire for her.

Before he returned his attention to Liam—who now, strangely enough, spoke of a pair of draft horses he'd purchased solely for the journey on the off chance of a heavy snowfall—North watched Miss Sutherland pull up her glove once more.

That glove. Watching it slip down, inch by inch, was like the veil dance he'd witnessed during his travels to India. Only this was much slower and, surprisingly, more erotic. He was becoming obsessed with the flesh hidden beneath that glove. He wanted to dip his fingers inside and peel the garment from her arm.

"What are your thoughts on the matter?" Liam asked.

North didn't hesitate to respond. "I wonder why you didn't purchase a sleigh instead. The vehicle's performance on snowy terrain is unsurpassed."

"Hmph. I thought you weren't listening," Liam said with a smirk, his gaze skimming to Miss Sutherland's general direction and then back again.

She slipped her arms behind her back and thrummed her fingers together. Once more, her glove slid down. North grabbed a glass of merlot from a passing tray, downed it in one swallow, and replaced the empty glass before the footman was out of arm's reach.

North made sure his expression was perfectly bland. "Have I given the appearance of rudeness or preoccupation?"

"No," his cousin answered, scrutinizing him. "And you never do. It's just that most of the time, I have the feeling that your mind is busy on other tasks."

An astute observation, North mused. Perhaps both he and Liam shared another similarity. However, North wasn't about to admit anything. He didn't have to—*he* was the duke. "I believe that we should speak with Edith and find out which one of us has earned her censure."

"I already know it isn't me," Liam said with a grin before he set off on a direct path toward their aunt.

North, however, took a slight detour.

Unable to fight the urge, he walked in Miss Sutherland's direction. At the same time, he calculated the nearest footman's route. Just as he'd anticipated, both the footman and he arrived in the narrow path behind her in the same instant. Then, in the second that transpired, he graciously allowed his servant to pass, while he himself skirted within a hairsbreadth of Miss Sutherland, his front to her back.

There was no time for an exchange. Or even for him to make his presence known. There was only time for a breath—filled with the sweet scent of persimmons perfuming her simple coiffure—and a single touch.

The pad of his index finger grazed the warm, soft flesh of her arm and dipped, ever so slightly, *beneath* the cuff of her glove.

A hedonistic shudder wracked him in that briefest of moments. And he was already several steps away before he heard her gasp.

Chapter Three

"I DO NOT WISH to be late to the concert," Lilah said from the door to their chamber the following evening. "Aunt Zinnia would not be pleased. She left a quarter of an hour ago."

In the dressing room, Ivy hunted for her other slipper. It had to be here, somewhere beneath the array of petticoats, stockings, and chemises strewn about. She'd seen it only a moment ago . . . "Since your aunt prides herself on pedestrianism, she must leave inordinately early. We, on the other hand, have no qualms over employing a quick pace when the need arises."

Ah ha! She spotted the blue silk toe peeking out from beneath the chair in the corner. Rushing over, she snatched it and slipped it on as she hopped toward the bedchamber.

"It may sound strange to your ears, Ivy, but some of us prefer not to arrive winded and gasping for breath . . ." Lilah's friendly scolding stopped when Ivy appeared. "I thought you asked the maid to press your sea-green gown for this evening."

Ivy smoothed her hands down the fine blue satin and adjusted the darker velvet sash beneath her breasts. That same velvet trimmed her sleeves, hem and bodice. Where the red gown last evening had helped her feel confident, this gown made her feel calm. Right now, she needed as much calm as she could manage. "I changed my mind. Sea green is such a turbulent color. I don't think it suits me."

Lilah laughed but kept her comment to herself. "You will be wearing gloves this evening, won't you?"

"Of course." Yet at the mention of gloves, Ivy felt her face heat. She turned away from Lilah and crossed the room toward the bed. Surreptitiously, she withdrew the folded pair of evening gloves that she'd tucked beneath her pillow last night. Slowly, she pulled them on.

All day long, she'd been trying not to think about the duke's inadvertent touch last evening. The problem was, not thinking about it turned into thinking about it. Often. And in those moments, she'd come to the conclusion that his touch had not been an accident. The swift, warm graze of his flesh against hers had felt entirely too purposeful. Not to mention intimate. Especially when he'd delved *beneath*.

Ivy glanced down at the underside of her arm, certain that a mark had been left behind. She could still feel the path his finger had taken. Still feel the hot frenzy of tingles beneath her flesh. Incomprehensible though it seemed, her pale skin was unmarked by anything other than the appearance of a long blue vein. That vein must, assuredly, lead to her heart, because its rapid palpitations kept tempo with the tingles.

When Ivy walked to the door, Lilah eyed her with speculation. "Do you always keep your gloves beneath your pillow?"

"I didn't want to misplace them. After all, I knew you'd be in a rush," Ivy answered on a single breath, hoping to distract her friend. Then, linking arms with Lilah, she made haste down the corridor. If they didn't hurry, they would surely be late for the concert.

"That *I'd* be in a . . ." Lilah stopped on a huff, slipping free of Ivy. "You know very well that I value punctuality, whereas you are the one making us tardy."

Ivy tossed a grin over her shoulder. Occasionally it was easy to fluster *and* distract her friend at the same time. "If that is true, then why am I four steps ahead of you?"

Lilah wanted to be cross—Ivy could tell by the set of her jaw—but in the end she rolled her eyes to the ceiling and mouthed the word *incorrigible,* giving up a smile in the process. Yet there was something altogether mischievous in that small curl of her lips. "Perhaps because you are heading in the wrong direction. Again. Therefore, I am four steps— *now five, six*—ahead of you."

This time, Ivy was the one who stopped. Sure enough, she peered down the corridor in the direction she was heading and saw a narrow window in the distance. *Drat!* This castle had her turned completely around. "Perhaps I know of a shortcut."

"Like the one we took last night? Thank you, Ivy, but no. I'd prefer to arrive at the concert tonight, not in the wee hours of tomorrow morning."

That wasn't entirely fair. Last night she'd been far too preoccupied to remember the way to their chamber. She blamed the duke. It was his fault. Completely. His errant touch had addled her. Even thinking about it now, she caught herself rubbing her palm over that place on her arm.

Abruptly, she dropped her hands to her sides. "Very well. We'll take your way."

Lilah laughed as they began their trek down the corridor that would eventually lead them toward the stairs to the ballroom. "Likely it is the *only* way. I'm glad one of us paid attention to the housekeeper's tour of the castle this afternoon."

"While you were studying architecture and listening to the history of the Norman Conquest, I was searching for your future husband." Unfortunately, Ivy had not caught a single glimpse of the duke all day. Part of her—the confused, tingly part—was relieved. Yet the rest of her was still determined for Lilah to marry the most eligible bachelor here. Vale was the obvious choice.

Ivy decided that she would just have to put her strange

reaction to him aside, conquer her inexplicable dizziness, and resume the focus that had brought her here in the first place.

"As the maid informed our group earlier," Lilah began, "the gentlemen had gone on a hunt early this morning. Therefore, searching for one would have been a futile endeavor."

One thing that had always confused Ivy about house parties was the fact that gentlemen and debutantes were, more often than not, kept apart. Supposedly, these gatherings were designed for the purpose of matchmaking. Yet the only moments the sexes spent together were typically before and during dinner. Ivy wondered how anyone managed to find a suitable spouse at all. "Our host was still here."

Lilah shook her head. "Ivy, I truly wish you would cease your pursuit. The duke is not going to marry someone like me."

"Well, he won't if *that* is your attitude," Ivy scoffed.

"It has nothing to do with attitude and more with interest. The duke is more likely to marry you than me."

Ivy tripped over her velvet hem and nearly stumbled into a suit of armor.

"Whyever would you say a thing like that? I'm not the least bit intrigued by the duke, and I certainly harbor no romantic notions about him. Not a single one." This time, when she said the words in a rush, her throat constricted. She tried to swallow, but the sensation would not abate.

"I didn't mean to suggest that you did . . ." Lilah hesitated, her eyes turning doelike and sorrowful. "Oh bother, Ivy. I know that asking you to attend this party was a selfish indulgence on my part. I should have realized how difficult it would be for you to be surrounded by marriage-minded debutantes, especially after what happened with my brother."

Now Ivy felt guilty for the way that her denial had sounded more like an outburst. "Don't be silly. You have no reason to apologize. I don't mind it here at all. In fact, the castle is lovely. If the party were to last ten years, then perhaps I could even tour it in its entirety. However, if you insist on being at fault for a nonsensical offense, you can make it up to me by inviting me to live here with you and your duke."

Lilah released an exhausted sigh as they reached a fork in the corridor. Automatically, Ivy turned left, certain that was the correct path. Everything inside of her told her to turn left. Behind her, however, Lilah cleared her throat. "The ballroom is this way, Ivy."

Ivy caught a glimpse of a man striding down the hall, heading in the direction she wanted to go. Even before her eyes recognized his form and his sure, purposeful stride, a jolt dashed through her, setting her off balance. In an instant, she knew it was the duke. Part of her wanted to flee to the ballroom. Yet another part knew that this was the perfect opportunity for Lilah. "We must go this way, for I believe that is the duke."

Beside her now, Lilah squinted. "At this hour, it is more likely a servant. Furthermore, the light is too dim. You cannot be certain."

But Ivy was. Even that path on her arm tingled again. "Our host is alone. There is no better time to make an exceptional impression on him."

"Thus far your methods have been far from impressive," Lilah grumbled.

"Think of those instances as part of a process. We keep going until we find one that works." Although Ivy hoped the process wouldn't take too long. Once the duke started to show clear interest in Lilah, Ivy could return home, where she could forget about errant touches, tingles, and dizzy spells.

"His Grace is walking in the opposite direction of the ballroom. I am certain he has no desire to be accosted.

Please come away," Lilah begged. "We must attend the concert. I know we are very late."

Ivy took a breath, preparing to use her most persuasive tone. "Your aunt will surely forgive you once you have secured a duke. Such a boon would reflect well on her, also."

Lilah glanced down the hall once more, appearing to waver. Then she shook her head succinctly. "No, for he has already turned that corner."

Oh, for mercy's sake! "He cannot have gotten too far. We could still—"

"I am leaving, Ivy," Lilah interrupted. "Are you joining me?"

NORTH WAS A man of science and purpose. He was not allowing an uncharacteristic reaction to Miss Sutherland to dictate his actions. The reason he was not seated in the ballroom, awaiting the concert to begin, was that he'd forgotten his gloves. It had nothing to do with the fact that Edith had arranged for him to sit next to Miss Sutherland and her friend all evening.

Nevertheless, he was thankful that he'd discovered the seating arrangement before he'd entered the ballroom. Moments ago, he'd stood in the hall at the back of the room, peering through a slivered opening of the French doors. The concert had already begun. Wall sconces and chandeliers had bathed the room in golden light. His guests had been seated in rows of cushioned fiddle-backed chairs, their lorgnettes poised—more for the purpose of gossip than for musical admiration, he'd been sure. That had been the reason he hadn't stepped inside. That and because there'd been three empty seats in between Edith and Lady Cosgrove. *Three*— most likely one for him, one for the tardy Miss Sutherland, and one for the equally tardy Miss . . . *whatever her name was*.

He never should have told Edith the truth earlier when

she'd asked if he'd spoken with Lady Cosgrove's niece and Miss Sutherland yet. *Damnation!*

Even now, striding away from the concert, he felt his pulse thicken at the thought of sitting beside Miss Sutherland. Just imagine the damage that could befall his plan if one of those lorgnettes spied him taking an indiscreet glance at a certain Miss Sutherland. Or worse, saw him touch her again.

That was precisely the reason he'd had to return to his study to don a pair of gloves. The fabric would likely be barrier enough to remind him of his position. If it did not, dire consequences awaited him. Tongues would surely wag. Some might even assume he was attracted to her beyond his control.

However, he knew the truth.

The epiphany had come to him a short time ago. Of course, this was after he'd caught himself requesting that the cook add a persimmon jelly to the menu for this evening. After he'd spent hours tinkering with his slipper stretcher. And after he'd found himself searching a map of Surrey for Norwood Hill in his private study—which was likely where he'd left his gloves.

Upon realizing his preoccupation, he'd summarily dismissed the cause as being linked to Miss Sutherland. It was far more likely that his fixation stemmed from his desire to prove his formula. His Fellowship was at stake, after all.

In the past, when he'd been on the precipice of revealing one of his own inventions to the Society for review, he'd usually found a minor flaw that would prevent him. The reason then had been that he hadn't been fully prepared. In his excitement, he'd rushed a few previous inventions. Yet with his formula, he'd taken his time. It was too important to rush. And in the end, his equation was flawless. Therefore, the obvious conclusion regarding his preoccupation with Miss Sutherland was that it was a form of self-sabotage. Nothing more. This time, however, he had proof that his formula worked. And over the course of the party, he would reveal his greatest achievement.

Now, on the way down the hall, North decided to test the stabilizing bars he'd added to the ascending room track to make for a smooth ascent and descent. Removing the key from his pocket, he opened the door. It was safer to keep a locked door in front of it, otherwise—if the room was not on the same floor—a gaping hole would greet you. That could be disastrous for anyone to happen upon.

Then, just as he stepped inside, he heard a rush of footsteps coming from around the corner. Holding the door open with one hand, he peered over his shoulder in time to see Miss Sutherland emerge, but she wasn't looking in his direction. Instead, she was looking over her shoulder.

"Tell your aunt that I will be late because I decided to wear the sea-green gown after all. And do not worry. Everything will be fine," she called out, and a voice replied in an indistinguishable murmur.

North opened his mouth to warn her, but he was suddenly preoccupied by the thought of her slipping out of this blue dress. He *could* offer his assistance . . .

By the time he cleared his head, Miss Sutherland was taking a few hurried backward steps. When she turned around, she ran headlong into him with a surprised *oh!* and then an *oof!*

North stumbled back into the ascending room. He did everything he could to remain upright. Planting his feet wide, he was forced to hold her against the sturdy column of his body. Forced to grasp her arms. Which, incidentally, were bare between her velvet-trimmed cap sleeves and elbow-length gloves. Bare beneath his hands. Bare, warm, and softer than goose down.

A shudder—that was more about untamed desire than preoccupation—quaked through him to his very core. Staring down into her almond-shaped eyes, he watched as they widened and swept over his features, from brow to chin. Her gaze lingered a fraction longer on his mouth, as if she was waiting for him to speak or, perhaps, waiting for him to kiss her.

He took a moment to speculate whether it was the former or the latter. In the seconds that passed, he catalogued how her hands were *resting* against his chest, not pressing as if she wanted to gain her freedom but curled slightly as if trying to capture the beat of his heart in the cup of her palms. Also, she made no movement to separate from him. Her breathing was rapid—though perhaps that was the result of running down the hall. When she wet her lips, however, she provided an irrefutable answer.

Another surge coursed through him. It was a shame he could not act upon it.

"Good evening, Miss Sutherland." As if by rote, he set her apart from him and lowered his arms. Instantly, he wanted to haul her back. Yet he did not. He knew he should say something inanely polite and send her in the direction of the ballroom. Yet he could think of nothing. His mind had ceased to function once more.

Chapter Four

"GOOD EVENING, MISS SUTHERLAND."

Even though Ivy knew that the duke was bound to speak at one point or another, hearing him now left her a bit dazed. His tone matched his countenance perfectly—rough-hewn and darkly mesmerizing. His enunciation lived up to ducal standards, she was sure, but there was something of an underlying growl to each word. The sound of it made her want to close her eyes and hear it whispered to her. "Your Grace. At last, we complete our introduction."

Instead of him staring at her as if she were a madwoman, her impertinence earned an unexpected smile. That smile formed two distinct creases alongside his mouth, like a tutor's brackets marking an important passage in a lesson. She was inclined to agree with this imaginary tutor, because the duke's broad mouth was certainly worth further study.

He inclined his head. "Northcliff Melchior Bromley, the fifth Duke of Vale, Marquess of Edgemont and Viscount Barlow, at your service. Forgive me for not introducing myself properly yesterday. I was . . . unaccountably distracted."

"With a name like yours to remember, I'd have been distracted as well," she said, the words tumbling out heedlessly.

His smile remained, deepening to three creases on each side, and his magnetic eyes crinkled at the edges. *Oh dear.* The combination did far worse things to her equilibrium than mere dark intensity had. "Are you lost, Miss Sutherland?"

"Lost? No, I—" Still standing near him, she didn't feel lost at all. Nor had she been lost when she'd chased him down in the hall. However, she could admit to neither. "Actually, yes. I believe I am. Though I imagine you employ a servant rescue brigade below stairs, whose sole purpose is to aid wayward guests."

He shook his head, his expression turning thoughtful. "Alas, they are all on another mission at the moment, so you are left with me. Luckily, I hardly ever get lost."

Surprised by his quick wit, she laughed. "*Hardly ever* is better than I have managed thus far."

"I'll tell you a secret, Miss Sutherland," he said, leaning in a fraction. He lifted his hand to her elbow and turned her to face the hall at her back. "Each hallway is comprised of a specific décor. The one leading to your chamber is, I believe, host to suits of armor. The one leading to the ballroom is adorned with statues in various dance poses. Others have urns, marble busts, paintings, topiaries . . ."

"That's actually quite brilliant," she said, turning to face him.

She might have said more to that effect, too, but she ended up breathless instead when he flashed those creases at her again. Reaching out, she placed a hand against the door frame. That was when she looked around at their close quarters. It appeared that they stood inside a closet. With the only light source coming from the hall behind her and a single lamp suspended from the ceiling, all she could see was unfinished walls with vertical tracks of metal and dangling ropes exposed, along with a small bench secured to the floor. A floor which—alarmingly enough—shifted beneath her feet. "Either the floor is moving, or your spell-casting abilities are even greater than I first imagined."

Wait a moment, did I say that aloud?

His gruff laugh was answer enough. "The floor is indeed shifting. A degree of movement allows for subtle changes in the frame and structure, providing a smoother elevation or descent—much like a carriage ride is smoother because the supports bounce and give instead of remaining rigid."

Ivy felt her cheeks heat, doubtless with that unfortunate scarlet color. It was less about embarrassment over what she'd said aloud and more about the alteration in him. His enthusiasm for his subject matter was obvious. The amount of passion in his voice enthralled her, stirred her, heated her. So much so, in fact, that it took her a moment to grasp what he was saying. "A carriage?"

"The term being used for the one being built in Regent's Park is *ascending room*. Essentially, this room is an elevator like those used in coal mines . . ." During his explanation, he never once looked away from her. He seemed as eager to tell her as she was to learn of it. Then he held out his hand. "Would you care to join me?"

She slipped her fingers into his palm without the barest thought of refusing. Had she still been a debutante, such an act could have ruined her. She had no chaperone, and to be alone in a gentleman's company was strictly forbidden. Even *on the shelf*, the same fate could befall her. With all the guests distracted by the concert, however, she doubted anyone would know. Unless . . . "Will it take long?"

He lifted his brows as he drew her farther inside toward a small cushioned bench. "Are you always in a rush, Miss Sutherland?"

"Always," she answered immediately, which earned her another chuckle.

"Then I will have you at the concert before you are missed." His grasp lingered for a moment before he released her.

Ivy's stomach trembled when the floor shifted once more. Her legs shook, too, forcing her to sit down on the bench. Even though she had an impulsive nature and enjoyed trying new experiences, it did not mean she never felt warned against them. Usually when she ignored this feeling, it tended to transform into one of exhilaration. She rather liked that part.

He moved to the door and turned the key in the lock, closing them inside. Anticipation swelled. Still, she felt compelled to ask, "Should there not be an inner door as well?"

"I'd thought of that, but it might give some the feeling of being caged in." He shifted to the right and opened a wall-mounted box that contained a lever.

While his statement made sense, when she looked around the small, dimly lit room, she could see how easy it would be to get a hand or foot trapped in the space between the floor and the wall. *Stop it, Ivy. You're beginning to worry like Lilah.*

Nevertheless . . . "Some might say that the purpose of a cage is to offer a semblance of security, while giving the illusion that one's freedom is within reach."

"You are quite safe, Miss Sutherland. The steam engine is not directly below us. Besides, this time of year, the water used for cooling the condenser is quite cold, thereby limiting the possibility of explosion. Plus, I have installed a series of bumpers to slow down the carriage should the supports give way."

"*Explosion? Give way?*" she gasped, having second thoughts.

Too late. The room jolted into motion. A harsh metallic clacking sound accompanied it. Her gaze lifted toward the sound to find a flat, black ceiling overhead. The room suddenly resembled a coffin. The candle flame cast undulating shadows on the unfinished walls, but the ceiling seemed to devour the light, reflecting nothing.

"Fear not," he said gently, drawing her gaze. "I have operated this room dozens of times, including twice today, without a mishap. I've run through every conceivable catastrophe and put forth methods of prevention."

Something Lilah would appreciate, Ivy thought absently. He sounded so sure of himself that she felt foolish for being alarmed.

Then another sound rang out above them. This time it was a grinding metal on metal, and a high, piercing shriek. Perhaps like a rope stretched to the point of snapping.

The carriage jerked to a stop with enough force that she bounced on the bench. "Please tell me that was supposed to happen."

The duke did not answer. He faced the lever instead, feet planted wide as if bracing himself. A series of clicks followed the up-and-down movement of his arms. Lifting the lever up—*click*. Down—*click*. Again and again. His broad shoulders strained against the seams of his coat. His breathing became harsh. He expressed an oath. Then suddenly he turned, took her by the shoulders, and lifted her to her feet.

"Hold on to me," he growled in her ear. His arms snaked around her waist and tucked her head into the crook of his shoulder. Then another marrow-chilling grinding sound ripped through the room.

Ivy clung to him. The first instant of their descent, her feet lifted off the floor. Time seemed suspended by a mutual intake of breath. The metallic shrieks grew deafening. Her feet returned to the floor, but her stomach was still elevated, held aloft by the force of their sudden fall. She remembered a similar feeling from when she'd raced down the hill in the gardener's wheelbarrow. It had been truly terrifying and then exhilarating, but only *after* she'd awoken and found herself still alive.

She closed her eyes now, hoping for the same result.

The carriage jerked on a groan and the crack of splintering wood.

"First bumper," the duke whispered, tightening his arms around her.

Another jerk followed. *Groan. Crack.*

"Second bumper. We're slowing now."

Slowing? How could he tell?

Another jerk. *Groan . . . crack.*

"Third bumper. Hold tight."

The carriage jerked. Hard. *Groan . . .*

She waited to hear the *crack*. When it did not come and their descent paused, she lifted her head. The candle flame had flickered out, enshrouding them in darkness. "How many bumpers are there?"

"Four. We are resting upon the last now, but fear not, it is quite sturdy and not a great distance from the bottom of the shaft." The nod of his head brushed her temple. "A survivable fall."

She should have been furious. She should have railed at him for putting her life in danger. Yet right that moment, a cool, tingly feeling of exhilaration poured through her. *I am alive,* she thought. *I'm alive, and his arms feel wondrous around me.*

Ivy drew in a deep breath and tilted her head back. She absorbed every sensation. Her heart pounded hard, like horses galloping over a moonlit path. The air smelled cold, damp, and delicious. The superfine wool of his coat was warm and soft beneath her fingertips. And where he cradled her body against his stomach, hips, and thighs, it felt hot and right. She never wanted it to end.

He cleared his throat and shifted, drawing himself apart from her. He took the tantalizing heat with him, too. "I think perhaps we are out of danger."

Since his hands were slowly leaving her waist, she supposed that was a hint to stand on her own and release him as well. On a disappointed breath, she did. Yet now she had that tingly feeling trapped inside her without any way to purge herself of it.

It was a dreadful feeling to keep inside. It made her feel edgy and irritable. Perhaps she was too old and out of practice to enjoy the elation after surviving an ordeal. Or perhaps if the duke would simply pull her into his arms once more, she might not feel this way.

"Regrettably," he began, "it appears we are between floors."

That meant they truly were blocked in. *No!* She was imprisoned here, when she would much rather run through all the corridors of this castle until she was bent over and breathless.

"It is my understanding that actual carriages are equipped with brakes," she grumbled. "For what is a smooth ride if there is no way to stop it?"

In the moment that passed, he exhaled audibly. "Duly noted, Miss Sutherland. For your information, I did employ a brake. Unfortunately, the speed of our descent caused it to fail."

The warmth vanished from his tone. Hearing him speak each word with cold, precise enunciation only added to her irritation. "Then perhaps it would be wise to design one that *reacts* to a rapid descent."

"I am all eagerness to hear your design modifications. A scientist never has enough ideas on his own," he drawled, not sounding the least bit eager.

She ignored his sarcasm. "A clamp of sorts would do the trick."

He did not respond, leaving her in this battle alone. The silence seemed to drag on and on until she could no longer stand it.

"I do not like this confined space," she said after a full minute. "I prefer to move about. Taking the staircase would have been a much better option."

"And yet *you* accepted my invitation." He scoffed at her. *Scoffed!*

"Do not make it sound, sir, that it is *my* fault we are in this predicament."

"That was not my intention." The accusation edging his tone did not convince her that he was in earnest. To her, he sounded as irritable as she was. But what could be his reason?

It was only then that she realized she might have wounded his ego. It was his ascending room, after all. And from what she had gathered from his aunt, he was rather proud of his modern contraptions. Not only that, but apparently he'd endured ample criticisms in his life.

A small twinge of guilt pinched her conscience.

"I'm somewhat impulsive, and you are rather persuasive. It is a dreadful combination," she explained.

He murmured a sound of agreement.

Then they were silent for another minute or two in the darkness. She could feel that he was close, because the space in front of her was warm, but she dared not reach out for fear of clinging to him once more. "What do we do now?"

"Wait for Mr. Graves," he said. "Someone from below stairs would have heard a crash and notified him."

Sure enough, within seconds a man's voice called down to them from above. "*Your Grace! Are you hurt?*"

"I am fine, Mr. Graves, though"—the duke hesitated—"I am not alone. Please fetch a ladder but with the utmost discretion."

Mr. Graves summarily left, promising to return in due haste.

The enormity of what had happened was starting to settle upon Ivy. Sure, she'd survived the clutches of death, but what now? If anyone should find out she spent any time alone with the duke, her reputation would be ruined. Worse, Lilah's would be tainted. No doubt Lady Cosgrove would ask Ivy to leave . . . and just when the party was starting to get interesting.

"I'm dreadful at waiting," she said.

"Somehow that does not surprise me. Have you always been impatient *and* impulsive?"

"Even as a child, I'm afraid," she admitted, nodding to herself. "I could not wait for the next footrace over the hill, or the next adventure. I could not stand to linger in bed when I was wide awake, even when it was before dawn. Nor could I tolerate being kept from my slumber when that was the only thing keeping me from beginning a new day."

Caught in a memory, she continued. "There was one summer, many years ago, when my aunt, uncle, and younger cousin came to stay with us. She had a pet frog that she kept in a box by her bedside table. She had an absurd notion that if she gave him a kiss, he would turn into a prince, but she was waiting for the day when she had the courage to find out. Apparently, the sound of constant croaking did not hinder my cousin's sleep. Across the hall, it had the opposite effect on me. Therefore, I decided to liberate the frog from his confines.

"In my own defense," she said after a short pause, "I never thought the frog wouldn't be able to hop from such a distance."

"What was the distance?" the duke asked, his tone warmer and suspiciously amused.

"A third-floor window," she murmured. "Over a stone patio."

Vale laughed, a hearty, rough-hewn sound that shook the small room. Automatically, she reached out for support and, as luck would have it, he was the closest thing to seize. His hand settled on her hip, steadying her. Gradually his laughter died, but she could still feel his warm puffs of air against her cheek. "Your cousin never had the chance to see if her frog was a prince in disguise."

"Oh, he wasn't. I made sure of it . . . just in case," she whispered. The obvious path of her thoughts would be to remember the moment that she'd held the bleating, wriggling frog in her hands as she'd kissed that cold, wet mouth. Instead, Ivy could think only of how close she was to Vale. So close that she could stand on tiptoe and press her lips to his. And she would, too. She was certainly impulsive enough. However, Ivy didn't want to break the spell.

The two kisses in her life had both yielded unpleasant outcomes. The first was the slimy frog, and the second was when she'd foolishly kissed Jasper, just weeks before his death.

With an angry swipe of his hand, Jasper wiped her kiss away in front of her. "No, Ivy. That is not done," he scolded. "A young woman does not kiss a man. If his passions are stirred, then he will kiss her. I have given you no indication that you stir mine! And now your actions have disappointed us both."

Thinking about that now, Ivy took a step back. It was the last thing she wanted to do, but it couldn't be helped. The duke's pleasant grasp disappeared. Unfortunately, she forgot about the bench directly behind her and she stumbled against it. Reaching out, she braced her hand against the wall—then felt a sharp prick pierce her thumb through her glove.

She drew back on a hiss.

"What has happened?" As if he had no trouble seeing in the dark, the duke returned her to his embrace.

Like before, she felt the heat of his hands on the bare flesh below the sleeve of her dress. For a breathless moment, she forgot the question. Then when the pad of her thumb began to throb, she remembered. "I touched the wall. I think . . . I have a splinter in my thumb."

"Then we must remove it." Already his hand shifted to cradle the elbow of her left arm, as if detecting which hand she was protecting. His fingertips brushed the exposed flesh above her glove. "This one?"

Her breath caught in her lungs. The thrill-seeking, impatient aspects of her nature wanted to strip off her glove and toss it to the floor so that she could feel more of his touch. *Now.* Her pulse began to purr in her ears, swift and hot. Yet it was the quieter and more prudent part of herself that spoke. "Yes, but it is likely nothing."

Of course, she said the words without trying to free herself. She might have even turned her arm in order to feel his finger travel down the same path as last night.

"Hmm," he murmured. "I am of a nature that certainty is paramount."

He delved beneath her glove, his movements gradual and cautious. The heat and slight roughness of his flesh elicited a flood of tingles throughout her body. Her flesh, blood, and bone all quivered in unison. He took his time, slowly drawing the soft leather down her arm, baring her flesh, inch by inch. Every subtle shift felt like a new caress. Even though the reason for his thorough examination was likely to keep from alarming her, for some reason, she had the sense that he was enjoying this.

Then one of his fingers traced the same path as last night. The touch was so reminiscent that she suddenly knew it had been no accident. That knowledge sent another rush through her, fluttering low in her stomach.

"This room is too dark. You'll never be able to"—the glove slipped from her fingers—"find it." A soft mew of surprise escaped her. She felt naked, as if he'd stripped far more than her glove from her flesh.

His hand cupped her elbow, and another grasped her wrist. His thumb slipped naturally into the center of her palm. Unable to help herself, she rolled her hand forward, rubbing against his touch. The hand at her elbow skimmed upward to capture her, gently holding her hand immobile.

"Your skin is incredibly delicate, soft as orchid petals," he said, his low voice rougher now, hoarse as he gradually lifted her hand upward. "These gloves are too thin to offer a proper amount of protection." His heated breath coated her palm. If not for the evident concern in his tone, his suggestion might have riled her. Instead, it warmed her.

"Ah. That explains it. You were bothered by my ill-fitting glove last evening," she teased, her voice nothing more than a purr in her throat. More than anything, she wanted to curl her fingers closed, hold each breath he released into her palm, and keep them. But he held her hand open, exposed to him. It made the sensation almost unbearable.

"Bothered? Yes, but not in the way you mean." His throat issued a rumble of amusement that licked her flesh. "I notice that you are wearing the same pair this evening."

"I only brought the one pair—likely ruined now."

"The flesh beneath is far more important." And then, he pressed his lips to her palm.

Ivy gasped but did not pull away. She was too eager for more. "What are you intending to do?"

"A purely scientific examination," he said as his lips grazed her, trailing a path from the center of her hand up the slender length of her thumb. "Our mouths are quite perceptive. Have you ever noticed how infants first put things to their mouths in order to unlock the object's mysteries? The same principle works in this circumstance. If you have a splinter, I will be able to detect it easier this way."

He sounded so confident that it was impossible to argue. Then again, she doubted she would have argued regardless. Her eyes drifted shut as he brushed his lips over the pad of her thumb. It was no longer throbbing. Likely, her injury had only been a small depression from the head of a nail and had not broken the skin. She'd suffered enough stumbles to know the difference. Yet she couldn't seem to find the words to tell him.

IF NORTH WERE a man given to foolish romantic notions, then he might have imagined that fate had a hand in placing Ivy Sutherland at his party. Of course, he was not such a man.

His momentary lapse in rational thought, not to mention his actions, stemmed from an escalation in his pulse, he was sure. Not to mention, the heightened sensitization of his nerves was the likely result from the sudden plummeting of the elevator. It was all perfectly understandable.

So why, then, was he finding it difficult to release her?

He brushed a kiss over the flesh of her thumb, examining her closely. The sweet citrus scent that he'd noticed from her hair last night was here as well. A low, hungry sound growled in his throat. In response, she rolled her wrist once more, pressing her thumb to his mouth, inviting him to draw her in. He did, reveling in her gasp and the feel of her body molding against him. His hand splayed over her back while his tongue explored her unmarred, silken flesh.

Under the circumstances, his actions were quite reasonable. How else would he be able to detect a splinter, here in the dark? Of course, Mr. Graves would likely arrive with the ladder at any moment and North *could* examine her then . . .

However, everything inside of him was compelled to hold her this closely and to press his lips to her. Any part of her. Every part of her.

Unfortunately, Mr. Graves chose that moment to arrive with the ladder.

The commotion heard overhead was enough to remind North of his position in society, not to mention his purpose for hosting this party. He was supposed to be proving his formula, not allowing his baser instincts to wreak havoc with his careful plan.

As the sound of footfalls began to near and a sliver of lamplight bled through the seam in the hatch on the ascending room's roof, North set Ivy apart from him. She, however, kept her thumb to his lips, curling her impossibly soft hand around his jaw. What else could he do but press one more kiss to her palm?

"I detected no splinter or the faintest mark on your flesh." He should know, he'd been quite thorough.

As if his statement jolted her, she drew back quickly. "Oh, yes. Of course. I am quite . . . relieved, as I ought to be, and not the least bit disappointed that further examination is unwarranted."

North grinned as her words tumbled out in a rush. A ready quip was on his lips, but to release it would be to extend their flirtation and venture into dangerous territory. This wasn't merely a physical attraction, after all. She was clever, too. A brake clamp that reacted automatically to a rapid descent? He should have thought of that himself. But if he had, his fall with Miss Sutherland would have been all too fleeting.

If logic hadn't conquered his romantic notions earlier, hearing proof of her brilliant mind might have sent him over the edge.

Fortunately, Mr. Graves lifted the hatch before North could reach for her once more. Lamplight spilled down into the small chamber, illuminating Ivy's bright eyes and flushed cheeks. Any other woman might have become pale and drawn from the harrowing fright. Not Ivy. Instead, she seemed even more vivacious.

"Miss Sutherland, I should like to introduce you to Mr. Graves," North said, standing at her side. He noted that she kept her hands at her back, one gloved and the other bare. By chance, the other glove was tucked neatly into his own pocket. "You may not realize it, Graves, but you are standing in the presence of a genius. Miss Sutherland has come up with an impressive idea for a braking system for passenger elevators such as this."

Graves possessed a single, thick black eyebrow, and it rose at this information. "My sister's boy would love to hear of it, miss. He is forever making inquiries about His Grace's inventions," he explained to Miss Sutherland. "Young Master Otis dreams of being a master builder and inventor someday. And if it would keep Sir safe, then I would like to learn of your idea, too."

"By all means. Although I'm afraid my *genius* has been overstated." She glanced up at North, her expression tender. "I have far more knowledge of falling than of preventing it."

Mr. Graves assured her with a nod. "Sir has a sense about these things."

Right now, North wasn't certain he had a sense about anything, because he wished they were still trapped.

Yet, without a word of confession, he assisted Ivy to the ladder.

Before she mounted the first rung, she looked over her shoulder at him. "This was quite the adventure, Your Grace."

"It was indeed, Miss Sutherland." A stranger now stood in his skin. North wondered if he would ever feel like himself again, or if he'd been changed forever.

Chapter Five

THE CHRISTMAS EVE Ball was only a few days away.

Ivy, Lilah, and the debutantes had spent most of the following day gathering greenery to decorate the hall. Red apples and white ribbons adorned garlands of pine and fir boughs over doorways and along the main stairs. Holly branches tied with silver bows made wreaths for wall sconces. The leftover pieces were clustered together with sprigs of rosemary to form a ball that hung from the foyer chandelier. Some of the young ladies even set about on a hunt for mistletoe, hoping for a kiss that might bring about a wedding within the year. Unfortunately for them, there was none to be found.

Ivy was a bit disappointed, but only for Lilah's sake. Claiming a kiss and a mistletoe berry could have done just the trick. Especially since Ivy hadn't done her part in securing a husband for her friend.

Even when she'd had the perfect opportunity to catalogue Lilah's innumerable qualities last night, Ivy had neglected to do so. In fact, while alone with the duke last night, she'd completely forgotten her entire purpose for being here. Worse yet, she hadn't behaved as an unmarried woman in society ought to have done. Instead, she'd been herself, which likely didn't bode well for Lilah either.

This evening, however, she was determined to make amends. She would forget about the events of last night. She would forget about the connection she felt. And she would forget about—

Ivy's thoughts abruptly veered backward. Had he felt a connection, too? Or had his actions merely been dictated by circumstance? What if, like with Jasper, the duke now was ashamed of his actions and hers? And what if, upon seeing her this evening, the duke pretended not to know her?

Awash in these turbulent thoughts, Ivy donned her sea-green gown for dinner and stepped out of the dressing room in search of her slippers. "I was sure I left them by the bed."

"You have been preoccupied all day." Lilah smoothed the front of her cream-colored gown and pointed to the marble console by the door, where a pair of green satin slippers waited. "Are you still unwell?"

Spotting the gold-tasseled slippers, Ivy realized that she must have left them on the table when she'd dropped one of her earbobs on the floor. Inexplicably, the thumb on her left hand—the one that he'd kissed—hadn't ceased tingling today, which had made it difficult to accomplish certain tasks, donning earbobs among them. "The very blossom of health. As you know, it is not unusual for my thoughts to drift."

After the ascending room experience, she'd come to this chamber and sent a maid with a note stating that she was ill. Yet in truth she hadn't been able to imagine sitting still for a concert, not with her entire being overbrimming with exhilaration. Nor would she have been able to sit still beside *him,* pretending nothing had happened between them.

Then, later, she'd hardly been able to sleep. She'd still been awake when Lilah had returned from the late supper that had followed the concert. Still awake and dreaming of the duke.

Ivy slipped into her shoes as Lilah pulled on a pair of gloves. That was the moment Ivy recalled that she only had one of her gloves. *Oh dear!* She'd left the other one behind last night. She'd brought other gloves, of course, but they were of the shorter variety. She'd only had her maid pack one pair of long evening gloves. Quite honestly, she'd never imagined needing another pair.

"I overheard Aunt Zinnia and the dowager duchess speaking of how our host was equally distracted last evening," Lilah said absently. "Though, from my own observations, His Grace appeared no different than he has been since our arrival."

Hearing the barest mention of the duke sent a wondrous thrill through Ivy. It started in her stomach and speared straight through her heart on its ascent. "You said nothing of him all day. Tell me, did he speak to you?" *Did he ask about me?*

Lilah shook her head. "Not a word. He did, however, glance down at my shoes once or twice. I don't think he remembers my name."

"Oh." That thrill turned into a hard lump of guilt. Ivy swallowed. How could her conscience permit her to wonder if the duke had asked about her when her sole focus should be Lilah?

Surely she could have thought of one thing to say on behalf of her dearest friend last night. An interesting tidbit that would have enticed him. Perhaps while standing in his embrace and plummeting down the shaft, Ivy could have mentioned Lilah's bravery—spiders never had bothered her one whit. Or perhaps when he'd tenderly stripped the glove from Ivy's arm, she could have mentioned how lovely Lilah's hands were—her fingers were quite elegant, and she played the harp beautifully.

Yet Ivy did not want to think of the duke's lips on Lilah's thumb.

The duke. After what had transpired between them, she should call him Vale, perhaps. At least in her mind . . . but no. The nature of her thoughts demanded more intimacy. *Northcliff,* perhaps, or simply *North.* She wondered which he preferred. Then again, asking him such a question assumed an intimacy between them, and if there was one thing that made Ivy timid, it was making an incorrect assumption.

She wondered—if Mr. Graves had returned just a few minutes later—would the duke have kissed her? And if he had, would he have been as disappointed as Jasper had been? Would North ultimately have discovered that she did not stir his passions either?

Ivy tried to clear away the clutter of depressing thoughts in her mind. "I will think of something, Lilah. Surely tonight he will speak to us." *Unless,* Ivy thought, *he regrets every moment last night and desires to avoid me . . .*

In the mirror, Lilah sighed and adjusted the coral comb in her coiffure. "If I begged you not to, would it make a difference?"

Ivy thought about her guilt and knew her answer. She was here for one purpose, and from now on, she would try harder for Lilah's sake. "Likely not, but there is always a chance."

Lilah said nothing, while Lady Cosgrove's voice called out from the other room. "Miss Sutherland, would you come here, please?"

Lady Cosgrove sat at her vanity, having her hair dressed. With an elegant, though minute, lift of her hand, she pointed to the door. "One of the maids left a mended glove for you on the table by the door. Though I did not know you tore your glove last evening. I thought you'd been ill."

Ivy drew in a sharp breath and fixed her gaze on the long white glove across the room.

"Yes, my lady, I . . . I had a dizzy spell, and when I reached out to steady myself, I snagged my glove." The statement was true enough, but she stumbled over the words regardless. Had North sent her glove to be mended?

She wanted to rush across the room and press the soft ivory leather to her lips, but her trembling legs kept her pace slow. Lifting her glove from the table, she noted the fine stitching on the thumb. When she slipped it on, she realized something was inside. Withdrawing it, she held a short stickpin, like a cravat pin, with a bit of cork around the point to keep it from piercing her glove. She looked closely at the small design on the other end and nearly laughed. It was a jade frog wearing a tiny gold crown.

A frog prince . . . Even though she dared not allow it, something tender and shivery swirled beneath her breast, making her feel lighter than air. Surely such a gift meant something. In the very least, that he would acknowledge their acquaintance.

Now, more than ever before, she dearly hoped that she would not see regret on the duke's face this evening.

DURING DINNER, NORTH had decided that having a single table capable of seating over one hundred guests was more hindrance than a point of pride. Miss Sutherland had been seated at the opposite end, near Aunt Edith. At such a distance, he'd only been able to make out the bluish-green hue of her gown—nothing of her expression, or whether or not she'd turned her head in his direction.

He'd found himself glancing equally as often at the clock, calculating the duration between courses and the interim period where the ladies would retire to the parlor in the west wing, leaving the gentlemen to their port and cheroots.

Now, dinner was over and a suitable time had passed for the requisite separation of the sexes. When a footman notified him that the ladies were awaiting them, North was the first out the door.

"Your step is rather eager, cousin," Wolford said from beside him in the archway leading to the parlor, his green eyes glinting with mischief. "Tell me, is there a certain debutante who has caught your fancy?"

North had endured enough of his cousin's teasing over the years to know better than to take him seriously. Yet a frisson of apprehension rolled over him as he wondered if his countenance gave anything away.

He collected himself, hesitating on the threshold. Upon first examination of the room, he noted Miss Sutherland's absence. A keen sense of disappointment trudged through him. "Such a development would be to the detriment of my formula. It is far more likely that the reason for my haste is simply to bring the evening to a close, sooner rather than later."

"What with Baron Cantham's snide remarks about your bloodline, it is no wonder," Wolford growled.

His cousin's defense of him caused North to forgive his more annoying characteristics. "Though he may be a purist, it is rather telling that both he and his daughter accepted my invitation." After dinner, he'd paid little heed to Cantham's thinly veiled slander. North had had far more important matters on his mind, like clock watching and—

Suddenly, Miss Sutherland emerged from a connecting doorway at the far side of the room. She stood arm in arm with her friend—whose name he could never seem to remember. Ivy's gaze darted around, seeking, until it collided with his. And held.

Something akin to elation stirred within him when she did not look around for anyone else. His chest grew warm and tight at once. Perhaps the port in the glass he still carried had turned. Although when her smile appeared, tentative and questioning, he forgot all about his drink. Instinctively he knew that she wondered if he would acknowledge their acquaintance. In order to protect her reputation, their time in the ascending room had to remain a secret. Therefore, he could do nothing more than hold her gaze as a measure of reassurance. Yet that was not enough for him. So he inclined his head a fraction as well.

She smiled in earnest now. If the sun dawned behind her this very instant, the star would appear dim and cold by comparison. And were he elevated to king right then and there, with all of England at his feet, the feeling could still not compare to this.

Suddenly, he felt like the most important man in the entire world. Every cell in his body told him to go to her. Now. To plow through the obstacles between them, seize her, and—

"At last, you are caught," Wolford said in a conspiratorial chuckle. "I see that your gaze is fixed on that cluster of blushing maids by the door."

North stiffened. "Is a host not meant to acknowledge the presence of his guests?"

"Even more damning than that, I was speaking all manner of nonsense, and you gave no reply."

North's heart thudded in his chest. He was still focused on the idea of taking Ivy Sutherland in his arms. It was not like him to entertain such thoughts. Not only that, but acting upon impulse was not something he did. Ever. Discounting, *of course,* last night's compulsion to invite Miss Sutherland into the ascending room. He was a methodical, planning sort. If he behaved in a manner so out of character, his guests would likely assume that he was ill. Or worse, that he'd been carried away by a romantic notion.

For his formula to have any merit at all, he could never do such a thing. Yet knowing this still did not remove the unexpected, consuming desire.

"I have turned a deaf ear to your nonsense," North readily explained. "As you know, I am not a man ruled by passions. Nor am I of an impractical nature."

"Aye. We are the same in that," Maxwell Harwick, Marquess Thayne, drawled as he sidled up to their small group just inside the parlor. He set down his empty snifter on a rosewood wine table with enough force that he nearly sent it toppling. "Leave the romantic notions to the women who want to marry a title and riches. They deserve what they get in return."

With a slow shake of his head, Wolford clucked his tongue at Thayne. "Apparently, you are forgetting that you are now a man with a title and riches. Worse yet, your mother is determined to find you a bride. Perhaps even here at this very party."

North allowed himself to expel a breath of relief when Liam's keen attention turned from him to their mutual friend. Now that the other gentlemen were filing into the parlor, it would not bode well for North's formula if his cousin's deliriums were overheard.

As for Thayne, North felt a sense of commiseration with him. Thayne had never expected to inherit a marquessate from a distant fourth cousin. Since receiving his title, he, too, had fallen under scrutiny. Every event of his past was analyzed beneath a microscope.

Thayne offered a none-too-friendly grin. "Do not look now, Wolford, but you are also a man with a title and riches."

Wolford made a show of brushing off the reminder from his waistcoat. "Like my father before me, I will marry at the ripe age of one and sixty, and no sooner."

While Thayne and Wolford continued their repartee, North abandoned them and crossed the room toward Aunt Edith. Fortuitously, she stood within a group that included Miss Sutherland, her friend, and Lady Cosgrove.

"Nephew, your hearing astounds me," Edith began. "Not a moment ago, I made the comment that I wished to gain your attention. Then, before I had even finished the sentence, you were striding toward us."

"How serendipitous," he said with a polite bow before greeting each of them in turn. Miss Sutherland's name was the last to leave his lips, and it lingered there for a moment. The hue of her gown turned her blue eyes stormy and dark. He noted the subtle parting of her lips on a breath that lifted the creamy swells of her breasts, and desire flooded him. "I was heading this way to make amends for being an abominable host. I could not allow another evening to go by without offering my sincerest apologies to both Miss Appleton and Miss Sutherland for my inattentiveness. From this moment forward, I will make every effort to ensure your enjoyment."

Edith patted his hand and smiled adoringly. "That pleases me, nephew, though with nearly three dozen debutantes all vying for your attention, I fear you will wear yourself thin."

"Never fear, Aunt Edith. I'm quite resilient." He glanced at Ivy, then down at the small jade pin she'd placed in the center of her bodice. It was nestled there so perfectly that he felt a pang of jealousy. "Rather like a . . . frog that has frozen in a pond for winter, but at springtime hops away."

At the mention, Ivy lifted her gloved hand to touch the pin.

"You always were fond of frogs," Aunt Edith said. "Your mother even taught you to speak German through a folk tale about a frog. I seem to recall that '*Der Froschkönig*' was your favorite as a child."

"Yes, 'The Frog King' was my favorite." North watched Ivy's eyes widen and a blush color her cheeks. "Though, in the English translation, he became a prince. I'd always felt sorry for him when he was thrown against a wall. Now I suppose he was fortunate to have found the one girl who was not annoyed by his incessant croaking, or else he might have been dropped from too great a distance instead."

A bubble of laughter escaped Ivy. "It could have been a much different tale for our poor prince, Your Grace."

"Ah, Miss Sutherland," the dowager duchess said with delight, "only now have I noticed your pin. Are you also fond of frogs?"

"Inexplicably, yes, ma'am," Ivy answered without hesitation, keeping her gaze fixed on his. "Very much so."

Elation expanded inside his chest, drawing it so tight that he could hardly bear the sensation. It caused a wave of panic to wash through him. He knew he should not have been feeling this way—whatever *way* this was. His sole focus needed to remain on gaining a Fellowship. Only proving his formula mattered.

Therefore, he forced himself to turn away from Miss Sutherland, at least marginally, in order to concentrate on the others within the group.

"I find it rather surprising that frogs are considered good omens for a happy marriage, don't you? After all, they are not the most romantic of creatures," Edith offered to the group, though with a sly glance toward North. When he cleared his throat in warning, she continued and discreetly fluttered her hand in a gesture over his shoulder. "With the use of my nephew's *Marriage Formula,* however, luck is not needed, I can assure you, Lord Basilton."

The man in question joined the group just as she spoke. He was of a short, solid build, with wiry brows and a carefully groomed beard.

"Yes, indeed, ma'am," Basilton said. "That is precisely the reason I ambled this way."

North stepped to the side to allow more room. The fact that he moved closer to Ivy was nothing more than happenstance. The sweet fragrance of persimmons filled his every breath. Mere inches separated them. He switched his port to his other hand so that he might accidentally brush her arm when he lowered his to his side. And when he did, he cursed the barrier of gloves between them. Yet at the same time, he noted with pleasure that Ivy did not pull away.

Unable to resist, his index finger discreetly arced out to capture her pinky, all too briefly, before he renewed his focus on the task at hand. "Basilton, I've been told that your daughter is quite the accomplished violinist."

Miss Basilton emerged from behind her father and looked down shyly. As of yet, North had heard nothing more than a quiet murmur from her, and only when prodded. He found that he preferred young women who could not contain their thoughts. And, perhaps, those who had a penchant for impulsive decisions.

Basilton's mustachio twitched in something of a grin. Puffing out his chest, he hooked a thumb between the buttons of his waistcoat and thrummed his fingers over the copper-colored silk. "We've had our share of exceptional musicians in our family. I'm pleased to add Hortencia to the list. Say, are musical abilities factored into your formula?"

North had waited years to gain Basilton's interest. This was the first real indication that the *Marriage Formula* might gain him a Fellowship. "They do, yes. The formula is designed to focus on the important factors of monetary assets, including property as well as dowries; lineage; *and* interests."

The moment he said *lineage,* North heard a snort of derision from Baron Cantham, who stood within a separate circle, which seemingly had their ears carefully tuned to *this* circle. North ignored the reaction, knowing that a number of his guests were purists when it came to noble blood.

Oddly enough, North had a place in his formula for men like Cantham. The sole purpose of the result was to benefit all parties involved—a pure and basic exchange of marital goods of monies, property, and lineage security. Adding in the *interest* portion of the formula had been an afterthought to appease his aunt.

"How does it work?" Ivy asked, turning to North and casting a perturbed glance over his shoulder to Cantham.

North felt a lump of guilt swell in his throat. Because—while there was a place for men who cared only for matters of lineage—the equation as it stood now never would have produced a match for Ivy.

It had never been intended for the names in the red ledger. There was simply too little data to analyze.

"It's a matter of filling out a card where each individual would rank their preferences," he began. "From there, it becomes a matter of calculation. That is when the *Marriage Formula* truly takes form. The resulting answer corresponds to another party's similar result. It's actually quite—"

North intended to finish his oration with the word *simple*. However, when he paused to clear his throat and gauge the reaction of those around him, he heard Ivy whisper, "Brilliant."

And he was not the only one who'd heard. Her declaration earned a few turns of the head. Her eyes went wide. "Do go on, Your Grace."

"I won't allow it. I must hear more of Miss Sutherland's opinion," Wolford said cheekily when he and Thayne found their way into the group. Wolford angled himself in such a way to effectively separate North from Ivy. "Surely, most members of your sex would not agree with the *brilliance* of my cousin's formula. Other young women rant endlessly on the merits of a gentleman's charm, character, and money. Only the last of the three can be determined on a card."

North glanced at Basilton long enough to see his speculative frown, then North turned a glare on Wolford. Unfortunately, he only received the back of his head.

"A wise young woman is not fooled by charm, my lord," Ivy said to Wolford. "My own mother has said that what might first charm you in a ballroom can become tedious after more than twenty years of marriage."

Edith snickered and tapped Lady Cosgrove with her fan as they shared a nod. Basilton chuckled, the sound more like a wheezing cough. And North felt that pressure again in the center of his chest, expanding more and more.

"In addition," Ivy went on, seemingly oblivious to the eager attention she'd gained, "if a gentleman has a dishonest character, then who is to say that he would not be dishonest in filling out a character question on his card?"

"I couldn't agree more." Juliet Granworth joined their ever-increasing group and settled a hand on Ivy's shoulder, as if in support. "There is no judgment of a gentleman's character better than witnessing it firsthand."

"The same could be said of women," Thayne said as he set another empty glass on the nearest table. Uncharacteristically, he'd been drinking more than his share, and North wondered if it had to do with Juliet Granworth's presence. After all, few could forget the once-famous kissing scandal that had involved Juliet and Max shortly before she'd married another man.

"Though with Vale's formula," Thayne continued, his voice rising, "at least there is a better chance of marrying for what truly matters in the end."

"And what truly matters is character." Juliet squared her shoulders.

Thayne laughed without humor and gestured with a sweep of his hand to encompass the flattering gold silk gown she wore. "Or perhaps ascertaining *character* is merely an excuse to indulge in a Season, to wear new gowns each year, and to promenade through ballrooms in order to collect scores of fawning admirers."

"As usual, you are making assumptions on my character. I see the years have not changed you," she said quietly. Then her gaze turned cold and remote, and she turned her head, as if she could not bear to look at him.

Instantly, Wolford—charmer that he was—offered a wry laugh and clutched Thayne's shoulder. "I daresay it is easy to guess which pair would never find a match, formula or not."

"Without a doubt," Thayne grumbled in agreement.

Basilton appeared oblivious to the exchange and turned fully to North. "To prove your formula, do you plan to use it to find a bride for yourself, Vale?"

The group—in addition to a few of those mingling along the outskirts—fell silent. They were eager for his answer. All except for Ivy, it seemed.

Without even a glance in his direction, she slipped away,

disappearing into the music room. The urge to follow her ran rampant through him. His legs jerked in preparation, his left foot lifting off the floor. North had to force himself to think of the consequences. Force himself to ground his foot firmly to the floor.

Drawing in a breath, North returned his focus to the question at hand. He knew that if he chose to marry Basilton's daughter, a Fellowship would likely follow. Call him old-fashioned, but North would rather succeed on his own merit. "Of course I will use my own formula. When the time comes."

Chapter Six

"Every girl must take a turn and stir the pudding," Miss Pendergast said. The spinster chaperone clapped her petite hands with maniacal enthusiasm, rousing Ivy from a trance. The kitchens of Castle Vale were bursting with debutantes this afternoon. Yesterday, Miss Pendergast had spoken of a tradition that any unwed maid who stirred the Christmas pudding would find her true love in the new year. As an alternative, Ivy suggested that they could all take part in the tradition and then deliver the puddings to the duke's tenants. Miss Leeds had been quick to offer her agreement.

The only problem was, Ivy had had no idea that making a pudding would be so difficult. The eggs, milk, and treacle were not mixing well with the suet. Adding the flour turned into a disaster of lumps. She must not have stirred fast enough. Looking over her shoulder at Lilah, her pudding partner, she sheepishly shrugged. "Perhaps whoever receives our pudding will believe that the lumps are currants."

"I just hope the person owns a pig to feed it to," Lilah said with a laugh. Tomorrow, on Christmas Eve, they would set off for the village in order to deliver them to the duke's tenants, along with a fat pheasant or goose, whichever the gentlemen were able to kill today while on another hunt.

Staring down at the soupy mess in the bowl, Ivy was glad that Lilah hadn't pinned all of her marital hopes on the magic of the pudding. Obviously it hadn't worked to gain Miss Pendergast a husband. Then again, perhaps Miss Pendergast *had* been in love once, only to have been spurned most cruelly. Such a trial was difficult to overcome, Ivy knew. Likely it was terrifying even to think of falling in love again. And Ivy feared it was happening to her.

She couldn't stop thinking about North . . . or Northcliff. Worse, she'd taken to wearing the frog pin each day, but tucked in the folds of her chemise, close to her skin. Close to her heart.

"Ivy, you are going to spill the pudding," Lilah warned in her ear. "We do not want ours to come up short."

"I'm sure Miss Sutherland doesn't think such traditions matter, since she favors a mathematical equation over a chance of marrying for love," Miss Leeds sneered from across the oak plank table. Those around her wore similar expressions.

Ivy had not earned much favor with the debutantes in the past two days since the duke had explained his formula. Her support of his idea had not been well received. As for the duke, however, the gentlemen had inundated him with questions. In fact, the constant flow of interested parties had left no room for her to stand within his circle, as she had the previous night. Knowing how much his formula meant to him, Ivy was pleased for his sake. Anyone could see it in the passionate way he expressed himself.

"I do not see why His Grace's formula cannot coexist with tradition. Nothing within it states that parties are forbidden. And wouldn't it be nice to know that your dance partner was a potential *perfect match*? It would allow you to see him in a wholly new light." At her words, some of the debutantes showed interest, offering tentative nods and curious murmurs to their pudding partners. However, a number— bearing frowns and crossed arms—still firmly demanded their Seasons, their parties, and, most importantly, their new trousseaux.

"One has to wonder how lineage is even a factor when nobility runs so thin in . . . *certain* people." Miss Leeds sounded very much like her father, Baron Cantham.

Ivy's hand curled around her spoon. She desperately wanted to hurl a clump of suet and flour at Miss Leeds's head. "None of us know the specifics of the equation, but the result is for the benefit of us all."

"*All?* What does it matter to you, Miss Sutherland? From what I understand, you have no interest in marrying."

"Not that it is any concern of yours, Miss Leeds," Lilah said, her shoulders as stiff as a stair tread, "but she is here to support *my* endeavors."

"Don't you see?" Miss Pendergast said gently. "Miss Sutherland's circumstances might very well have been changed if the formula had been in existence before she was past the marrying age."

While the chaperone's intentions were kindly meant, Ivy suddenly felt a weight settle over her breast. It was as if someone had stacked all the pudding crocks on her at once. She could hardly breathe. And, to her horror, the sting of tears pricked the corners of her eyes. Deep down she knew that even if the formula had existed when Jasper had been alive, he still wouldn't have married her. More than that, she feared that the formula wouldn't have found anyone for her to marry.

Hastily, she turned around under the pretense of gathering a bowl of dried plums and currants for the pudding, then dabbed the moisture from the corners of her eyes. Unfortunately, her actions did not go unobserved. For in that same moment, she saw the duke standing in the doorway, his gaze missing nothing.

NORTH WATCHED IVY quickly lower her hand and brush her damp fingertip over her apron. She offered something of a smile before she dipped into a curtsy.

"Your Grace, what an unexpected pleasure," Miss Pendergast said, following suit. As did the rest of the room.

He felt unaccountably annoyed at the lot of them—all except Ivy, of course—and for what he'd overheard. Unfortunately, it wasn't true. His formula would not have found Ivy a match of any sort. Part of him was glad of it—glad she was here and not making Christmas pudding in another man's home—glad even though it made him a selfish monster.

Selfish or not, he still wanted to comfort her. Wanted to pull her into his embrace. Wanted to kiss those damp lashes and then her mouth. Ever since leaving the ascending room the other night, he'd regretted not kissing Ivy. He'd squandered an opportunity that he might never have again.

Not able to do that, however, he stepped past Ivy. Surreptitiously, he held his folded handkerchief behind his back where only she could see. Her fingers brushed his as she slipped it out of his grasp and whispered a soft *thank you* for his ears alone.

He cleared his throat. "Ladies. I heard tale that dozens of puddings were being made and will soon find their ways into the homes of my tenants. For that, I wanted to offer my appreciation to each of you."

A collection of smiles and tittering commenced, most of the debutantes expressing their desires to *only be of service, Your Grace.* At least he assumed that was what Miss Basilton had murmured, gaze fixed to the table while she blushed.

Seeing her reminded him of his conversation with Lord Basilton earlier this morning. Because of the formula, Lord Basilton and his daughter—the only female born into a family with seven sons—were now gravitating toward Baron Nettle, a widower with four daughters and desperate need of a well-dowried bride who was young enough to produce a son and heir.

In addition, Lord Pomeroy's eldest son was turning his attention toward Miss Bloomfield, who recently inherited a goodly sum from a late grandmother.

North knew that gossip and the natural progression of information might have eventually led Basilton and Pomeroy on this same path. However, once North had worked out the formula with the few guests who'd filled out cards, he was able to make the process much simpler. Now, his Fellowship was closer than ever.

Everything was going according to plan. So then why wasn't he thrilled?

Perhaps it was because his formula was working too well. He had proof of its validity, which meant that he had been right all along. It also meant that he'd earned this on his own merit. Most men would find comfort in that. A week ago, he would have been one of those men. Now everything that was supposed to be good and right suddenly felt wrong.

"We are all looking forward to this evening's play, Your Grace," Miss Leeds said, squinting at him in an attempt to bat her lashes. "You've provided us with such a wealth of entertainment during this party that it saddens me to know it must end."

North found himself nodding in agreement, but his thoughts were of Ivy leaving in a matter of days. "Castle Vale will be empty without each of you. I daresay Mrs. Thorogood will be saddened to have fewer visitors to her kitchens as well."

Standing with her hands on her hips and shaking her head at the disastrous mess upon her worktable, the cook in question raised an eyebrow at him and huffed.

"Oh dear me," Miss Pendergast exclaimed, "I imagine it's well past time for these young ladies to rest before dinner. Not to mention, time to allow the cook to boil our puddings. We are ever so grateful, Mrs. Thorogood."

Grumbling, the cook picked up the first pudding and

walked through a narrow hall that led to the main kitchen with the ovens and stoves.

Gradually, the girls filed out, one by one, each pausing to curtsy, blush, giggle, or bat her eyes—with the exception of Miss Leeds, who did all four. He also overheard Ivy telling her friend that she would follow as soon as she added the currants and dried plums. Her friend hesitated, yet at the same time Miss Leeds intervened.

"Miss Appleton, since we have both been invited to tea with the dowager duchess, we should walk together." She sidled up to Ivy's friend and linked arms with her before maneuvering to stand before North. "Will you be coming to Her Grace's sitting room as well, sir? We would be eager for your escort."

North recalled his aunt inviting him to this tea. Now, however, he believed he would rather linger in the kitchens. "Alas, I must forgo the pleasure of your company, as I have business with Mrs. Thorogood."

Miss Leeds offered another curtsy-blush-giggle-bat, then pulled Miss Appleton away before she could finish her curtsy. Mrs. Thorogood trudged in for another pudding before disappearing again.

As he moved toward Ivy, she frowned in puzzlement. "I thought you wanted to speak with your cook."

Likely, he could think of something to tell Mrs. Thorogood, but the truth was, the only reason he'd come down to the kitchens was to see Ivy. "It can wait."

"Oh, then you must be waiting for this," Ivy said and reached under her sash to hold out his handkerchief. "Thank you. I don't know what came over me a moment ago. It must have been all the flour dust."

As guilt trampled through him, he said nothing but merely closed his fingers over hers. He held her hand in his for a moment, feeling the combination of her soft skin and a smudge of wet pudding. It took everything within him to resist lifting her hand to his lips and tasting her. Briefly, he wondered if their entire acquaintance would only be the sum of a few errant touches. He wanted so much more.

They stood in silence—all except for the constant clunking of pots and pans, the chatter and shuffling of a dozen kitchen maids and sculleries in the adjacent room.

When he heard the clack of Mrs. Thorogood's sturdy shoes, he reluctantly released Ivy's hand but put his thumb to his lips to taste the remains of the pudding. It was sweet and creamy, rather like her flesh. "Mmm . . . I'm certain this particular pudding is the most delicious of all."

While the cook came and went, Ivy's gaze dipped to his mouth and lingered. She wet her lips as if she, too, wanted a taste, but not of the pudding. North shifted nearer until he could feel the brush of her skirts against the fine buckskin of his riding breeches.

"You are too kind," she said, her voice a mere whisper. Then she shook her head and turned back to her bowl. "This pudding is the worst of the lot. I don't know what I did wrong. Lilah and I added all the same ingredients that the others did."

For the first time, North looked down at the runny brown liquid sluicing down the sides of the bowl as she vigorously stirred. The strange part was that the end of the spoon had a clumpy white mass stuck to it, which left the mixture interspersed with lumps. "Well, perhaps after it is boiled . . ."

She gave a wry laugh. "It will need to be boiled until Twelfth Night."

"Then I will have something to look forward to," he said honestly before a solemn truth struck him. He would not have until Twelfth Night with her. The day she would depart was fast approaching.

There was a commotion in the other kitchen, the crash of crockery and Mrs. Thorogood's grousing at the maids. All of which meant that he had a fraction of time alone with Ivy.

"I suddenly feel that now is not the most opportune time to ask the cook about my lumpy pudding." Ivy glanced at the doorway. "Besides, I really should be off . . ."

Without wasting a moment, North pulled her out of the room, stopping in the vestibule between the door and the hall. There were too many servants milling around.

Making no attempt to separate from him, Ivy lifted her face. "May I ask you a question?"

"You may ask me anything you wish." He turned her hand over and rubbed the pad of his thumb into the center of her palm, where it was warm and dewy.

"Do you prefer *Northcliff* or *North*?"

He grinned. The question was more revealing than his answer could be.

Then, as if she realized it as well, she went on in a rush. "It was only because I was thinking of you earlier—well, not thinking of you but more so *wondering*—if you had a preference. Not every name can be shortened, after all. Certainly not mine. And besides, you might have been scolded with your full name. Your mother might have said, 'Northcliff Melchior, what have you done with my curling tongs this time?'"

That wondrous, inopportune elation returned to North. He wanted to take her away with him to the nearest dark corner to kiss those rapidly moving lips and slow them down. "Curling tongs serve multiple purposes. They work wonders for holding a book open."

Curiosity brightened her expression, lifting the corners of her mouth. "I hadn't thought of that. But what of the binding?"

"*That* was when I would hear my full name, along with my father's reminder of how those books had once belonged to my fourth great-grandfather—Melchior had been his Christian name."

"It's quite fitting that you were given the name of one of

the three wise men, though I imagine you heard the word *incorrigible* a time or two in your youth," she said fondly. "But you still haven't told me if you prefer North to North-cliff."

Because he wanted to delay their parting for as long as possible. "First you must tell me your full name, Miss Ivy Sutherland of Norwood Hill."

"You will laugh," she warned. "I arrived in this world early, you see. My mother told me that she'd once had great hope that my impatience would be fleeting. Therefore she named me Ivy *Patience* Sutherland."

Something shifted inside him, and that too-full sensation in his chest began to burn and ache with a ferocity that demanded a cure. Unfortunately, he feared this particular ailment had no cure whatsoever. "What is it, Ivy Patience Sutherland, that makes you so impatient?"

She swayed closer to him, as if something had shifted inside her, too. "It's difficult to explain, but I am sometimes overcome with an urgent need to find out what will happen next."

"I understand. I have been overwhelmed with eagerness in the past, rushing headlong into a new invention. Over time, however, I realized how much more I enjoy the process than the result." His gaze drifted to her lips. "Therefore, taking my time, savoring what I enjoy, is the greatest reward."

Drawn in by that alluring citrus scent combined with the spices from the pudding, he wanted to lean forward. When Ivy's free hand fanned out over his lapel, he realized he had. And that he'd tilted his head in preparation to capture her lips.

"Your advice is sound, I am sure. But right this moment, all I want to know is what will happen next."

North did, too.

At the sound of footsteps nearby, North straightened immediately and released her. For a moment, he'd forgotten about the servants and the possibility of tainting her reputation. He could only think about how much he wanted to taste her, explore her. "I would hate to make you tardy for my aunt's tea," he lied. If he could do so without damaging her reputation, he would haul her away this instant. "As for me, I am assuredly late for a meeting with Baron Cantham."

Ivy's nose wrinkled. "Miss Leeds's father?"

"I was surprised by the request to complete an equation for her as well. Cantham comes from a lengthy descendancy who all possess the Leeds surname. He is a staunch advocate in bloodline purity."

"*His own*," she said with a shudder. "Though how insulting for you to endure his public scorn even when, it appears, his prejudice can be pushed aside if his daughter were to become a duchess."

Her defense of him warmed North. "Such comments are not the barbs they once were."

She tilted her head, gazing at him with tender scrutiny. Whether she believed his lie or not, she said nothing. Instead, she drew in a breath. "I wish you were attending your aunt's tea. F-for Lilah's sake, of course. You've not had much of an opportunity to become acquainted with her."

He grinned, loving the way she ran out of breath while saying things she likely didn't mean. "Unfortunately, this evening I have private appointments with others who share Cantham's way of thinking. I will likely not attend the play."

"Oh," she said, her gaze mirroring his own longing and disappointment. "It is wonderful, though, that your *Marriage Formula* has gained such a following. How proud you must be." He offered a nod, but before he could make a comment, she continued. "Then I will simply see you tomorrow evening at the Christmas Eve Ball?"

Time was slipping away too quickly. He was at odds with

his desire to spend more time with her, and his desire to take the steps to earn his Fellowship. "Perhaps I should request your first dance now before anyone else has the chance."

"And perhaps, before you come to your senses, I should say yes."

Chapter Seven

THE CHRISTMAS EVE Ball at Castle Vale had begun. As usual, Ivy was running late. This time, however, she was not looking for her slippers. She was looking for the duke's study instead.

She hadn't passed a single servant here in the east wing, but when she saw that the hall was lined with paintings of scientists at their worktables, she knew she was on the right track. Hesitating at an open pair of glossy walnut doors, she smoothed her hands over her skirts.

This evening, she wore layers of silvery gray silk organza with little puffed sleeves that rested at the very crests of her shoulders. Her pale, straight hair had been curled, coiffed, and secured by silver combs. Unfortunately, the small oval mirror in the hallway reflected that a few strands had unwound and now lay limply against her temples. Not only that, but her cheeks were flushed as well.

She made a face and shrugged. At least when she arrived later to the ball, her unrefined appearance would only corroborate the story she'd told Lilah about feeling a trifle ill.

Now was not the time to be worried about her appearance, however. Ivy needed to decline the duke's offer for the first dance. What business did she have dancing with him, when she needed to help Lilah win him?

Stepping over the threshold of the study, she prepared to do just that. Yet after a glance about the room, she realized the duke was not here. Disappointed, she was about to turn around when she saw him emerge from a narrow doorway on the far side of the room near the fireplace.

For a moment, he stilled and blinked at her, as if he was as surprised as she. Then those creases appeared on the sides of his mouth.

He crossed the room, leaving the narrow door behind him ajar. "Miss Sutherland, what brings you to the east wing? Shouldn't you be patiently waiting for the first dance?"

At the word *patiently,* she knew he was teasing her. Yet as he neared, she felt a tremor of apprehension. What if her plan worked too well? Could Ivy's heart bear to see North marry her friend? "Actually, I was hoping to speak with you about that."

"Oh?" He stepped past her and peered into the hallway before closing the door.

Ivy knew that being alone with him, *again,* wasn't at all proper. His closing the door was even less proper. Perhaps she should mention it. Perhaps they should hold their conversation in the open doorway . . . yet when he gestured for her to accompany him into the other room, she forgot to mention it.

"It was Lilah," she began along the way, "*Miss Appleton's* idea to take the puddings to your tenants, though I'm certain Miss Leeds would like to take the credit." If Ivy had to endure the sight of him marrying anyone, she would rather it be Lilah than that dreadful Miss Leeds. Though neither thought made her happy.

A smirk appeared, looking perfectly at home on his lips. And when she drew close enough to pass through the narrow doorway, something hot and pleased shone in his eyes. "Actually, Mrs. Thorogood told me that the idea was yours."

"Well . . . it was Lilah who whispered it to me," Ivy said quickly, forgetting all about the cook being present for her idea. *Drat!* Continuing, she tried to make up for all the times she'd missed the opportunity to bring Lilah to his notice. The way she should have been doing all along. "As you might have guessed, I have the propensity to say whatever idea is on my mind, even if the idea isn't mine in the first place. Lilah is incredibly kind and generous. Not only that, but—like you—she is fond of numbers and equations."

"Is she?" He grinned in earnest now as he closed this second door as well.

Most assuredly *this* was not at all proper. Yet Ivy said nothing to reproach him. She wanted to be here. It was a cozy space, cast in the glow of firelight. Floor-to-ceiling shelves lined the semicircular walls. Unevenly stacked papers and leather books with worn bindings poked out in complete disarray. A few jars were tucked in here and there, along with assorted sizes of microscopes and other scientific paraphernalia. Yet all the clutter appeared to have function and order. There were no plates with half-eaten dinners. There were no forgotten teacups. The room was not a dirty mess. It was a sort of organized chaos. It felt like stepping into the mind of a genius. *His* mind. She realized quite suddenly that this room was an extension of him. "Do you often bring your guests here?"

"Never," he said as he moved toward his desk and leaned back against the one place that wouldn't cause papers to topple. "My aunt has invited herself on a few occasions, and Mr. Graves is permitted at my request."

Those intense, magnetic eyes held hers in an unspoken communication that Ivy felt in the center of her heart. She hadn't been imagining the uniqueness of their connection. He felt it, too. Which made what she had to do all the more difficult.

"Lilah has quite the head for figures, indeed. Since her brother and father passed away, she's been overseeing her family's estate ledgers," Ivy said, drifting toward his desk, where an assortment of contraptions rested. The first one looked like a miniature ascending room, built out of wood. Picking it up, she toyed with the button-sized pulley and small ropes.

"Hmm . . . and what other accomplishments does your friend possess?" As he spoke, North reached over and compressed the pulley. The action sent the miniature ascending room on a swift descent, slipping down a few inches until it suddenly caught and held. Then, flipping the contraption over, he brushed his fingertip over what looked like four diminutive clamps.

Ivy beamed. *Brakes.* Somehow he'd come up with a design from her suggestion in only a matter of days.

"That's ingenious. However did you—" Lifting her gaze, she found him staring at her. Another moment passed in silent communication that made her want . . . *everything.* She wanted so much more than she could ever have.

"I was inspired by a fascinating and brave young woman," he said, setting aside the model to take her hand, drawing her to stand before him.

She cleared her throat and went on with her task. "Lilah is brave. Do you know that I've never seen her flinch in the presence of a spider? She has other fine qualities, too."

"I'm certain she does." He expelled a rasp of air that was just shy of a laugh. "Miss Sutherland, I am not going to marry your friend."

"That isn't what I—" Ivy stopped, already seeing in his perceptive expression how easily he'd read her intention. "Whyever not?"

Something tender softened the flesh around his eyes and the creases around his mouth. "I suppose the simplest reason is that Miss Appleton and I are not in the same ledger."

Ledger? Before she could ask what he meant, he reached behind him to a stack of ledgers in three colors on his desk and held them up, one after the other. "You see, for my formula, there are certain people who automatically enter the black ledger—those with high-ranking titles, a good deal of property, and wealth. The brown ledger contains members of the lower-ranking aristocracy and the landed gentry." He stopped then, his gaze fixed on the trio.

"And what about those in the red ledger?"

He shook his head. "They have little, if any, hope of marrying at all."

"Please do not tell me that Lilah is in the red ledger."

He blinked at her. "You needn't worry. If my formula is correct, your friend would find her match among those in the brown ledger."

No. That couldn't be right. Ivy wanted Lilah to be in the black ledger. After everything she'd been through, her friend deserved the very best. "Have you finished her equation? Isn't it possible that her number would pair with yours?"

"I have not, but I already know the answer. And I think you do, as well." He set the ledgers back down. Gently, he took her other hand as well. "Now, tell me the real reason you want me to marry your friend."

She didn't like thinking about the past, and she certainly never spoke of the life-altering incident, yet she found herself wanting to tell North. It would be better for him to understand.

Ivy exhaled. "It's because of Jasper, her brother."

North's brow furrowed. "I don't recall the mention of his name."

"He had an unfortunate . . . accident and died a couple of years ago." Reluctantly, Ivy released North's hands and turned away. "You see, since we were children, I'd always planned to marry Jasper."

"And he is the reason why you are not married now?"

She nodded even though the answer was more complicated. She began to amble around the room, stopping at a bookshelf full of sideways stacked books, and jars filled with all sorts of things. She picked up one that contained a green branch dotted with small white berries that looked suspiciously like mistletoe. "I'd always planned to take care of Lilah, too. Her parents were not very kind. After Jasper died, they became worse.

"Within the year, her father died as well, and for a while I thought she might have a reprieve from the demands put upon her. However, then came the reading of her father's will. After Jasper's death, Lilah's father added a codicil, stating that the line had to be preserved. Lilah has to marry a man of noble blood, or she will essentially lose everything. Worse yet, if she doesn't find a titled gentleman to marry by the end of this coming Season, she will be forced to marry her licentious cousin, who holds her father's estate."

When she turned around, North was there beside her. He lifted a hand to cup her jaw. "I am sorry for your friend. If you like, I will work her equation and find a match for her. In addition, I will introduce her to as many of my unmarried friends as possible. You must know that I would do anything . . ."

His touch stirred so many sensations within her. She wanted to lean against his hand and close her eyes. Fighting the impulse was next to impossible. "Anything other than marry her yourself."

"I am sorry, Ivy."

He wouldn't marry Lilah. Ivy's entire purpose for attending this party was to save her friend, and she had failed. So then why was joy leaping inside her heart?

"No. I am the one who should be sorry, because hearing those words from your lips fills me with blissful relief, when it should fill me with agony instead." It was no use. She lifted her hand to cover his, to urge him to linger. "I am a terrible friend. I failed Jasper, and now I have failed—"

"How did you fail?" North shook his head, his gaze frank and earnest. "Even in the short duration of our acquaintance, I feel as if I know you. You cannot fail at anything, because you are the kind of person who does not give up when something matters to you. I know you, Ivy, to the very core of my being. You weave the world around you into a fabric of light that blankets anyone who stands near. Your vivacity is as charming as it is infectious. Your heart is warm and open. And your curiosity might even rival my own. There is nothing within you that could fail."

Embarrassed, she wanted to look away so that she wouldn't have to face the truth. She even attempted to step back but found herself against the bookcase. Yet even with North so close, his hand still curled beneath her jaw, she did not feel trapped. Surprisingly, she found his nearness comforting. If ever there was a time to admit her dreaded secret, now was it.

"But I did fail," she said. "For years, I tried hard to be perfect. To let Jasper know that I was the bride for him. I was patient. You may not believe it, but I was. Nearly ten years went by before my impulsive nature finally consumed me. And when I kissed him on that last night we ever spoke, he scolded me and told me that I did not stir his passions."

North slowly shook his head, his gaze drifting to her mouth, lingering. "That is not possible."

"It is true, I tell you. I must have done it wrong. All I know is that I wasn't enough for him. And there you have it."

"Not possible. I simply do not believe it." His thumb swept against the underside of her bottom lip. "Your mouth is far too perfect."

Ivy held her breath. "Apparently not."

"It is a matter of simple mechanics." His gaze lifted to hers. He edged closer by degrees. With one hand propped on the shelf beside her head, and the other sliding to the back of her neck, his fingertip dipped into the hollow at the base of her skull. A riot of tingles traversed her spine, plummeting all the way to her toes. "I'll show you."

And then he kissed her. Her lips parted on a soundless

gasp of pleasure. The press of his mouth was brief, but warm and pleasantly firm. When he withdrew, the sensation of his lips upon hers lingered. A current zinged through her. She imagined that she knew what an electric-coil felt like, all tingly and warm.

Reeling from it, she was almost afraid to ask his thoughts. Instead, she prolonged the moment. She licked her lips to see if she could taste him, and the barest hint of port teased her tongue.

His gaze darkened. The hand at her nape tightened ever so slightly. His nostrils flared and his breath rushed against her lips, but he said nothing.

Surely something that felt so wondrous to her couldn't have been a complete failure. Could it? Ivy closed her eyes before she asked, "Well?"

"I'd say the experiment was a complete success. However . . ."

Her eyes snapped open. "*However?*"

"It was only *one* kiss," he said with a slight lift of his brow, as if uncertain. Yet one of those creases made an appearance beside his mouth. "A scientist must experiment multiple times in order to come to a definitive conclusion. I believe we should make another attempt, for further study, of course."

He hesitated only long enough for her to agree with a nod before he took her mouth again. This time, he angled his head the other direction, kissing her once—*twice,* nuzzling the corner of her mouth. By the time he concluded, she was out of breath and clinging to his shoulders.

"Hmm . . ." he murmured, the low sound vibrating through her. "Another successful experiment."

She moved closer, her hands sliding down from the breadth of his shoulders beneath his coat to wrap around his torso. This new position molded her body to his. Beneath the solid wall of his chest, his heart pounded. Her breasts ached and her back arched so that she felt the firm rise and fall of his breaths. And lower, she felt the unyielding, intriguing heat of him. "Though . . . perhaps further study is in order."

"In great depth." His hand abandoned the shelf and settled on her hip. He shifted, his feet on either side of hers. "I must warn you—this may take a while."

This time, he did not wait for her response. Instead, he kissed her again. But it was more than a kiss. Their entire bodies were involved. While their mouths eagerly fused, nipped, devoured, she could not stop the impulse to arch against him. His hand splayed over her lower back and pulled her closer, lifting her. In the same motion, his stance altered, his foot sliding in between hers. Her skirts made a shushing sound as their legs tangled and their hips connected like interlocking pieces.

"*North*," she moaned, her head falling back as his kisses continued down her chin to the column of her throat. The feel of his heated lips on her flesh did terrible, wondrous things to her, making her breasts throb and ache, turning her body liquid where their hips aligned. "Or do you prefer Northcliff? You never told me."

"When you are in my arms, you may call me whatever you like," he said, his lips tracing the line of her collarbone. The hand at her nape drifted down to tease the edge of her gown, nudging it off the crest of her shoulder. He stroked the newly exposed flesh with the pad of his thumb. Lifting his head, he captured her lips once more.

At the first touch of his tongue, a soft murmur of surprise escaped her, jolting her. He drew back a fraction to look at her, as if gauging her reaction. He must have seen something that pleased him, because he grinned and slowly sampled her again. Taking his time, he delved past her lips in leisurely strokes.

This was all new to her. She mimicked his actions, tentatively slipping her tongue into his mouth and gliding sinuously over his flesh. He issued a low, hungry groan of approval.

The sound fed her impulsive nature and made her eager to further her own studies. She sucked the tip of his tongue, swirling hers around to feel the variant textures, from the ridged top to the silken underside. Wanting to explore more, she suckled him deeper into her mouth.

North responded with a growl. Matching her eagerness, he tilted her head back, claiming her mouth. His hips rolled against hers. A swift shock of desire speared her, sending hot tremors throughout her body. Even her mind quivered, making her dizzy. She clung to him tighter still, her hands finding his shoulders again as the full-body kiss went on and on.

Unfortunately, she needed to catch her breath. From the sound of his deep inhales and exhales, North did, too. The motions of his hips stilled, though he remained firmly pressed against her where the pulse of her body throbbed incessantly.

She broke away, pressing her cheek against his, her fingertips skimming the soft, short hair at the back of his neck. "I wish you had a sofa in here."

"A sofa?" He laughed, the sound rough, as if it caused him pain.

"I feel dizzy and everything inside of me is telling me to lie down. And then we could continue . . . with our experiment."

North's fingertips curled over her hips, and the soft flesh waiting beneath the layers of her gown. He rocked against her once more, then eased away and released a slow exhale. "I would need hours with you, Ivy. Days. Weeks. Months . . ."

With a nod, she rose up on her toes to kiss him. She agreed to his terms unequivocally, willing to give anything to continue just like this.

He laughed softly, pulling back far enough to brush her

hair from her forehead and to press a kiss there as he cradled her face. "Dearest Ivy, even if I were to take just a few more hours with you, I would be forced to marry you."

She flinched at his choice of words.

He seemed to notice and quickly continued. "Or rather, *we* would be forced to marry."

"*Forced*"—as in, against his will—"I see."

"Perhaps *expected* is more accurate."

A gradual numbness began to settle over her as she saw his expression alter from passion to something that looked like regret. She'd seen Jasper give her that look. A ghost of the pain she felt that day came to haunt her now. "I would never force you to do anything against your will."

"Nor I you, which is precisely why I never should have—" He didn't finish. Then again, he didn't have to. Ivy already knew. *I never should have kissed you . . .*

She slipped away in the space between the duke and the wall, keeping her gaze averted. When she shifted to put her sleeve back in place, she felt the tines of that frog pin scrape against her flesh.

He stepped in front of her and grasped her arms, his gaze imploring. "So much is at stake for me. I've worked hard for the Fellows of the Royal Society to acknowledge me. I cannot afford to lose my head, or my heart, and behave irrationally. My entire formula is proof that none of that nonsense is necessary. Don't you see? I could lose the one thing I want more than anything else."

More than anything actually meant *more than I want you*. North wanted his Fellowship, just as Jasper had wanted someone else. Anyone else, as it had turned out. She'd been fooling herself to imagine that the duke was one person who could want her *more than anything else*.

However, she couldn't fault him for it. Because, up until a moment ago, she hadn't even realized that was what she wanted. Up until a moment ago, her only worry was that

Lilah might be in the red ledger. Now she worried that her own name was there.

"I wouldn't want to ruin your chance to gain a Fellowship. Resentment would be sure to follow, and for what? A few hours of kissing that would likely never be repeated?" She shrugged, and his hands dropped to his side.

He closed his eyes and scrubbed the side of his fist over his forehead. "Ivy, I don't think you understand what those hours would entail—"

"Besides, you and I would never suit," she interrupted, not wanting to hear about what might have been if only she had never mentioned the sofa. Restlessness filled her, forcing her to move around the room or risk feeling the pain inside her heart. It was a slow pain—a terrible, squeezing ache. She knew her heart wouldn't survive long under the pressure, but part of her wished it would just shatter in a flash so that she could be done with it. But apparently, a breaking heart had all the time in the world.

"You need someone who will tenderly scold you about your disorganized mess of a study." Ivy attempted a laugh in order to sound worldly, as if things like this happened all the time and she was used to it. "Yet if you were to see the chaos I left in the dressing chamber upstairs, you would realize that I would have no right or inclination to scold you. Not only that, but I would constantly want to inspect your inventions—which might very well lead to their destruction. Even our names are opposites. Surely a man named Northcliff should never be forced to marry a woman whose surname is Sutherland."

"Now you're just spouting nonsense," he hissed, his words clipped.

Surreptitiously, she dabbed at the sudden well of moisture along the lower rim of her eyes. "I do that frequently. Yet another one of my flaws."

"Ivy . . ."

She didn't know what he was going to say, but some-how she knew she couldn't bear to hear it. "Most of all, you need a person who fits into your formula, a person who possesses the qualities that matter to you. You need some-one who doesn't suddenly wish that, all along, you'd set out to disprove your own theory, to prove instead that there is more to someone's worth than lineage, property, and wealth. And, perhaps, that matters of happenstance—like a fateful pairing of hearts in a single moment—might have been the truest answer all along."

She didn't know why she hesitated at the door. Perhaps she thought he might want to stop her. After a moment, how-ever, he didn't say anything more. Ivy left the room without looking back.

Chapter Eight

NORTH CROSSED THE room and closed the door, letting Ivy go. He didn't know what else to do. Because if he stopped her, he didn't know what he might say. A number of irrational phrases filled his head, and he was afraid of them spilling out.

"Don't go. Forgive me . . ."

"You make me question my sanity. I might already be accustomed to the madness. I crave it . . ."

"I need you in my life. Stay. Forever . . ."

He pressed his forehead to the door as more thoughts continued along the same vein that ran directly to his heart. They twisted knots inside his mind. The pressure within his chest now felt condensed and weighted, crushing him. He preferred the elation, no matter how uncontrolled and incalculable it was. But as he straightened and moved away from the door, he suddenly knew he would never feel it again.

At his desk, he lifted the scale model of the ascending room, remembering Ivy's smile of pleasure when she'd seen the changes in his design. He'd done them for her. The errand of a romantic fool. She was his inspiration. He'd worked on it without sleep for an entire day, stopping only to see her at dinner.

He pulled on the strings to elevate the diminutive room once more. Yet the pulley string snagged. He tugged again.

Then, before he could stop it, the top of the model cracked, collapsed, and crumbled.

He stared down at the broken pieces as it fell apart in his hands. It was useless now. The entire model would have to be rebuilt. Yet this wasn't even *his* invention. It belonged to someone else. North was merely modifying it. The pointlessness of it hit him hard.

Suddenly angry, he closed his fist and crushed the model further. Yet that was not enough. So he hurled it into the fire. The flames flared, leaping up in a shock of orange, consuming the wood in an instant.

A rush of primal satisfaction tore through him, feeding this inexplicable rage.

Striding back to the desk, he snatched up the model of a guillotine and hurled it into the flames as well. He crossed the room to the shelves. The slipper-stretcher went next, landing with a clunk against the other logs. It was too solid to incinerate in a flash, so he began crumbling papers and tossing them into the fire. Heaps and stacks of designs and potential patents went up in flames. Everything he'd worked on for years.

He grabbed the jar of mistletoe, his arm reeling back, preparing to smash it to bits. But then he remembered her kiss—*their kiss,* those moments of utter contentment—and suddenly, he couldn't release the jar.

"This is madness!" he shouted to the empty room. "My formula is what matters. *All that matters.*"

Then, seeing the ledgers on his desk filled him with a mixture of purpose and loathing. "*You need someone who doesn't suddenly wish that, all along, you'd set out to disprove your own theory, to prove instead that there is more to someone's worth than lineage, property, and wealth . . .*"

He gripped the black ledger, his fingertips white from the force. Then he hurled it into the flames.

The brown one followed.

Picking up the red ledger, he shook it at the ceiling. There was only one name on its pages. One single name that should be of no consequence. "This was a brief aberration that is over now. She was not my match. It could not have lasted. *Ha!* It was never meant to begin."

At once, he lowered his arm and stared at the red ledger in confusion. *Lasted?* Why had he said that? It wasn't as if he'd given any thought to marrying Ivy Sutherland of Norwood Hill. Or any thought to spending hours, days, weeks, *years* . . . kissing her, touching her, listening to her ideas, having her rush impatiently into his arms, feeling elation each and every day for the rest of his life. No. Not a single thought. He was a rational, scientific man. When it was time for him to marry, he would use his formula to find a suitable candidate.

Taking up the quill pen, he dipped it into the inkpot and worked Ivy's equation, needing her number. He already knew it would yield nothing, because she met none of the criteria. She only had insubstantial goods to bring to a marriage. Only her vivacity, her winter-blue eyes, her warmth, her heart, her mind, her laugh . . .

His formula was an insufficient tool to measure these qualities. His formula . . . was lacking in everything that mattered.

Suddenly, he realized that he was a complete fraud.

All the breath left North's body as he sank to his knees. His formula didn't work.

WHEN IVY HEARD the door to the other room open, she leaped up from the window seat and rushed across the room to douse the lamp. She didn't want Lilah to see that she'd been sobbing like a complete idiot.

"Are you feeling better—" Lilah stopped cold the instant she spotted her. "Oh, dearest, what is the matter? You've been crying."

Ivy shook her head. "Nothing more than a headache."

Carefully, Lilah looked over her shoulder and closed the door to the dressing chamber. "I hope this doesn't have anything to do with the duke."

"Of course it doesn't have anything to do with . . . Why would you even think that?"

Lilah sighed. "I know you wanted me to marry him."

"Oh." Ivy pinched the bridge of her nose and sat heavily on the bed, playing the part of a headache victim, and certainly not someone with a broken heart. "You must forgive me. I did not realize how foolish my notion was until this evening."

Apparently she was convincing, because the concern lifted from Lilah's expression.

"Then you have heard, as well." Lilah tsked as she plucked her gloves off one finger after the other. "I cannot believe our host would abandon his own party. There were whispers that he rode away on his horse."

Ivy lowered her hand, her attention riveted. "The duke left in the dead of night?" That did not sound like something he would do.

Lilah nodded and removed her combs from her hair, shaking it free before she sat down beside Ivy.

"I don't understand," Ivy said. "Why would you think it had something to do with his not wanting to marry?"

"Either his interests lay elsewhere, or he has no intention of marrying any of us. If he did, he would have attended his own Christmas Eve Ball."

Thinking of what he wanted *more than anything,* Ivy offered a solemn nod. "I believe you are correct on both counts."

"There now, it is done. You mustn't think of him anymore, and you must stop hoping that he will marry me."

Ivy's shoulders slumped forward, and she settled her face in the cup of her hands. "Lilah, I've been such a fool. I never really wanted him to marry you. Not since the moment we were introduced."

"If it's because you thought his manners abominable, then I certainly agree."

"No." Ivy shook her head and turned toward her friend. "My failing is much worse, and I hope you can forgive me."

"Of course. What is there to forgive?" Lilah smiled and squeezed Ivy's shoulder.

"I think . . . for just a moment"—Ivy drew in a breath and slowly released it—"*I* wanted to marry him."

Lilah covered her mouth on a gasp. "You wanted to— But that means that you—Is it possible that you've fallen in love?"

Not love. Whatever this was, it was much worse and it had no name, only a combination of symptoms: dizziness, exhilaration, bliss, consuming desire, misery, pain, heart-wrenching agony, despair . . . "You must know that I could never love again after Jasper."

"But that was not love, silly." Lilah offered a tender smile. "That was one of those childhood dreams we hold on to for far too long. You thought of him as your Prince Charming, no matter how many times he proved otherwise. But he re-mained a boy who was determined to gather as many hearts as he could, filling his pockets with them until they over-flowed and fell to the dirt at his feet."

Jasper had enjoyed women. That had been one of the rea-sons why his unequivocal rejection of Ivy had hurt so much. Why hadn't he wanted her, too?

"Right before he left with that married harlot," Lilah con-tinued, "I begged him to set you free, once and for all. It wasn't fair the way he kept you . . . forever in his pocket."

"You asked him to set me free?" Ivy stared, agape. She replayed the set-down he'd given her and how it had left her feeling like a failure. She'd never heard Jasper sound cruel.

In fact, he'd sounded more like his father in that moment. Now, Ivy understood why.

"I suppose he did set me free," she said. "That was his last noble act, only I was too stubborn to see it. Perhaps Jasper did love one of the women whose hearts he collected. He loved his sister."

"Of course he did," Lilah said on a watery laugh, wiping away a sudden sheen of tears. "I'm an incredibly loveable young woman. And one day I might even find a man who realizes it."

"I will make sure of it," Ivy vowed as she hugged her friend.

"Oh, please, Ivy. Don't."

Ivy was in the midst of convincing her friend of a perfect plan for her upcoming Season, when the door from the dressing chamber suddenly opened. More surprising than that was having the dowager duchess step inside the room.

"There you are, Miss Sutherland. I am in a fretful state, to be sure," she said, wringing her hands. Strands of silver hair stuck out from her coiffure. "I am taking it for granted that you have already heard the rumors of my nephew's leaving this evening. Let me say that over the years, he has disappeared into his study when working on an invention, but he has never left the house without a word. Worse, he did not pack a bag, inform his valet, or even order a carriage. It is now very late, well past two o'clock on Christmas morning, and still he has not returned."

Ivy stood, her own alarm mounting. She hadn't entirely believed that he'd left, but was likely in another part of the castle. What errand could have sent him out of doors on Christmas Eve? Glancing at the starlit night beyond the frost-rimmed window, she worried that it had something to do with the agitated state she'd left him in. "Do you have any idea where he could be, Your Grace?"

The dowager duchess shook her head. "I was hoping you would shed some light on the situation."

"Me, ma'am?"

"His study is in complete disrepair. Many things destroyed, or burned in the fireplace."

Ivy gasped. "Was there an assault? Did someone break into his study? Is he hurt?"

"I have been assured by the groomsman who saddled his horse that my nephew was alone and appeared unhurt, though disheveled. When asked where he was going, my nephew responded that he needed to clear his head." The dowager duchess stepped forward, lifting an object in her grasp. "My only clue is inside this red ledger, which sat squarely in the center of his desk."

"I don't understand. What does that red ledger have to do with me?" Ivy asked as a sinking feeling settled into the pit of her stomach. She wanted to step back from it.

"Perhaps if you looked inside, you could offer your insight."

Reluctantly, Ivy took the ledger, her hands already cold and trembling.

"You'll see that there is only one name in that entire ledger, and it is yours."

Numbly, she opened the book. True enough. The first page read: MISS IVY SUTHERLAND OF NORWOOD HILL—NO CONSEQUENCE.

"*And what about those in the red ledger?*" she'd asked him a few hours ago.

"*They have little, if any, hope of marrying at all.*"

"Mr. Graves found the remains of the other two ledgers in the ash," the dowager duchess said. "I know they were an integral part of his formula. One can only presume that some dire result caused such destruction."

Dire, indeed. For the third time in her life, her kiss had brought about a calamity. Only this was the worst of all.

Where could North be? Was he hurt? Or did he clear his head enough to forget her entirely?

Miss Ivy Sutherland of Norwood Hill—no consequence. It was true. She possessed no title, no property, no dowry— none of the things that mattered to North.

You don't understand, Ivy, we would be forced to marry.

The grip around Ivy's heart intensified until she felt it shatter beneath the pressure. Strangely, she remained composed on the outside. Inside was a wholly different story. Inside, she was on her knees, sobbing. "I wish I could help, ma'am, but I do not know where the duke is, though I pray for his safe return."

And she did, even when he saw no redeeming quality in her existence.

"Pray . . . Yes, we must all pray. If my nephew has not returned by dawn, then I will send out a search party."

Chapter Nine

NORTH WAITED IN the hall outside Jack Marlowe's rooms in his lavish estate. After riding on horseback for four hours in sleet, North was wet and cold to the bone. But this was a matter of importance that he could not delay one moment longer.

After a short interval, Marlowe emerged from a gilded doorway, securing a blue silk banyan around his waist as he swaggered, barefoot, into the hall. With a careless rake of his hand, he pushed back a golden mane of hair from his forehead. "Vale, do you have any idea what time it is?"

North didn't want to waste time by answering unimportant questions. "Marlowe, what do you think of my formula?"

They'd been friends for years, and he trusted Marlowe to speak plainly. He would have spoken with Wolford, but his cousin tended to laugh too often when the matter required severity. Thayne had been too distracted since Juliet Granworth's return to society. And as the bastard son of the Earl of Dovermere, Marlowe hadn't wanted to attend the party, knowing that his father was there. So it had been up to North to come to him instead.

Marlowe's tawny brow furrowed. "You rode all the way here in the dead of night for me to stroke your ego? Come now, Vale, I must get back to"—he turned his head toward the bedchamber door—"darling, what is your name?"

"*Minerva*," came the singsong reply, along with a giggle.

Marlowe shrugged. "I must get back to Minerva. She's an opera girl and was just showing me how long she can hold a single note."

"This won't take long," North said, losing his patience. He started pacing around the marbled hall, his booted steps echoing around him. "I want my formula to have merit and lasting value. What I've created is a simpler, surer method than the notion of marrying for love would be."

"I agree. Love has no place in a marriage. Marriages are all about drawing new lines on old maps and ensuring that blue blood continues to bleed from inbred veins for generations to come. At least with your formula those *highest of high* on the ladder rungs needn't marry their cousins. And there you have your answer," Marlowe concluded with a brush of his hands.

North stopped pacing. "We don't all marry our cousins."

"Enough of you do it to put a stain on the whole lot. Want a drink?" Marlowe poured from a decanter sitting atop a mahogany and gold inlaid secretary along the far wall.

Absently, North shook his head. There was something in the words Jack chose that sparked his interest. "Even though you think love has no place in marriage, you still believe it exists?"

"I fall in love all the time. Ask any of my paramours." He nodded toward the bedchamber door as he tipped back his glass.

"I'm speaking of true, honest, soul-deep love. The kind that takes you by surprise and changes the entire course of your life in an instant."

"Vale, the night air has gone to your head. You are speaking of supposition and theory instead of facts. At school, I bore witness to many of your recitations against *prattling poets* whose craniums were—in your opinion—*overflowing sop buckets*." Marlowe laughed and poured himself another drink. "Why are you really here? Why come all this way when you likely already knew my answers to your questions?"

"I needed to hear from a fellow analytic. To feel grounded once more."

"Hmm . . . And you couldn't have found a single one beneath your own roof? It sounds as if you've stumbled on an error in your calculations."

"No. The equation is flawless," he admitted, feeling a sense of despair roll over him.

"Then congratulations are in order. Soon you will have scores of the unwed who want to remove the risk of being wrong. You must be thrilled. I know you've worked hard on this for a while now."

North scrubbed a hand across his brow. "I am thrilled."

"It's strange, though. Your jubilation looks rather like disappointment," Marlowe said on a wry laugh.

North lowered his arm and glared at his friend, agitated. "You're wrong. *This* is what elation looks like. I set about to create a formula that provides clarity and simplicity instead of needless frippery and feelings. *Disappointment?* You make it sound as if I'd wanted to disprove my own theory all along—"

Then it hit him.

All the years of criticism regarding his common blood, of having to prove himself worthy of the dukedom and wanting desperately to gain a Fellowship, but to what end? He never would have been satisfied. His brain would have continued to turn with whatever invention he could begin next. The only time he'd ever stopped to live in one single moment— the only time he'd felt a true purpose in his life—had been during those moments with Ivy Sutherland of Norwood Hill. "*Damn.*"

"Well then, I'm glad I could help. Next time, be a chap and wait until calling hours." Marlowe paused on his way back to his chamber. "Say, do you need a room, a fresh horse?"

"A fresh horse, I'll take. As for the room"—North paused to calculate his next move—"I won't know until I've concluded my business."

Marlowe walked to the bellpull and rang for a servant. "What business could you have on Christmas Eve? The only other estate for miles belongs to Lady Binghamton, the archbishop's sister."

North had already been aware of that before he'd left Castle Vale.

"Your horse. My business." Then, before Jack could slip away, North held up a hand to stay his friend. Withdrawing a pencil from his pocket, he took out a card. "Do me a favor, Marlowe? When you're back in London, send a bouquet of flowers to Miss Lilah Appleton. I wrote her street on this card."

Marlowe took the card and flashed a smile. "Is she my Christmas present?"

"No, and I only want you to send her flowers. Just the once, and make no other contact with her. Besides, she is far different from the type of woman you prefer. She is respectable."

Marlowe made a sour face. "Then why are you bothering with the flowers?"

"*You* are sending the flowers," North corrected. "And the reason for that is because I promised her friend that I would do whatever I could for her."

"You have me intrigued."

"No, Marlowe, I absolutely forbid you to be intrigued. For the sake of our friendship, I need to know that I can rely on you to behave with honor."

"Send her flowers. Leave her be. Understood. Now I must get back to . . . to . . ."

"*Minerva,*" the woman huffed from the room beyond.

"Ah yes, the opera girl. She was quite interested in acquainting herself with a man in possession of an *immense*"—Marlowe's brow arched suggestively—"fortune."

With a reluctant laugh and a shake of his head, North turned away and called out, "Happy Christmas."

"Indeed, for the rest of the chorus will be arriving later today," Marlowe said before disappearing into his bedchamber.

As for North . . . he was feeling rather impulsive, but completely certain as well. He hoped to find the archbishop in a particularly giving mood this Christmas morning.

Chapter Ten

"THE DUKE HAS returned! The duke has returned!" The pageboy's joyous shouts rang out through the corridors of the castle.

Tears welled up in Ivy's eyes, and a stuttered breath of relief left her. Yet, knowing that Lilah was studying her closely, Ivy turned toward the window. A fresh dusting of snow had fallen in the wee hours of the morning. The first glimmer of Christmas touched her heart, but the ache deep inside remained. "Then he is safe. That is good news. I'm certain the dowager duchess is quite glad."

Before she allowed herself to dwell on pointless musings, she went to the basin and splashed frigid water onto the swollen, tender flesh around her eyes. In the looking glass, her complexion appeared too pale against the sable trim of her red dress. It could not be helped, she supposed. A broken heart hardly aided one's complexion.

Lilah came up beside her, her reflection tinged with sorrow. "Ivy, when are you going to admit that you're in love with him?"

She shrugged. "Whatever for? Love serves no purpose. If it did, it would be in the duke's formula."

"Well . . . saying the words might cheer you up."

Lilah looked so hopeful that it was hard not to indulge her. More than that, however, Ivy wanted to say the words aloud, to get them out of her heart so that the pain would subside.

"All right, then, I love him." *Cheer* did not make an appearance. Nor did her heartache lessen. She wasn't surprised. "We don't want to be late for chapel. I am impatient to finish this day so that we may leave tomorrow."

Lilah said nothing more about love as they donned their redingotes and bonnets in preparation to walk to the small chapel on the grounds. Nor did she say anything about the fact that they were likely the last ones to exit the house because, as usual, Ivy had made them late.

Outside, the sunlight glanced off the freshly fallen snow in a blinding display. A blast of cold, crisp air sent a few flakes swirling over the path, glistening like diamonds being strewn over the ground. That same blast of air turned toward her and Lilah.

Ivy's breath arrested in her lungs. She closed her eyes as tiny ice crystals washed over her, clinging to her mouth, nose, and eyelashes. A shadow crossed in front of her, blocking the sunlight for a moment. Reaching up to brush the snowflakes away, she was surprised to feel the warmth of a hand touch her cheek, her brow, her lashes. A man's hand. A familiar hand. There was a certain thoroughness to the caress that could belong to only one person. *The duke.*

"Happy Christmas, Ivy," he whispered, his tone surprisingly cheerful.

She felt as if he was mocking her pain. Her eyes snapped open, and she took a step back. The only thing that kept her from walking away was the fact that he looked terrible. His pale complexion and the purplish bruises lining the underside of his eyes told her that he hadn't slept either. A tender warmth filled her heart.

However, before she could allow herself to feel a semblance of hope at this knowledge, she remembered the true cause of his lack of sleep. And it had nothing to do with his having a broken heart.

"I hope you enjoyed your escapade. Though you might

have had more consideration than riding off in the middle of the night and worrying"—she drew in a stuttered breath—"your aunt."

It was only then that Ivy realized she'd raised her voice. She looked around to find that Lilah had slipped away and the courtyard was empty. The bell in the chapel tower rang, startling her. "The service has begun. I must go, Your Grace."

She offered a perfunctory curtsy, never expecting him to reach out and take her hand.

"I prefer *North*," he said. "And I would like you to sit with me in church this morning."

A moment passed when he gazed at her with a mixture of trepidation and expectation. Such a request was not a matter to be taken lightly and quickly forgotten.

"I cannot." She slipped her hand free and took *two* steps back this time. "The front pew belongs to you and the dowager duchess. Your rank—your lineage—dictates your place. As you know, those of no consequence sit many rows behind you. I saw the red ledger. I know my place."

She strode away before she gave in to either anger or tears. Neither would serve her.

He kept pace beside her. "Then I shall sit in your row."

"To do so would risk what matters most to you."

"Hmm . . . then how else can I speak with you? You are walking at such a fine clip that we will be within the chapel before I have said all that I planned."

On a huff, she stopped and turned to him. "Then say it now and be done."

"I've been thinking a great deal about our frog and his chances of survival—should he have chosen the wrong young woman—and I have come to a conclusion."

She blinked, confused. "Pardon me?"

"I believe there was more to it than happenstance," North continued, as if he was making perfect sense. "After all, it was quite a risk on the frog's part. Especially if you take into account the damage that can be caused by a tremendous fall."

"Are you speaking of the fairy tale?"

He lifted his brows in a way that suggested she already knew the answer. In that moment, she realized that it was their tale he was telling.

North took a step closer. "I believe that all his concerns and calculations were cast aside when he first beheld a pair of winter-blue eyes and first heard her speak about something as absurd as pinching slippers. In that instant, his entire world changed. He knew that he had to risk everything and reveal himself to her in the hopes that she wouldn't throw him back without at least giving him a kiss first."

"In the tale, she *did* throw him," Ivy reminded. "What she needed was to find a frog who would be transformed by the fall."

"You're absolutely right. I've recently discovered that falls of all kinds can do that. The most transforming of all is falling in—"

"*Cousin!*" Before North could finish, the Earl of Wolford rushed down the path, the snow crunching beneath his boots. "I received the most interesting missive from Jack Marlowe just now. He wants to know if you've altered your formula."

"You may tell Marlowe *yes, I have,*" North said without removing his gaze from Ivy.

"He also asked—strangely enough—whether or not you found the archbishop agreeable or—"

"*Wolford,*" North interrupted, "please take your seat in the chapel."

The earl departed without another word. A stunned awareness began to creep upon Ivy. "Did you ride off in the middle of the night to see the archbishop?"

"I did."

This time, she took a step closer. "Whyever would you do such a thing on Christmas Eve?"

"I can think of only one reason."

So could she, but it made no sense. Not unless . . . "I was never going to speak of our kiss. As I said last night, I would never force a man to marry me." Hearing her own words rekindled the hurt and anger she'd felt last night. "I am perfectly content as I am. I certainly do not need to resort to tricks in order to claim a husband. I may be of no consequence to you, but I have wonderful traits that are worth more than a fine lineage, vast property, or any amount of wealth. Your formula was wrong about me."

"I know. I am a fraud, Ivy." North took her hands, tugging off her gloves so that he and she were flesh to flesh, and lifted them to his lips. "You were right. I wanted someone to disprove my formula. You made me see what truly matters, perhaps not for anyone else, but for me."

When another gust of wind stole the warmth from her, she pulled her hands free. "That is a fine, pretty speech, and I thank you. I will be able to leave here without any bitterness in my heart."

"I am in earnest," he said. "And though my method is somewhat disorderly, when I asked you to sit beside me in church, I wasn't just asking for today. I want you there beside me always."

A lovely thought. However, that, too, was a fairy tale. "Even if I could, there would be no other opportunity. I leave on the morrow."

He laughed. "Ivy, I am asking you to marry me."

She couldn't have heard him correctly. "But your formula . . . the red ledger . . ."

"I failed to calculate the one factor that overrides all others—*love*. I fell in love with you in that first moment. I've come to love you more and more in each moment since. You are my perfect match in every way."

Dumbfounded, she didn't know what to think or how to respond.

"I can see that there is only one way to convince you," he said, glancing toward the chapel. He drew in a breath and nodded. "You are all that matters, Ivy."

He walked away from her and into the chapel. Then Ivy found herself standing at the open doors. The melodic sounds of hymns drifted out into the courtyard. At the front, the vicar had yet to climb to the pulpit. And she watched as North strode down the center aisle and faced the congregation.

"Good morning, all," North said. "Before we begin to celebrate this glorious day, I have a confession to make. As you know, I invited you all here to learn of my *Marriage Formula*. This formula was originally designed with an honest desire to enhance our society by simplifying matters of marriage down to the basic desired elements . . ."

Numbly, Ivy walked forward. Awareness crept over her as she realized what he was saying. And more importantly, what he was risking. She couldn't let him do it.

"However," he continued, ignoring the fervent shakes of her head, "I have recently discovered that my calculations were—"

"Frog!" she shouted, drawing startled gazes in her direction, along with a few gasps. She pointed to the floor, gesturing beneath the pews. "I saw one just there."

As luck would have it, Ivy was standing near the corner of Lilah's pew. "Please pretend there is a frog in your lap," Ivy whispered.

"Why must—*Oh, Ivy, you truly are incorrigible.*" Lilah sighed in exasperation, then suddenly leaped up from her seat. "Frog!"

Beside her, Lady Cosgrove stood, but likely only out of necessity. Nevertheless, it started a reaction among the guests. A few squeals erupted. They all began to stand, scatter, and search the floor. Even the vicar shook out his robes.

Ivy rushed to North's side. "I couldn't let you do it."

"Why not?" While the creases on the sides of his mouth revealed his amusement, there was a measure of trepidation in his gaze.

She could tell him how she believed that his formula had merit and that, with a little tweaking to include the names from the red ledger, it would be even better. However, instead of saying all that, she simply told him, "Because I love you."

Without warning, he picked her up and spun her around in a circle. Right there, in front of the entire congregation. When her feet returned to the floor, she suddenly realized that the frog hunt was over. Everyone was staring at them. She even heard a few people whispering unsavory things about *common blood*. That was when it occurred to her that he could still lose the Fellowship he'd worked so hard to gain.

"And this is because I love you," North whispered, smiling down at her before he addressed his guests. "As I was saying before, I have recently discovered that my formula—"

"Is a success," Ivy interrupted. Again. Boldly, she took his hand. "The results of the duke's formula brought us together."

Which wasn't a *complete* fabrication and, therefore, was acceptable to say in church. The only thing she would have to repent was the small lie about the frog . . .

An odd, warbled bleating sound interrupted her thoughts, and she looked down. Much to her surprise, a fat green toad hopped into the aisle. Then the melee began once more.

Ivy looked up at North. He seemed equally shocked. Then his gaze slid to the doorway, and he grinned as the Earl of Wolford bowed. "My cousin is rather resourceful in a pinch. He had to have sprinted all the way to the warm springs by the hillside."

This morning, she never would have imagined her heartache transforming into the happiest day of her life. "Riding off in the middle of the night to see the archbishop was rather impulsive of you. Not only that, but you automatically assumed that I would be equally as impulsive to marry you by special license."

He flashed those creases. "Call it a *leap* of faith."

"After all this, I suppose I should say yes." She laughed, overflowing with that wonderful feeling of exhilaration. "If a frog is a good omen for a happy marriage, then it would be a shame to waste a perfect opportunity."